299 8

WORDSWORTH CLASSIC
OF WORLD LITERATURE

General E

F

D0626379

JOHANN WOLFGANG
VON GOETHE

Faust

A Tragedy in Two Parts

*with the unpublished scenarios
for the Walpurgis Night
and the* Urfaust

❖

*Translated, with an Introduction
and Notes, by John R. Williams*

WORDSWORTH CLASSICS
OF WORLD LITERATURE

For my husband
ANTHONY JOHN RANSON
with love from your wife, the publisher
Eternally grateful for your
unconditional love

Readers who are interested in other titles from
Wordsworth Editions are invited to visit our
website at www.wordsworth-editions.com

For our latest list and a full mail order service contact
Bibliophile Books, Unit 5 Datapoint,
South Crescent, London E16 4TL
Tel: +44 (0) 20 74 74 24 74
Fax: +44 (0) 20 74 74 85 89
orders@bibliophilebooks.com
www.bibliophilebooks.com

This edition published 2007 by Wordsworth Editions Limited
8B East Street, Ware, Hertfordshire SG12 9HJ

ISBN 978 1 84022 115 2

Wordsworth Editions is
the company founded in 1987 by
MICHAEL TRAYLER

Typeset in Great Britain by Antony Gray
Printed and bound by Clays Ltd, St Ives plc

CONTENTS

INTRODUCTION

Johann Wolfgang von Goethe (1749–1832) is Germany's most celebrated writer, and his dramatic poem *Faust* his most celebrated work. Born into a prosperous family of lawyers and civic administrators in Frankfurt am Main, Goethe studied at the universities of Leipzig and Strasbourg, and by the age of twenty-four had earned an international literary reputation with his historical drama *Götz von Berlichingen* (which Walter Scott translated into English in 1799) and his best-selling novel *The Sufferings of Young Werther*. In 1775 he moved to the small Duchy of Sachsen-Weimar at the personal invitation of the Duke Karl August, where, except for extended journeys to Italy, Switzerland, and to other parts of Germany, he spent the rest of his life.

During his first decade in Weimar Goethe produced dozens of minor works, many for the entertainment of the Weimar court, wrote many poems, and became increasingly involved in the political administration of the state, busying himself with official duties in diplomacy, mining and forestry, roads and finance. He was made a Privy Councillor of the Duchy in 1779, and was ennobled in 1782, with the honorific von Goethe. Major literary projects were started during these years, but few were completed; in 1786 the pressure of official literary and political burdens became so great that he left Weimar for an extended tour of Italy, living in Rome as an artist and travelling the length of Italy for some twenty months.

On his return from Italy Goethe settled to life in Weimar with his mistress Christiane Vulpius, whom he met in 1788, but only married in 1806. He accompanied his Duke, who held the rank of General in the Prussian army, as an observer during the Coalition Wars against revolutionary France in 1792, and saw the Battle of Valmy that turned the tide of the French Revolution when the Austro-Prussian counter-revolutionary army was forced to retreat from France. In 1808 he met Napoleon, whom he admired enormously, and as his literary fame grew he met and corresponded with the leading political, intellectual, artistic and scientific figures of his day. His friendship with Friedrich Schiller, until Schiller's death in 1805, led to one of the most productive literary partnerships ever known. During the rest of his life Goethe's vast energies were devoted to a prodigious output of poetry, novels, dramas, letters, writings on art and literature, to the management of the Weimar Court Theatre, and to his wide scientific studies. He developed a theory of colours that set out (unsuccessfully) to refute Newton's optics, and studied botany, zoology, geology and meteorology. He enjoyed mutually respectful relations with Alexander von Humboldt, in spite of their fundamentally differing scientific beliefs; his studies in comparative anatomy were acknowledged by Charles Darwin in *The Origin of Species*.

The writing of *Faust* occupied Goethe sporadically for most of his creative life. It grew from a fragmentary dramatic account of the man who made a pact with the Devil into a vast dramatic poem that represents some of his last (and some of his first) thoughts on humanity, on human history and institutions, on the grandeurs and follies of the human condition, its hopes and despairs, its values and illusions, its scope and its limitations, its nobility and criminality.

The legend of Faust, or Dr Faustus, was based on the reported life of a notorious but obscure magician who probably lived c. 1480–1540. By 1587 his sensational and blasphemous career was chronicled by an anonymous author who presented the *History of Dr Johann Faust, the Notorious Magician and Nigromancer* in the spirit of the German Reformation as 'a terrible warning to all Christians' against the snares of the Devil, who 'as a roaring lion, walketh about, seeking whom he may devour' (1 Peter 5:8). The *History* was a warning against arrogance and pride, against the sin of Adam or Lucifer; it was also – within the expectations of the time – an entertaining, even exciting story that presented sensational and risqué material within a moral and religious framework of the strictest Lutheran orthodoxy. Unsurprisingly, it quickly became an international best-seller, translated into several languages; an English version by an author identified only by his initials, P. F., provided Christopher Marlowe with the material for his *Tragical History of Dr Faustus* (c. 1592).

By now Faust had become an ambivalent and composite figure who represented almost emblematically the contradictions and tensions of the age. On the one hand he was the post-Renaissance scholar, the speculative seeker after truth beyond scholastic or humanist traditions, the astrologer exploring new worlds on earth and beyond, the magus searching for the Philosopher's Stone, the talisman of the highest philosophical and scientific wisdom; on the other hand, for the religious forces of the Reformation and the Counter-Reformation he was the godless apostate, the renegade intellectual whose presumption and pride had led him to arrogate to himself powers beyond those properly given to him, to defy God and to ally himself with the Devil.

Marlowe's play was subsequently re-imported into Germany by English travelling players, and provided a literary quarry from which increasingly garbled versions were taken to be performed in the German popular theatre and as puppet-plays until well into the nineteenth century. Goethe did not know Marlowe's play at first hand until 1818, well after his *Faust* Part One was completed; he first experienced the story of Faust in a puppet version as a child in Frankfurt. But the narrative of the Faust legend had also survived in various versions into the eighteenth century, and it was from these two traditions, the moralising narrative and the popular and sensational theatrical versions, that Goethe derived the impetus for his own treatment of the story of Dr Faust. Other contributory factors include the real-life public execution for infanticide of a young woman, Susanna Margaretha Brandt, in Frankfurt in 1772; the enormous influence of Shakespeare on the young Goethe; his enthusiasm for folk song and folk ballad; his early interest in alchemy, astrology and occult traditions; and his enthusiasm for the thriving culture of the German Reformation, the age of Martin Luther, Hans Sachs, Albrecht Dürer, and the Emperor Maximilian I.

From the obscure figure of Faust, who haunted the fringes of Reformation Germany, Goethe created a symbolic figure for the modern age who embodies both the restlessly enquiring mind of the eighteenth-century Enlightenment and the passionate assertion of individual emotional and existential freedom that is the hallmark of the German *Sturm und Drang* ('Storm and Stress'): an ambivalent and flawed individual who struggles to assert himself against the cynical nihilism of his diabolical companion. In the figure of Mephistopheles, Goethe has also created a figure of fascinating complexity who is both the spirit of perpetual negation and the divinely-sanctioned taskmaster whose function is to spur Faust out of lethargy and self-satisfaction, who works to bring Faust to damnation while also driving him relentlessly towards his ultimate salvation, and who mocks Faust's lofty pretensions and illusions with all his weaponry of wit, sarcasm and down-to-earth humour. Goethe's Devil has many of the best lines, and some of the scenes involving Mephistopheles are among the most hilarious in German literature.

URFAUST: THE EARLY MANUSCRIPTS

Goethe began work on *Faust* when he was in his early twenties; he finished work on Part Two just before his death at the age of eighty-two. *Faust* Part One was completed in 1806, when Goethe was fifty-seven, and published in 1808. He had, however, worked sporadically on the play for many years, and had frequently read parts of the uncompleted work to his circle of friends. At some point, probably around 1775–6, Luise von Göchhausen, a lady-in-waiting at the Weimar court, borrowed Goethe's manuscripts and made a copy – whether with his knowledge or consent, is not clear. Goethe eventually destroyed his draft manuscripts, and the Göchhausen copy lay unknown for more than a century. It was re-discovered among her papers by the Goethe scholar and editor Erich Schmidt – a sensational find that he immediately published in 1887 as *Goethe's Faust in its Original Form after the Göchhausen Transcript*. It became known as the *Urfaust*.

The *Urfaust* is a fascinating document that allows a glimpse into the young Goethe's earliest work on the subject of Faust. It is not a play complete in itself, although it does contain much of the material that went to make up the final version of Part One: Faust's alliance with the Devil Mephistopheles (though no formal pact appears in this version); his performance of magic tricks in Auerbach's Cellar (a Leipzig inn associated with the early Faust legend, which Goethe knew well as a student, and which still exists); and Faust's disastrous love-affair with Margareta (Gretchen), as a result of which her mother is poisoned and her brother murdered, she is abandoned by Faust, kills her new-born child, and is sentenced to public beheading for infanticide – a crime (and a punishment) not uncommon in Goethe's day.

The *Urfaust* is the original core of *Faust* Part One, which Goethe elaborated and extended in the final version, but which remained remarkably unchanged in its details and its structure. It does not represent *the* early version of Part One, but only *an* early version, and a fragmentary one at that. There may well have been other early material that Goethe did not hand over to Fräulein von Göchhausen – or perhaps even some that she did not care to copy out; there is hearsay evidence to suggest that Goethe read to his friends material that did not appear in either the *Urfaust* or the final version of Part One. Nevertheless, the fragmentary and sporadic structure of the *Urfaust* has not prevented its frequent performance on the stage as a powerfully brief and swift version of *Faust* Part One. Brecht, impressed by its social and literary radicalism, regarded the *Urfaust* as a dramatic masterpiece, and adapted it in his own manner for performance by the *Berliner Ensemble*.

FAUST, PART ONE

When Goethe came to complete Part One between 1797 and 1806, he preserved most of the *Urfaust* material, but added much more (a provisional, unfinished version, *Faust. A Fragment*, had been published in 1790). The opening poem Dedication, the Prelude on the Stage and the Prologue in Heaven were added as a framework; it should be noted that these prefatory scenes were evidently intended to frame not simply Part One, but also a second part that Goethe was already planning by about 1800, even if he was not to complete it until more than thirty years later – the first scene in Faust's study is headed *The First Part of the Tragedy*. Also added was a large body of text dealing with the introduction of Mephistopheles. The hilarious and satirical scene between Mephistopheles (playing the professor) and a student was revised; the scene of Faust's rejuvenation in the Witch's Kitchen was added, as was his introspective soliloquy in Forest and Cavern. The death of Gretchen's brother Valentin was filled out, and two scenes (Auerbach's Cellar and the final prison scene) were revised and versified. Some scenes were transposed from their positions in the early versions. Otherwise, the *Urfaust* material (Faust in his study; Faust and Wagner; Mephistopheles and the student; Auerbach's Cellar; the tragic drama of Gretchen) survive remarkably into the final version – which indicates, apart from anything else, what an accurate copyist Fräulein von Göchhausen was. The most startling and sensational new material introduced by Goethe into the final version of Part One was, however, the Walpurgis Night – the witches' sabbath on the Brocken – and its controversial sequel, the Walpurgis Night's Dream.

Walpurgis Night, or St Walburga's Eve on the night of 30 April, is by German folkloric tradition the night when the creatures of darkness assemble on the summit of the Brocken (or 'Blocksberg') in the Harz Mountains to worship Satan. Although it was not a feature of the original legend, Goethe clearly thought such an episode appropriate to the story of Faust; it would represent the attempts of Mephistopheles to distract Faust from the appalling sufferings of Gretchen, the lapse of a whole year during which she bears his child, kills it in her distracted grief, and is tried and sentenced to death. It may well be that the Walpurgis Night would also have represented another agenda for Faust: his attendance at, or at least his observation of, a satanic ritual – which might also have included a nightmarish phantom enactment of Gretchen's execution. However, for reasons that are still contentious, Goethe chose not to include the more extreme and sensational scenes he evidently planned, or at least considered, for the Walpurgis Night – possibly because he feared, reasonably enough, that such material would give profound offence to a contemporary public on both moral and religious grounds. Indeed, even the published version of Part One was attacked, in Germany and Britain, for indecency and blasphemy; it was from a fear of such charges that Coleridge abandoned a plan to translate Part One into English. Shelley and Byron loved it; Shelley translated some scenes, and Byron declared he 'would give the world' to be able to read it in the original German.

The Walpurgis Night, as it appears in the published version, begins vividly enough, as Faust and Mephistopheles make their way towards the summit of the Brocken through an eerie landscape, accompanied by witches, warlocks, will-o'-the-wisps, and other demonic creatures. But although there are (for Goethe's day, at least) bold passages of explicit and implicit ribaldry and diabolism, although we are told that Satan is enthroned on the summit, Mephistopheles (of all people!) distracts Faust from this apotheosis of evil, and instead ushers him towards a bizarre amateur theatrical performance of the masque of Oberon and Titania's Golden Wedding, which is itself only the flimsy pretext for an extraordinary satirical revue, a parade of eccentric and ludicrous figures representing a spectrum of literary, philosophical and political individuals and types – a collection of those Goethe had, as it were, wished onto the Brocken in order to pay off some old scores. Although some of these satirical verses are witty enough, the dramatic result is that the powerful impetus of the satanic revels is diluted to a whimsical masquerade, and critics have been forced to devise ingenious explanations to justify its place in the work (in theatrical performance the whole Walpurgis Night's Dream is more often than not cut out altogether).

Goethe left behind a body of material, some in fair copy in his own hand, some in a copyist's hand, some barely legible on scraps of paper, which has been assembled as *paralipomena* (leftovers or 'out-takes'). Fragmentary and disjointed though these largely are, it is still possible to reconstruct imaginatively something of what Goethe might have had in mind for his original conception of the Walpurgis Night (or at least as an *alternative* conception): a ribald and blasphemous scenario for a satanic ceremony on the summit of the Brocken. The translations given in this edition represent a cautious selection from the more coherent surviving fragments, which is not intended to suggest definitively what course the Walpurgis Night might have taken, but to give a glimpse of a possible scenario Goethe might at one stage have had in mind. (A distinguished German scholar, Albrecht Schöne, has published a more coherent but speculative and controversial version of the whole Walpurgis Night as Goethe might have intended it – see the list for further reading below).

A possible scenario for the alternative Walpurgis Night runs as follows. Faust and Mephistopheles in fact proceed to the summit of the Brocken, where they witness a sensational spectacle accompanied by violent pyrotechnics: the triumphant arrival of Satan himself, who enacts a blasphemous travesty of Judgement Day, dividing the he-goats to his right and the she-goats to his left, and haranguing the respective sexes on the twin urges of greed and sexual lust. After a ribald exchange between Mephistopheles and a puzzled young girl, Satan receives from one of his subjects a peculiar act of homage – his vassals are expected to kiss his backside. This was a commonly reported feature of satanic ritual as outlined in accounts of witch trials in the sixteenth and seventeenth centuries, which Goethe read widely for this episode; here it is represented as a ribald travesty of a loyal vassal kissing his lord's hand – or as a blasphemous travesty of the kiss of Papal homage. There may also be some contemporary political reference to those purported 'democrats' or bogus radicals who were prepared to accept power or patronage under an autocratic system.

A grisly apparition sets the scene for an *auto-da-fé*, an execution witnessed (and presumably initiated) by a chorus of Black and Grey Friars – the Dominicans and Franciscans who were notoriously involved in witch trials and executions. The apparition assumes nightmarish dimensions as it appears to anticipate Gretchen's own execution, a spectacle that might have been designed to remind Faust of the woman he has abandoned, to alert him to her fate, and to prompt his futile efforts to rescue her from prison: the final indication of this section ('Faust. Mephistopheles') is the original *Urfaust* heading of the prose scene 'Gloomy Day. A Field' in *Faust* Part One. Where the Walpurgis Night's Dream intermezzo was to be included in this sequence, if at all, is unclear; but one of the fragmentary outlines does suggest that the satanic scenes were to take place 'after the intermezzo'. A quatrain also indicates the break-up of the Walpurgis Night, with the witches flying home; and a further quatrain suggests that Mephistopheles proposes to take Faust away from the Nordic, Gothic demonic environment to a southern setting – a brief but inconclusive anticipation of Faust's future adventures in *Faust* Part Two, where he travels to Greece to encounter Helen of Troy in her homeland.

It seems that Goethe juggled at various times with various options for his Walpurgis Night episode; but it is improbable that he ever seriously intended to include such scabrous material in his published version of Part One. It is more likely that he was toying with alternative scenarios for his own amusement and that of his close friends (though he must also have known that such material would come to light one day). Even so, it is right that the interested reader of this extraordinary and (even without these fragments) sensational drama should have the opportunity to read this material which, although published in most standard German editions of Goethe's works, has been virtually inaccessible in English.

The other major additions Goethe made to the *Urfaust* and *Fragment* material during his final phase of work on Part One were designed to fill out what he called the 'great gap' in the early versions: Faust's despair after his rejection by the Earth Spirit, his abortive attempt at suicide, the introduction of Mephistopheles in the shape of a black dog, and the crucial terms of the agreement between them that provide the impetus of the action – an agreement which, taken together with the theological and metaphysical issues presented in the Prologue in Heaven, raises questions of interpretation that are still controversial today.

It is almost certain that by the time he wrote the Prologue in Heaven and the pact scene around 1800, Goethe already not only intended to extend the drama into a second part, but also envisaged Faust's salvation – or at least wished to keep the issue open. Indeed, in the Prologue in Heaven, it seems that the Lord anticipates, and might even guarantee, Faust's salvation: continual striving, unremitting effort, a refusal to sink into self-satisfied sloth or idleness, are necessary, though perhaps not sufficient, conditions for salvation. In this divine scheme, the Devil is an unwilling agent of God's purpose; his task is to goad humanity into activity and, as Devil, to further the divine will. Mephistopheles, of course, resists this role; and Goethe uses the model laid down in the Book of Job (1: 6–12) to suggest the possibility of Faust's damnation. The Devil issues a challenge to, or makes a bet with, the Lord (the wager is more explicitly formulated in the Lutheran version than in the King James Bible) that he can bring Faust to perdition – a wager that the Lord may or may not accept, but which results in his allowing Mephistopheles a free hand as long as Faust lives.

Because he wished to leave the issue of Faust's redemption or damnation open, Goethe clearly could not formulate the pact between Faust and the Devil in the terms of the traditional story – which were that the Devil agrees to serve Faust for a fixed term (usually for twenty-four years), at the end of which he will claim Faust's soul. Instead, the agreement arrived at in the so-called 'Pact

Scene' (lines 1530–1867) is complex, ambiguous and open-ended. Mephistopheles accepts a wager or challenge from Faust that he can never delude or satisfy him so completely with pleasure that he will bid the passing moment stay (lines 1699–1706); if the Devil succeeds, then Faust (who is in any case indifferent to his fate after death) will be his. The fundamental paradox here is that Mephistopheles should accept a wager which, on the terms of the Prologue in Heaven, he cannot possibly win: it is his divinely-ordained task to spur men out of sloth into activity, and yet he accepts a wager that challenges him to reduce Faust to just such a state of passive self-satisfaction.

We must remember, however, that this puzzling wager or challenge is not the only agreement reached between Faust and Mephistopheles. A little earlier in the same scene (lines 1656–59), Mephistopheles has carefully formulated a formal pact or contract – which he also carefully ensures is signed, in the traditional way, in Faust's own blood: not that he will serve Faust for a fixed term of twenty-four years, but that he will serve him in this world, provided that Faust will do the same for him in the hereafter. Since Faust cares little for the hereafter, Mephistopheles has no difficulty in securing Faust's signature on his master-servant contract – by which, in contracting himself to serve Faust, he has also bound Faust to him for the rest of his life. This, it appears, is the most important part of the arrangement – at least for Mephistopheles.

The British scholar Eudo C. Mason has perceptively cut through the contradictions and paradoxes of the wager by suggesting that Mephistopheles does not take Faust's conditions at all seriously: '... the only thing that matters in his eyes is that Faust has committed himself to him *on any terms*. Ignoring those conditions, he sets about procuring Faust's damnation by the good, old-fashioned, and well-tried method of involving him in guilt, crime and sin – just like any other normal devil; not by the strange, paradoxical method of trying to make him so contented that he might feel inclined to say to the passing moment: "Stay, you are so fair"' (Mason, p. 307). Michael Beddow takes this argument a stage further by suggesting that Mephistopheles has no intention of winning his 'spurious' wager with Faust; indeed, he is intent on losing it in order to win the far more important wager he has made with the Lord in the Prologue in Heaven (Beddow, pp. 54–59).

There are several factors that support this interpretation. Firstly, nowhere in the drama does Mephistopheles invoke Faust's conditions for the wager – not in the Gretchen episode, nor in the Helen episode, nor at Faust's death; he speaks only of his contractual bargain, of 'that lofty soul that pledged itself to me' (line 11830), or of the deed Faust signed in his own blood (lines 11613–14). Secondly, the strategy adopted by Mephistopheles throughout is entirely consistent with this purpose: far from trying to satisfy Faust, he goes out of his way to keep him dissatisfied, to blight his aspirations, and to contrive disastrous outcomes for his ventures, 'thereby goading him on to further ceaseless activity and striving, as the Lord had intended' (Mason, p. 306). Thirdly, this strategy is also consistent with the import of Mephistopheles' vicious and triumphant monologue at the end of the pact scene (lines 1851–67) – a passage that is all too often disregarded, and one in which, we may safely assume, Mephistopheles shows himself in his true colours, since he has no reason to dissimulate as he does in Faust's presence. Here, Mephistopheles promises to feed Faust with illusion and trivial banality – not in order to satisfy him, but to frustrate him, to exploit his insatiability and drive him to perdition. For, as he concludes with diabolical confidence, such a man does not even require the Devil's services to bring him to damnation: 'And even if he hadn't pledged himself to me, / He'd still be damned for all eternity' (lines 1866–7).

There are clearly several perspectives on the issues of the pact, of the two wagers (in heaven and in Faust's study), and of Faust's salvation generally: those of Faust, of the Lord, of Mephistopheles, and of the reader or audience. In any case, as Goethe is reported to have said, the question of Faust's salvation is not one that informs either the whole drama or each individual scene; it was not his way to hang such a richly diverse and variegated theme as that of Faust on the meagre thread of a single idea. As he also put it somewhat facetiously (again on the not entirely reliable evidence of Eckermann's report), in the end it is 'the old gentleman's prerogative of mercy' that intervenes 'to bring the whole to a most happy conclusion.'

FAUST, PART TWO

The writing of Part Two was less protracted and more concentrated than that of Part One. In 1800, while he was still working on Part One, Goethe wrote a fragment of 269 lines entitled 'Helen in the Middle Ages', an episode in iambic trimeter and choral odes that corresponds quite closely to the opening section of the third act of *Faust*, Part Two (lines 8488–8802). He may also have planned, and even written out, some sections of the fifth act; but between 1806 and 1825 he did very little work on the project, except to dictate in 1816 a rough scenario that represents his early conception of Part Two. In 1825, however, urged by his publisher Cotta and his loyal diarist Johann Peter Eckermann, and perhaps inspired by the death of Byron at Missolonghi the previous year, he used the 1800 fragment as the starting point for an episode that was to become the third act of Part Two, which was completed in June 1826 and published separately as 'Helen: Classical-Romantic Phantasmagoria: Interlude to *Faust*'. From May 1827 he worked intensively on what he now designated his *Hauptgeschäft* (principal task). Act One was completed by early 1830, and Act Two by June of that year; Acts Five and Four (in that order) were ready by July 1831. The manuscript was sealed, and *Faust* Part Two was published posthumously in 1832.

It is almost immediately clear to the reader or audience that Part Two is fundamentally different in character from Part One. This is not to deny any overall unity or continuity between the two parts; quite clearly, there are echoes and references between them. The figures of Faust and Mephistopheles are common to both parts; the action is still broadly encapsulated within the framework of the Prologue in Heaven and the pact and wager between the two protagonists. The second part represents Faust's experiences in the 'wider world' after the 'small world' of Part One, according to the undertaking given to Faust by Mephistopheles in line 2052; it is the continuation of, or the sequel to, Part One, in that it is the extension of the story of Faust into the world of public affairs. It is the continuation of his struggle to assert himself against confusion and despair, against the cynical nihilism of the spirit of denial who is his constant companion; it is the continuation of Faust's striving. But the second part is drastically, indeed bafflingly, different from the first in structure and characterisation, in literary idiom and style, in scope and treatment.

Goethe himself repeatedly stressed these differences. The second part, he claimed, was less fragmentary than the first; it engaged the mind more than the first part, it was designed to appeal to the reader's intellect, learning and education. The story was more conceptual; the first part had dealt with the specific, the second tended towards the generic. The first part was 'almost entirely subjective', it concerned a 'passionate' individual; the second part revealed a 'higher, wider, brighter, less passionate world.' For all its unconventional 'open' structure, Part One is – just – within what Brecht called the 'Aristotelian' canon of drama, demanding a degree of empathy with its characters and their fate as the action moves relentlessly towards its conclusion.

In the second part, the action is broader and more discursive, more dispassionate. It is an epic panorama of Faust's involvement in national, indeed international affairs: affairs of state, of politics and culture, wars and revolution, commerce and technology. The action of the second part is symbolic rather than mimetic, allegorical rather than dramatic (though it is at times highly theatrical). The Faust of Part Two, while not entirely purged of human individuality, is quite different from the psychologically – and erotically – motivated personality of the first part; he is less an individual in a dramatic context than an emblematic figure whose experiences are not simply those of a single person, but rather those of modern western man, just as the whole action of Part Two is an allegorical representation of certain phases of Western European history and culture within the scope of Goethe's knowledge and experience.

Faust appears in a series of roles, each determined by the symbolic or allegorical context in which he moves: as Plutus, as court financier and necromancer, as a travelling philhellene, as the lover of Helen of Troy in the guise of a Frankish crusading knight, as the Emperor's 'military adviser', as trader, colonist, and civil engineer. Helen is, similarly, a composite symbolic and emblematic figure who plays her role in an extended and complex allegory of the reception of the classical heritage in the Western European imagination. Mephistopheles continues in Part Two his function as

Faust's negative alter ego; his characterisation is still determined by his nihilistic contradiction of Faust's illusions and aspirations. If at times he appears to be more positive in helping Faust to realise his ambitions, this is also consistent with his role from the beginning, with the terms of his contract with Faust; Mephistopheles is in a long comic tradition of servants who contrive at once to further and to frustrate their masters' commands and wishes. But he too appears in a bewildering series of roles or (at times literally) of masks: as court jester, as Zoilo-Thersites, as Avarice, as Sheherezade, as university professor (again), as the negative polarity to the beauty of Helen in the hideous mask of Phorkyas, as Faust's military agent, as bailiff of his estates, and finally in burlesque as the Satan of traditional superstition. In Act Three he is also the agent or demon of cultural and historical change, moving the allegorical action on from ancient Greece to the Middle Ages, and from the Renaissance to the modern era.

Faust Part One was essentially a product of late eighteenth-century German literature, of the Enlightenment, the so-called 'Sturm und Drang', and – up to a point – of 'Weimar' classicism. Though there may be allusive references to the French Revolution (in the Witch's Kitchen and in some of the quatrains of the Walpurgis Night's Dream), it is a pre-revolutionary work. Part Two, however, is a product of post-revolutionary Europe, a work of the early nineteenth century, adumbrating in Act One the crisis and imminent collapse of the *ancien régime* in the previous century; in Act Three, the reception of classical culture in Europe, the meeting of north-west and south-east in the successive assimilations of ancient Greece by other cultures, up to and including the short-lived but momentous period of Goethe's and Schiller's Weimar Classicism between 1795 and 1805; in Act Four, the political turbulence of the Napoleonic wars and invasions, and the restoration of the old order in post-Congress Europe; and in Act Five, the beginnings of agricultural and industrial revolution, of exploitation, colonisation, and technological revolution – until the drama finally returns to the quasi-theological premises and issues with which it opened.

Part Two is a 'Gesamtkunstwerk' *avant la lettre* (it was frequently read and avidly discussed by Richard and Cosima Wagner). It is a multi-media work, drawing on street theatre and pageant, on German, Italian and classical carnivals, court festivals and *trionfi*; on all manner of sources in the visual arts (representations of Leda and the Swan, of marine triumphs, of anchorites in the Theban desert, of the Madonna in glory); it teems with intertextual literary references – Homer, Attic tragedy, Dante, Shakespeare, Calderon, Milton, Klopstock, Byron, and of course the Bible; and it reverts frequently to music, even to opera. Much of the text (as also in Part One) is devoted to song, and music is prescribed for the Florentine masquerade of Act One; the Classical Walpurgis Night of Act Two, and especially the concluding marine pageant, calls for songs and operatic effects; in the Euphorion episode of Act Three, the dialogue is clearly in part written as operatic libretto, and music is specifically prescribed from lines 9679 to 9938. Goethe wistfully remarked that Mozart would have been the ideal composer for Part Two; he also mentioned Mayerbeer or Rossini as possible collaborators.

The problems of performance and production for *Faust* are clearly enormous, if only because of its sheer length, but they are not insuperable (the first integral stage performance of both parts was not until forty-four years after Goethe's death, under Otto Devrient in Weimar). To students who almost invariably raised this question, my (somewhat evasive) answer was: if Wagner's *Ring* cycle can be produced on stage, then surely both parts of *Faust* can be. In Britain alone over the last twenty years, I have seen (severely abridged and adapted, but otherwise successful and entertaining) performances of both parts at the Citizens' Theatre Glasgow, at the Lyric Theatre Hammersmith, and the Swan Theatre Stratford-on-Avon – as well as a truly execrable production in 2006 at the Royal Lyceum in Edinburgh. The most successful performance I have seen was Peter Stein's exhilaratingly original production at Hanover in 2000, in which every line of *Faust* (albeit based on Albrecht Schöne's eccentric edition of Part Two, and with some strange textual affectations) was performed over two days in a vast exhibition hall, with the most imaginative possible use of separate areas and spaces, whereby the audience moved from one scene to the next, with the action at times continuing around them as they went. Rarely can such justice have been done to a vast and complex drama.

NOTE ON THE TRANSLATION

Although Goethe's *Faust*, and Part One in particular, has been translated dozens of times into English, I know of only six other translations of the *Urfaust*. The earliest known translation of the *Urfaust* is *Goethe's 'Faust' (the so-called First Part, 1770–1808); together with the Scene 'Two Imps and Amor'; the variants of the Göchhausen Transcript; and the Complete Paralipomena of the Weimar Edition of 1887. In English, with Introduction and Notes*, by R. McLintock, London, 1897. McLintock's version is remarkable in that it appeared only ten years after Erich Schmidt's discovery and publication of the *Urfaust* in Germany. Even fewer translations of *Faust* include the unpublished scenarios for the Walpurgis Night – though Luke (1987, p. 173) and Constantine (2005, pp. 180–1) provide summaries. It is extraordinary that two nineteenth-century translators offered English versions of the scenarios – McLintock and Bayard Taylor (1871, pp. 246–8) – though these were, inevitably, very heavily bowdlerised. (Bayard Taylor never knew of the *Urfaust*, having died in 1878, nine years before its discovery).

It would be wearisome to attempt a survey of English versions of *Faust*; for twentieth-century translations, the reader is referred to Derek Glass's bibliography of Goethe translations into English. The most notable translations of recent years are by Stuart Atkins (1984 and 1994), which is in unrhymed metrical verse; by David Luke (1987 and 1994), which is in rhymed and metrical verse, and includes an extensive introduction and explanatory notes; and by David Constantine (Part One, 2005), which is in half-rhymed metrical verse, with introduction and notes.

In this translation I have sought to reproduce as closely as possible the rhymes, metres and verse forms of Goethe's text. Clearly, these constraints render a literal translation impossible; but a literal translation would scarcely be appropriate in any case. I have exercised a cautious freedom of expression, but have taken pains to remain faithful to the essential meaning of the text. In the more colourful and ribald exchanges of Auerbach's Cellar, for instance, I have taken some licence in rendering those passages that would sound alien to a present-day reader (whether German or English) into a modern equivalent.

I have also exercised the same freedom that Goethe allowed himself in the basic verse form of the drama by varying the metrical length of lines and the rhyming patterns, using lines of four, five or six stresses, occasional lines of two or three stresses, and even some isolated unrhymed lines (known in German as *Waisen*: orphans). This is the so-called 'madrigal verse', the flexible iambic form in which the greater part of *Faust* is written. But the drama also exploits a huge variety of other verse forms: *Knittelvers*, Goethe's free adaptation of Hans Sachs's sixteenth-century octosyllabic rhyming couplets (e.g. lines 354–429, 1868–1967, 2815–60); *ottava rima* (1–32, 59–74); free verse (468–74, 3438–50, 3776–3834); unrhymed iambic pentameter or 'blank verse' (3217–50); adonics (dactyl + trochee, 1447–505); dactylic sequences (737–41, 749–61, 785–807); folk song strophes (949–80, 2759–82); the liturgical sequences of the *Stabat Mater* and the *Dies Irae* (3590–601, 3798–9, 3813–15, 3825–7); prose ('Gloomy Day. A Field' – and, in the *Urfaust*, 'Auerbach's Cellar' and 'A Dungeon'); and all manner of interpolated songs and jingles.

Part Two is, in the apt words of a German critic, even more of a 'metrical pandemonium' than Part One. I have not cared to count the number of different metrical forms in the whole of *Faust*, but it is safe to say that no other serious work of European literature has such astonishing prosodic variety; in the final scene alone there are some sixteen changes of metre and verse form. The principal form of Part Two is, as in Part One, iambic madrigal verse – though here it tends towards a more regular form of predominantly five, occasionally four, stressed syllables per line. This basic dialogue form is frequently broken by a great variety of lyrical forms, strophic or stichic, trochaic, iambic or dactylic – many of which are designed to be sung; in particular, the masquerade scene of Act One and the Classical Walpurgis Night – especially the marine festival that concludes it – display a wide metrical variety, as do the Euphorion episode of Act Three and the final scene of the drama.

Part Two also draws on certain verse forms with distinct historical or cultural resonance: *terza rima* (lines 4679–727); the classicising forms of iambic trimeter (7005–39, 10039–66, in Act Three 8488–515 and *passim*), choral ode (8516–23 and *passim*), and trochaic tetrameter (8909–29 and *passim*); and alexandrines (10849–11042). These forms are discussed in more detail in the relevant sections of the commentary to Part Two. Finally, the wooing of Faust and Helen in Act Three, the symbolic merging of classical and romantic, of ancient and medieval cultures, is expressed in prosodic terms, as Faust instructs Helen in the art of end-rhyme unknown to classical antiquity. I have attempted to reproduce all these forms as scrupulously as possible, in order to give some impression of the enormous vitality and variety of Goethe's poetic expression.

The translation is based – with some minor emendations – on the text of Ulrich Gaier's edition (*Faust-Dichtungen, vol. 1*). I am most grateful to Tom Griffith, General Editor of Wordsworth Classics of World Literature, for his invaluable guidance; to the late Derek Glass of the Department of German, King's College, London, for bibliographical information; and to my wife Elizabeth, who has looked through the manuscript with meticulous care. Finally, I wish to dedicate this translation with affection and gratitude to three friends and colleagues who, in their very different ways, have helped and encouraged me, perhaps more than they might realise (or indeed more than I might realise) in the course of my career: Raymond Furness, Francis Lamport and Barry Nisbet.

JOHN R. WILLIAMS
St Andrews

SUGGESTIONS FOR FURTHER READING

ENGLISH TRANSLATIONS OF *FAUST*

Faust: A Tragedy. Translated in the Original Metres by Bayard Taylor, third edn, London, New York and Melbourne: Ward, Lock, and Co., 1890.

Faust I & II, ed. and trans. Stuart Atkins, Boston: Suhrkamp/Insel, 1984 (paperback: Princeton University Press, 1994).

Goethe: Faust, Part One, trans. and introd. David Luke, Oxford World's Classics: Oxford University Press, 1987.

Goethe: Faust, Part Two, trans. and introd. David Luke, Oxford World's Classics: Oxford University Press, 1994.

Faust. The First Part of the Tragedy, trans. and introd. David Constantine, Penguin Classics: London, 2005.

Glass, Derek: *Goethe in English: A Bibliography of the Translations in the Twentieth Century*, Maney: Leeds, 2005, for the English Goethe Society and the Modern Humanities Research Association.

WORKS IN ENGLISH

The Historie of the damnable life, and deserued death of Doctor Iohn Faustus, Newly imprinted . . . according to the true Copie printed at Franckfort, and translated into English by P. F., Gent., London, 1592. In: Philip M. Palmer and Robert P. More, *The Sources of the Faust Tradition from Simon Magus to Lessing*, Oxford University Press, 1936, pp. 134–236.

Christopher Marlowe, *Doctor Faustus and Other Plays*, ed. D. D. Bevington and E. Rasmussen, Oxford World's Classics, Oxford University Press, 1995.

Beddow, Michael: *Goethe: Faust I*, London: Grant & Cutler, 1986.

Bishop, Paul (ed.): *A Companion to Goethe's 'Faust'*, Rochester, NY: Camden House and Woodbridge, Suffolk: Boydell & Brewer, 2001.

Boyle, Nicholas: *Goethe: Faust, Part One*, Cambridge University Press, 1987.

Boyle, Nicholas: *Goethe: The Poet and the Age, vol. 1: 1749–1790,* Oxford University Press, 1991; *vol. 2: 1790–1803,* Oxford University Press, 2000.

Butler, E. M.: *The Fortunes of Faust,* Cambridge University Press, 1952. New edn, 1979.

Durrani, Osman: *Faust: Icon of Modern Culture,* Robertsbridge: Helm Information, 2004.

Geary, John: *Goethe's Faust. The Making of Part One,* New Haven, Conn.: Yale University Press, 1981.

Mason, Eudo C.: *Goethe's Faust: its Genesis and Purport,* Berkeley and Los Angeles: University of California Press, 1967.

Reed, T. J.: *Goethe,* Oxford University Press, 1984. New edn, 1998.

Sharpe, Lesley (ed.): *The Cambridge Companion to Goethe,* Cambridge University Press, 2002.

Swales, Martin and Swales, Erika: *Reading Goethe: A Critical Introduction to the Literary Work,* Rochester, NY: Camden House and Woodbridge, Suffolk: Boydell & Brewer, 2002.

Williams, John R.: *Goethe's Faust,* London: Allen & Unwin, 1987.

Williams, John R.: *The Life of Goethe. A Critical Biography,* Oxford: Blackwell, 1998.

WORKS IN GERMAN

Benz, Richard (ed.): *Historia von D. Johann Fausten, dem weitbeschreyten Zauberer und Schwarzkünstler* [Frankfurt am Main: Spies, 1587], Stuttgart: Reclam, 1964.

Gaier, Ulrich: *Johann Wolfgang Goethe, Faust-Dichtungen,* 3 vols, Stuttgart: Reclam, 1999.

Michelsen, Peter: *Im Banne Fausts. Zwölf Faust-Studien,* Würzburg: Königshausen & Neumann, 2000.

Schmidt, Jochen: *Goethes Faust, Erster und Zweiter Teil: Grundlagen – Werk – Wirkung,* Munich: Beck, 1999.

Schöne, Albrecht: *Götterzeichen – Liebeszauber – Satanskult. Neue Einblicke in alte Goethetexte,* Munich: Beck, 1982. New edn, 1993.

FAUST. A TRAGEDY

DEDICATION

Once more I sense uncertain shapes appearing,
Dimly perceived in days of youth long past.
Now in my heart I feel the moment nearing
When I can hold those phantom figures fast.
The haze and mist that swallowed them is clearing,   5
They gather round me, bodied forth at last.
Within me now a youthful passion surges
As from a magic spell their throng emerges.

They bring back scenes of youthful jubilation,
And with them many well-loved shades appear;   10
A half-forgotten distant intimation
Of those in early times I held so dear.
The grief returns, once more the lamentation
Of life's obscure and wayward course I hear
For those capricious fortune cruelly treated,   15
Who all too soon of joy and life were cheated.

They cannot hear the songs within these pages,
Those souls to whom I sang; I sing alone.
That friendly throng was scattered to the ages,
And those first echoes on the wind were blown.   20
My sorrow now the stranger's mind engages,[1]
Whose praise I cannot in my heart condone;
And some by whose applause my gifts were flattered,
If they still live, to the world's ends are scattered.

And now I feel a long-forgotten yearning;   25
That solemn, quiet world calls me once more,
Its spirit music to my lips returning
Like the Aeolian harp's uncertain chord.
I tremble, and my cheeks with tears are burning,
The stern heart softens, melted to its core.   30
What I possess now vanishes before me,
And what was lost alone has substance for me.

PRELUDE ON THE STAGE

DIRECTOR, POET, CLOWN

DIRECTOR   You two have stood beside me now
For years and shared my troubles all the way.
I'd like to have your views on how   35
To make our mark in Germany today.
I want to entertain the crowd out there –
They put up with an awful lot, you know.
The posts and boards are up, so let's prepare
To give the audience a proper show.   40
They're all agog and sitting patiently,
Something spectacular is what they want to see.
How to please the public – that's the test,
But nowadays I find I'm in a fix;
I know they're not accustomed to the best,   45
But they've all read so much they know the tricks.
How can we give them something fresh and new
That's serious, but entertaining too?
I love to see a crowd of people pour
Into the theatre like rolling waves,   50
And painfully like new-born babes
Squeeze themselves through that narrow door;
At four o'clock, in broad daylight,
Breaking their necks to get a seat,
Pushing and shoving as they fight   55
Like starving beggars for a piece of meat.
And who can work this miracle? I say
The poet can: my friend, do it today!

POET   Don't talk to me about the many-headed,
My spirit fails me at the very sight.   60
Preserve me from that motley mob, the dreaded
Rabble that puts poetry to flight.
The poet to the silent Muse is wedded,
In heavenly peace he finds his true delight,
Where love and friendship godlike forge and cherish   65
The blessings of the heart that never perish.

And what our hearts from deep within created
Or what our timid lips had sought to say,
No matter if it's good or bad, is fated
To be forgotten in the present fray,   70
And only when the tide of time's abated
Appears in its true form another day.
What glitters for the moment is but passing;
Posterity will value what is lasting.

CLOWN   I don't want to hear about posterity!   75
And even if I did, what's it to me?
It's here and now they want to have some fun,
That's what they like, what they're entitled to.
That's just the sort of thing a lad like me can do –
It's what I'm best at, when all's said and done.   80
If you can get across to them, then you can cope
With anything the audience throws at you,
And a full house will give you much more scope
To entertain them – and to move them, too.
So don't be shy and write a proper play.   85
Let your imagination weave its magic spell,
Let sense and reason, love and passion have their say –
But let us have a bit of fun as well.

DIRECTOR   But most of all, put in a lot of action!
That's how to get your audience satisfaction –   90
Don't give them an excuse for getting bored.
They like to see things happen on the stage;
Just keep them happy, you'll get your reward –
They'll love you, you'll be all the rage.
A lot of people like a lot of stuff   95
To choose from, and they have to be presented
With a spectacle that has enough
For everyone – then they'll go home contented.
Let's have a play that plays to every taste!
It's easy to concoct a tasty stew.   100
Get busy with your scissors and your paste;
Don't try to get it perfect – if you do,
The public will demolish it for you.

POET   You've no idea what it does to me
To prostitute my talents in this way;   105

You want the sort of rubbish you can see
In any West-End theatre every day.
DIRECTOR   I'm not offended by such taunts as these;
I want to put a show on that will run,
And I don't really care much how it's done.   110
The public isn't difficult to please;
Just try to keep your audience in mind.
Some of them come here simply to unwind,
Some have just stuffed themselves with food;
And if they've read the papers, then you'll find   115
They can be in a very nasty mood.
These people don't want anything too arty,
They come because they're curious to know
What's on; the women think they're at a party,
Parading around – it's all part of the show.   120
Why are you poets all such dreamers, though?
Doesn't a full house give you a big thrill?
Just take a close look at our patrons, and you'll know
Some don't appreciate us, others never will.
After the play they'll trot off to some gambling den,   125
Look forward to a wild night with their floozies.
You needn't look too far for inspiration, then –
I don't know why you bother the poor Muses.
I tell you, give them lots and lots of action
And rivet their attention, that's the way.   130
They only want a few hours of distraction –
You'll never satisfy them anyway.
Now what's the matter? Are we having a contraction?
POET   Oh, go and find yourself another slave!
You want the poet to betray his Muse?   135
The highest birthright nature ever gave
You'd have him wantonly abuse?
How does the poet move all people's hearts?
Command the elements with all his arts?
It is the harmony that dwells within us   140
So that the whole world is reflected in us.
When nature's spindle twists the thread of ages,
Indifferently she spins the endless strand,
And when the world's discordant clamour rages

In dire confusion none can understand –   145
Who then enlivens that monotony
And makes it pulse with rhythmic motion?
Who summons every voice, united in devotion,
And blends them into glorious harmony?
Who makes the furious tempest rage and sing,   150
Gives solemn meaning to the sunset glow?
Who scatters all the lovely flowers of spring
At the beloved's feet wherever she may go?
Who weaves the modest laurel leaves that crown
The heads of those whose deeds set them apart?   155
Preserves Olympus and the gods' renown?
Man's power, embodied in the poet's art!

CLOWN   Why don't you use them then, these splendid
                            powers?
Let's see them in this theatre of ours!
Approach your story like a love-affair;   160
You meet, you feel attracted, so you hang around,
And gradually you find you really care.
Of course, you'll find it has its ups and downs;
There's pain and pleasure, if you're truly smitten –
Before you can turn round, you'll have a novel
                         written.   165
That's the kind of play we ought to give –
The whole parade of life that people live!
Plunge in and take it as it is, and you
Can offer something interesting and new.
Some vivid scenes, a measure of illusion,   170
A grain of truth and plenty of confusion,
That's the surest way to mix a brew
To please them all – and teach them something, too.
Our finest youth will flock to see your play,
Expecting some momentous revelation;   175
Their melancholy minds will soak up what you say
And in your words they'll find sweet consolation.
Arouse their feelings for them, and reveal
Their own emotions – that's what will appeal.
They're young enough to move to tears or laughter,   180
Excitement and illusion's what they're after.

You'll never please the older ones, I know —
Impressionable minds will love it, though.

POET   Then give me back the time when I was young,
When all my life before me lay,   185
A constant stream of words and song
Burst from my lips with every passing day,
When clouds of glory hid the world from view,
And budding youth still found it all so new;
When flowers in thousands seemed to fill   190
The fields for me to gather them at will.
Though I had nothing, what I had was this:
The urge for truth, delight in make-believe.
Give me those passions back, let me retrieve
The keenest pangs of adolescent bliss,   195
Extremes of love and hate, of joy and pain —
Give me back my youth again!

CLOWN   Such youthful energy, my friend, you'll find
Is needed in the frantic heat of war,
Or when some pretty girl might feel inclined   200
To take you in her arms and ask for more;
Or in the race before your weary eyes
You see the finish and the winner's prize,
Or when the whirling dance is at an end
You spend the night carousing with a friend.   205
But if you've confidence enough to play
A graceful tune and let us hear your voice,
Or let your pleasant fancy stray
Towards a destination of your choice —
That is a task for the maturer man,   210
And we respect you for it all the more.
They say age makes us childish — but it can
Make truer children of us than before.

DIRECTOR   You've bandied words enough, now let me see
Some action from you both for once.   215
We could have spent the time more usefully
While you two were exchanging compliments.
What's all this talk of inspiration in the end?
You can't just sit and hope it might descend.
If you're a poet, as you claim to be,   220

Get on with it and write some poetry.
You know exactly what we have to do –
To give them something with a kick in it,
So hurry up and make a decent brew.
Don't leave it till tomorrow, stick at it –   225
Today will pass you by before you know.
You've got to grab your chance, or else it's gone,
It doesn't come round twice, so don't be slow,
And once you've taken it, don't let it go;
That's the only way to get things done.   230

On German stages, everybody knows,
They like to try out anything that goes;
And so today let's have some splendid scenery
And plenty of spectacular machinery.
We'll have the sun and moon – use all the lights –   235
And lots of stars, as many as you want,
Fire, water, rocky mountain heights,
And birds and animals – just be extravagant.
This narrow stage is wide enough to gird about
The whole of God's creation. Very well: 240
Go carefully but quickly – measure out
The way from heaven through the world to hell.

PROLOGUE IN HEAVEN

The LORD, *the Heavenly Host, then* MEPHISTOPHELES.
The three Archangels step forward.

RAPHAEL   With choirs of kindred spheres competing,
The sun intones its ancient sound,
And runs its thunderous course, completing   245
Its preordained diurnal round.
This vision none has comprehended,
Though angels quicken at the sight;
These high and wondrous works are splendid
As when the world first shone with light.   250

GABRIEL   The earth in majesty rotating
Spins on itself as swift as light,
Celestial radiance alternating
With dread impenetrable night.
In rocky depths the foaming ocean   255
Surges with elemental force,
Swept on by the eternal motion
That speeds the worlds upon their course.

MICHAEL   And mighty tempests rage unceasing
From sea to land, from land to sea,   260
A furious clash of power, releasing
A chain of vast causality.
Before the crash of rolling thunder
The flashing bolts blaze out the way;
But we, thy angels, watch with wonder   265
The peaceful progress of thy day.

ALL THREE   Thy vision none has comprehended,
Though angels quicken at the sight;
Thy mighty works, O Lord, are splendid
As when the world first shone with light.   270

MEPHISTO.   Since, Lord, you deign to visit us once more
To find out how we manage our affairs,
And since you've always welcomed me before,
I've come to join your household staff upstairs.

I'm not much good at lofty words, I fear,   275
It doesn't worry me if they all sneer.
Pathos from me would make you laugh – although
I know you gave up laughing long ago.
I can't sing hymns about the universe,
I only see how people go from bad to worse.   280
He hasn't changed, your little god on earth –
He's still peculiar as the day you gave him birth.
He'd live a better life, at least,
If you'd not given him a glimpse of heaven's light.
He calls it reason – which gives him the right   285
To be more bestial than any beast.
Saving your gracious presence, Sire, I'd say
He's like a silly grasshopper in the hay.
He chirps and sings and flitters to and fro,
And chirps the same old song and jumps about;   290
If only he were satisfied with that – but no,
In every pile of filth he dips his snout.

THE LORD Why are you telling me all this again?
Do you always come here to complain?
Could there be something good on earth that
                                        you've forgotten? 295

MEPHISTO. No, Lord! I'm pleased to say it's still completely
                                        rotten.
I feel quite sorry for their miserable plight;
When it's as bad as that, tormenting them's not right.

THE LORD Do you know Faust?

MEPHISTO.   The Doctor?

THE LORD   Yes – my servant.

MEPHISTO. He serves you in a very curious way indeed.   300
It isn't earthly nourishment he seems to need;
His fevered mind is in a constant ferment.
Half-conscious of his folly, in his pride
On all the joys of earth he wants to feed,
And pluck from heaven the very brightest star.   305
He searches high and low, and yet however far
He roams, his restless heart returns dissatisfied.

THE LORD Though in confusion still he seeks his way,
Yet I will lead him to the light one day.

	For in the budding sapling the gardener can see	310
	The promise of the fruit upon the full-grown tree.	
MEPHISTO.	What would you wager? Will you challenge me	
	To win him from you? Give me your permission	
	To lead him down my path to his perdition?	
THE LORD	While he's on earth, while he is still alive,	315
	Then you may tempt him – that is my condition.	
	For man will err as long as he can strive.	
MEPHISTO.	I take up your kind offer, Sire, most gratefully;	
	The dead are of no interest to me.	
	I like them fresh and full of life, well fed.	320
	A corpse is very boring; I'm like a cat, you see –	
	It's no fun once the mouse is dead.	
THE LORD	Well then, it shall be left to you.	
	Entice this spirit from its primal source,	
	And drag him down, if you are able to,	325
	Upon your own infernal course;	
	With shame you will confess to me one day,	
	A good man, though his instincts be obscure,	
	Is still quite conscious of the proper way.	
MEPHISTO.	So be it! And it won't take long, I'm sure.	330
	I have no doubts about my wager, none –	
	And I will come before you when it's done,	
	Triumphant with the glory that I've won.	
	He shall eat dust, and on his belly I will make	
	Him go, like my old aunt, the celebrated snake.	335
THE LORD	I give you freedom to appear at will;	
	For you and for your kind I feel no hate.	
	Of all the spirits of denial and of ill,	
	Such rogues as you I can well tolerate.	
	For man's activity can slacken all too fast,	340
	He falls too soon into a slothful ease;	
	The Devil's a companion who will tease	
	And spur him on, and work creatively at last.	
	But you, true sons of God, attend your duty:	
	Rejoice in rich creation's living beauty!	345
	The vital process that eternally informs	
	All things, embrace you with the bonds that love	
	has wrought;	

To what appears in evanescent forms
Give substance with the lasting power of thought.

Heaven closes, the Archangels disperse

MEPHISTO. I like to drop in on him if I can,   350
Just to keep things between us on the level.
It's really decent of the Grand Old Man
To be so civil to the very Devil.

THE FIRST PART OF THE TRAGEDY

Night. In a high-vaulted narrow Gothic room
FAUST *sits restlessly at his desk.*

FAUST Medicine, and Law, and Philosophy –
You've worked your way through every school,   355
Even, God help you, Theology,
And sweated at it like a fool.
Why labour at it any more?
You're no wiser now than you were before.
You're Master of Arts, and Doctor too,   360
And for ten years all you've been able to do
Is lead your students a fearful dance
Through a maze of error and ignorance.
And all this misery goes to show
There's nothing we can ever know.   365
Oh yes, you're brighter than all those relics,
Professors and Doctors, scribblers and clerics;
No doubts or scruples to trouble you,
Defying hell, and the Devil too.
But there's no joy in self-delusion;   370
Your search for truth ends in confusion.
Don't imagine your teaching will ever raise
The minds of men or change their ways.
And as for worldly wealth, you've none –
What honour or glory have you won?   375
A dog could stand this life no more.
And so I've turned to magic lore;
The spirit message of this art
Some secret knowledge might impart.
No longer shall I sweat to teach   380
What always lay beyond my reach;
I'll know what makes the world revolve,
Its inner mysteries resolve,
No more in empty words I'll deal –
Creation's wellsprings I'll reveal!   385

Sweet moonlight, shining full and clear,
Why do you light my torture here?
How often have you seen me toil,
Burning last drops of midnight oil.
On books and papers as I read,   390
My friend, your mournful light you shed.
If only I could flee this den
And walk the mountain-tops again,
Through moonlit meadows make my way,
In mountain caves with spirits play –   395
Released from learning's musty cell,
Your healing dew would make me well!

But no, you're stuck inside this lair,
In this accursed dungeon, where
The very light of heaven can pass   400
But dimly through the painted glass.
Immured behind a pile of books,
Motheaten, dusty, in the reek
Of papers stuffed in all these nooks –
This is the wisdom that you seek.   405
These jars and cases row on row,
Retorts and tubes and taps and gauges,
The useless junk of bygone ages –
This is the only world you know!

And still you wonder why this pain   410
Constricts your heart and hems it in,
Why agonies you can't explain
Sap all life's energies within?
When God created us, he founded
His living nature for our home;   415
But you sit in this gloom, surrounded
By mildewed skull and arid bone.

Escape into a wider sphere!
This book of secrets will provide
The magic writings of the Seer;   420
Let Nostradamus be your guide.

If nature helps us, we can seek
The paths the stars in heaven go;
Through her we have the power to know
How spirits unto spirits speak.   425
Your dusty learning can't expound
The magic symbols written here.
The spirits hover close around:
Now answer me, if you can hear!

He opens the book and sees the Sign of the Macrocosm[2]

Ah, what ecstatic joy at this great sight   430
I feel at once through all my senses flowing!
What vital happiness, what sheer delight
Through veins and nerves with youthful passion
                                              glowing.
Was it a god that wrote these signs for me?
The raging in my soul is stilled,   435
My empty heart with joy is filled,
And through some urgent mystery
All nature's forces are revealed.
Am I a god? My mind's so clear!
With mystic vision now I see concealed   440
In these pure symbols nature's rich activity.
At last I grasp the wisdom of the Seer:
'The spirit world is with us still,
Your mind is closed, your heart is dead.
Up, worldly scholar, drink your fill –   445
At heaven's gate the dawn is red!'

He studies the Sign

How all into a wholeness weaves,
Each in the other moves and lives!
The powers of heaven ascending and descending,
And to each other golden vessels sending,   450
With fragrant blessings winging,
From heaven to earth their bounty bringing –
In harmony the universe is ringing!

Ah, what a vision! But a vision, and no more.
I do not feel the pulse of nature, nor 455
Feed at her breasts. The springs of life that nursed
All things, for which creation yearns,
To which the flagging spirit turns,
They flow, they suckle still, but I must thirst!

> *Disconsolately he turns the pages and*
> *sees the Sign of the Earth Spirit*

I see more inspiration in this sign! 460
Earth Spirit, we are of a kind.
I feel new energies, my mind
Now glows as if from new-fermented wine.
Now I can dare to face the world again,
To share in all its joy and all its pain. 465
Into the eye of storms I'll set my sail,
And in the grinding shipwreck I'll not quail.
Clouds gather overhead,
The moon conceals its light!
The lamp burns low! 470
Mist swirls around! Red flashes flicker
About my head. A chill shiver
Blows down from the vault above
And grips me!
I feel your presence round me, 475
Great Spirit, you have found me –
Reveal yourself!
It tears my heart, my senses reel
And burn with passions new. I feel
My heart goes out to you, I have no fear; 480
If it should cost my life, you must appear!

> *He seizes the book and with mysterious words*
> *invokes the Sign of the Earth Spirit. A red flame*
> *flickers, the Spirit appears in the flame.*

SPIRIT   Who calls me?
FAUST   [*turning away*] A dreadful shape I see!
SPIRIT   Your potent spells have brought me here;
            You sought to draw me from my sphere,

And now –

FAUST   You are too terrible for me!   485

SPIRIT   With sighs you begged me to appear,
          My voice you would hear and my face you would see;
          Your mighty pleas have summoned me.
          I'm here! But now – what piteous fear
          Has seized you, superman? The soul that cried
                                        for me, where   490
          Is it now? The heart that in itself could bear
          A whole created world, and in its swollen pride
          Puffed up, with us, the spirits, would have vied?
          Where are you, Faust, whose voice reached to
                                        my sphere,
          Who summoned all your powers to draw me here?   495
          This is you? who scarcely felt my breath,
          And quake as if you go to meet your death,
          A frightened worm that twists and writhes!

FAUST   Creature of flame, to you I'll not give in;
          I, Faust, I am your equal, am your kin!   500

SPIRIT   In all life's storms and surging tides
          I ebb and flow
          From birth to grave,
          Weave to and fro,
          An endless wave   505
          Through all life's glowing
          Fabric flowing.
          On time's humming loom, as I toil at the treads,
          For God's living garment I fashion the threads.

FAUST   Industrious spirit, to the world's furthest end   510
          You rove; how close you seem to me!

SPIRIT   You match the spirit that you comprehend,
          Not me!   [vanishes

FAUST   [shattered] Not you?
          Who then?   515
          I, made in God's image,
          No match for you?

                    A knock at the door

Oh death! It's my assistant at the door.

To turn my highest bliss into despair,
Dissolve these teeming visions into air,   520
It only needs that plodding bore.

WAGNER *in nightgown and nightcap, holding*
a lamp. FAUST *reluctantly turns to him.*

WAGNER Forgive me, but I heard your voice –
It sounded like a tragedy in Greek.
That is an art that I would learn by choice.
These days one has to know just how to speak   525
One's lines; an actor, people often say, could teach
A parson in the art of how to preach.

FAUST Why, surely – if the parson's only acting,
And many times I daresay that's the case.

WAGNER But all this study I find so distracting;   530
One scarcely sees the world beyond this place,
And only from afar – so how can all our arts
Of eloquent persuasion guide men's hearts?

FAUST If you don't feel, your words will not inspire;
Unless from deep within you speak sincere,   535
And with a charismatic fire
Compel the hearts of all who hear.
Oh, you can sit there glueing bits together
Or mixing cold leftovers in a stew,
Blowing at the ashes, wondering whether   540
There's any fire left to warm your brew.
Yes – fools and children you'll impress –
If that is really what you want to do;
But you will never know another's heart, unless
You are prepared to give yours too.   545

WAGNER A good delivery can help the speaker, though;
I feel there's still so much I ought to know.

FAUST Speak honestly, speak from the heart!
Your foolish tricks are all in vain!
Good sense and reason – they don't need the art   550
Of eloquence to make their meaning plain.
If with sincerity you speak,
Why, then for words you need not seek.
The dazzling rhetoric a speaker spins,

Cut

	The frills and flourishes with which he weaves	555
	His spell, are all as barren as the frosty winds	
	That play among the arid autumn leaves.	
WAGNER	Ah God, but art is long,	
	And short our life's duration!	
	In all my critical deliberation	560
	I often fear the way I chose was wrong.	
	How hard it is to get the method right	
	To follow learning to its very source;	
	Before we're half-way through our course	
	We'll surely die and never reach the light.	565
FAUST	The manuscripts, are they the sacred springs	
	From which one drink will slake your thirst for ever?	
	You'll find no profit in these things	
	Unless your own heart flows with fresh endeavour.	
WAGNER	Forgive me, but it's such delight	570
	To bring the spirit of the past to light,	
	To study all the thoughts of history's wisest men –	
	And marvel at the progress we have made since then.	
FAUST	Oh yes, we've reached the stars! And yet	
	The past, my friend, by which you set	575
	Such store, is a book with seven seals to us.	
	It is a mirror that reveals to us	
	Only the minds of those who seek	
	This spirit of the past of which you speak.	
	Believe me, all you'll find is bunk,	580
	A lumber-room stuffed full of junk,	
	At best a blood–and–thunder play	
	From which most audiences would run away;	
	A catalogue of pompous commonplaces,	
	A puppet–play that's full of empty phrases.	585
WAGNER	Yes – but the world! The human heart and mind!	
	We all seek knowledge, surely, in this sphere?	
FAUST	Why, yes, however knowledge is defined.	
	But who will dare to speak the truth out clear?	
	The few who anything of truth have learned,	590
	And foolishly did not keep truth concealed,	
	Their thoughts and visions to the common herd	
	revealed,	

Since time began we've crucified and burned.
But please, my friend, it's deep into the night,
And I must sleep now – if I can.   595

WAGNER   I'd gladly stay much longer, for it's such delight
Exchanging thoughts with such a learned man.
But then tomorrow, as it's Easter Day,
I'll put more questions to you if I may.
I've studied very hard, and yet, although   600
I know a lot, there's so much more to know.   [*exit*

FAUST   [*alone*] How is it that his mind can take such pleasure,
Forever dabbling in these shallow terms.
He digs so avidly for hidden treasure,
And then rejoices when he digs up worms.   605
Why is it that this tiresome nuisance can
Dispel the throng of spirits gathered round me?
And yet for once I'm glad the wretched man
Came in and broke the magic spell that bound me.
His interruption saved me from despair   610
That threatened to destroy my shattered mind.
The mighty vision I confronted there
Showed me the pygmy stature of mankind.

And I myself, made in God's image, thought
That I had glimpsed eternal truth's reflection,   615
Exulting in the radiance of heaven, sought
To shed all earthly imperfection;
I, higher than Cherubim, imagined I was free
To surge through nature's very veins, I vied
With gods in their creative power, and tried   620
To share their joy – I pay now for my pride!
That voice of thunder has annihilated me.

Your peer, great Spirit, I can never be.
Although my powers could summon you, I fear
I had no power to hold your presence here.   625
That moment was sublime beyond compare,
I felt myself so small and yet so great;
But cruelly you drove me back to share
Humanity's obscure uncertain fate.

Who now will counsel me or warn me? Who?   630
Should I obey that urge that drives me on?
Not just our sorrows, everything we do
Confines the course our lives would freely run.

Against our spirit's loftiest conception
Some foreign element continually conspires;   635
The good to which the soul on earth aspires,
The better part of it is vain deception.
The glorious feelings that life gave us, all emotion
Is numbed and coarsened in the world's commotion.

Once our imagination boldly sought   640
To reach eternity; but now a tiny scope
Is all it needs. The swirling tide of time has brought
An end to all our joy and all our hope.
Deep in our hearts is lodged the worm of care,
It works its secret pain and worry there.   645
In ever-changing guises it appears,
Gnaws at our peace of mind and turns our joys
                                          to tears,
As house and home, as child and wife,
As fire or flood, as poison or as knife;
We tremble at the things that never harmed us yet,   650
And what we never lost we bitterly regret.

I am not like the gods! Too well I know
That I am like the snake that eats the dust,
That must for ever on its belly go
And by the feet of those who pass be crushed.   655

These drawers, these cluttered shelves that line the wall
Confining me inside this dismal cell,
This useless and motheaten bric-à-brac, and all
This junk surrounding me – is this not dust as well?
Shall I discover what I seek in here?   660
And should I read a thousand books to find
How men have agonized in vain, or hear
Of one or two to whom fate has been kind?
You empty skull, I see you grinning down;

Perhaps your brain, like mine, sought in confusion   665
The light of day, but in the gloomy twilight found
Your joyful urge for truth had ended in delusion.
Those instruments that hang there mocking me,
That cobwebbed tangle, clamps and pulleys,
                                        cogs and wheels –
With these I thought I could unlock the seals   670
That guard the door to nature's mystery.
But it was barred; the veil that shrouds from sight
All nature's secrets cannot be dispelled,
And what from your inquiring mind she has withheld
These screws and levers will not bring to light.   675
This rusty apparatus I've retained
Only because it's from my father's time;
The lamp that gutters on my desk has stained
This ancient parchment black with soot and grime.
Far better to have squandered what I had than stay   680
And struggle with the useless junk of yesterday!
What we inherit from our fathers should
Be ours to have and hold, to use it as we would,
Or else it is a millstone that we carry with us;
We can use only what the here and now will give us.   685

Why do my eyes turn to that place again?
Is it that phial that attracts me so?
Why do I sense a sudden lightening, as when
The darkness of the woods is bathed in
                                        moonlight's glow?

I take you down with reverent devotion,   690
And welcome you, most precious, rarest potion!
In you I honour human skill and art,
Quintessence of all kindly opiates, austere
Tincture of subtlest poisons, play your part –
Do one last service for your master here!   695
I see you, and all pain is stilled at last;
I hold you, and my restless striving ceases.
The surging of my mind is ebbing fast,
Borne on fresh tides to ocean's furthest reaches.

Here at my feet the shining waters stretch away,   700
And to a new shore beckons now a bright new day!

A chariot of fire descends on buoyant wings
And finds me ready! Soon I shall be free
To soar aloft to realms of higher things,
To other spheres of pure activity.   705
You who were as a worm, do you deserve such bliss,
Such radiant life, such godlike joy as this?
Yes, turn your back on earth, and resolutely go
Into a sunlight such as here you'll never know!
Now you must dare to fling those portals wide,   710
The gates through which none willingly would go;
Now is the time to act, and by your action show
That man is fit to stand at the immortals' side,
And not to quail before that gloomy cavern, where
Imagination damns itself to torment and despair;   715
Press on towards that passage from which none returns,
Around whose narrow mouth all hell-fire burns.
To make that awful journey freely I decide,
Although oblivion await me on the other side.

Come down, you glass of purest crystal bright!   720
Out of your ancient case I bring you to the light.
For all these years you lay forgotten here;
You sparkled at our fathers' banquets long ago,
And brought those solemn gatherings good cheer
When as a loving-cup from hand to hand you'd go.   725
It was the drinker's duty to convey in rhymes
The richly wrought engravings round the bowl,
Then in one draught to drain the cup – how you recall
For me those far-off youthful times!
Today I shall not pass you to a fellow-guest,   730
Nor try my wit against the figures round your rim;
This darker juice that fills you to the brim
Inebriates more swiftly than the rest.
I made it well, and choose it for this final test:
With all my heart I bring, as day is dawning,   735
My festive greeting to this solemn morning!

He sets the cup to his mouth. The sound
of bells and a choir are heard.

CHOIR OF ANGELS   Christ is arisen!
Joy he has brought for us
Sin he has fought for us
Salvation sought for us   740
In his dark prison.

FAUST   What distant voices, what exalted singing
Now from my eager lips have snatched this cup away?
Are those deep-throated bells already ringing
The first glad message of the Easter Day?   745
You early choirs, you sing as once the angels sang
When from the dark night of the tomb there rang
Assurance of a covenant renewed that day.

CHOIR OF WOMEN   With fragrant lotion
Gently his limbs we dressed,   750
With true devotion
Laid our dear Lord to rest,
Clean linen round him
Binding with loving care.
Alas, we found him   755
No longer there.

CHOIR OF ANGELS   Christ is arisen!
Saviour who loves us best
Ever thy name be blessed
Who for us stood the test   760
In thy dark prison.

FAUST   You gentle, potent choirs of heaven, why do you seek
To visit me within this dusty cell?
I hear your message, but my faith is weak;
Go, on more tender minds to cast your spell   765
And work the miracles that faith loves well.
I do not dare to reach towards those spheres,
Your gracious gospel calls to me in vain;
And yet these sounds bring memories of early years
That call me back to life on earth again.   770
Then, in the solemn stillness of the sabbath day

I felt the loving kiss of heaven descend on me;
The pealing bells rang out the sacred mystery,
And with a fervent joy I knelt to pray.
I did not understand the joyful urge   775
That drove me out to wood and field and lane,
Or why I wept a thousand tears to feel the surge
Of life as if a world was born in me again.
Those songs would promise carefree childish play,
And herald the unfettered joys of spring;   780
The memories of childhood innocence they bring
From that last solemn step turn me away.
Sweet choirs of heaven, your hymns were not in vain;
My tears run free, I am restored to earth again!

CHOIR OF DISCIPLES   Though in the tomb he lay,   785
                     All was not ended;
                     Our loving Lord today
                     Heavenward ascended.
                     Now through his second birth
                     Glad transformation nears,   790
                     But we remain on earth
                     Still in this vale of tears.
                     We who were not reborn
                     Languish here comfortless;
                     We who were left to mourn   795
                     Envy his bliss!

CHOIR OF ANGELS   Christ is arisen
                     Out of corruption's woe.
                     Now from your prison
                     Joyfully go,   800
                     Praises declaring
                     Loving and caring
                     Brotherhood sharing
                     His gospel bearing
                     Heaven's joys preparing.   805
                     For you the Lord is near,
                     See, he is here!

OUTSIDE THE CITY GATE

All kinds of people walking out

SOME APPRENTICE TRADESMEN Why are you going out that way?

OTHERS We're going to the hunting lodge today.

IST GROUP We're going to walk as far as the mill.   810

APPRENT. The watergate's a better bet.

2 APPRENT. The path's no good, it's far too wet.

2ND GROUP Are you coming with us?

3 APPRENT.   I don't think I will.

4 APPRENT. Let's go up to Bergdorf, there's better beer
And prettier girls than you get down here.   815
They have good fights up there as well.

5 APPRENT. If I were you, I'd just go steady –
You've had two hidings there already;
I'd avoid the place like hell.

SERVANT GIRL Oh come on! Let's go back to town.   820

2ND SERVANT GIRL I'm sure he's waiting by that tree.

IST GIRL And anyway, it's not much fun for me,
It's you he always hangs around.
He'll only ever dance with you –
There's nothing much for me to do.   825

2ND GIRL Oh, he won't be the only one up there,
He said he'd bring that boy with curly hair.

STUDENT My God, just watch those girls go by!
Come on, let's give them both a try.
I like a pint and a damn good smoke, but still   830
There's nothing like a housemaid dressed to kill.

A MIDDLE-CLASS GIRL What is it with the boys around these parts?
There's lots of nice girls, they could take their pick –
But they go chasing after those two tarts.
It really is enough to make you sick!   835

2 STUDENT [*to the first*] Hey, not so fast! Look at the other two,
They're really smart. I've seen that one before –
Yes, she's the pretty one that lives next door.
I fancy her – the other one's just right for you.
They're in no hurry, leave it all to me;   840

	They'll let us go along with them, you'll see.	
I STUDENT	Oh no, it's boring when you have to be polite.	
	Come on, don't let those two birds out of sight.	
	They're much more fun; believe me, if you want	
	to score,	
	These working girls know what their hands are for.	845

I STUDENT Oh no, it's boring when you have to be polite.
Come on, don't let those two birds out of sight.
They're much more fun; believe me, if you want
                                        to score,
These working girls know what their hands are for.   845

A CITIZEN No, I don't like our present Burgomaster,
Since he got in, he's just been a disaster.
Whatever good has he done for the town?
Things go from bad to worse, and every day
There's something else for which we have to pay.   850
He gives his orders – we just have to knuckle down.

A BEGGAR [sings]   Fair ladies and fine gentlemen
With rosy cheeks and pretty dress,
I beg you, spare a thought for them
That suffer hunger and distress.   855
You're lucky if you have the choice
To help the poor, a Christian deed;
On Easter Day, when all rejoice,
Give charity to those in need!

2 CITIZEN What I like best when I'm on holiday   860
Is talk about a bloody foreign war,
In Turkey or some country far away –
The din of battle and the cannon's roar!
You sit at the window with a glass of beer,
And on the river watch the ships go by,   865
Then in the evening go home with a grateful sigh
And thank the Lord that things are peaceful here.

3 CITIZEN Yes, neighbour, that's the way I see it.
Just let them fight among themselves, I say,
And make a mess of things – so be it –   870
As long as we can go on in the same old way.

AN OLD WOMAN [to the middle-class girls]
Well now, young ladies! All dressed up today?
Why not, to make the young lads gawk at you!
But not so hoity-toity now, that's not the way;
Just come to me, I'll make your dreams come true.   875

IST MIDDLE-CLASS GIRL   Agatha, come on! I don't like to be seen
                 Talking to witches like her in the street.
                 But still, she showed me just last Hallowe'en
                 The boy I'd marry; he was really sweet.
THE OTHER   She showed me mine once in her crystal ball,   880
                 With all his cheeky friends – a soldier, I could swear.
                 But it's no good, I've looked around them all,
                 I just can't find him anywhere.

SOLDIERS   Castles with mighty
                         Ramparts and towers,   885
                         Girls proud and flighty
                         Force overpowers
                         And makes them ours!
                         Bold enterprises
                         Win the best prizes.   890

                         We stick together,
                         We're always willing,
                         Whether it's pleasure,
                         Whether it's killing.
                         A girl or a castle,   895
                         Tough ones or tender,
                         After a tussle
                         They all surrender.
                         No one is bolder,
                         We take the prize –   900
                         And then the soldier
                         Says his goodbyes.

FAUST *and* WAGNER

FAUST   The ice has melted, the streams and rivers,
                 Released from the frozen hills, now bring
                 To the valleys the hopeful promise of spring.   905
                 Old winter, defeated, retreats and shivers
                 High in the desolate mountain snows,
                 And from his bitter exile blows
                 His icy blasts in feeble showers
                 That turn the green fields hoary white.   910
                 The sun will put his frost to flight,

And soon will paint the meadows bright.
All round us new life stirs and grows;
But now in the fields instead of flowers
A motley throng of people flows.   915
Here from this rise we can look down
And see them pouring in full spate
Through the dark and narrow gate
Out of the confines of the town.
They celebrate with one accord   920
The resurrection of the Lord,
For they themselves are now reborn;
Away from the workshops and counting-tables,
From narrow hovel and dismal room,
Out of the shadow of roofs and gables,   925
Out of the churches' pious gloom,
Out from the squash of the streets they swarm,
All streaming out into the light,
Into the open countryside –
How eagerly they take their flight!   930
See, on the river far and wide
The painted boats go sailing past,
And packed with revellers they glide
Until they're lost to sight at last.
You see the tiny figures crawl   935
Along the mountain tracks up there,
And hear the noisy village fair.
This is a paradise for all;
They all proclaim on every side
What joy it is to be alive!   940

WAGNER   Doctor, although it makes me very proud
          To keep you company and hear your learned talk,
          Alone I would not care to come and walk
          With this uncouth and vulgar crowd.
          Their shouting, fiddling, bowling and the rest,   945
          It grates upon my ears, I have to say.
          They rant and shriek as if they were possessed,
          And take their pleasures in this raucous way.

PEASANTS *under the linden tree, dancing and singing*

> The shepherd in his Sunday best
> In coloured coat and ribbons dressed, 950
> I'm really smart, he says, oh!
> Around the linden tree the boys
> And girls were dancing – what a noise!
> Diddle dee! Diddle dee!
> And fiddle-me diddle-me dee! 955
> That's how the fiddler plays, oh.
>
> He joined the dance and in a while
> He sees a girl, and with a smile
> He digs her in the stays, oh.
> The lively lass she turns about 960
> And says, stop that, you stupid lout!
> Diddle dee! Diddle dee!
> And fiddle-me diddle-me dee!
> Just watch your cheeky ways, oh.
>
> Then round and round the couple flew, 965
> They danced and danced the whole
> night through –
> Her skirts fly as she sways, oh!
> They danced until they both got warm,
> And lay together at the dawn.
> Diddle dee! Diddle dee! 970
> And fiddle-me diddle-me dee!
> On her thigh his hand he lays, oh.
>
> Now, don't be so familiar, you!
> I'm not so sure you love me true.
> The girl it is that pays, oh. 975
> But he coaxed her on, and very soon
> From the linden tree you heard this tune:
> Diddle dee! Diddle dee!
> And fiddle-me diddle-me dee!
> All shout and the fiddler plays, oh. 980

OLD PEASANT Doctor, we be very proud
> That such a learned man today
> Should come and join our merry crowd.

We welcome you, and bid you stay,
And beg you, Sir, to be the first   985
To sample this, our finest cup.
We hope that as you drink it up
It will do more than quench your thirst;
May it as many drops contain
As years on earth to you remain.   990

FAUST   I thank you for your welcome here;
I drink, and wish you all good cheer.

The people gather round

OLD PEASANT   Indeed, it is a fitting thing
That you should be with us on this glad day,
For you have helped relieve our suffering   995
In former times on many a bad day.
There's several of us be here still
Your father treated with devoted care
When fever raged, and with his healing skill
Saved them from death, and saved us from despair.   1000
And you yourself were then a young man, you
Would visit the plague-houses without fear,
Among the dead and dying all night through
You toiled, and lived to work among us here.
Through all those many trials you endured,   1005
And many of us with God's help you cured.

ALL   Good health to a true and trusted friend,
May he be with us to the end!

FAUST   Give thanks to God in heaven above,
Who helps and heals us with his love.   1010

He walks on with WAGNER

WAGNER   What pleasure it must give you, Sir, to find
Such honour and respect among the crowd!
How happy is the man who is allowed
To use his talents in the service of mankind.
The father shows you to his son,   1015
They rush to see you, every one.
The music stops, the dance is done,
They crowd around you everywhere you go

And doff their caps with reverence – why,
You'd almost think they'll kneel as though   1020
The Sacred Host were being carried by.

FAUST   We'll walk a few steps further to that stone,
And then we'll sit and rest awhile up there.
Here deep in thought I've often sat alone
In agony of mind, with fasting and with prayer.   1025
So rich in hope and strong in faith I thought
To force God's will, and heaven I besought
With pleas and tears and pious abstinence
To put an end to that vile pestilence.
How hollow in my ears their plaudits ring!   1030
If you could read my inmost thoughts, you'd learn
How little son or father did to earn
The praises that these simple people sing.
My father was a decent man who strove
To fathom holy nature's secret lore;   1035
His honest but eccentric efforts drove
Him to a science occult and obscure.
In the dark workshop of his trade
With his initiates he hid away,
And from some ancient formulae   1040
Repellent and arcane concoctions made.
There in a warm solution he would wed³
The lily to the lion, white to red,
Then both were forced with open flame
Through narrow bridal chambers time and time again. 1045
And if the glowing colours then revealed
The young queen in the phial deep inside,
That was the medicine – but the patients died,
And no one thought to wonder who was healed.
And so with hellish brews and deadly skills   1050
Among these valleys and these hills
We did more mischief than the plague could ever do.
I gave the poison to a thousand men who died;
Now to my shame I have to listen to
The praises of the murderers sung far and wide.   1055

WAGNER How can you be disturbed by such a thought?
It's quite enough for any honest man

To practise scrupulously as he can
The skills and disciplines he has been taught.
As young men we respect our fathers' guidance,   1060
And from their teachings willingly we learn;
If then as grown men we extend their science,
Our sons will surely further it in turn.

FAUST   How fortunate are those who can still hope
To rise above this sea of error all around!   1065
For what we need to know is quite beyond our scope,
And useless all the knowledge we have found.
But with such dismal thoughts let us be done,
And marvel at the bounty that this evening yields!
See how the glory of the setting sun   1070
Touches the huts among the lush green fields.
It dips and sinks, completes its daily round,
And brings new life to lands still plunged in night.
If only I had wings to lift me from the ground,
To soar and track it on its onward flight!   1075
In everlasting sunset I would greet
The quiet world spread out beneath my feet,
The valleys hushed, the mountain summits glowing,
The silver streams to golden rivers flowing.
For nothing then could check my godlike flight,   1080
No rocky peaks or chasms interrupt my gaze,
And soon the ocean with its balmy bays
Reveals itself to the unfettered sight.
Again the fiery disk begins to sink,
And with fresh energies I hurry on to drink   1085
And quench my thirst in its eternal light,
The day before me, and behind me night,
The heavens above me, under me the waves!
A glorious vision, even as it fades.
The sullen body's burden always brings   1090
To earth the impulse of our spirit's wings.
Yet every creature's by its nature led
To strive and climb beyond its earthly ties;
The lark pours out its shrilling descant overhead,
Lost in the azure spaces of the skies;   1095
On spreading wings the soaring eagle seeks

	The solitude of fir-clad mountain peaks;	
	Towards its distant home the wandering crane
	Flies onward over forest, lake and plain.

WAGNER   I've often felt a certain restlessness,   1100
But not an urge like that, I must confess.
You soon get tired of woods and fields and
                                      suchlike things,
And I would never envy birds their wings.
For I prefer more intellectual delights;
From book to book, from page to page I go –   1105
It helps me pass the bitter winter nights.
For as I read, I feel a warming glow;
And if I find a manuscript of any worth –
Why, then it's like a very heaven on earth.

FAUST   You only know that single urge; far better so –   1110
That other impulse you should never seek to know.
Two souls are locked in conflict in my heart,
They fight to separate and pull apart.
The one clings stubbornly to worldly things,
And craves the pleasures of our carnal appetites,   1115
The other has an inborn urge to spread its wings,
Shake off the dust of earth and soar to loftier heights.
If there are hovering spirits that hold sway
In the sublunary regions of the sky,
Oh, come down from the golden clouds and let me fly 1120
With you to new adventures far away!
Or if I had a magic cloak at my command
To lift and take me to some distant land,
I'd not exchange it for a cloth of gold,
For a king's ransom, or for wealth untold!   1125

WAGNER   Do not invoke that too familiar swarm
Of demons that infest the atmosphere,
And bring from every quarter and in every form
The countless ills and perils that we fear!
From the cold north the spirit hordes descend   1130
With cutting teeth and arrow-pointed tongues;
And from the east a barren drought they send
That shreds and feeds upon our gasping lungs;
From southern deserts comes the heat that overpowers

	And sears us with its torrid glow;	1135

And sears us with its torrid glow;   1135
The west brings us relief with drenching showers
That drown us and the crops just as they grow.
They listen well, on mischief always bent,
Obey our call, beguile us to believe
They speak with angels' tongues, as if from heaven sent 1140
To serve us here – but only to deceive.
But come, let's leave; the world is grey and still,
The mist is gathering and the air is chill.
At such times I appreciate my cosy room.
You look amazed, why do you stop and stare?   1145
Can you see something out there in the gloom?

FAUST   You see that black dog running through the
                                  stubble there?

WAGNER   That's nothing odd; I noticed it a while ago.

FAUST   Look carefully! What kind of creature can it be?

WAGNER   It's just a poodle running to and fro   1150
And picking up its master's scent, it seems to me.

FAUST   It's running circles round us; there, look back –
It's getting closer to us all the time.
I seem to see a streak of red, a line
Of fire marking out its track.   1155

WAGNER   It's just a stray black poodle that has found us;
I daresay it's an optical illusion, have no care.

FAUST   It seems to me it's weaving magic lines around us,
To draw us into some infernal snare.

WAGNER   It doesn't know us, so it feels unsure,   1160
Because it was its master it was looking for.

FAUST   The circle's getting smaller now, it's coming near!

WAGNER   You see – a dog! There is no witchcraft here.
It growls and cowers, wags its tail, lies flat
Upon its belly – every dog does that.   1165

FAUST   Perhaps you're right; then let it come with us.

WAGNER   It's just a silly dog that wants some fun with us.
It stands and waits there every time we stop,
You speak to it, it begs and does its tricks.
It'll bring back anything you drop,   1170
Jump in the river just to fetch some sticks.

FAUST   I see no evil spirit in it, sure enough;

It's just a dog that's trained to do its stuff.

WAGNER   There is no reason why a learned man
Should not approve a well-trained poodle, too;   1175
The students teach him everything they can,
Just as the students learn so much from you.

[*they go in through the city gate*

FAUST'S STUDY

FAUST enters with the poodle

FAUST

The fields and pastures now lie still,
And night its canopy has spread;
The solemn darkness seems to fill   1180
Our better soul with holy dread.
Our wilder impulses are stilled,
And all our hasty actions, when
The peaceful heart with love is filled
For God and for our fellow men.   1185

Be quiet, poodle! Stop running everywhere!
Why are you snuffling around the door?
Sit by the stove, Sir, over there –
I'll put my best cushion on the floor.
This running and jumping and sniffing about   1190
Was all very well out there on the hill;
You're welcome here, but I'll turn you out
If you can't settle down and just lie still.

When the friendly lamp burns bright
Confined within this narrow cell,   1195
The heart that knows itself aright
Can find enlightenment as well.
Then hope once more within us swells,
And reason speaks again, it seems;
We long to seek the deepest wells   1200
Of life, and drink from living streams.

Poodle, stop growling! These animal cries
Disturb the calm and reverent mood
That fills my mind in this solitude.
We know that men only mock and despise   1205
What they don't understand or never knew;
In the minds of most there is no place
For goodness, beauty, love or grace –
Do such things make dogs uneasy, too?

But though my spirit wills it, still I cannot find   1210
That true contentment and serenity of mind.
Why must we thirst and search in vain, and why
Must every source of hope run dry?
How often have I sought such consolation,
How often have my efforts been in vain!   1215
And so we look beyond this world again
And seek the witness of God's revelation,
The truth that with majestic beauty shines
In the Evangelist's most solemn lines.
A reverent impulse now inspires me   1220
To take the ancient text, and with sincerity
Translate the Holy Gospel of St John
Into my own beloved native tongue.

He opens a large volume and begins to write

I read: In the beginning was the Word. But here
Already I must hesitate. The mere   1225
Word for me has no such resonance;
I must translate it in a different sense.
Now, if the spirit guides me right, I ought
To say: In the beginning there was Thought.
Consider well; the deeper truth escapes   1230
The hasty pen. For is it thought that shapes
And drives creation at its very source?
Far better: In the beginning was the Force!
Yet something tells me even as I write
That this is not the meaning that I need.   1235
The spirit helps me, now I see the light,
I have it: In the beginning was the Deed!

If I'm to share this room with you,
Poodle, stop growling
And stop your howling!   1240
I won't have such a hullabaloo,
So stop your fuss,
Or one of us
Will leave the house, and quickly, too.
You don't have to stay here, you know –   1245

The door is open, you can go.
But what's this apparition that I see?
Is it real or is it fantasy?
It can't be natural, there's magic in it –
The poodle's getting bigger by the minute!   1250
It's heaving and swelling violently –
That's not a dog in front of me!
It's like a hippopotamus in size,
With fearsome teeth and glowing eyes.
What kind of spirit have I let in here?   1255
But I know how to make your sort appear:
Solomon's Key[4] is just the spell
To exorcise the powers of hell.

SPIRITS   [*in the passage outside*]
    There's somebody trapped in there!
    Stay out, don't follow him, beware!   1260
    It's the old hell-hound, like a fox
    Caught in a box!
    Listen to me:
    Fly high and low,
    Weave to and fro,   1265
    And he'll soon be free.
    Help him, don't let him
    Just sit there, they'll get him!
    He's helped us before,
    Done us favours galore.   1270

FAUST   First I'll need the fourfold spell
To summon up this beast of hell:

    Salamanders aglow,
    Undines so fair,
    Sylphs of the air,   1275
    Kobolds below!
    You represent
    Each element,
    Through your powers
    The gift is ours;   1280
    Spirits will fall
    Under our thrall.

Vanish in the fiery glow,
Salamander!
With the rippling waters flow,   1285
Undine!
Like a glorious meteor blaze,
Sylph!
Show your helpful homely ways,
Incubus! Incubus!   1290
Be done, and show yourself to us!

None of the four
Dwells in the beast,
It leers and lies there just as before –
I haven't hurt it in the least.   1295
But I can weave
A stronger spell.

My friend, I believe
You're a minion of hell.
This sign can quell⁵   1300
The hordes that dwell
In the pit beneath.

Ah! Now it's bristling and showing its teeth.

Vile creature, it seems
You know what it means: 1305
The uncreated one,
Undesignated one,
Through all heavens glorified,
Infamously crucified.

Now behind the stove it goes,   1310
And like an elephant it grows.
It fills the room, it swirls and flows,
Like mist it seems to disappear.
It rises to the roof again –
Now, at your master's call, come here!   1315
You see, my threats were not in vain –
I'll singe your fur with holy flame!
Do not invite
The threefold glowing light,

Do not invite   1320
The most commanding spell of all!

MEPHISTOPHELES *steps out from behind the stove*
as the mist clears, dressed as a travelling scholar

MEPHISTO.   Why all the fuss? I'm here, Sir, at your call.
FAUST   So that was what the poodle had in it –
            A travelling scholar! Well, I like your style.
MEPHISTO.   Congratulations to you; I admit   1325
            You had me rather worried for a while.
FAUST   What is your name?
MEPHISTO.   The question seems absurd
            For someone who despises the mere word,
            Who treats appearances as vain illusion
            And seeks the truth in such remote seclusion.   1330
FAUST   But with you gentlemen the name
            And nature's usually the same,
            And we can often recognize
            The Liar, the Destroyer, or the Lord of Flies.
            Who are you, then?
MEPHISTO.   A part of that same power that would   1335
            Forever work for evil, yet forever creates good.
FAUST   And does this riddle have some explanation?
MEPHISTO.   I am the spirit of perpetual negation.
            And that is only right; for all
            That's made is fit to be destroyed.   1340
            Far better if it were an empty void!
            So – everything that you would call
            Destruction, sin, and all that's meant
            By evil, is my proper element.
FAUST   You call yourself a part? You seem entire to me.   1345
MEPHISTO.   I'm telling you the simple truth. You see,
            While man, that poor deluded soul,
            Imagines he's a perfect whole,
            I am part of that part that at the first was one,
            Part of the darkness from which light has sprung,   1350
            Proud light, that now competes with Mother Night
            For room and status, and disputes her ancient right.
            But it will not succeed, because it clings

To sullen matter, to corporeal things.
Matter reflects its beauty to the eye, 1355
But matter hinders its triumphant course;
It cannot last for ever, and perforce
When matter perishes, then light must die.

FAUST   Ah, now I see what you're about; you fail
To bring wholesale destruction to the universe, 1360
And so you work your mischief on a smaller scale.

MEPHISTO.   Indeed; but frankly, things just go from bad to worse.
This awkward world, this object, this obstruction,
Resists all my best efforts at destruction.
Whatever harm I do to it, it seems 1365
Quite unaffected by my nihilistic schemes.
Flood, fire or earthquake, storm – whatever I can send
To ravage land or sea, they calm down in the end.
And that accursed brood of man and beast –
That rabble I can't cope with in the least. 1370
I've buried millions in my time, but then
They breed and multiply – I have to start again!
So it goes on, it drives you to despair;
In water, in the earth and in the air,
A dry, a moist, a cold or warm environment, 1375
A thousand germinating seeds are sown.
If fire were not my native element,
There would be nothing left to call my own.

FAUST   I see; against the ever-living power
That tends and nurtures all creation, 1380
You rage in vain with all the sour
Malice of your cold negation.
Strange son of chaos! No, you ought
To change your strategy and start again.

MEPHISTO.   Indeed, I'll give the matter careful thought, 1385
And we'll go into it more fully then.
But now, with your permission, may I go?

FAUST   I don't see why you need my leave.
We've got to know each other – so
Feel free to visit when you please. 1390
There's the door, and there's the window – you
Could surely get out through the chimney, too?

MEPHISTO.   Well – yes, there is a snag, I have to say;
            There's just one little obstacle in the way.
            That magic sign drawn on the floor –   1395
FAUST   Is it the pentagram [6] that keeps you in?
            So tell me then, you son of hell and sin,
            However did you get in through the door?
            How could a demon let himself be fooled?
MEPHISTO.   Take a close look; it's not perfectly ruled.   1400
            That corner pointing out into the street –
            As you can see, the two lines don't quite meet.
FAUST   Now that's a very fortunate mistake!
            I've caught the Devil, and he can't escape –
            And quite by accident, it would appear.   1405
MEPHISTO.   The poodle didn't notice when he came in here;
            But now the situation's changed, and so
            The Devil could get in, but he can't go.
FAUST   You could leave by the window, I'd have thought.
MEPHISTO.   Demons and spirits have their code; we may   1410
            Come in just as we please, but then we're caught;
            We have to leave the house by the same way.
FAUST   So hell has its own laws and regulations too?
            That's very good! So tell me – I dare say
            It's possible to make a pact with you?   1415
MEPHISTO.   Indeed; if you negotiate with us,
            You'll find the offer tempting – and we never cheat.
            But these things can't be rushed, so we'll discuss
            The matter in more detail the next time we meet.
            For now, I would respectfully require   1420
            Your kind permission to retire.
FAUST   Come, stay a little longer; you can tell me
            Something about the bargains you might sell me.
MEPHISTO.   Please let me go – I'll soon be back again,
            And you can ask me all about it then.   1425
FAUST   I didn't trick you into coming here, you know –
            You got yourself into this snare.
            It isn't often that you get the Devil where
            You want him – so you don't just let him go.
MEPHISTO.   If that is what you wish, I will remain   1430
            And keep you company a while.

On one condition, though – that I can entertain
You with my talents in the proper style.

FAUST
Why, yes, of course, you must feel free;
I hope you've something pleasant, though, to offer me.   1435

MEPHISTO.
My friend, in just one hour tonight
You'll have more sensual pleasure and delight
Than in a year of everyday monotony.
What these airy spirits sing you,
And the visions that they bring you   1440
Are no empty magic dream.
Sweetest perfumes will beguile you,
All your senses ravish while you
Feast on fruits you've never seen.
You're here – you don't have to rehearse your part;   1445
Now, spirits of the air, show us your art!

SPIRITS
Let the dark ceiling
Over us vanish!
Blue sky revealing,
Sweetly appealing   1450
Comforting light!
If the concealing
Clouds we could banish,
Stars would be gleaming,
Milder suns beaming   1455
Through the dark night.
Spirit perfection,
Heaven's reflection,
Gracefully swinging,
Overhead winging.   1460
Yearning affection
After them sighing;
Ribbons are flying,
Draperies streaming,
Scattered like flowers   1465
Garland the bowers.
See lovers dreaming,
Pledging together
Love that's for ever.

Green leaves surround them,   1470
Tendrils wind round them,
Heavy grapes cluster,
Ripe for the treading,
Vats overflowing.
Now the wine gushes,   1475
Foaming in fountains
Through the rocks' lustre
Trickling, it rushes
Down from the mountains
Streaming and pouring,   1480
Into lakes spreading,
Round the hills flowing,
Emerald glowing.
Birds above soaring
Sunwards are streaming,   1485
Effortless motion
Blissfully winging
Where in the gleaming
Waters of ocean
Islands are dreaming,   1490
Where we hear singing
Joyfully ringing,
Soft pipes are playing,
Dancers are straying
Through the fields gliding,   1495
Stepping and swaying.
Some we see striding
Over the mountains,
Others are playing
In the cool fountains,   1500
Others are soaring,
All are adoring,
Stars high above us
Cherish and love us,
Bless us with grace.   1505

MEPHISTO.   Well done, my gentle spirits of the air!
He's sleeping like a babe without a care.

For this recital I am in your debt.
You're not the man to hold the Devil yet!
Now plunge him in an ocean of delight,   1510
Entrance him with deluded fantasy.
But here I need a rodent's teeth to bite
The magic charm around this door for me.
They'll not take long to answer to my call –
I can already hear one rustling in the wall.   1515

The master of all rats and mice,
Of flies and frogs and bugs and lice,
Commands you to come forth and gnaw
That symbol chalked upon the floor.
There, where I mark it with a drop   1520
Of oil; ah, yes, he's coming, hippety-hop!
Now, get to work! The point that's holding me
Is on the edge, right at the top. Now then,
Another bite, and I'll be free.
So, Faust, dream on until we meet again!   1525

FAUST [*waking*] Have I been cheated then once more,
And has my throng of spirits vanished into air?
Did I only dream the Devil was there,
And was it just a poodle that I saw?

FAUST'S STUDY

FAUST *and* MEPHISTOPHELES

FAUST   Who's there? Come in! Now who the devil's
                                          pestering me?   1530
MEPHISTO.   It's me.
FAUST   Come in!
MEPHISTO.   Just one more time, to make it three.
FAUST   Well, come in then!
MEPHISTO.   And here I am, you see.
            I hope we shall get on together, you and I;
            I've come to cheer you up – that's why
            I'm dressed up like an aristocrat   1535
            In a fine red coat with golden stitches,
            A stiff silk cape on top of that,
            A long sharp dagger in my breeches,
            And a cockerel's feather in my hat.
            Take my advice – if I were you,   1540
            I'd get an outfit like this too;
            Then you'd be well equipped to see
            Just how exciting life can be.
FAUST   In any costume I would still despair
            Of life, its misery and care.   1545
            I am too old to kindle youthful fire,
            And yet too young to be beyond desire.
            What has this world to offer me, what sort of choice?
            You must forgo, renounce, abstain –
            That is the tedious refrain   1550
            That echoes in our ears, that dismal song.
            Hour after hour we hear its croaking voice,
            It mocks and follows us our whole life long.
            Each morning when I wake, I wake with dread,
            With bitter tears I greet the day that brings   1555
            No promise and no hope of better things,
            No wish fulfilled, not one, for hope is dead;
            The day whose leering grimace only stifles
            The faintest inkling of delight or joy.

The warmest promptings of the heart it can destroy   1560
With all its stubborn and capricious trifles.
And even when night falls, and on my bed
Fearful and uneasy I must lie, I find
No welcome rest to comfort me – instead
Wild dreams will come to haunt my anxious mind.   1565
The God who dwells within me and who fires
My inner self, my passionate desires,
The God who governs all my thoughts and deeds,
Is powerless to satisfy my outer needs.
This weary life, this burden I detest;   1570
I long for death to come and bring me rest.

MEPHISTO. Death is not always such a welcome guest.

FAUST   How happy is the blood-stained hero who
Meets death in furious battle face to face,
The man who's wildly danced the whole
                        night through,   1575
And finds death in a woman's passionate embrace.
That night I saw the Spirit in the flame,
If only I had fallen lifeless at its feet!

MEPHISTO. And yet that very evening, all the same,
A certain potion didn't taste so sweet.   1580

FAUST   You have some talent as a spy, I see.

MEPHISTO. I don't know everything; but much is known to me.

FAUST   That night I heard familiar voices call
To save me from my terrible confusion,
And childhood memories, a sweet illusion   1585
Of happiness long past held me in thrall.
But now I curse that power whose spell
Deludes our souls with its enticing wiles,
And with its false alluring tricks beguiles
Us in this dreary cavern where we dwell.   1590
I curse the self-conceit and pride,
The high opinions of the mind!
I curse appearances that blind
Our senses to the truth they hide!
I curse the dreams of vain obsession,   1595
Of reputation, fame or merit,
I curse our pride in all possession,

Of wife or child, and all that we inherit.
A curse on Mammon's glittering treasures
That spur ambition on to reckless things,   1600
And on the sybaritic pleasures,
The luxury that his indulgence brings!
I curse the honeyed nectar of the grape,
The grace of love for which all creatures thirst,
A curse on hope, a curse on faith –   1605
Above all, patience be accursed!

CHORUS OF INVISIBLE SPIRITS   Alas! Alas!
                    You have destroyed
                    This lovely world!
                    A demigod has smashed it,   1610
                    His fist has dashed it
                    To pieces and hurled
                    Them into the void!
                    Ours is the duty
                    To gather the fragments and mourn   1615
                    The lost beauty.
                    Great son of earth,
                    Give it new birth;
                    Let it be born
                    More splendid still   1620
                    Within your heart again.
                    And with fresh will
                    And vision then
                    New life begin;
                    New songs we'll sing   1625
                    To ring it in!
MEPHISTO.   My little creatures
                    Are wise little teachers.
                    They promise you action,
                    Delight and distraction;   1630
                    Leave this seclusion,
                    That withers body and mind;
                    Out in the world you'll find
                    Life in rich profusion!

Stop toying with this misery in your scholar's den,   1635

It's like a vulture gnawing at your heart.
Even in the worst company you'll find a part
To play among your fellow men.
But that's not what I have in mind,
Simply to mingle with the crowd;   1640
I'm not so very grand, but if I were allowed
To keep you company, you'd find
That I could help you on your way.
I would be glad to travel by your side,
Attend to everything you say,   1645
Be your companion, be your guide,
Supply you with whatever you might crave –
In short, I'd be your servant, nay, your slave.

FAUST   And what would you want from me in return?
MEPHISTO. There's time enough for that, I should have thought. 1650
FAUST   Oh no! The Devil's not the altruistic sort.
You have to treat such offers with suspicion;
He'll scarcely do you a good turn
Unless he's going to get a fat commission.
So tell me straight, then: what is your condition?   1655

MEPHISTO. I undertake to serve you *here* most faithfully,
Fulfil your every wish in every way,
Provided you will do the same for me
When we meet over *there* one day.

FAUST   It doesn't worry me, your 'over there';   1660
If you can manage to destroy
This world, the next can have its turn for all I care.
This world's the source of all my joy,
This sun shines on my anguish and despair,
And if I have to leave it all behind one day,   1665
So be it – let it happen, come what may.
I am not curious in the least to know
That in a future life there will be hate or love,
Whether it's in the regions up above,
Or in the other places down below.   1670

MEPHISTO. Then take a chance – what are you waiting for?
Sign up with me, and you can feast your eyes
On everything my talents can devise.
I'll show you things no one has seen before.

FAUST   Poor devil, what have you to offer me but lies?   1675
        The highest aspirations of the human mind,
        Such things mean nothing to your kind.
        Oh, yes – I'm sure you've food that never satisfies,
        Or liquid gold that instantly will melt and run
        Like quicksilver between my fingers,   1680
        A game that no one's ever won,
        A girl who even while she lingers
        In my arms, makes eyes at someone new;
        Or meteoric fame, and honour too,
        That blazes once before it fades away.   1685
        Show me the fruit that rots before it's ripe,
        And trees that put out new leaves every day!

MEPHISTO.   Of course I can provide you with that type
        Of thing – you only have to say.
        But they soon pall, and then, my friend,   1690
        We look for something that will give more
                                        lasting pleasure.

FAUST   If I should ever choose a life of sloth or leisure,
        Then let that moment be my end!
        Or if you can beguile or flatter me
        Into a state of self-contented ease,   1695
        Delude me with delight or luxury –
        That day shall be my last. These
        Are my terms.

MEPHISTO.   It's done!

FAUST   So let it be:
        If I should bid the moment stay, or try
        To hold its fleeting beauty, then you may   1700
        Cast me in chains and carry me away,
        For in that instant I will gladly die.
        Then you can sound my death-knell, for you will
        Have done your service and be free.
        Then let the hands upon the clock stand still,   1705
        For that will be the end of time for me!

MEPHISTO.   Consider well; we don't forget these things, you see.

FAUST   That is a right you are entitled to.
        This is no frivolous adventure that I crave;
        If I succumb to lethargy, I'll be a slave –   1710

	Whether to another, or to you.	
MEPHISTO.	I'll serve you dutifully when you dine	
	At the graduation feast tonight.	
	There's just one thing; if you would sign	
	A document for me – I like to do things right.	1715
FAUST	Why, how pedantic! Have you never heard	
	That you can take a man's word as his bond?	
	It's not enough to stake my fate here and beyond	
	Upon the honour of my spoken word?	
	Life rushes past us on its headlong course –	1720
	Why should a promise have such binding force?	
	But in our hearts we all cling to that whim,	
	From such illusions we are never free;	
	An honest man will not regret his own integrity,	
	Nor all the sacrifices that are asked of him.	1725
	But such a document, drawn up with stamps and seals –	
	That is a daunting spectre, for the word congeals	
	And freezes as it's written by the pen;	
	Vellum and wax are all that matter then.	
	Well, evil spirit, what is it to be?	1730
	Bronze, marble, parchment, paper – what you will.	
	Do I use a chisel, stylus or a quill?	
	The choice is yours, it's all the same to me.	
MEPHISTO.	What an extraordinary display!	
	Don't let your rhetoric carry you away.	1735
	Any scrap of paper here will do, I think;	
	We'll use a drop of blood instead of ink.	
FAUST	If you think it will be of any use,	
	I'm willing to join in your comic act.	
MEPHISTO.	Blood is a very special kind of juice.	1740
FAUST	You needn't fear that I will break this pact;	
	I undertake to strive with all my heart	
	And all my energy to play my part.	
	I was too swollen with conceit and pride;	
	The mighty Spirit has rejected me,	1745
	And now I see my place is at your side.	
	All nature's secrets are concealed from me,	
	The thread of thought is broken, for	
	Henceforth all knowledge I abhor.	

	To satisfy my seething passions I'll explore	1750
	The very depths of sensuality;
	Reveal your wonders and your miracles to me
	Behind impenetrable veils of mystery!
	We'll plunge into the headlong rush of time,
	Into the whirling turmoil of each day.	1755
	Let pain or joy, the monstrous, the sublime,
	Success or failure, triumph or vexation
	Follow each other as they may;
	Such restless striving is our true vocation.
MEPHISTO.	There are no limits, no restrictions in your way;	1760
	Dip into everything and sample every dish,
	Grasp every opportunity without delay,
	Do as you please, take what you wish –
	Just help yourself, and don't be coy.
FAUST	Listen: it's not on happiness I'm bent.	1765
	I want a frenzied round of agonizing joy,
	Of loving hate, of stimulating discontent.
	Learning and knowledge now I leave behind;
	I shall not flinch from suffering or despair,
	And in my inner self I wish to share	1770
	The whole experience of humankind,
	To seek its heights, its depths, to know
	Within my heart its joys and all its woe,
	Identify myself with other men and blend
	My life with theirs, and like them perish in the end!	1775
MEPHISTO.	Believe me, many thousand years I've had to chew
	That rancid stuff; that's long enough to know
	That from the cradle to the grave not even you
	Could ever manage to digest such sour dough.
	You have the Devil's word that such totality,	1780
	Such wholeness is for God alone, for he
	Dwells in a realm of everlasting light,
	While we were banished to the darkness down below –
	And all you ever see is day and night.
FAUST	But that is what I want!
MEPHISTO.	Bravo!	1785
	There's just one problem, I'd have thought,
	For art is long, and life is short.

You haven't got all that much time, and so
I think you'd better go and hire a poet,
Who'd let his wild imagination go –   1790
And he could soon provide, before you know it,
Every noble quality to your liking:
Bold as a lion,
Swift as a stallion,
Passionate as an Italian,   1795
Tough as a Viking.
He would teach you how to reconcile
High-minded generosity with subtle guile,
Or if you want to fall in love, he'd fashion
A scheme for you to satisfy your youthful passion.   1800
I'd like to meet a gentleman like that;
I'd call him 'Mr Universe' and raise my hat.

FAUST   What am I then, if it's not possible to earn
The crown of human life for which I yearn
With all my senses and with all my heart?   1805

MEPHISTO. You are – just what you have been from the start.
Wear a full-bottomed wig and play the sage,
Put on high heels and strut about the stage –
You're still the same, whichever way you act the part.

FAUST   In vain it seems to me that I have strained   1810
To grasp the riches of the human mind, for when
I pause to reckon what I might have gained,
I feel no new vitality within my breast,
I am no further in my futile quest –
The infinite is still beyond my ken.   1815

MEPHISTO. My dear Sir, that's a very common view
Of things – but come now, we must try
To find a more imaginative plan for you,
Before life's pleasures pass you by.
Why, damnit man, your hands, your feet,
                       your name,   1820
Your head, your arse, are yours alone;
But all the other things we use and own –
Are they not ours just the same?
Look, it's like this: suppose I can
Afford six horses, then it's just as though   1825

Their strength were mine. I could put on a
                                        proper show –
I'd be what you might call a six-horse-power man.
So cheer up! Let your brooding be,
And come out into the wide world with me.
A man who speculates like that, you know,   1830
Is like a beast grazing on barren ground;
Some evil spirit leads it round and round,
While all about it lush green pastures grow.

FAUST   Where do we start?

MEPHISTO.   We just leave, here and now.
What kind of prison is this anyhow?   1835
What sort of life is this for you,
Boring yourself – and all your students too?
Just let your paunchy colleagues do it,
It's time to leave this treadmill, so go to it!
In any case, you mustn't talk too loud   1840
About the best things that you know – it's not
                                           allowed.
You've got a student here already at the door.

FAUST   I cannot possibly see him today.

MEPHISTO. Come, the poor lad's been there an hour or more,
He'll be so disappointed. Don't send him away;   1845
Give me your cap and gown, I'll see him for a while –
This sort of fancy dress is just my style.

                        [*he dresses in Faust's costume*

I'll use my wits and tell him something wise.
A quarter of an hour is all I need; meanwhile
Go and prepare yourself for our great enterprise!   1850

                                        [*Faust leaves*

MEPHISTOPHELES *in Faust's long gown.*

Reason and knowledge, the highest powers of
                                        humankind,
You have rejected, to oblivion consigned.
Now let the Prince of Lies confuse you,
With magic spells and fantasies delude you –
And I will have you then once and for all.   1855
For fate has given him a mind

So restless, so impetuous, so unconfined
That his impatient spirit, like a waterfall,
Pours headlong over all the pleasures life can give.
I'll plunge him into such distraction, he will live   1860
A life so futile, so banal and trite,
He'll flap and flutter like a bird stuck tight.
He is insatiable, and so I'll tantalize
Him, dangle food and drink before his greedy eyes.
In vain he'll beg relief on bended knee,   1865
And even if he hadn't pledged himself to me,
He'd still be damned for all eternity!

A STUDENT *enters*

STUDENT I've recently arrived at College
  In my earnest quest for knowledge;
  On you, Sir, with respect I call –   1870
  You are acclaimed by one and all.
MEPHISTO. Well, your politeness pleases me;
  A man like other men you see.
  You've had a good look round the place?
STUDENT Please take me on, if you've the space!   1875
  I'm young and eager, keen to please,
  And I've enough to pay my fees.
  My mother was sad to see me go,
  But there's so much that I want to know.
MEPHISTO. Why, then you've come to the right door.   1880
STUDENT But to be frank, I'm not quite sure.
  These rooms and walls, so gaunt and tall,
  I just don't like it here at all.
  They hem you in, and you can see
  No green leaves, not a single tree.   1885
  The lecture halls are all so grim
  I get confused, my mind goes dim.
MEPHISTO. You'll soon get used to it, you know.
  A baby's often very slow
  To suckle at its mother's breast,   1890
  But in the end it feeds with zest.
  Just so at Wisdom's breasts you will
  Quite soon be glad to drink your fill.

STUDENT	I'll feed from her with joy; but will you say,
	Just what I have to do to find my way?	1895
MEPHISTO.	Well, first of all, it seems to me
	You need to choose a Faculty.
STUDENT	I'd like to study every sphere
	Of nature and learning while I'm here,
	And find out all there is to know	1900
	Of the heavens above and the earth below.
MEPHISTO.	Well, yes, you've got the right idea;
	But you must be careful how you go.
STUDENT	I'll do my best, I promise you –
	Although of course I have to say	1905
	I'd like some fun and freedom too,
	Whenever there's a holiday.
MEPHISTO.	Use your time well, for time so quickly passes.
	A little discipline will help you with your classes;
	And so, young friend, my pedagogic	1910
	Judgement is, you start with Logic.
	For there your mind is trained aright;
	It's clamped in Spanish boots so tight
	That henceforth with a clearer head
	The wary path of thought you'll tread,	1915
	And not like Jack o' Lantern go
	Hopping and flickering to and fro.
	For here with rigour you'll be taught
	That things you'd never given a thought,
	Like eating, drinking and running free,	1920
	Must be done in order: one, two, three!
	The mind, however, needs more room;
	It's like a master-weaver's loom.
	A thousand warps move as he treads,
	The shuttle flies, and to and fro	1925
	The fibres into patterns flow –
	One stamp combines a thousand threads.
	Send for a philosopher, and he
	Will prove to you that it must be:
	The first is thus, the second so,	1930
	Ergo: the third and fourth we know.
	If first and second were not here,

Then third and fourth would disappear.
The students love it, I believe –
But none of them have learned to weave.   1935
To know what nature is about,
First you must drive the spirit out;
And when you've pulled it all apart,
What's missing is the vital spark.
'Nature's knack!'[7] the chemists cheer –   1940
But that just means they've no idea.

STUDENT   I'm not quite sure I follow you.

MEPHISTO.   Don't fret, my boy, you'll still get through
When you've learned the tricks and when you're able
To simplify things and give them a label.   1945

STUDENT   I'm afraid I've simply lost the thread;
It's like a mill-wheel grinding in my head.

MEPHISTO.   And after Logic, what should you do?
Ah! Metaphysics is the thing for you;
You'll learn without the slightest trouble   1950
Stuff that would make your brain-cells bubble.
For notions that won't fit inside your head,
You'll find a splendid word instead.
But this first term, whatever you read,
A strict routine is what you need.   1955
Five hours a day – it's not a lot,
Be in the classroom on the dot;
Prepare the texts at home with care,
And study all the details there –
You'll know without even having to look   1960
He's reading straight out of the book.
But write it all down, concentrating
As if it were the Holy Ghost dictating!

STUDENT   I'm sure that's very good advice,
And you won't have to tell me twice;   1965
If you've got it down in black and white,
You can take it home to read at night.

MEPHISTO.   But now you must choose a Faculty!

STUDENT   I don't think Law is quite the thing for me.

MEPHISTO.   I can't say that I blame you, for the Law,   1970
Believe me, is a monumental bore.

	Those dreary statutes, rights and cases,	
	Like a congenital disease are handed on	
	Through generations from the father to the son.	
	They spread like germs to other places,	1975
	Turn sense to nonsense, bad to worse;	
	If you inherit them, your heritage is a curse.	
	The human rights that you were born with, though –	
	Those are the rights that you will never know.	
STUDENT	All that you say confirms my previous view.	1980
	How fortunate I am to be advised by you!	
	I rather think Theology's the course for me.	
MEPHISTO.	I'm not too sure that that's the way	
	You ought to choose, for in that discipline, you see,	
	It is so easy to be led astray.	1985
	The subtle poison it contains is so refined,	
	The antidote is difficult to find.	
	It's best if you have only ever heard	
	One teacher, and then take him at his word.	
	In other words, words are the things to hold to,	1990
	And if you swallow everything he's told you,	
	Then you will never doubt that what he says is true.	
STUDENT	But surely words must have some meaning too!	
MEPHISTO.	Perhaps – don't let that worry you a bit;	
	For even if the meaning's problematic,	1995
	Then you can always find a word for it.	
	With words you can be so dogmatic,	
	With words you can be systematic.	
	You can believe in words, with words all can	
	be proved;	
	Not one iota from a word may be removed.	2000
STUDENT	Forgive me if I pester, you're so kind.	
	But I would much appreciate your view	
	Of whether Medicine is the thing to do,	
	For it's a course I also have in mind.	
	Three years can very soon be past,	2005
	And one must learn it all so fast.	
	They say the course is very tough;	
	With your advice I'd cope, I know.	
MEPHISTO.	[aside] I'm tired of all this academic stuff;	

Now let the Devil have a go.   2010
[*aloud*] It's not too hard to learn a Doctor's skill;
You study till there's nothing left to know,
And in the end you let things go
According to God's will.
But all that science doesn't get you very far;   2015
We all learn willy-nilly what we can –
But if you learn to seize your chance, you are
The up-and-coming man.
You're well-built, a good-looking chap,
You've got a saucy manner, too;   2020
Self-confidence, that's the secret, that
Will give your patients confidence in you.
The women are the ones to make for;
They're always ready to complain
About a little pain –   2025
I'm sure you know the remedy they ache for.
And if they think you understand,
You'll have them eating from your hand.
There's nothing like a Doctor's title for
Persuading them they really can respect you,   2030
And in your first examination you'll explore
Places that others would take years to get to.
You take her hand to check the pulse is steady,
Look deep into her eyes, and then be ready
To slip your arm around her slender waist,   2035
Just to make sure she's not too tightly laced.

STUDENT   That sounds much better! That makes sense to me.
MEPHISTO. Listen, my friend: the golden tree
           Of life is green, all theory is grey.
STUDENT   I never dreamed I'd learn so much today!   2040
           I'd like to come along another day
           To hear more of your wisdom, if I may.
MEPHISTO. What I can do, it shall be gladly done.
STUDENT   Just one thing more; and I'll be gone.
           I've got my album here; please could you say   2045
           Some words to help me on my way.
MEPHISTO. Of course.   [*he writes and hands back the book*
STUDENT   [*reading*] Eritis sicut Deus scientes bonum et malum.[8]

He shuts the book reverently and takes his leave.

MEPHISTO. 'You'll be like God'; my aunt, the serpent, was
             quite right.
  Just heed her words, and one day you'll get such
              a fright! 2050

FAUST [*enters*] Now where do we go?
MEPHISTO.   Wherever you like; just come with me.
  We'll see the small world first, and then the
            wider scene.
  Pleasure and profit await you, sights you've
           never seen –
  For my beginner's course there's no tuition fee!

FAUST With this long beard I shall stick out a mile, 2055
  I haven't got the confidence or style.
  This crazy scheme of yours won't work at all,
  I never was at ease with other men;
  In company I always feel so small
  And so inadequate – you'll have to think again. 2060

MEPHISTO. My dear friend, that will come in time;
  Self-confidence is all you need, and you'll be fine.

FAUST And how do we travel, how do we get away?
  You've got a coach and horses out there, I daresay.

MEPHISTO. We simply spread our cloaks, and they will bear 2065
  Us up as we sail gently through the air.
  Just one thing, though – we mustn't carry too
          much weight,
  That makes it difficult to navigate.
  Some flame for hot air, which I shall provide,
  Will give us lift-off. Spread your arms out wide; 2070
  We've shed our ballast, and the sky is clear –
  Congratulations on your new career!

AUERBACH'S CELLAR IN LEIPZIG

Drinkers carousing

FROSCH   Come on, drink up, let's have a ball!
              What's the matter with you all?
              I've never seen such po-faced gits –   2075
              You'd get on anybody's tits.

BRANDER   Well, you're not much fun, anyway –
              No laughs or filthy jokes today.

FROSCH   [*tips a glass of wine over his head*]
              You asked for it!

BRANDER   You bloody swine!

FROSCH   Well, it was your idea, not mine!   2080

SIEBEL   Whoever quarrels gets thrown out!
              Let's have a sing-song, drink and shout!
              Holla la la la!

ALTMAYER   God, what an awful din!
              Give me some cotton wool, or pack it in.

SIEBEL   When the deep bass voices start to sing,   2085
              The echoes make the vaulting ring.

FROSCH   Yes – if you make any trouble, you're out on the street!
              Ah! Tra la! Tra la la!

ALTMAYER   Ah! Tra la la!

FROSCH   We're all in tune, now watch the beat.

              [*sings*] To the Holy Roman Empire – but whatever,   2090
                   I ask you, holds the dear old thing together?

BRANDER   Urgh! What a rotten song! That's political blether!
              You should thank God every night, and every
                                               morning, too,
              That the Holy Roman Empire's nothing to do
                                               with you!
              I pity the poor sod who's got to be   2095
              Emperor or Chancellor, that's not the job for me.
              Still, someone's got to be the boss round here;
              We'll have a drinking contest, wine or beer –

The last one standing who can hold a glass
Will be the Pope, and we'll all kiss his arse.   2100

FROSCH   [*sings*]   Oh nightingale, fly to my love,
                        A thousand kisses for my turtle dove.

SIEBEL   Not for mine there ain't, don't give me all that crap!
FROSCH   A thousand kisses – just you shut your trap!

            [*sings*]   Open up! The coast is clear.   2105
                        Open up! Your lover's here.
                        Slide the bolt when morning's near.

SIEBEL   Yes, go on, tell us all about her, sing her praises!
            One day the laugh will be on you.
            She led me on, the bitch – you'll get the treatment too. 2110
            I'd give her a hobgoblin, she can go to blazes
            Or meet him at the crossroads – he'd know what to do.
            A randy goat who's been up on the Brocken could
            Give her a galloping for all I care.
            A normal decent bloke is much too good   2115
            For her, the little tart. It's just not fair.
            I'll smash her window with a brick before
            I send her any kisses, that's for sure.

BRANDER   [*banging on the table*] Now then! Now then!
                                        Just let it be!
            I know a thing or two, you'll all agree.   2120
            Some people here appear, unless I'm wrong,
            To be in love, and so it falls to me
            To serenade these lovers with a song.
            So here's a new one I've just written for us –
            And you can all join in and sing the chorus.   2125

            [*he sings*] In a cellar once there was a rat
                          Who lived off lard and butter.
                          She grew and grew, she got as fat
                          As Doctor Martin Luther.
                          The cook put poison down the drain,   2130
                          And soon she felt an awful pain –
                          As if love's dart had stuck her!

CHORUS   [*exuberantly*]
                          As if love's dart had stuck her!

BRANDER	She twitched as if she'd had a fit	
	And drank from every puddle,	2135
	She chewed and scratched and gnawed and bit,	
	Her wits were in a muddle.	
	She jumped till she could jump no more,	
	And very soon lay at death's door –	
	As if love's dart had stuck her!	2140
CHORUS	As if love's dart had stuck her!	
BRANDER	In panic then at break of day	
	She ran into the kitchen,	
	And by the fireside she lay	
	In agony a-twitchin'.	2145
	The cook just laughed and said 'Oh my,	
	That rat is surely going to die –	
	As if love's dart had stuck her.'	
CHORUS	As if love's dart had stuck her!	

SIEBEL	Whatever are you laughing at?	2150
	Well, I don't think it's very nice	
	To go and poison that poor rat.	
BRANDER	I take it you're quite fond of rats and mice?	
ALTMAYER	Poor Siebel here, he's getting bald and fat,	
	And love has made him suffer terribly.	2155
	He's gone all soft, and so that rat	
	Reminds him of himself, you see.	

FAUST *and* MEPHISTOPHELES

MEPHISTO.	It's most important you should be	
	In entertaining company,	
	And see the common folk at play;	2160
	For this lot, every day's a holiday.	
	They're pretty witless, but they have their fun,	
	They drink a lot, and like small cats they run	
	In circles chasing their own tails – and then	
	Next day they have a hangover again.	2165
	As long as their credit with the landlord's good,	
	They're quite a happy little brotherhood.	
BRANDER	These two are on a journey of some kind –	
	There's something odd about the way they're dressed.	
	I'll bet they've just arrived in town today.	2170

FROSCH	You're right, they've come to Leipzig, it's the best!
	They call it Little Paris, 'cause we're so refined.[9]
SIEBEL	They're strangers – but what sort of folk are they?
FROSCH	Leave it to me! We'll have a drop to drink,
	And I'll soon worm it out of them, you'll see – 2175
	Easy as pulling milk-teeth, I should think.
	They look like aristocrats to me,
	They've got that surly stuck-up sort of look.
BRANDER	Get on! They're cheapjacks from the fair!
ALTMAYER	Maybe.
FROSCH	Just watch me, I'll soon have them on the hook! 2180
MEPHISTO.	[to Faust] These people never know the Devil's
	in the place,
	Even when they're looking at him face to face.
FAUST	Good evening, gentlemen!
SIEBEL	The same to you.
	[aside, looking askance at MEPHISTOPHELES]
	That fellow's got a limp – look at his shoe.
MEPHISTO.	We'll join you at your table, if we may. 2185
	If we can't get a decent drink, at least we can
	Enjoy your conversation, anyway.
ALTMAYER	You seem to be a very choosy man.
FROSCH	When you left Rippach, was it late at night?
	You'll have had supper with old Hans there, right? 2190
MEPHISTO.	No, we didn't call on him today,
	But when we saw him last, he had a lot to say
	About his cousins who live over here,
	And told us we should wish them all good cheer.
	[he bows to Frosch
ALTMAYER	[aside] So much for you – he knows the joke!
SIEBEL	He's pretty fly! 2195
FROSCH	Just wait a bit, I'll have him by and by.
MEPHISTO.	I thought I heard – correct me if I'm wrong –
	Some well-trained voices raised in song.
	It must be fine to hear the echoes ring
	Around this splendid vaulting when you sing. 2200
FROSCH	I suppose you think you're quite a virtuoso?
MEPHISTO.	Oh no! I love it, but my voice is only so-so.

ALTMAYER   Give us a song!

MEPHISTO.   I'll give you three or four.

SIEBEL   But let's have one we haven't heard before!

MEPHISTO. We've just come from abroad, we haven't been

                                        back long –   2205
           From Spain, the lovely land of wine and song.

           [*sings*] Once upon a time there was a king,
                   Who had a great big flea –

FROSCH   Did you hear what he said? A great big flea!
           I wouldn't ask a flea to live with me!   2210

MEPHISTO. [*sings*] Once upon a time there was a king,
                   Who had a great big flea.
                   He loved him more than anything,
                   More than a son did he.
                   He said to his tailor, listen to me –   2215
                   Get busy with tucks and stitches;
                   Just measure him up and make my flea
                   A pair of silken breeches!

BRANDER   You'd better tell the tailor, too –
           Just measure him good and proper,   2220
           'cause if there's any creases, you
           Will surely get the chopper!

MEPHISTO.   So soon that flea was kitted out,
                   In finest velvet dressed,
                   With silks and ribbons fitted out,   2225
                   And medals on his chest.
                   They gave him a knighthood, called him Sir –
                   He really was a swell;
                   And all of his relations were
                   Created peers as well.   2230

                   The court was in a dreadful stew,
                   They weren't allowed to fight 'em;
                   The Queen and all her ladies, too –
                   The fleas knew where to bite 'em!
                   They itched and scratched, but not a man   2235
                   Could harm the little blighters.

But we can catch 'em if we can,
And squash 'em when they bite us!

CHORUS   [*exuberantly*]
But we can catch 'em if we can,
And squash 'em when they bite us!   2240

FROSCH   Bravo! Bravo! Very fine!
SIEBEL   That's how to deal with fleas, it never fails!
BRANDER   You squash 'em in between your fingernails!
ALTMAYER   Here's to freedom! Here's to wine!
MEPHISTO.   I'd gladly drink a toast to freedom – but I fear   2245
I just can't drink the wine you get round here.
SIEBEL   Don't let us hear that kind of talk again!
MEPHISTO.   Well, if I didn't think the landlord would complain,
I'd offer our respected guests a choice selection
Of some of the best wines in our collection.   2250
SIEBEL   Don't worry about that, I'll see to him.
FROSCH   If you provide us with a drop of the right stuff,
We'll be quite happy; but you must give us enough.
I like a glass that's full right to the brim,
And then I can appreciate it properly.   2255
ALTMAYER   [*aside*] These guys are Rhinelanders, if you ask me.
MEPHISTO.   Fetch me a gimlet!
BRANDER   Now what's all this for?
I suppose you left your barrels just outside the door?
ALTMAYER   The landlord's tools are in a basket over there.

MEPHISTOPHELES *takes the gimlet*

MEPHISTO.   [*to Frosch*] Well, what can I offer you then, Sir?   2260
FROSCH   What do you mean? What wines have you got?
                                                    Where?
MEPHISTO.   It's up to you – just say which you prefer.
ALTMAYER   [*to Frosch*] Licking your lips already then, you
                                            greedy swine?
FROSCH   Well, my choice would be something from the Rhine.
The fatherland produces the best wine.   2265

MEPHISTOPHELES *bores a hole in the table where* FROSCH *is sitting*

MEPHISTO.   We need some stoppers – get some wax here, quick!

ALTMAYER   Oh God, it's just another conjuring trick.

MEPHISTO.   [to Brander] And you?

BRANDER   Champagne, if it's not too much trouble –
            And nice and fizzy, 'cause I like to see it bubble!

> MEPHISTOPHELES *bores a hole. Someone has meanwhile made*
> *the wax stoppers and plugs the holes.*

BRANDER   You must admit sometimes, I know it's sad,   2270
            But foreign stuff is really not that bad.
            Us Germans just can't stand the Frogs, but then
            We like to drink their wine now and again.

SIEBEL   [as Mephistopheles approaches him]
            I must say, I don't like my wine too dry.
            Have you got something nice and sweet to try?   2275

MEPHISTO.   [bores a hole] I've just the thing for you – a good Tokay!

ALTMAYER   Now gentlemen, be honest, look me in the eye;
            Don't play your tricks on us, we're not so dumb.

MEPHISTO.   Play tricks on such distinguished guests? Oh, come!
            I wouldn't dream of taking such a liberty.   2280
            But tell me, quick, what can I offer you?
            I'm sure you'd like a taste of something, too.

ALTMAYER   Oh, anything is good enough for me.

MEPHISTO.   [with mysterious gestures]
                   Luscious fruit the grapevine bears,
                   Curly horns the billy-goat wears;   2285
                   Juice comes from the wooden vine –
                   A wooden table can give us wine.
                   Just believe, and you will see
                   Nature's deepest mystery!
                   Now draw the plugs and let it pour!   2290

> *They draw the plugs, and the chosen wine flows into each glass.*

ALL   Fountains of wine! There's wine galore!

MEPHISTO.   Be careful! Not a drop must fall upon the floor!

> *They drink again and again*

ALL   [sing] We're all as pissed as cannibals,
                   And happy as pigs in clover!

MEPHISTO.	Man is born free – and how he loves his liberty!	229
FAUST	I want to go, there's nothing here for me.	
MEPHISTO.	Just watch a while, and you will see	
	A demonstration of man's bestiality.	
SIEBEL	[drinks clumsily, the wine spills on the floor and turns	
	to flame] Help! I'm on fire! Help! These are	
	flames from hell!	
MEPHISTO.	[addressing the flame]	
	Down, friendly element! Obey my spell.	230
	[to the drinkers] That was just a little taste of purgatory.	
SIEBEL	What's going on here? Nobody does that to me!	
	You don't know how unfriendly I can be.	
FROSCH	Don't try that one on us again!	
ALTMAYER	We need to get this bloke outside, and quick.	230
SIEBEL	You have the cheek to walk in here, and then	
	You try to scare us with that stupid trick!	
MEPHISTO.	Quiet, you old wine-tub!	
SIEBEL.	You beanpole!	
	He's trying to insult us now as well!	
	Just wait, we'll kick you right back down to hell.	231
ALTMAYER	[pulls one of the plugs out of the table; a flame shoots	
	up at him]	
	Help! I'm burning!	
SIEBEL	Sorcery! Don't let him	
	Scarper, he's an outlaw, he's fair game. Let's get him!	

They draw their knives and advance on MEPHISTOPHELES

MEPHISTO.	[with a solemn gesture]	
	Confuse the eye, deceive the ear,	
	Make a different scene appear.	
	Be there and here!	231

They stand amazed and look at each other

ALTMAYER	Where am I? What a lovely place!	
FROSCH	Vineyards! I'm seeing things!	
SIEBEL	Grapes right in front of your face!	
BRANDER	Underneath the leaves here I can see	
	A luscious bunch of grapes, and all for me!	

He takes hold of Siebels's nose. The others do the
same to each other and raise their knives.

MEPHISTO. [*as above*] Illusion, let them be! I hope that shows   2320
           The lot of you you don't mess with the Devil!

He disappears with FAUST; *the drinkers let each other go.*

SIEBEL   What is it?
ALTMAYER   Eh?
FROSCH   Is that your nose?
BRANDER   [*to Siebel*] And I've got yours! This isn't on the level.
ALTMAYER   I felt a shock, and then I seemed to freeze.
           Get me a chair, I feel weak in the knees.   2325
FROSCH   But what the hell was going on just then?
SIEBEL   Where is he? If I see that bloke again
           He won't perform his tricks here any more.
ALTMAYER   I saw him ride out of the door
           Astride a barrel – well, that's what I thought I saw.   2330
           I just can't move my feet, they feel like lead.
           [*turning to the table*]
           D'you think there's any more wine left in there?
SIEBEL   It was a trick. We've all been fooled. Let's go to bed.
FROSCH   But I did drink some wine, I swear.
BRANDER   And what about those grapes we saw?   2335
ALTMAYER   And people say they don't believe in magic any more!

A WITCH'S KITCHEN

A low hearth with a large cauldron on the fire. In the steam rising
from it various shapes can be seen. A female monkey sits by the
cauldron and skims it, taking care not to let it boil over. The male
monkey sits and warms himself by the fire with his young ones.
The walls and ceiling are decorated with the weird
paraphernalia of witchcraft.

FAUST *and* MEPHISTOPHELES

FAUST	These magic spells and tricks of yours repel me!	
	You think I'll find recuperation, then,	
	Here in this bedlam, in this witch's den?	
	You think an ancient crone can tell me	2340
	How I'm going to shed some thirty years,	
	Or brew some potion that will make me young again?	
	But you have nothing else to offer, it appears,	
	And you have only raised my hopes in vain.	
	Is there no natural remedy, has no great mind	2345
	Devised an elixir to meet my need?	
MEPHISTO.	My friend, this ranting isn't very clever.	
	There is a natural way to make you young, indeed –	
	But that's another story altogether,	
	From a mysterious book of a quite different kind.	2350
FAUST	Well, tell me then.	
MEPHISTO.	The other way is cheap,	
	It needs no medicine and no magic. You just go	
	Out into the fields, you dig and hoe,	
	And plough and harrow, sow and reap;	
	You keep yourself and all your thoughts confined	2355
	Within the limits of your small domain,	
	Take nourishment of the most frugal kind,	
	Live as a beast among your beasts, and don't disdain	
	To fertilize the land you work with your own dung.	
	That's the best way, believe me – you will find	2360
	You'll live for eighty years, and still be young!	
FAUST	I'm just not used to it, I couldn't stand	

	A narrow life like that, it's not for me –	
	And I could never work upon the land.	
MEPHISTO.	Then you must take the witch's remedy!	2365
FAUST	But does it have to be this ancient crone?	
	Why can't you brew a potion of your own?	
MEPHISTO.	You don't think I've got that much time to spare!	
	I've rather more important things to do, indeed.	
	It's not just skill and knowledge that you need,	2370
	But time and patience, and a lot of care.	
	The spirit must ferment for many years until	
	The mixture is mature and powerful enough,	
	And then it's ready to distil.	
	The witches can do all that tedious stuff –	2375
	The Devil hasn't got the knack, although	
	The Devil taught them everything they know.	

                                     [he sees the animals

	Look, what a charming family!	
	This is the servant, that's the maid, I see.	
	[to the animals] And your dear mistress, where is she?	2380
ANIMALS	Can't see you,	
	Gone to a do	
	Up the chimney-flue!	
MEPHISTO.	Out gallivanting! How long will she be?	
ANIMALS	As long as it takes to warm a paw.	2385
MEPHISTO.	*[to Faust]* How do you like this pretty pair?	
FAUST	The most repulsive animals I ever saw!	
MEPHISTO.	Oh come, my friend, that's hardly fair;	
	I like their lively repartee.	
	[to the animals] So tell me, little imps from hell,	2390
	What have you got in that foul brew?	
ANIMALS	We're cooking watery beggars' stew.	
MEPHISTO.	You'll have a lot of customers – I hope they like	
	the smell.	

MALE MONKEY *[approaches Mephistopheles ingratiatingly]*

                  Let's throw the dice,
                  It would be nice   2395
                  To have a pot
                  Of gold, and then

                        I'd have a lot
                        Of sense again.

MEPHISTO.   How happy would this little monkey be   2400
            To have a winning ticket on the lottery!

        Meanwhile the young monkeys roll a large ball around.

THE MALE MONKEY   The world's so small,
                   It's like a ball,
                   Up and down
                   It rolls around.   2405
                   It gleams like brass,
                   It's brittle as glass.
                   It shines like tin,
                   It's hollow within.
                   I live, but you,   2410
                   My son, beware
                   The danger there;
                   You must die too.
                   It's made of clay,
                   It'll break one day.   2415

MEPHISTO.   And what's this sieve?
THE MALE MONKEY [*takes down the sieve*]

                        If you're a thief, it'll give
                        You away.

    He runs to the female monkey and makes her look through it.

                        Look through the sieve!
                        It's my belief he's a thief,   2420
                        But his name you mustn't say.

MEPHISTO.   [*approaching the fire*] And what's in this pan?

THE TWO ANIMALS   That's a pot,
                   You silly clot!
                   He can't tell a pot from a pan!   2425

MEPHISTO.   You cheeky pair!

THE MALE MONKEY   Here, take this fan
                   And sit in the chair!

He makes MEPHISTOPHELES *sit down.* FAUST *has
meanwhile been standing in front of a mirror,
moving towards it and stepping away again.*

FAUST   What is this heavenly vision that I see
                 Reflected in the magic glass in front of me?   2430
                 Oh Love, lend me your wings to spread them wide
                 And fly me swiftly to her side!
                 Alas, when I approach her, when I dare
                 To reach out to that lovely vision there,
                 The image blurs and fades into the air!   2435
                 How is it possible, can any woman be
                 So beautiful, her shape so heavenly?
                 Shall I find anything on earth so fair?
                 In this recumbent body do I see
                 The very essence of all paradisal bliss?   2440

MEPHISTO.   Of course – if God toils for six days without a break
                 And then congratulates himself, you'd think he'd make
                 A sight worth looking at like this.
                 Well, go ahead and feast your eyes. I can provide
                 A sweetheart for you just like her,   2445
                 And you shall have her – or, if you prefer,
                 You might be glad to take her as your bride!

FAUST *continues to gaze into the mirror.* MEPHISTOPHELES
lounges in his chair and plays with the fan.

MEPHISTO.   I sit here like a monarch on his throne;
                 I've got my sceptre, but no crown to call my own.

THE ANIMALS *have meanwhile been up to all sorts of strange antics.
They bring* MEPHISTOPHELES *a crown with loud screeches.*

                          Oh Sir, if you could,   2450
                          Please mend the crown
                          With sweat and blood.

*They fumble and drop the crown. It breaks in two,
and they dance round with the pieces.*

                          You clumsy clown!
                          We chatter and curse
                          And speak in verse.   2455

FAUST   [*looking at the mirror*]
           I'm driven to distraction at this sight!
MEPHISTO. [*pointing to the animals*]
           I must admit, my own head feels unsteady, too.

ANIMALS   If we get it right
                   Why, then we might
                   Think just like you!   2460

FAUST   [*as above*] My heart's on fire, I just can't stay
           In here. Come on, let's get away!
MEPHISTO. [*as above*] You've got to hand it to the little beast –
           He's quite a poet, and his verses rhyme, at least.

          The cauldron, which the She-Monkey has neglected, starts
          to boil over; a great flame shoots up the chimney. THE WITCH
          comes tumbling down through the flames, screaming horribly.

WITCH   Ow! Ow! Ow! Ow!   2465
           A curse on you, you bloody sow!
           You let the cauldron boil, you've burnt me now!
           You stupid cow!   [*she sees Faust and Mephistopheles*

                   So who are you?
                   And you as well?   2470
                   Where did you two
                   Get in here, how?
                   I'll shrivel you
                   With fire from hell!

          She thrusts the ladle into the cauldron and sprays flame at FAUST,
          MEPHISTOPHELES *and the animals. The animals whimper.*

MEPHISTO. [*takes the other end of the fan and lashes out at the pots*
           and glasses]

                   Take that, and that!   2475
                   I'll spill your brew
                   And smash your glasses flat!
                   You carrion, you old bat,
                   I'll call the tune for you
                   To whistle to.   2480

[THE WITCH *retreats in fury and terror*]
You skeleton, you gargoyle, can't you recognize
Your lord and master right before your eyes?
Why should I stop, why not smash you to bits as well,
Thrash you and your demon monkeys back to hell?
Doesn't the red doublet call for more respect? 2485
And can't you see my face, you loathsome dame?
You see this cockerel's feather? Do you expect
Me to announce myself by name?

WITCH   Oh Sir, forgive my rude reception, pray,
I didn't see your cloven hoof at all - 2490
And your two ravens, where are they?

MEPHISTO.   Well, this time we'll forget our little brawl.
It's been some time now since I went away.
We haven't seen each other for a while,
And these days fashions change from year to year – 2495
Even the Devil has to change his style.
Your northern Gothic Devil's out of date, I fear,
I just can't wear a tail or horns round here.
But I can't go without my foot, I wish I could –
It doesn't do my reputation any good. 2500
And so for years, as many young men do,
I've worn a fashionably built-up shoe.

WITCH   [*dancing*] I'm all of a dither, I could throw a fit –
Squire Satan here! That's really made my day.

MEPHISTO.   That name's not to be mentioned, by the way. 2505

WITCH   Why? What the devil's wrong with it?

MEPHISTO.   It only comes in fairy stories nowadays.
But even so, humanity's no better off –
The Evil One has gone, they've kept their evil ways.
Just call me Baron, that will do for me – 2510
I move in the best circles now, I'm quite a toff;
I think you know my noble pedigree,
I've got a coat of arms as well – this is my crest!
                       [*he makes an obscene gesture*

WITCH   [*laughs immoderately*]
Ha Ha! Ha Ha! Yes, that's what you do best!
You're still the same rogue that you always were. 2515

MEPHISTO.   [*to Faust*] Just take a note of this, my friend, and you

	Will know the way to deal with crones like her.	
WITCH	Now tell me, gentlemen, what can I do?	
MEPHISTO.	We want a glassful of your special brew –	
	But one that's been a long time on the shelf.	2520
	Its strength increases with the years, I know.	
WITCH	Of course! Here's one I brewed up long ago,	
	I often take a drop of it myself.	
	It doesn't smell at all bad, I assure you –	
	I'd be delighted to mix up a cupful for you.	2525
	[aside to Mephistopheles]	
	But if he's not prepared, this stuff could fuck him up;	
	A single drop could kill him on the spot.	
MEPHISTO.	Well, he's a friend of mine, I need to buck him up,	
	So let him have the very best you've got.	
	Now draw your circle, say your magic spell,	2530
	Give him a proper dose and make him well!	

THE WITCH *with weird gestures draws a circle and puts strange
objects in it. Meanwhile the glasses start ringing and the cauldron
makes a musical sound. Finally she brings a large book, makes
the monkeys stand in the circle, and uses one of them
as a lectern. The others hold torches.*
She beckons FAUST *to her.*

FAUST	[to Mephistopheles] Oh no, what is this rabid stuff?	
	These signs and gestures are absurd!	
	I hate this crazy ritual, I've heard	
	It all before, I know it well enough.	2535
MEPHISTO.	Don't take it all so seriously! You know	
	It's not for real, it's just for show.	
	She needs some mumbo-jumbo, as all doctors do,	
	To make her potion work – it's nothing new.	

He pushes FAUST *into the circle.* THE WITCH *begins
to recite solemnly from the book.*

WITCH	So hear me, then!	2540
	From one make ten,	
	And let two be,	
	The same with three –	
	You're rich, you see!	

	The four is nix,	2545
	From five and six	
	The witch can mix	
	A seven and eight,	
	That's got it straight!	
	From nine make one,	2550
	And ten is none.	
	That's the witches' one-times-one!	

FAUST The old woman's raving now, she's had a fit.

MEPHISTO. There's plenty more of it to go,
The whole damn book is full of it.   2555
I've wasted time on it myself, so I should know.
I've always found that you can fox
A wise man or a fool with paradox.
It's an old trick, but it works all the same,
And every age has tried time and again   2560
To spread not truth, but error and obscurity,
By making three of one and one of three.
And so the fools can preach and teach quite
                                   undisturbed –
Who wants to argue with them? Let them wander on;
Most men believe that when they hear a simple word, 2565
There must be some great meaning there to ponder on.

WITCH [*still reading*] The mystery
Of alchemy
From all the world is hidden.
But if it's sought   2570
Without a thought,
Then it will come unbidden!

FAUST What is this nonsense that she's spouting for us?
She's giving me a headache with her blether.
It's like a hundred thousand idiots in chorus   2575
All gibbering and chattering together.

MEPHISTO. Enough, most excellent of Sibyls, stop!
Just bring your potion over here, and please
Be sure to fill the bowl right to the top.
The stuff won't hurt him, let him drink his fill,   2580

        For he's a man with several degrees –
        He's drunk a lot before and not been ill.

THE WITCH *with much ceremonial pours the liquid*
into a bowl; as FAUST *sets it to his lips, a gentle*
flame rises from it.

MEPHISTO.   Down with it, quickly! Come on, drink the brew,
        And that will make your heart feel young again.
        If you rub shoulders with the Devil, then   2585
        A little bit of fire shouldn't worry you.

THE WITCH *breaks the circle.* FAUST *steps out of it.*

MEPHISTO.   You must keep moving now, so off we go!
WITCH   I hope my little mouthful puts you right!
MEPHISTO.   [*to the Witch*] I owe you one for this; just let me know –
        I'll see you at the next Walpurgis Night.   2590
WITCH   Here's a song for you; you sing it twice a day –
        It heightens the effect enormously, they say.
MEPHISTO.   [*to Faust*] Come on now, quickly, you must
                            move about;
        You've got to sweat the potion out
        So it works through your system all the way.   2595
        Then you'll be able to appreciate your leisure,
        And all the more intensely feel the pleasure
        When Cupid stirs you up and lights your fire.
FAUST   Let me look in that mirror just once more!
        That lovely woman's all that I desire.   2600
MEPHISTO.   No, leave that phantom, and I promise you'll enjoy
        A real woman as you never have before.
        [*aside*] A drop of that stuff in your guts, my boy,
        And every woman looks like Helen of Troy.

A STREET

FAUST. MARGARETA *walks by.*

FAUST   Fair lady, you are all alone;   2605
             May I take your arm and see you home?
MARGARETA   I'm not a lady, nor am I fair,
             And I can find my own way there.
                              [*she pulls herself away and goes*
FAUST   That girl is just so lovely, she
             Has really captivated me.   2610
             Demure and virtuous, you can tell –
             But with an impish look as well.
             And such red lips and cheeks so bright,
             How could you ever forget that sight!
             The bashful look she had just now,   2615
             It touched my heart, I can't say how.
             She sent me packing, and quite right –
             But that's what gave me such delight!

MEPHISTOPHELES *enters*

FAUST   I've got to have that girl, d'you hear?
MEPHISTO.   Which one?
FAUST   The one that just went by.   2620
MEPHISTO.   But she came straight from church! I fear
             The priest just gave her the all clear.
             I listened to them on the sly;
             She's just too innocent, I guess –
             She had nothing whatever to confess.   2625
             I can't touch her, she's far too pure.
FAUST   But she's over fourteen, that's for sure.
MEPHISTO.   My, what a lecher we've become!
             He thinks he can pick them one by one.
             His head's so turned by his conceit   2630
             He thinks they'll all fall at his feet.
             It's not as simple as all that.
FAUST   Yes, you can preach and you can scoff,
             But spare me all that moral chat,

	And just you listen carefully:	2635
	If you can't get that girl for me,	
	And by tonight, I tell you, we	
	Are finished, and the deal is off.	
MEPHISTO.	Be reasonable, you randy beast.	
	I'll need a good two weeks at least	2640
	To sniff around and see what's what.	
FAUST	I don't need you to show the way;	
	I wouldn't take more than a day	
	To bed a little girl like that.	
MEPHISTO.	You're getting a bit French, my friend!	2645
	Why are you so impatient, though?	
	You mustn't rush these things, you know –	
	You'll get your pleasure in the end.	
	Take time to talk her round to it,	
	Impress her, flatter her a bit.	2650
	Soften her up with little advances –	
	That's how Italians get their chances.	
FAUST	I can do without all that.	
MEPHISTO.	But seriously, I tell you flat,	
	You can't just have that girl today;	2655
	You've got to plan, prepare the way.	
	You'll never get in there by force –	
	We'll think of a more subtle course.	
FAUST	Get me something of hers to keep,	
	Show me where she lies asleep,	2660
	Get me a scarf that's touched her breast,	
	A garter, anything she's possessed!	
MEPHISTO.	Well, I'll do everything I can	
	To help you on your lovesick way.	
	We'll not waste time; I have a plan	2665
	To take you to her room today.	
FAUST	And shall I see her? Have her?	
MEPHISTO.	No.	
	Tonight she's at a neighbour's, so	
	For a few minutes you can go	
	And breathe the atmosphere at leisure,	2670
	And dream about your future pleasure.	

FAUST   Can we go now?
MEPHISTO.   No, I'll say when.
FAUST   Get me a present for her, then.   [*exit*
MEPHISTO.   A present, already? Good! That's what I like to see!
               I know a place where there might be   2675
               Some buried treasure to be found.
               I'll go and take a look around.   [*exit*

EVENING

A small, tidy room

MARGARETA [*plaiting and tying up her hair*]
      I wonder who that man could be
      Who stopped today and spoke to me.
      A handsome gentleman he was,   2680
      A nobleman, I'm sure, because
      He had a certain air, I knew –
      And he was very forward, too.   [*exit*

Enter MEPHISTOPHELES *and* FAUST

MEPHISTO. You can come in now, the coast is clear.
FAUST   [*after a pause*] Just leave me for a moment here.   2685
MEPHISTO. [*prying around*]
      Tidier than most girls are, it would appear.   [*exit*
FAUST   [*gazing around him*] The gentle light of evening falls
      Into this sanctuary. Within these walls
      Love's pangs clutch at your heart, but you
      Must still your cravings with hope's meagre dew.   2690
      This peaceful homestead seems to breathe
      A sense of order and content.
      Such poverty is wealth indeed,
      And there is bliss in such imprisonment!

He throws himself into the leather chair by the bed.

      How many generations has this seat   2695
      Borne through all the years of joy and care!
      Her forebears sat upon this very chair,
      A throng of children playing at their feet.
      Perhaps my love, when Christmastime was near,
      With pious thanks and childish cheeks so sweet   2700
      Would kiss the feeble hand that rested here.
      Dear child, I sense your presence all around me,
      Integrity and order everywhere.
      The traces of your daily tasks surround me;
      The table that you set with loving care,   2705

The sand you scattered on the flagstones there.
One touch of your dear hand, and in a trice
This humble dwelling is a paradise.
And here! [*he raises the curtain round the bed*]
          Ah, what a shiver of delight!
Here I could sit for hours and dwell   2710
On dreaming nature's magic spell
That fashioned that angelic sight.
As she lay here, the glowing surge
Of life pulsed in her gentle breast,
And here a pure creative urge   2715
God's image on the child impressed.

And you! What brought you to her door?
What do you want? Why is your heart so sore?
What feelings hold you in their sway?
Ah Faust, poor fool, I fear you've lost your way.   2720

Is there some magic spell around me?
I lusted for her, and I find
A dream of love comes to confound me.
Are we the playthings of a breath of wind?

And what if she should come while you are here?   2725
You'd answer for your recklessness, and all
Your bold bravado would just disappear –
Abject and sighing at her feet you'd fall.
MEPHISTO.   Quickly! She just came through the gate.
FAUST   I'll never come back here again. Let's go!   2730
MEPHISTO.   Here is a box of jewels – just feel its weight;
I got it from – well, from a place I know.
Put it in this cupboard here; I swear
She'll fall into a faint, your little dove.
The finery I put in there   2735
Was meant to win another woman's love –
But then, they're all just kids at heart.
FAUST   I don't know if I should.
MEPHISTO.   Oh please, don't start!
D'you want to keep it for yourself? Then,

Lecherous Sir, I beg of you,   2740
Think what you really want to do,
And please don't waste my time again.
I hope you're not a miser, too!
I rack my brains and toil away –
[*he puts the casket in the cupboard and locks it up again*]
Now, come with me!   2745
So you can have your wicked way
With that sweet child, and all I see
Is the sort of miserable expression
You wear before you give a lesson,
As if physics and metaphysics too   2750
Were standing there in front of you.
Come on!   [*exeunt*

MARGARETA *with a lamp*

It feels so close and stuffy here,   [*she opens the window*
And yet outside it's not so warm.
I don't know why, I feel so queer –   2755
I wish my mother were at home.
You silly girl, you're shivering –
You really are a timid thing!
[*she sings as she undresses*]

> There was a king in Thule, he
> Was faithful to the grave.   2760
> To him his dying lady
> A golden goblet gave.
>
> He would drink from no other,
> It was his dearest prize;
> Remembering his lover   2765
> The tears would fill his eyes.
>
> And on his death-bed lying,
> To his beloved son
> He left his lands, but dying
> He gave the cup to none.   2770
>
> And many a faithful vassal
> And knight sat by his knee

In his ancestral castle
Beside the northern sea.

One last time he drank up then,   2775
His cheeks with wine aglow,
And hurled the sacred cup then
Into the waves below.

He watched it falling, sinking
Beneath the ocean deep;   2780
Then he had done with drinking –
His eyes were closed in sleep.

She opens the cupboard to put her clothes away, and sees the casket.

Whoever put that casket there?
I locked the cupboard up, I swear.
That's very strange! What can it be?   2785
Perhaps it was left as surety,
And mother lent some money for it.
And here's a ribbon with a key –
Well, really, I can't just ignore it.
But what is this? Ah, glory be!   2790
I've never seen such jewels before.
All this expensive finery
Was made for some great lady, that's for sure.
I wonder how they'd look on me?
But who can it belong to, though?   2795

She tries on some jewels and stands in front of the mirror.

I'd love to have these earrings – oh,
What a different girl you are!
But youth and beauty, what's it worth?
It's not your fortune on this earth;
It doesn't get you very far.   2800
They flatter you and call you pretty,
But it's gold they crave,
For gold they slave –
And poverty they pity!

AN AVENUE

FAUST *pacing up and down, deep in*
thought, then MEPHISTOPHELES

MEPHISTO.	By all frustrated love! By all hell's fires, and worse!	2805
	I wish I knew more dreadful things by which to curse!	
FAUST	What is it now? What's biting you today?	
	I never saw a face as black as yours.	
MEPHISTO.	I'd go to the Devil right away –	
	That is, if I weren't one myself, of course.	2810
FAUST	Has something happened to disturb your mind?	
	This snarling and spitting suits you well, I find.	
MEPHISTO.	That box of jewels I got for Margaret –	
	A bloody priest has snaffled it!	
	Her mother found the jewels last night –	2815
	They gave her quite a nasty fright;	
	That woman smells brimstone a mile away,	
	She's forever kneeling down to pray.	
	She only needs to sniff a chair	
	To tell the Devil's been sitting there.	2820
	As for our jewels, well, that's clear –	
	She knows there's something fishy here.	
	'Gretchen', she says, 'ill-gotten gold	
	Corrupts the heart, ensnares the soul.	
	The Blessed Virgin must have this hoard,	2825
	And manna from heaven be our reward.'	
	Poor little Gretchen nearly weeps –	
	She thought her gift horse was for keeps,	
	And whoever put it in her drawer	
	Can't be all that bad, for sure.	2830
	Her mother summons up the priest;	
	He'd hardly heard her out, the beast,	
	When he began his peroration:	
	'A Christian act! For there's no question	
	That victory lies in abnegation.	2835
	The Church has an excellent digestion;	

	It's gobbled up countries by the score,	
	But still has room for a little more.	
	Only the Holy Church, dear ladies,	
	Can properly digest the Devil's wages.'	2840
FAUST	That's the way it is, it's true –	
	But Jews and kings can do it too.	
MEPHISTO.	He raked those rings and bangles in	
	As if they were just bits of tin;	
	He packed them up and took them away	2845
	As if this happened every day.	
	'Heaven will surely reward you,' he sighed –	
	And they, of course, were greatly edified.	
FAUST	And Gretchen?	
MEPHISTO.	She's unhappy, too;	
	Doesn't know what she ought to do.	2850
	Thinks of her jewels night and day –	
	But even more, who put them in her way.	
FAUST	The darling girl! It's such a shame.	
	Well, go and get more of the same;	
	The first ones weren't much, anyway.	2855
MEPHISTO.	Oh yes, to you it's just child's play!	
FAUST	Now listen, do exactly what I say:	
	Get to know her neighbour, act the pimp –	
	I never knew the Devil was such a wimp.	
	And get more jewels – do it now, today!	2860
MEPHISTO.	Your slightest wish is my command, my lord.	

[exit *Faust*

That lovesick fool's completely lost his wits;
Just in case his girlfriend might get bored,
He'd blow the sun, the moon and all the stars to bits.

[e*xit*

THE NEIGHBOUR'S HOUSE

MARTHA   [*alone*] May God forgive my husband, he   2865
            Has not done the right thing by me.
            He took off one day on his own,
            He left me flat, and all alone.
            I didn't nag, and never took the huff;
            God knows, I loved him well enough. [*weeping*]   2870
            And if he's dead, I'm in a sorry state –
            I haven't even got a death certificate!

MARGARETA [*enters*] Oh, Martha!

MARTHA   Gretchen, what's the matter, pet?

MARGARETA Oh Martha, I'm in such a sweat;
            There's another box of jewels for me!   2875
            A lovely box, it's made of ebony,
            Such precious things in it, I swear
            They're even finer that the others were.

MARTHA   Don't show them to your mother, then,
            Or else she'll give them to the priest again.   2880

MARGARETA Look at this necklace! And this ring!

MARTHA   [*dressing her in some jewels*]
            Oh Gretchen, you're a lucky thing!

MARGARETA I can't wear them in public, that's forbidden,[10]
            Or to church – I'll have to keep them hidden.

MARTHA   Just you come over to my place   2885
            Whenever you like, and put your jewels on,
            See yourself in the mirror and do up your face –
            We'll have our little bit of fun.
            Then maybe at a wedding or a party
            You gradually start to dress a bit more smartly –   2890
            A gold chain first, then pearl drops in your ear;
            We'll tell your mother that they weren't too dear.

MARGARETA Who could have brought two jewel boxes, though?
            There's something not quite right, I know.

A knock at the door

MARGARETA Oh God! Is that my mother at the door?   2895

MARTHA   [*peering through the curtain*]
                Come in! It's a man I've never seen before.
MEPHISTO.   [*enters*] May I come in? Oh, please ex**c**use me, Miss.
                It's very rude of me to walk straight in like this.

                He bows respectfully to MARGARETA

                It's Mrs Martha Schwerdlein that I called to see.
MARTHA   How can I help you, Sir? For I am she.   2900
MEPHISTO.   [*aside to Martha*] Ah yes, of course, I could
                                                    have guessed.
                But you're entertaining a distinguished guest;
                Forgive me, I'll retire right away,
                And come again – around noon, shall we say?
MARTHA   [*aloud*] Now, child, there's a compliment for you –   2905
                This gentleman thinks you're a lady, too!
MARGARETA   You're quite mistaken, Sir, I fear;
                I'm just a girl who lives round here,
                And all this finery's not my own.
MEPHISTO.   Ah, but it's not the jewels alone;   2910
                It's in your bearing, in your gracious smile –
                How fortunate that I can stay awhile.
MARTHA   What is your business, may I ask?
MEPHISTO.   I only wish I had a happier task.
                I hope the messenger won't get the blame;   2915
                Your husband's dead, but greets you all the same.
MARTHA   He's dead? The poor man's gone, you say?
                My husband's dead! Oh, what a dreadful day!
MARGARETA   Oh Martha dear, please don't despair.
MEPHISTO.   Would you like to hear the tragic story?   2920
MARGARETA   I'll never fall in love, I do declare;
                I'd die of grief if my love died before me.
MEPHISTO.   But joy and grief are never far apart.
MARTHA   Please tell me of my husband's sad demise.
MEPHISTO.   Of course, dear lady. Now, where shall I start?   2925
                In Padua at St Anthony's he lies,
                And in that cool and pleasant spot
                He rests for ever in a consecrated plot.
MARTHA   And have you nothing else for me?
MEPHISTO.   Oh yes – a serious and solemn plea   2930

	To say three hundred Masses for his soul.	
	But otherwise I fear, dear lady, that is all.	
MARTHA	What! Not a single keepsake, not a ring?	
	What every poor apprentice carries in his kit,	
	A token of affection, some small thing	2935
	He'd rather starve or beg than part with it?	
MEPHISTO.	Madam, I have to say with great regret,	
	It wasn't trifling sums that got him into debt.	
	He saw the error of his ways, it's true –	
	But then, he blamed it all on bad luck, too.	2940
MARGARETA	I find it sad that fate is so unkind.	
	I'll pray for him, say lots of Masses for the Dead.	
MEPHISTO.	You are a lovely child, it must be said.	
	Have thoughts of marriage never crossed your mind?	
MARGARETA	Oh no, Sir, I can't think of such a thing.	2945
MEPHISTO.	If not a husband, what of a lover's charms?	
	It is the highest gift that heaven can bring	
	To hold such a sweet creature in one's arms.	
MARGARETA	That's not the custom in these parts, for shame!	
MEPHISTO.	Custom or not, it happens all the same.	2950
MARTHA	But tell me about my husband!	
MEPHISTO.	Ah yes, I was at his side.	
	It was as a good Christian, repenting, that he died.	
	Confessed his sins as he lay there upon some	
	filthy straw –	
	But then, he had so many he could scarcely keep	
	the score.	
	'Alas!' he cried aloud, 'it is a wicked thing I've done,	2955
	To quit my trade, my home, and leave my poor	
	wife all alone!	
	It tortures me to think of it, and now before I die	
	I pray that she'll forgive my sin.'	
MARTHA	The dear man! I've forgiven him.	
MEPHISTO.	'But then, God knows,' he told me, 'she was more	
	to blame than I.'	2960
MARTHA	The liar! What, he lied when he was at death's door?	
MEPHISTO.	He was delirious at the end, I'm sure;	
	I've seen it happen many times before.	
	'I never had a minute's rest,' he said,	

| | 'With her and all her children to be fed, | 2965 |

          'With her and all her children to be fed, 2965
          And always wanting more –
          I never had the peace to eat my share.'

MARTHA   Had he forgotten all the love and care,
          The way I slaved for him by day and night?

MEPHISTO. Oh no, dear lady, he remembered that all right. 2970
          He told me: 'As we left Valletta Bay,
          I prayed most fervently for wife and children too,
          And heaven heard me, for that very day
          We took a Turkish vessel, who
          Had some of the Great Sultan's wealth on board. 2975
          And as I wasn't backward in the fight,
          When it was over, as was only right,
          I got my proper share of the reward.'

MARTHA   Oh, fancy! Did he bury it, d' you think?

MEPHISTO. Gone with the wind, on women and on drink. 2980
          When he was in Naples feeling lonely,
          A pretty lady took him as a friend,
          And she was kind and loving to him, only –
          Love left its mark on him right to the end.

MARTHA   The wretch! With children and a wife to feed, 2985
          He left us here in poverty and need.
          Oh, what a shameless life he led!

MEPHISTO. Well yes, you see – that's why he's dead.
          If I were you, if you'll take my advice,
          I'd mourn him for a year or so, 2990
          And then look round for someone really nice.

MARTHA   I'll never find another like him, though,
          I'm sure of that, however hard I try.
          He was a scamp, but still I liked him fine.
          He never could stay put, I don't know why, 2995
          And chasing other women too, and all that wine,
          And gambling everything he earned.

MEPHISTO. Well, many couples get on well like that.
          If he'd been easy-going, if he'd turned
          A blind eye to whatever you were at – 3000
          Why, I myself, on that condition
          Might be prepared to make a proposition.

MARTHA   Ah, you will have your little joke with me!

MEPHISTO.   [*aside*] It's time to go; this tough old bird
             Would take the very Devil at his word.   3005
             [*to Gretchen*] And you, Miss – all alone and fancy-free?
MARGARETA   Sir, what do you mean?
MEPHISTO.   [*aside*]   Sweet innocence of youth!
             [*aloud*] Goodbye then, ladies.
MARGARETA   Good night!
MARTHA   No, wait! I need some proof!
             I need a death certificate to show
             How, when and where my loved one passed away.   3010
             I want to put it in the paper, too, you know –
             One must do these things properly, I always say.
MEPHISTO.   Madam, of course; two witnesses will do
             To prove in law that what they say is true.
             I have a good friend living near –   3015
             He'll tell the magistrate just what you want to hear.
             I'll bring him here tonight.
MARTHA.   Oh, do!
MEPHISTO.   And this young lady, will she be here too?
             He's a fine lad, well-travelled, very charming;
             The ladies find his manners quite disarming.   3020
MARGARETA   Oh, I would only blush if we should meet.
MEPHISTO.   You needn't blush before a king, my sweet.
MARTHA   Until this evening in the garden, then.
             We shall expect you – shall we say, at ten?
                                              [*they all leave*

A STREET

FAUST. MEPHISTOPHELES

FAUST	Well, what's the news? Did you get anywhere?	3025
MEPHISTO.	Ah, bravo! All on fire – that's what I like to see!	
	Soon Gretchen will be yours, I guarantee.	
	At Martha's place, this evening – she'll be there.	
	That woman's born to be a go-between,	
	By far the finest pimp I've ever seen.	3030
FAUST	All the better!	
MEPHISTO.	There's a small price to pay.	
FAUST	Well, one good turn deserves another – so?	
MEPHISTO.	We have to swear a solemn oath and say	
	What's left of her dear husband here below	
	Now rests in Padua – at least till Judgement Day.	3035
FAUST	Oh, brilliant! Now we've got to go to Italy.	
MEPHISTO.	*Sancta simplicitas!* Of course we don't – [11]	
	Just swear, and leave the rest to me.	
FAUST	You want me to commit perjury? I won't!	
MEPHISTO.	Oh, what a Holy Joe! Is that your problem, then?	3040
	You mean you've never told a lie before?	
	Was it the truth you told your students, when	
	You spoke of God, the world, the hearts and	
	minds of men,	
	And heaven knows what else that lay beyond	
	your ken,	
	When you defined your terms with such authority,	3045
	With brazen confidence and great superiority?	
	And if the truth were told, you lied with every breath;	
	If you were honest, you'd admit you knew no more	
	Of all these matters than of Schwerdlein's death.	
FAUST	The Devil always deals in sophistry and lies.	3050
MEPHISTO.	Oh yes, with you of course it's otherwise.	
	Tomorrow, I suppose, in all sincerity,	
	With all the tricks of the seducer's art	
	You'll try to capture little Gretchen's heart?	
FAUST	And I shall mean it, too.	

MEPHISTO.   That's as may be.   3055
          You'll swear undying love and true emotion,
          Assure her of your passionate devotion –
          Will that stand up to closer scrutiny?
FAUST   Indeed it will, for that is truly what I feel.
          If I can't find the phrases to confess   3060
          This fevered love that makes my senses reel,
          And search in vain for ways that would express
          This passion burning deep inside me,
          And if I grasp at lofty words to guide me,
          And swear that love's for ever, that it never dies –   3065
          Is that a tawdry pack of Devil's lies?
MEPHISTO. I beg to differ.
FAUST   You always do, of course,
          So hold your tongue and bottle up your spite.
          You talk and never stop to listen, so perforce
          You're always right.   3070
          I'm tired of all this talk, I'll spare my voice –
          And you are right, because I have no choice.

A GARDEN

MARGARETA *on* FAUST'S *arm,* MARTHA *strolling
to and fro with* MEPHISTOPHELES

MARGARETA I feel, Sir, that you only speak to me
                So kindly and so condescendingly
                Because a travelled man like you   3075
                Believes it is the proper thing to do.
                My conversation's dull, it is so shaming –
                I can't think why you find it entertaining.
FAUST   One look, one word from you diverts me more
                Than all the wisdom that the world could store.   3080
                                                    [*he kisses her hand*
MARGARETA Oh no, how could you? You embarrass me.
                My hands are rough, and unattractive, too;
                It's all the housework that I have to do –
                My mother's so particular, you see.   [*they walk on*
MARTHA   And you, Sir, always travelling, I dare say?   3085
MEPHISTO.   Indeed, we visit many different places.
                But then business and duty summon us away,
                And it is sad to leave such friendly faces.
MARTHA   Ah yes, for younger men it can be fun
                To roam the world alone and see its ways;   3090
                But soon one's years of travelling are done,
                And as a lonely bachelor to end one's days –
                Why, that's a dismal thought for anyone.
MEPHISTO.   A distant prospect that I dread to contemplate.
MARTHA   Then make your plans before it is too late.   3095
                                                    [*they walk on*
MARGARETA But out of sight, I'll soon be out of mind.
                You're very gracious and polite to me,
                But you have many friends of your own kind
                Far cleverer than I could ever be.
FAUST   Oh dearest! Cleverness isn't all, you know;   3100
                It's often vain and superficial –
MARGARETA   Oh?
FAUST   While innocence and sweet simplicity

Are rarely valued as they ought to be.
Humility and modesty – they
Are the highest gifts that loving nature gave us, when – 3105

MARGARETA If you can think of me just now and then.
I shall have time enough when you're away.

FAUST And are you often on your own?

MARGARETA Oh yes, our household's very small, but even so
It doesn't run itself alone.   3110
We have no maid, I have to knit and sew
And cook and clean, all day I'm on my feet;
My mother wants it all so very neat
And tidy, too.
She doesn't really need to scrimp and save at all,   3115
We have far more than many others do.
My father left us well provided for –
A little house, a plot outside the city wall.
But still, it's very quiet here, it must be said;
My brother is a soldier in the war,   3120
My little sister's dead.
She gave me so much trouble while she lived, and yet
I'd do it all again for her, the little pet.
I loved her so.

FAUST   An angel, if she was like you.

MARGARETA I brought her up, she loved me dearly too.   3125
The little thing was born after my father died;
We feared the worst, my mother was so ill.
We nursed her, I was always at her side,
And slowly she recovered, by God's will.
But then she couldn't even think   3130
Of feeding the poor creature at her breast,
And so I had to do my best
And gave it water mixed with milk to drink.
She grew up in my arms, smiled up at me,
And squirmed and wriggled when I held her on
                                        my knee.   3135

FAUST Those must have been such happy times for you!

MARGARETA Yes, but we often had our troubles, too.
Her cradle always stood beside my bed;
She only had to stir once in the night,

I'd wake up, and she wanted to be fed.   3140
I'd take her into bed with me and hold her tight,
And if she wouldn't settle, out of bed I'd creep,
Walk up and down and rock her back to sleep.
Then in the mornings I would have to sweep
And wash and cook, and go to market, too;   3145
All day and every day I had enough to do.
It's hard work, and there's not much time for fun;
But then, we eat and sleep the better when it's done.

                                        [*they walk on*

MARTHA   It's hard for women who are all alone;
            You bachelors seem quite happy on your own.   3150
MEPHISTO.   But it might only take someone like you
            To make me see a different point of view.
MARTHA   On all your travels, Sir, you mean to say
            You never lost your heart along the way?
MEPHISTO.   Proverbially, of course, we're told   3155
            A good wife and a home are worth their weight in gold.
MARTHA   But have you met no one for whom you really care?
MEPHISTO.   I've always found a civil welcome everywhere.
MARTHA   I mean, have you been seriously committed?
MEPHISTO.   To trifle with a woman's heart is not permitted. 3160
MARTHA   Oh, you don't understand!
MEPHISTO.   You mustn't mind;
            I understand – that you are very good and kind.

                                        [*they walk on*

FAUST   My angel, so you knew me at first sight
            The moment that I came in here tonight?
MARGARETA   You must have noticed how I hardly dared to look. 3165
FAUST   And you don't mind the liberty I took?
            You weren't disturbed by what I had to say
            When you came out of church the other day?
MARGARETA   I *was* put out, I thought it rather rash.
            I thought: there's something forward, something brash 3170
            About me that this gentleman's detected,
            To talk to me like that. It was so unexpected
            To be approached so boldly in the street
            Like any common girl, it seemed so indiscreet.
            I was confused, I must admit, but still   3175

	I couldn't bring myself to wish you ill.
	And I was angry with myself, because I knew
	That I could not feel angry towards you.
FAUST	My sweet love!
MARGARETA	Wait a moment.
	[*she picks a daisy and plucks off the petals one by one*]
FAUST	What is this?
MARGARETA	You'll laugh at me, it's just a game.
FAUST	But what? 3180
	[*she plucks and murmurs*]
	What are you whispering?
MARGARETA	[*half aside*] He loves me – loves me not –
FAUST	You sweet and lovely vision of heaven's bliss!
MARGARETA	[*continues*] Loves me – not – loves me – not –
	[*plucking the last petal, joyously*]
	He loves me!
FAUST	Yes, my dear child. Let the flowers spell
	The judgement of the gods, for it is this: 3185
	He loves you! Loves you more than he can tell!
	[*he takes her hands in his*]
MARGARETA	I'm shivering!
FAUST	Oh no, don't tremble! Let this look,
	Let one touch of my hands convey
	What words cannot express. 3190
	Just trust your feelings, don't resist
	This ecstasy that has to be for ever!
	Ever! To end it would be to despair.
	No, it must never, never end!

MARGARETA *presses his hands, tears herself away and runs off.*
He stands for a moment in thought, then follows her.

MARTHA	[*enters*] It's getting dark.
MEPHISTO.	Ah yes, and we must go. 3195
MARTHA	I'd ask you to stay longer, both of you,
	But it's a spiteful neighbourhood, you know.
	You'd think these folk had nothing else to do
	But watch their neighbours like a hawk –
	And how they talk! 3200

You can't turn round before the whole street knows.
And our young couple?

MEPHISTO.   Fluttered off up there
Like wanton butterflies!

MARTHA.   He seems quite fond of her.

MEPHISTO.   And she of him. And that's the way it goes.

A SUMMERHOUSE

MARGARETA *runs in breathless, hides behind the door, holds a finger to her lips and peers through a crack in the door.*

MARGARETA He's coming!

FAUST   [*enters*]   Where are you? Don't be such   3205
           A tease! [*he kisses her*]

MARGARETA [*puts her arms round him and returns the kiss*]
                      Oh dearest man, I do love you so much!

MEPHISTOPHELES *knocks*

FAUST   [*stamps his foot*] Who's there?

MEPHISTO.   A friend.

FAUST   A beast!

MEPHISTO.   It's time to go, you two.

MARTHA   [*enters*] Yes, Sir, it's late.

FAUST   May I not come with you?

MARGARETA What would my mother say! Goodbye!

FAUST   I'll have to leave you, then.
           Goodbye, my love.

MARTHA   Good night!

MARGARETA   Until we meet again!   3210
                              [*Faust and Mephistopheles leave*

MARGARETA Dear God, I'm sure I never heard
           A man so clever, so well-bred,
           And I can only nod my head
           And scarcely say a single word.
           It makes me blush, I just can't see   3215
           What he finds in a simple girl like me.   [*exit*

FOREST AND CAVERN

FAUST   [*alone*] You gave me, sublime Spirit, gave me all
         I asked of you; and it was not in vain
         You turned your face upon me in the fire.
         You gave me glorious nature as my kingdom,   3220
         The power to feel it and delight in it.
         No cold encounter, no mere spectacle
         You granted me, for nature's very heart
         Is like the bosom of a friend revealed.
         Creation's ordered scale of life you've shown me;   3225
         I learn to know my brother creatures here
         In quiet woods, in streams and in the air.
         And when the forest shudders in the storm,
         The mighty fir-tree falls, and falling tears
         Its neighbours with it, crushing all around,   3230
         Its thundering echoes booming from the hills –
         Then I find refuge in this cavern, where
         I see into myself, and in my heart
         Deep mysteries and wonders are unveiled.
         And when the pure moon rises overhead   3235
         Within its soothing beams the silver forms,
         The hovering spirits of the past emerge
         From mountain crags and mossy woods to ease
         The austere pleasure of my contemplation.

         But now I see that we can never know   3240
         Perfection here on earth. For with this bliss
         That brings me ever closer to the gods,
         You gave that cold and insolent companion
         From whom I can no longer free myself,
         Who makes me feel my shame and my disgrace,   3245
         And turns your gifts to dross with every breath.
         He fans the flames that burn within my heart,
         And fires my longing for that lovely form.
         I satisfy desire with pleasure, then
         In pleasure languish for desire again.   3250

MEPHISTO. [*enters*] This outdoor life is really not for you –
Haven't you grown tired of it yet?
It's all right for a while, but then you get
The urge to go and sample something new.

FAUST I wish you could find something else to do   3255
Than spoil my day by pestering me here.

MEPHISTO. Why, you can rest all day, and all night too,
As far as I'm concerned; you make yourself
quite clear.

I wouldn't miss your company at all,
You're so uncivil, so erratic and ill-bred.   3260
It's no fun being at your beck and call –
I can find better things to do instead.
I can't tell what you want just from your attitude.

FAUST That's rich! You even want my gratitude
For ruining what peace I might have had?   3265

MEPHISTO. Poor mortal fool! What kind of life would you
have led

Without my help? You should be glad
I've cured your whimsical imagination
Of all that harebrained speculation.
And if I hadn't intervened, you know,   3270
You would have left this planet long ago.
Whatever makes you come here like an owl to brood
Among these crags and caverns all this time?
You're like a toad that sucks its food
From soggy moss and rocks that drip with slime.   3275
I can't imagine that you're having fun –
You're still a professor, when all's said and done.

FAUST Can you not understand what new vitality
This barren solitude inspires in me?
Of course, if you had any inkling, you   3280
Would use your devil's tricks to cheat me of it, too.

MEPHISTO. Oh yes! It must be heavenly to sit the whole
night through

Out on the mountainside among the dew
Embracing earth and heaven with ecstatic bliss,
Imagining a god must feel like this,   3285
Whose spirit penetrates the marrow of the earth,

Rehearsing in yourself creation's very birth.
You feel no limits to your grand ambition,
Love's heady rapture holds you in its sway;
All earthly crudities just melt away,   3290
Till finally your lofty intuition
[*with a gesture*] Ends in – well, I hardly like to say.

FAUST   You are disgusting! Shame on you!

MEPHISTO.   And shame
On your hypocrisy! You prudes are all the same;
Chaste ears must never hear us speak about   3295
What no chaste heart can ever do without.
In any case, I've really no objection
If now and then you need a little introspection.
But you won't stand it long, my friend,
And you will realise you must   3300
Escape from it, or you will end
In madness, horror and disgust.
Enough of that! Your sweetheart sits at home,
She feels shut in, bereft and all alone.
She thinks about you all the day,   3305
And loves you more than she can say.
Your passion overwhelmed her at the start,
Just like a mountain torrent fed by melting snow;
It poured into her unresisting heart –
But now your stream is running very slow.   3310
It would become Monsieur much better, though,
Instead of lording it out in the wild
To go and comfort that poor child,
And give her something to reward her love.
Beside the window in her room she stands,   3315
Watching the clouds as they go by above,
And time hangs very heavy on her hands.
'I wish I were a bird with little wings'
All day and half the night she sings.
Sometimes she's happy, other times she's glad,   3320
Sometimes she can only sit and weep;
Then she'll calm down and go to sleep –
But it's always, always love that makes her sad.

FAUST   You snake! You serpent! You are vile!

MEPHISTO.	[*aside*] Yes – and you'll feel my fangs in just a while.
FAUST	You monster, get out of my sight!
	Don't mention her, and let that lovely woman be.
	Don't tempt me with the thought of the delight
	That her sweet body might have given me.
MEPHISTO.	What do you want? She thinks you've done a flit –
	And that's at least half true, you must admit.
FAUST	I'm always close to her, no matter where
	I go, and she will be with me forever.
	I envy the very body of the Lord whenever
	She puts it to her lips in prayer.
MEPHISTO.	Ah yes! And the two young twins like roes that feed
	Among the lilies – those I envy you indeed.
FAUST	Get out, you pimp!
MEPHISTO.	Come, spare me your derision.
	For God himself approved that laudable vocation;
	When he created girls and lads, he made provision
	To give them opportunity for procreation.
	Get on, let's have less of this gloom!
	You're going to see your girl tonight,
	And not to meet your doom!
FAUST	Though at her breast I might feel heaven's bliss,
	And in her arms the warming passion of her kiss,
	I would still feel the pity of her plight.
	I am accursed, a homeless refugee,
	An aimless outcast driven relentlessly
	Like a cascading torrent over rock and precipice,
	Raging and seething into the abyss.
	And in a peaceful meadow by that stream
	She lived her simple life, her daily round
	And all the childish thoughts that she could dream
	In that small world were safely hedged around.
	And I, whom God has cursed,
	Was not content to thunder
	In a foaming rage and burst
	The tumbling rocks asunder.
	I had to undermine that girl's tranquillity –
	That was the sacrifice that hell required of me.
	What must be done, let it be quickly done,

3325

3330

3335

3340

3345

3350

3355

3360

Now, Devil, help me end this agony;
My fearful destiny and hers are one,
And she is doomed to share my fate with me.   3365
MEPHISTO.   Oh, what a boiling stew we're in again!
Go in and comfort her, my friend.
A fool like you just needs to lose the plot, and then
He thinks the world is coming to an end.
You're quite a devil now – but mind   3370
You keep your nerve; for there
Is nothing more deplorable, I find,
Than a devil who's been driven to despair.

GRETCHEN'S ROOM

GRETCHEN *at the spinning wheel, alone*

My peace is gone,
My heart is sore,   3375
It's gone for ever
And evermore.

Whenever he
Is far away,
The world for me   3380
Is cold and grey.

And my poor head
Is quite bemused,
My scattered wits
Are all confused.   3385

My peace is gone,
My heart is sore,
It's gone for ever
And evermore.

It's him I look for   3390
On the street,
It's only him
I go to meet.

And in his walk,
Such dignity.   3395
His gracious talk
Bewitches me.

And when he smiles
At me, what bliss,
To feel his hand –   3400
And ah, his kiss!

My peace is gone,
My heart is sore,
It's gone for ever
And evermore.   3405

Here in my heart
I long for him,
And if I could
Belong to him,

I'd hold him and kiss him   3410
All the day,
Though in his kisses
I'd melt away!

MARTHA'S GARDEN

MARGARETA, FAUST

MARGARETA Tell me something, Heinrich.
FAUST   Gladly, if I can.
MARGARETA What is your faith? I feel I ought to know.   3415
          You're such a good and kindly man;
          You seem to have no true religion, though.
FAUST   Oh, do not ask! You know I love you well, indeed
          For those I love I'd hazard life and limb,
          And never seek to hurt their feelings or their creed.   3420
MARGARETA But that's not right, you must believe in Him!
FAUST   Must we?
MARGARETA   I wish I could persuade you to
          Respect the Holy Sacraments as I do.
FAUST   I do respect them.
MARGARETA   Yes – but is your faith sincere?
          You don't go to confession or to Mass, I fear.   3425
          Do you believe in God?
FAUST   My love, who can
          Say such a thing?
          Go ask the cleverest priest, the wisest man –
          Their answers only mock our questioning,
          And mock us too.
MARGARETA   You have no faith, I see.   3430
FAUST   Sweet child, you misinterpret me.
          For who can name,
          Who can proclaim
          Belief in Him?
          Who can reveal   3435
          He does *not* feel
          Belief in Him?
          All-embracing
          And all-preserving,
          Does He not hold   3440
          And keep us all?
          Is not the vault of heaven above us,

The earth's foundation here below?
Do not eternal stars smile down
Upon us as they climb the skies?   3445
And when I look into your eyes, do you
Not feel how all things
Flood your heart and mind all through,
And weave their everlasting spell
Unseen, yet visible beside you?   3450
Just let it fill your heart, and when
You feel the highest bliss, why, then
You call it what you will:
Joy! Heart! Love! God!
I have no name for it;   3455
Feeling is all,
A name's mere sound, a haze that veils
The radiance of heaven from view.

MARGARETA I daresay that's all very true;
The priest says more or less the same thing, too –   3460
He doesn't put it quite the same way, though.

FAUST You'll hear it everywhere you go,
As far as heaven's light can reach,
All hearts, all languages will teach
That message; why should I not speak in mine?   3465

MARGARETA Yes, put like that it all sounds very fine,
But still it doesn't seem quite right; you see,
It's not what I think of as Christianity.

FAUST Dear child!

MARGARETA   It's always troubled me
To see you in that person's company.   3470

FAUST But why?

MARGARETA   That man you call your friend
Is deeply hateful to me, and I can't pretend
To like him, for in all my life
I never saw a face so grim;
His look goes through me like a knife.   3475

FAUST My sweet, you mustn't be afraid of him.

MARGARETA His presence chills the very blood in me.
I always think the best of folk, but he –
Although I long to be with you, I swear,

| | It makes me shudder when I see him there. | 3480 |

It makes me shudder when I see him there. 3480
I've thought he was a villain all along –
May God forgive me if I do him wrong.

FAUST   He's odd – no more than many others, though.

MARGARETA How you can live with him, I just don't know.
He only has to come in here 3485
With such a mocking look, a sneer
About his lips, and you can tell
He cares for nothing, wishes no one well.
It's written on his face, it's plain to see
That he could never love his fellow men. 3490
I feel so safe when you are holding me,
So free, so loving and so warm, but then
I freeze and shiver when I feel his presence.

FAUST   You angel! Ah, what knowing innocence!

MARGARETA It overwhelms me more than I can say. 3495
I even think, whenever he is here,
My very love for you might ebb away,
And I could never pray when he is near.
That is what really tears my heart in two –
But Heinrich, you must feel his menace too. 3500

FAUST   You have a loathing for him, that is clear.

MARGARETA And I must go now.

FAUST   Ah, my dear,
If only we could have one hour tonight
To lie together, hold each other tight.

MARGARETA If I were on my own, for sure, 3505
I'd willingly unlock my door.
My mother sleeps so lightly, though;
I'd die upon the spot, I know,
If she should come and find us there.

FAUST   My angel, we can easily prepare 3510
For that; you only have to take
This bottle, put three drops into her drink tonight,
And she'll sleep undisturbed until daylight.

MARGARETA What would I not do, Heinrich, for your sake?
You're sure it won't be dangerous for her? 3515

FAUST   My love, would I suggest it if it were?

MARGARETA Oh dearest man, my love for you is such,

I would do anything you asked me to.
For your sake I've already done so much,
There's little more for me to give to you.   [*exit* 3520

MEPHISTO. [*enters*] The little monkey!

FAUST   Eavesdropping again, I see.

MEPHISTO. I have been listening most attentively.
Was that the catechism I heard you reciting?
I trust Herr Doktor found it to his liking.
These girls are keen on simple faith and piety,   3525
They think: if he's had a religious education,
He's much more likely to resist temptation.

FAUST   You monster, you have never known
How an angelic child like this,
Whose faith is pure and whole,   3530
Whose faith alone
Sustains her hope of heaven's bliss,
Could fear the one she loves might lose his soul.

MEPHISTO. What supersublimated sensuality!
A little girl has got you on a string.   3535

FAUST   You misbegotten spawn of hell-fire and depravity!

MEPHISTO. She's good at reading faces too, the cheeky thing!
She feels a bit uneasy when I'm there;
She looks at me, and seems to see
A touch of genius, a certain flair –   3540
She might even suspect some devilry in me.
Well, and tonight?

FAUST   That's no concern of yours.

MEPHISTO. I like to have my fun – it's all in a good cause.

AT THE WELL

GRETCHEN *and* LIESCHEN *carrying pitchers*

LIESCHEN	And what about Barbara? Haven't you heard?	
GRETCHEN	No, not a word; I don't get out as much as you.	3545
LIESCHEN	Sibyl told me today – it's true!	
	At last she's got what she deserved,	
	Miss Hoity-Toity!	
GRETCHEN	What?	
LIESCHEN	It stinks!	
	She's feeding two when she eats and drinks.	
GRETCHEN	Oh, no!	3550
LIESCHEN	Oh yes, she came a cropper in the end.	
	That man she always went about with,	
	The one she boasted she was 'walking out with',	
	Going to fairs and dances with her 'friend' –	
	She always had to be the first in line.	3555
	He treated her to cakes and wine,	
	She thought she was so very fine.	
	And all those presents he gave her, too –	
	I'd be ashamed to take them, so would you.	
	And all those cuddles in the wood!	3560
	Well, now her flower's gone for good.	
GRETCHEN	Oh, the poor girl!	
LIESCHEN	Now don't be soft!	
	While you and I were spinning in the loft	
	Because we weren't allowed out after dark –	
	She was with her lover in the park.	3565
	Behind the house and in the alleyway,	
	For hours they were together, every day.	
	Next time she goes to church she'll have to do	
	Her public penance in the sinners' pew!	
GRETCHEN	But he will marry her, for sure.	3570
LIESCHEN	He's not so daft as that. And he's a likely lad	
	Who'll want the chance to look around for more.	
	And anyway, he's gone.	
GRETCHEN	Oh, that's too bad!	

LIESCHEN   And if she does catch him, she'll still be had.
            The boys will snatch her wreath, and at the door   3575
            Instead of flowers we'll throw bits of straw.   [*exit*
GRETCHEN   [*walking home*] If some poor girl got into trouble, you
            Would always scoff and gossip like that too.
            And you were always quick to lay the blame
            And wag your tongue at someone else's shame!   3580
            And though their sin was black as black could be,
            It never could be black enough for me.
            I crossed myself and felt so proud –
            And now my own sin cries aloud!
            But what I did, dear God in heaven above,   3585
            It was so good – and it was all for love.

A SHRINE

In a niche in the city wall a sacred image of the
Mater Dolorosa with vases of flowers in front of it.
GRETCHEN *puts fresh flowers into the vases.*

Our Lady, thou
So rich in sorrows, bow
Thy face upon my anguish now!

Thy heart transfixed,   3590
Thy gaze is fixed
Towards thy son upon the Cross.

The Father beseeching,
Thy sighs are reaching
To heaven to assuage thy loss.   3595

Who can feel
And who reveal
Such pain, such bitter woe?
Why my heart with fear is shaking,
Why it's yearning, why it's quaking,   3600
Only you can truly know!

Wherever I may be,
I feel such misery
Within my bosom aching.
When I am on my own   3605
I weep, I weep alone,
My fearful heart is breaking.

The early sun was shining
When I rose from my bed.
In grief and sorrow pining,   3610
What bitter tears I shed!

The boxes in front of my window
Were watered with the dew
Of my tears as early this morning
I picked these flowers for you.   3615

Help! Keep me safe from death and blame!
Our Lady, thou
So rich in sorrows, bow
Thy gracious face upon my shame!

NIGHT

The street in front of Gretchen's house.
VALENTIN, *a soldier, Gretchen's brother.*

VALENTIN   When I was drinking with the rest,   3620
They used to argue who was best
Of all the girls they ever knew,
The way that soldiers always do.
And then they used to fill their glasses
And drink a toast to all the lasses.   3625
I'd sit there with a quiet smile,
And let them brag on for a while;
I'd stroke my beard and hide my thoughts,
And when they'd finished, I'd fill my jar
And tell them: Well, it takes all sorts.   3630
But of all the lasses near and far,
Not one could hold a candle to
My sister Gretchen – ain't that true?
He's right, they'd shout, let's drink a toast
To little Gretchen, she's the one,   3635
She's the girl we all like most.
And all the boasters sat there dumb.
But now! It drives you to despair,
It makes you want to tear your hair;
The neighbours talk, the gossips sneer,   3640
And every lout thinks he can jeer.
All I can do is look away,
Dreading every word they say.
And even if I knocked them flying,
I couldn't tell them they were lying.   3645

What's that? Who's lurking over there?
It must be him – the other one as well.
If I get hold of him, I swear
I'll send him and his friend straight down to hell.

FAUST, MEPHISTOPHELES

FAUST	Through that church window softly gleams	3650
	The warm reflection of the sanctuary light;	
	But here outside its ever fainter beams	
	Are smothered in the darkness of the night.	
	That darkness, too, encompasses my heart.	
MEPHISTO.	And I feel like a tom-cat in the dark,	3655
	Up on the roof-tops by the fire-escapes,	
	Padding along the walls and roaming free,	
	A bit of thieving, getting into scrapes,	
	Screwing around – that's just the life for me!	
	In all my limbs I feel these ghostly twitches –	3660
	Walpurgis Eve is just two nights away.	
	Now that's worth staying up for any day –	
	I just can't wait to get among those witches.	
FAUST	Perhaps by then you might have raised the treasure	
	That I see glowing dimly over there?	3665
MEPHISTO.	I promise, very soon you'll have the pleasure	
	Of dipping into it – you'll get your share.	
	I took a peep at it not long ago;	
	It's full of silver coins, a fine collection.	
FAUST	No jewels? Not a single ring to show	3670
	That lovely girl a token of affection?	
MEPHISTO.	Ah yes, indeed, I might have seen	
	Some jewellery – a string of pearls, it could have been.	
FAUST	I'm glad to hear it; when I go to see	
	My love, I like to take a gift with me.	3675
MEPHISTO.	I don't see why you should be too upset	
	If you don't have to pay for what you get.	
	But now, the stars are shining overhead –	
	I'll treat you to a little serenade,	
	A cautionary song about a lovesick maid.	3680
	It's sure to turn her pretty little head.	
	[*he sings to a guitar*]	

<blockquote>

Oh, Katie dear [12]
What brings you here
To your lover's door
Before the day is dawning?   3685
Be careful, or

</blockquote>

You'll be betrayed,
Let in a maid –
A maid no more by morning.

Sweet maid, begone, 3690
For when it's done
He'll up and run –
With you he will not linger.
Sweet maid, beware,
Don't go in there 3695
Unless you wear
A ring upon your finger.

VALENTIN [*comes forward*] You damned ratcatcher! Curse you, who
D'you think you're serenading to?
I'll send your instrument to hell, 3700
And then I'll send the singer there as well!
MEPHISTO. My poor guitar is ruined! What a shame!
VALENTIN And now you're going to get more of the same!
MEPHISTO. [*to Faust*] Come on now, Doctor, don't hold back!
Keep close to me, out with your snicker-snack! 3705
I'll parry, all you have to do
Is watch your chance and run him through.
VALENTIN Right, parry that!
MEPHISTO. Why, certainly.
VALENTIN And that!
MEPHISTO. Of course!
VALENTIN Is this the Devil fighting me?
What's going on? My hand's gone numb! 3710
MEPHISTO. [*to Faust*] Now thrust!
VALENTIN [*falls*] Ah God!
MEPHISTO. That's settled him! Now come,
We've got to get away from here before
They start to raise a mighty hue and cry.
I'm on good terms with the police, but even I
Can't get away with murder, that's against the law. 3715
MARTHA [*at her window*] Help! Help! Outside!
GRETCHEN [*at her window*] Quick, fetch a light!
MARTHA [*as above*] They're shouting in the street, there's
been a fight!

PEOPLE	There's someone lying here. He's dead!
MARTHA	[*coming outside*] Where are the killers? Have they
	cut and run?
GRETCHEN	[*coming outside*] Who's this?
PEOPLE	It is your mother's son. 3720
GRETCHEN	Almighty God, what have I brought upon my head?
VALENTIN	I'm dying! That's soon said,
	And even sooner done.
	You women, stop your wailing, and instead
	Hear what I have to say before I'm gone. 3725
	[*they all gather round him*]
	Gretchen, listen. You are young, and still
	Unable to distinguish good from ill.
	You've got yourself into a pretty mess. Before
	I die, I want to say, just between you and me,
	That you are nothing but a whore – 3730
	So go ahead and do it properly.
GRETCHEN	Brother! Dear God, what can you mean?
VALENTIN	Just leave God out of it. What's been
	Has been, what's done is done;
	But you'll go on as you've begun. 3735
	First you take a secret lover,
	And soon you think you'd like another.
	And when you've had a dozen or so,
	Then the whole town will want a go.

When you give birth to sin and shame,   3740
You never call it by its proper name;
You cover it with the veil of night,
And keep it hidden out of sight.
You want to stifle it, but then
It can't be hidden, and it grows,   3745
And in the light of day it shows
Itself in all its ugliness again.
And the more hideous your disgrace,
The more it seeks to show its face.

Indeed, I can foresee the day   3750
When decent folk will turn away

From you, you slut, and they will shun
You like the plague, yes, every one.
Your blood will freeze within you when
They look at you, your heart will quail.   3755
You won't wear any jewels then,
Nor stand and pray at the altar-rail!
At dances you won't show your face,
You'll not wear finery or lace –
You'll crouch in a corner in misery   3760
With cripples and beggars for company.
God may forgive you yet, but I
Give you my curse before I die!

MARTHA   Commend your soul to God in death!
            Would you blaspheme with your last breath?   3765

VALENTIN   If only I could lift my sword,
            You scrawny pimp, you shameful bawd,
            Then surely I could hope to win
            Forgiveness for my every sin.

GRETCHEN   Dear brother, ah, what misery!   3770

VALENTIN   I tell you, let your weeping be!
            You are dishonoured, and your fall
            Was the unkindest cut of all.
            I go to God, and to my grave,
            An honest soldier, true and brave.   3775

                                              [*he dies*

CATHEDRAL

Mass, organ and choir.
GRETCHEN *among a crowd of people.*
An EVIL SPIRIT *behind* GRETCHEN.

EVIL SPIRIT	How different, Gretchen, you felt	
	When you, still all innocent,	
	Came here to the altar	
	Thumbing the well-worn pages,	
	Lisping your prayers,	3780
	Half childish play,	
	Half pious worship!	
	Gretchen!	
	What's on your mind?	
	And in your heart,	3785
	What misdeed?	
	Are you praying for your mother's soul, which	
	Through your doing now spends long, long years in purgatory?	
	Whose blood is on your doorstep?	
	And there below your heart,	3790
	Can you not feel it quickening,	
	That fearful presence, boding ill	
	For both of you?	
GRETCHEN	No! No!	
	If only I could rid myself	3795
	Of these oppressive thoughts	
	That swarm around me!	
CHOIR	*Dies irae, dies illa* [13]	
	Solvet saeclum in favilla.	[*organ music*
EVIL SPIRIT	Dread fear grips you!	3800
	The trumpet sounds!	
	The graves gape!	
	And your heart,	
	From the ashes	
	Where it slept	3805
	Awakes to hell-fire	

	And quakes!	
GRETCHEN	I must get out!	
	The organ seems	
	To stifle me,	3810
	The chanting voices	
	Melt my heart within me.	
CHOIR	*Judex ergo cum sedebit,*	
	Quidquid latet adparebit,	
	Nil inultum remanebit.	3815
GRETCHEN	I'm suffocating!	
	The pillars	
	Press in on me,	
	The vaults above	
	Are crushing me! I need air!	3820
EVIL SPIRIT	You try to hide! Sin and shame	
	Cannot be hidden.	
	Air? Light?	
	Woe on you!	
CHOIR	*Quid sum miser tunc dicturus?*	3825
	Quem patronum rogaturus?	
	Cum vix justus sit securus.	
EVIL SPIRIT	The blessed	
	Turn their faces from you.	
	The pure	3830
	Shudder to reach out their hands to you.	
	Woe!	
CHOIR	*Quid sum miser tunc dicturus?*	
GRETCHEN	Neighbour! Your salts!	

[she falls in a swoon

WALPURGIS NIGHT

The Harz Mountains, near Schierke and Elend.
FAUST *and* MEPHISTOPHELES

MEPHISTO. A broomstick's what you really need –   3835
         Or a randy goat would make an even better steed.
         We'll never get there at this speed.

FAUST   I'll trust my own two legs to carry me,
         And this good stick to help me, that will be
         Quite adequate. And what's the hurry, anyway?   3840
         I find it very pleasant just to stray
         Along the winding valley, then
         To climb the rocky cliffs again,
         And see the never-ending torrents flow
         Foaming and dashing to the chasm far below.   3845
         The birches and the firs can feel the breath of spring –
         Why shouldn't our legs feel its bracing thrill?

MEPHISTO. To be quite honest, I can't feel a thing.
         For me it's deepest winter still;
         I like the frost and snow, the icy chill.   3850
         The waning moon is rising overhead,
         And casts a dismal glow of sullen red.
         It sheds no light, and we could break
         A leg with every step we take.
         These Jack o' Lanterns are a much more cheerful sight, 3855
         I'll go and ask one if he'd like to guide us.
         Hullo, my friend! Can we not share your light?
         We'd be most grateful if you'd walk beside us
         And help us to negotiate this slope.

WILL O' THE WISP   Why, I'd be honoured, Sir! I only hope   3860
         I can restrain my natural frivolity;
         We go in zig-zags as a rule, you see.

MEPHISTO. You imitate the human race, it would appear.
         Now, in the Devil's name, don't gad about –
         Go straight, or else I'll blow your lantern out!   3865

WILL O' THE WISP   I see you are the master around here.
         I'll do my best, Sir, not to go astray;

But don't forget the Brocken is bewitched tonight,
And if a Jack o' Lantern shows the way,
You mustn't be surprised if things don't go quite right. 3870

FAUST, MEPHISTOPHELES, WILL O' THE WISP [*chanting alternately*]

Wonderland of magic dreams
We have entered now, it seems.
Lead us well and show your paces,
So that we can safely go
Through these vast and barren places.   3875

See the fir-trees, row on row,
Speeding past us in the gloom.
Cliffs above us rear and loom,
Rocks like giants' noses soaring,
Hear them blowing, hear then snoring!   3880

Through the rocks and meadows pouring
Streams and torrents dash along.
In the rushing waters' song
Do we hear a sweet lament
For the days in heaven spent,   3885
Days of love and hope now gone?
From the past the ancient tales
Echo through the woods and vales.

Tuwhit! Tuwhoo! Here close by wails
The screech-owl, peewit and the jay;   3890
All have stayed awake today.
Long-legged newts with shiny tails
And bloated bellies crawl about.
Twisted roots come winding out
From the rocks and sandy soil,   3895
Slithering like snakes to seize
Stumbling walkers as they go.
From the gnarled and knotted trees
Living tentacles uncoil,
Twisting, writhing to and fro.   3900
Fieldmice in their thousands pour
Through the moss, across the moor;
Fireflies swarming in the dark

  Dance and flicker, flash and spark –
  But they do not light our way.   3905

  Now we can no longer say –
  Are we moving? Standing here?
  Everything around us races,
  Trees and rocks with grinning faces,
  Lights that float and sway and veer,   3910
  Blaze and flicker far and near.

MEPHISTO. Grab my coat-tails, Doctor, follow me!
  Stand up here and take a look around;
  Inside the mountain over there you'll see
  Mammon's palace glowing underground.   3915

FAUST How eerily that faint and spectral glow
  Glimmers among the chasms far below!
  Even the very deepest gorges seem
  To catch the last reflection of that gleam.
  Great swathes of smoke and vapour billow round, 3920
  A fiery shaft lights up the clouds, and then
  It flows, a slender thread, beneath the ground.
  And now it gushes like a spring again,
  And branches in a hundred veins that stream
  Along the valley to that narrow corner, where 3925
  It merges into one again, and there
  Becomes a single precious seam.
  Now sparks are flying ever higher,
  Like golden sand flung in the air,
  And higher still, look, over there –   3930
  The mountainside is all on fire.

MEPHISTO. Yes, Mammon's palace is a splendid sight,
  He does his best to give us all a treat.
  You're lucky to be here – and soon you'll meet
  Some of our wilder guests tonight.   3935

FAUST The storm is howling now, and I can feel
  It tugging at my back, it makes me reel.

MEPHISTO. Just cling on to the rock's old ribs like this,
  Or else you'll be swept into the abyss.
  The fog is dense, and dark the night,   3940
  Listen how the forests whine!

Startled owls are put to flight,
Pillars split in evergreen
Palaces of fir and pine.
Grating branches scrape and scream,   3945
Mighty trunks are cracking and groaning,
Heaving roots are creaking and moaning!
With a fearful crash they all
Topple others as they fall,
They choke the gorges, and the gale   3950
Whistles through them with its dismal wail.
Can you hear the voices everywhere,
Far and near, high in the air?
Yes, the whole mountainside is ringing
With the witches' furious singing.   3955

WITCHES [in chorus]
           Witches to the Brocken streaming,
           The stubble is yellow, the shoots are greening.
           To the summit swarms the witches' chorus,
           Up there Old Nick is waiting for us.
           Hurry to get there before they start!   3960
           The billy-goats stink and the witches fart.

A VOICE   Here comes Baubo, the ancient crone,
           Riding a sow, and all alone.

CHORUS   All honour then where honour's due;
           Old Mother Baubo, be our guide.   3965
           A sturdy pig with you astride –
           Lead on, and we'll all follow you!

A VOICE   Which way did you come?
A VOICE   By Ilsenstein!
           I looked in at the owl's nest as I flew by –
           She glared at me with her beady eye.   3970
A VOICE   Damn you, don't ride so fast, or go to hell!
A VOICE   The creature went for me as well –
           Just take a look at these scratches of mine!

WITCHES [in chorus]
           The way is broad, the way is long,
           Along it pours a giddy throng.   3975

       The broomstick scrapes, the pitchfork pokes,
       The mother bursts and the baby chokes.

WARLOCKS   [*half-chorus*]
       We creep along like weary snails –
       The women are faster than the males.
       If it's the Devil you're looking for,   3980
       They'll beat you by a mile or more.

THE OTHER HALF–CHORUS
       We needn't hurry; what's the fuss?
       Women need more time than us.
       They think the men are far too slow –
       But we can do it in one go.   3985

A VOICE   [*above*] You down by the lake, come up from below!
VOICES   [*from below*] We'd like to come with you, for sure;
       We wash till we're pure as driven snow,
       But we'll be barren for evermore.

BOTH CHORUSES   The starlight fades, the wind has died,   3990
       The dismal moon creeps out of sight.
       A thousand sparks blaze in the night
       As the witches to the Brocken ride.

VOICE   [*from a rocky chasm*]
       Stop! Wait for me! Oh, won't you stop?
VOICE   [*from above*] Whose voice is that from far below?   3995
VOICE   [*from below*] Let me come with you, please! Although
       I've climbed three hundred years or so,
       And still I haven't reached the top,
       I'd rather be with folk I know.

BOTH CHORUSES   A good stout broomstick carries you,   4000
       A pitchfork or a goat will do;
       If you can't get up there today,
       You'll never make it anyway.

HALF–WITCH   [*below*]   I trot along all on my own,
       And try to keep up with the crowd.   4005
       I can't get any peace at home –
       But then, up here it's just as loud.

WITCHES   [*in chorus*]
            The witch-grease gives us all a thrill,
            For a boat we use a rusty pail,
            And any old rag will make a sail.   4010
            If you don't fly now, you never will.

BOTH CHORUSES Around the summit we shall ride,
            And settle on the ground beneath.
            A swarm of witches far and wide
            Will cover all the blasted heath.   4015
            [*they land on the ground*]
MEPHISTO.   They're pushing and shoving and sliding and clattering,
            Jostling and squirming and hissing and chattering,
            They flicker and fizzle and stink like bitches –
            They're in their element, these witches!
            Hold on to me, or you'll get lost. Hold tight, I say!   4020
            Where are you?
FAUST   [*in the distance*]   Here!
MEPHISTO.   What, so far away?
            I'll have to show them who's the boss round here.
            Stand back! Squire Voland's here! Good folk,
                                            make way!
            Now, Doctor, take my hand! We must break free
            From all this milling crowd – I fear   4025
            It's too much, even for the likes of me.
            Look, by those bushes over there I see
            A cosy glow that looks much more inviting.
            Come on, you never know, it could be quite exciting.
FAUST   You spirit of perversity! All right,   4030
            Lead on – but it's not very clever, I must say,
            To come here to the Brocken on Walpurgis Night,
            When all we do is go our own sweet way.
MEPHISTO.   Look, what a cheerful blaze! And we're
            Part of a jolly club in here.   4035
            Just a small circle, but good company.
FAUST   Up there is where I'd rather be!
            The crowd streams upwards to the summit, where
            The Evil One is sitting in a fiery glow.
            What mysteries would be revealed up there!   4040

MEPHISTO.   New mysteries would be created, though.
            Just let the world outside go by, and we
            Will take it easy over here.
            For folk have always had a tendency
            To form small worlds within the wider sphere.   4045
            See those young naked witches over there, how sweet;
            The older ones, I'm glad to say, are more discreet.
            Now make an effort to be friendly, just for me;
            They'll give you a nice time – and it's all free.
            Is that an orchestra that I can hear?   4050
            We'll have to put up with the awful noise, I fear.
            Just come with me, we can't avoid the din;
            Come on, I'll go ahead and introduce you –
            I might find someone else who will seduce you.
            And take a look at this great room we're in,   4055
            It's huge, it stretches nearly out of sight.
            A hundred cheerful fires are burning bright,
            They're dancing, talking, flirting, drinking, eating –
            I tell you, this place takes a lot of beating.
FAUST   What role have you assumed for this surprise –   4060
            A conjuror, or the Devil in disguise?
MEPHISTO.   I often travel incognito, that is true,
            But I wear my decorations at a proper do.
            I haven't got the Order of the Garter – though
            My cloven hoof commands respect up here, you know.   4065
            You see this snail here slowly crawling by?
            It's only got those feelers in its face,
            But it can sense something, perhaps it knows
                                                  my limp –
            I can't disguise myself here even if I try.
            Come on, let's have a good look round the place;   4070
            You can be the punter, and I'll play the pimp.
            [*to a group sitting round a dying fire*]
            Now, gentlemen! What, sitting all alone?
            I am surprised at you! Why do you shun
            These youthful revels? Why not join the fun?
            If you wanted solitude, you should have stayed
                                                  at home.   4075
GENERAL   You cannot put your trust in any nation!

      Whatever you've done for them in your day,
      The people are just like the women – they
      Will always want the younger generation.
MINISTER They just don't do things properly these days.   4080
      When I think of the old traditional ways,
      There was a time when we had their respect.
      It was our Golden Age – in retrospect.
SOCIAL CLIMBER We took our chances when they came along,
      And did some shady business in the past;   4085
      But somehow nowadays it's all gone wrong,
      Just when we thought we'd made the grade at last.
AUTHOR They don't read anything I'd call
      Good literature or decent prose today.
      Young people now, they think they know it all – 4090
      They're just not interested in what you say.
MEPHISTO. [*suddenly looking very old*]
      To hear them talk, you'd think Doomsday was nigh!
      Indeed, I even feel my barrel's running dry.
      This is the last time I shall come up here;
      The world is coming to an end, I fear.   4095
PEDLAR-WITCH Wait, gentlemen! Don't pass me by,
      You'll miss your chance, so come and buy!
      Take a good look – knick-knacks galore,
      There's everything you need, and more.
      There's nowhere in the world you'll find   4100
      Such a well-stocked shop as mine.
      There's nothing here that hasn't done
      A serious injury to someone,
      No dagger here that hasn't run with blood,
      No cup that hasn't sent a deadly flood   4105
      Of poison scorching through some healthy veins.
               You'll find
      No trinket that has not seduced a sweet young maid,
      No sword that has not treacherously betrayed
      A friend, or stabbed a rival from behind.
MEPHISTO. Oh Grandma, you're just too set in your ways! 4110
      That stuff's old hat. Believe me, you
      Should try to offer people something new –
      It's novelty they look for nowadays.

FAUST	How I keep my wits about me, I don't know;	
	This really is a most amazing show!	4115
MEPHISTO.	They're making for the summit in a swirling throng,	
	You can't resist, you just get swept along.	
FAUST	Who is that woman I see over there?	
MEPHISTO.	Take a good look; it's Lilith.	
FAUST	Who?	
MEPHISTO.	Adam's first wife. You see her lovely hair?	4120
	That is her chief attraction – but take care!	
	If any young man falls for her, he should beware –	
	He'll be an old man by the time she's through.	
FAUST	That young witch, and the old one, sitting there together –	
	I saw them dancing just now hell-for-leather!	4125
MEPHISTO.	We're going to get no peace tonight, I know.	
	They're playing a new dance, come on, let's have a go!	

FAUST   [*dancing with the young witch*]

> A lovely dream once came to me;
> I thought I saw an apple-tree.
> I climbed it, and a gorgeous pair   4130
> Of apples I found hanging there.

PRETTY YOUNG WITCH

> You men like apples, I believe,
> Since Adam had a bite from Eve.
> I'm overjoyed, and very proud
> My garden is so well-endowed.   4135

MEPHISTO.   [*dancing with the old witch*]

> I had a wild dream some time back;
> I saw a tree with a great big crack.
> It had a gaping hole inside –
> I like a hole that's nice and wide.

OLD WITCH   You and your cloven hoof, Sir Knight,   4140
> Are very welcome here tonight.
> A hole like that needs a big stopper,
> So you can plug it good and proper!

SPOOKYBUM[14]   What impudence! Accursed crew!
> Haven't I proved that ghosts like you   4145

Can't walk around like normal folk –
And now you're dancing, too. This is beyond a joke!

PRETTY WITCH [*dancing*] What does he want up here with us?

FAUST   [*dancing*] Oh, he gets everywhere, and always
                                                    makes a fuss.
He likes to watch while other people dance;   4150
He analyses every step you take,
And criticizes every small mistake.
He gets annoyed whenever we advance –
If we dance round in circles, then he will
Admit it's better than just standing still.   4155
Going around in circles is what he does best;
He still expects our thanks though, the old pest.

SPOOKYBUM Are you still there? But this is an outrage!
Away with you! We live in an enlightened age.
This devil's rabble just ignores the rules. We've
                                                    proved   4160
They don't exist, yet Tegel's haunted still.
I've done my best to clear them out, but will
They go? It's scandalous! They simply can't be moved!

PRETTY WITCH   So stop annoying us and pack it in!

SPOOKYBUM I tell you spirits to your face,   4165
This spiritual tyranny is a disgrace;
It upsets all my spiritual discipline.
[*they carry on dancing*]
I see I shan't get anywhere today;
I'm going on a journey, and before I'm through
I'll have worked out the proper way   4170
To deal with devils – and with poets, too.

MEPHISTO. He'll go away and sit down in a puddle,
That's how he gets his wits out of a muddle.
And when the leeches have all feasted on his bum,
The ghosts have vanished – but his brain's gone numb. 4175
[*to Faust, who has left the dance*]
Why did you let that pretty girl escape just then?
She sang so nicely as you jigged about.

FAUST   She'd scarcely started singing to me, when
She opened up her mouth, and a red mouse
                                                    jumped out.

MEPHISTO.	Ah well, you can't be too particular today.
	You're lucky that the mouse was red, not grey.
	Lovers shouldn't notice these things, anyway.
FAUST	And then I saw —
MEPHISTO.	What?
FAUST	Look, Mephisto, can you see
	That lovely child, so pale and lonely over there?
	She shuffles awkwardly along; it seems to me
	She's wearing chains around her feet. I swear
	She looks like Gretchen. Can it be
	That she and I will meet again up here?
MEPHISTO.	No, stay away from her! Keep clear!
	She's just a magic phantom, an illusion. Those
	Who fall under her spell are terrified;
	Her lifeless stare will freeze your blood with fear
	And make your rigid limbs seem petrified.
	You've heard of the Medusa, I suppose?
FAUST	Indeed, her gaze is lifeless, cold and dead;.
	No loving hand has closed those eyes that cannot see.
	Yet that is the sweet body Gretchen gave to me,
	That is the breast on which I laid my head.
MEPHISTO.	You unsuspecting fool, that is her sorcery!
	For everyone she can take on a lover's shape.
FAUST	What anguish! And what ecstasy!
	This vision holds me fast, I can't escape.
	How strange! Around that lovely neck I see,
	No thicker than a blade, a single red
	And slender line drawn like a scarlet thread.
MEPHISTO.	Of course! That's nothing new to me.
	She puts her head under her arm as well;
	You fall for every magic spell!
	Perseus chopped it off for her, believe me.
	Come on, let's take a walk up there,
	You'll find as much fun here as any fair.
	And look, unless my eyes deceive me,
	They've even got a theatre set up for us.
	What's all this then?
LICKSPITTLE	We're just about to start.
	It's a new play, the seventh, and the last.

Line numbers: 4180, 4185, 4190, 4195, 4200, 4205, 4210, 4215

We have to give them seven, or they make such a fuss.
A dilettante wrote it, and the cast
Are dilettantes too – they all expect a part.
Excuse me now, I've got to raise the curtain –
I mustn't dilly-dally, that's for certain!   4220

MEPHISTO. Amateur theatricals on Walpurgis Night! Well yes –
The Brocken's where you all belong, I guess.

A WALPURGIS NIGHT'S DREAM, OR
OBERON AND TITANIA'S GOLDEN WEDDING

Intermezzo

STAGE MANAGER	We're Mieding's trusty band of men,[15]
	And we're on holiday.
	Ancient hill and misty glen –
	That's the scene today!
HERALD	Fifty summers have gone past
	Since their wedding year.
	Now their quarrel's done at last,
	Golden days are here!
OBERON	Elves and spirits all unseen
	Show yourselves and see
	Your Fairy King and Fairy Queen
	Rejoined in harmony.
PUCK	Puck has come to join the throng
	With his merry laughter.
	He dances right, he dances wrong –
	And hundreds follow after.
ARIEL	Ariel's songs will fill the air
	With pure ethereal sound;
	Monstrous shapes and creatures fair
	Gather all around.
OBERON	Couples all should take this test
	If they're brokenhearted;
	Learn from us that you'll love best
	When you have been parted.
TITANIA	A wife who never shuts her mouth,
	A husband who's a boor,
	Send him north and send her south –
	That's the only cure.
ORCHESTRA TUTTI [*fortissimo*]	
	Snout of fly and nose of gnat,
	All sorts and conditions,
	Croaking frog and squeaking bat –
	These are our musicians.

4225

4230

4235

4240

4245

4250

SOLO	Look, here comes the bagpipe now!	4255
	All blown up and groaning,	
	Making an infernal row –	
	His nose does all the droning.	
FLEDGLING SPIRIT	Paunch of toad and spiders' toes,	
	Stick some wings upon it;	4260
	It's not a creature, but who knows –	
	It might just make a sonnet.	
WEE COUPLE	Through scented honeydew we fly,	
	We hop and skip around;	
	We'd dearly love to soar on high,	4265
	But just can't leave the ground.	
INQUISITIVE TRAVELLER	Ah! A satirical revue!	
	And do my eyes deceive me?	
	Lord Oberon is up here too –	
	Whoever will believe me?	4270
ORTHODOX THEOLOGIAN	He's got no claws, no tail, but still	
	There's no doubt in my mind;	
	Just like the gods of Greece, he's still	
	A devil of some kind.	
NORTHERN ARTIST	My talents hitherto, I know,	4275
	Were scant and immature;	
	But soon it will be time to go	
	On my Italian tour.	
PURIST	This is a most distressing sight,	
	They're slovenly as pigs!	4280
	Of all the witches here tonight,	
	Just two wear powdered wigs.	
YOUNG WITCH	Your powder and your petticoat	
	Are for the old and paunchy;	
	I ride stark naked on my goat,	4285
	And show 'em something raunchy!	
MATRON	We're too experienced, too mature	
	To bandy words with you.	
	Your youthful bloom will fade for sure –	
	We hope you wither, too.	4290
CONDUCTOR	Snout of fly and nose of gnat,	
	Keep off that naked floozy!	
	Croaking frog and squeaking bat,	

Your tempo's gone all woozy!

WEATHER-VANE [*looking one way*]

You meet nice people at this do, 4295
There's pretty girls a-plenty;
There's lots of nice young men here, too –
And not one over twenty.

WEATHER-VANE [*looking the other way*]

Why can't an earthquake or hell-fire
Consume them all like Sodom? 4300
And if it won't, then I'll retire
To hell myself. God rot 'em!

SATIRES

Little insects bite and sting
With their sharpened claws;
Satan's our papa, we bring 4305
Honour to his cause.

HENNINGS

Satirists! God, what a crew,
So silly and malicious.
They claim to be good-hearted, too,
But mostly they're just vicious. 4310

MASTER OF THE MUSES

These witches, though – it seems to me
That they could have their uses;
If they were on my staff, they'd be
Less trouble than the Muses.

SOMETIME SPIRIT OF THE AGE

I'll take you on if you can write, 4315
There's talent here in masses;
You'd think the Brocken was tonight
A real German Parnassus.

INQUISITIVE TRAVELLER

Who's that man who stalks about
So rigid and austere? 4320
He snoops around – he's sniffing out
The Jesuits up here.

A CRANE

The pure and pious have the right
To fish in muddy waters;
That's why you see me here tonight 4325
Among the Devil's daughters.

A CHILD OF THE WORLD   The pious will choose any site
    To practise their affairs;
    All kinds of sects come here tonight
    To meet and say their prayers.   4330

DANCER   Like bitterns booming by the shore,
    I hear a distant drumming.
    Another choir? Oh, what a bore –
    Philosophers are coming!

DANCE-MASTER   See how they hop and skip and prance!   4335
    Each thinks he's got it right.
    The clumsy cripples try to dance –
    And don't they look a fright!

MERRY FIDDLER   They hate each others' guts, you know –
    Each one would kill his fellow;   4340
    Like Orpheus with his lyre, though,
    The bagpipes keep them mellow.

DOGMATIST   I won't be shouted down, d'you hear?
    Let carping critics doubt us;
    But devils must exist, it's clear –   4345
    We see them all about us.

IDEALIST   It's all a product of my brain,
    But still, it does amaze me;
    If this is me, then it's quite plain
    I must be going crazy.   4350

REALIST   This nonsense undermines my sense
    Of all reality;
    I can't believe the evidence
    Of what's in front of me.

SUPERNATURALIST   I'm overjoyed! I much prefer   4355
    To think all this is true.
    If there are devils, I infer
    There are good spirits, too.

SCEPTIC   They dig for gold and poke about,
    But truth is just a fiction;   4360
    It's D for devil and D for doubt –
    That sums up my conviction.

CONDUCTOR   Croaking frog and squeaking bat,
    Oh, damn these amateurs!
    Snout of fly and nose of gnat,   4365

	Just try to keep in time, Sirs!	
OPPORTUNISTS	We call ourselves the *Sans-Souci*,	
	We don't care how we're fed;	
	We can't stand on our feet, so we	
	Walk on our heads instead.	4370
THE HELPLESS	We used to fawn and mop and mow,	
	And snap up many a rare treat;	
	But now we're destitute, and so	
	We run around in bare feet.	
WILL O'WISPS	In the fetid swamps and meres	4375
	We originated;	
	Now we're dashing cavaliers,	
	Lionised and fêted.	
A SHOOTING STAR	Once I blazed across the sky,	
	Leaving trails of flame;	4380
	I fell to earth, and here I lie –	
	Who'll help me up again?	
THE HEAVIES	Stand back and give us room, or you	
	Will surely all be flattened;	
	Spirits can be clumsy, too,	4385
	Provided they're well-fattened.	
PUCK	Don't stamp about so heavily	
	Like elephants run wild!	
	Come, don't be clumsier than me,	
	Stout Puck, the sturdy child.	4390
ARIEL	Some have nature's wings, and some	
	The spirit lifts on high;	
	To the hill of roses come,	
	Follow where I fly!	
ORCHESTRA	[*pianissimo*] On drifting cloud and mist the day	4395
	Spreads its early gleam;	
	Whispering leaves and rushes sway –	
	All's vanished like a dream.	

GLOOMY DAY. A FIELD

FAUST. MEPHISTOPHELES

FAUST   In misery and despair! Pitifully wandering the country all this time, and now imprisoned! That sweet, hapless creature shut up in a dungeon like a criminal, exposed to appalling suffering! For so long, so long! And you kept this from me, you treacherous, despicable demon! Yes, stand there rolling your malevolent devil's eyes at me! Stand there and defy me with your insufferable company. In prison! In irredeemable misery! At the mercy of evil spirits and the pitiless judgement of humanity! And meanwhile you lull me with vulgar distractions, you conceal her growing misery from me and let her perish helplessly!

MEPHISTO.   She's not the first.

FAUST   You hound! You vile monster! Oh infinite Spirit! Change him, change this snake back into his dog's shape, when he would delight in trotting ahead of me in the night, rolling at the feet of harmless wayfarers and leaping onto their shoulders as they fell.[16] Turn him back into his favourite shape, so that he crawls before me on his belly in the sand, and I can crush the depraved creature under my feet! Not the first! Oh, misery! Misery such as no human soul can grasp, or understand how more than one creature has been plunged into such wretchedness, that the writhing death-agony of the first was not enough to atone for the guilt of all the others in the sight of ever-forgiving God! The suffering of this one creature sears me to the heart, and you grin calmly at the fate of thousands.

MEPHISTO.   Now we've reached our wits' end, the point where you humans lose your head. Why do you seek our company, if you can't handle it? You want to fly, but you have no head for heights. Did we force ourselves on you – or was it the other way round?

FAUST   Don't bare your ravening fangs at me! It revolts me! Great, glorious Spirit, you deigned to appear to me, you know my heart and soul, why did you fetter me to this infamous companion, who feeds on mischief and delights in destruction?

MEPHISTO.   Have you finished?

FAUST   Save her! Or woe betide you! The most atrocious curse on you through all the ages!

MEPHISTO.   I cannot undo the bonds or draw back the bolts of retribution. Save her? Who was it that dragged her to her ruin? I or you?

FAUST   [looks wildly about him]

MEPHISTO.   Are you reaching for thunderbolts? It's just as well they were not given to you miserable mortals. That is the way a tyrant seeks to relieve his fury, by crushing any innocent person who gets in his way.

FAUST   Take me to her! She must be freed!

MEPHISTO.   And what about the risks you run? Don't you realize that you're still wanted for murder in that town? Avenging spirits still haunt the grave of the man you killed, waiting for the murderer to return.

FAUST   I have to hear that from you! You monster, may the deaths and murders of the whole world come on your head! Take me to her, I say, and rescue her!

MEPHISTO.   I'll take you there, and let me tell you what I can do. I don't have power over everything in heaven and earth, you know. I will drug the gaoler, you take the keys and release her by human hand. I will keep a lookout. The magic horses will be ready, and I will get you away. That I can do.

FAUST   Away then!

NIGHT. OPEN COUNTRY

FAUST, MEPHISTOPHELES *storming past on black horses*

FAUST	What's going on around the gibbet there?	
MEPHISTO.	I don't know what they're stewing and brewing.	4400
FAUST	They're swaying about and stooping and bowing.	
MEPHISTO.	A witches' coven.	
FAUST	They're sprinkling and blessing.	
MEPHISTO.	Ride on! Ride on!	

A DUNGEON

FAUST *with a bunch of keys and a lamp,
in front of a small iron door.*

A long-forgotten shudder seizes me,   4405
I feel the very depth of human misery.
Within these dripping walls she is confined,
Her only crime a love that was too blind.
Are you reluctant to go in and free her?
Or is it that you are afraid to see her?   4410
Come! If you falter, death is close behind.
[*he grasps the lock, from within a voice is heard singing*]

> My mother, the whore, she's [17]
> Murdered me!
> My father, the villain, he's
> Eaten me!   4415
> My little sister found
> The bones that lay around.
> In a cool place she laid them down.
> I turned into a little bird that day.
> Fly away! Fly away!   4420

FAUST   [*unlocks the door*]
          She cannot know her lover's at the door

And hears the rattling chains, the rustling straw.

[*he goes in*

MARGARETA [*hiding her face in the straw*]
No! No! They're coming! Bitter death is near!

FAUST [*softly*] I've come to set you free! Hush, I am here!

MARGARETA [*throws herself at his feet*]
If you have human feelings, pity me. 4425

FAUST Hush! You will wake your gaolers. Hush, speak quietly!
[*he takes hold of the chains to unlock them*]

MARGARETA [*on her knees*] Who gave you, executioner, the right
To come so early to my cell
And fetch me in the middle of the night?
Have pity, let me live a little spell. 4430
The dawn will not be long – can you not wait?

[*she stands up*

I am so young, so young, but I
Am not, alas, too young to die.
Once I was beautiful, that was my fate;
My friend was with me, but he would not stay. 4435
My wreath is torn, my flowers blown away.
Don't lay such violent hands on me!
What have I done to you? Oh, let me be,
And spare my life, I beg you – for
I've never seen you in my life before. 4440

FAUST How can I bear this anguish any more?

MARGARETA You have the power over me, I know;
But let me feed my child before I go.
I held it in my arms all night;
They took it from me out of spite, 4445
And said I'd killed it, that was wrong
And wicked of them. Now they sing a song
About me, but it isn't true –
It's just a fairy tale that ends like that, you see.
Why do they put the blame on me? 4450

FAUST [*throws himself at her feet*]
Your love lies at your feet, imploring you
To come with him and end this misery!

MARGARETA [*kneels down with him*]
Oh, let us kneel and offer up a prayer!

The saints will guard us. Underneath the stair,
Below the threshold there,   4455
Hell seethes beneath the floor!
The Evil One is near,
His angry roar
Brings dread and fear!

FAUST   [shouts] Gretchen! Gretchen!   4460

MARGARETA [listens attentively]
That was my lover's voice! He's here!
[she jumps to her feet. The chains fall from her]
Where is he? Was he calling me?
No one can hold me now, for I am free!
To my love I'll fly,
In his arms I'll lie!   4465
'Gretchen,' he called, I heard him speaking.
Through all the devilish taunting and shrieking,
Through all the howling and clatter of hell
I heard that sweet voice I remember so well.

FAUST   I'm here!

MARGARETA   You're here! Say it once more. You're here! 4470
[she takes hold of him]
He's here! Now where is all my pain,
Where are my fetters now, my prison and my fear?
He's here! I've found my love again!
I'm free! —
I see again the little street where I   4475
First saw you passing by,
The pretty garden, and the gate
Where I and Martha used to wait.

FAUST   [urging her away] Come with me! Come!

MARGARETA   Don't go away!
I want to be with you so much, please stay!   4480
[she caresses him

FAUST   Hurry!
If you don't hurry, we shall miss
Our chance, and have a heavy price to pay.

MARGARETA What? Can you not kiss me any more?
We were not parted long, for sure;   4485
Have you forgotten how to kiss?

I feel so fearful in your arms. Why should that be?
Once, when you spoke, or when you looked at me,
I felt all heaven's rapture, heaven's bliss;
You stifled me with kisses, it was not like this.   4490
Oh, kiss me, do –
Or I'll kiss you!   [she embraces him
Oh no, your lips are cold
And dead.
Where has love fled?   4495
Oh tell me, say –
Who stole my love away?   [she turns away from him

FAUST   Dearest, take heart and follow me!
             I will save up a thousand kisses for you,
             But follow me this minute, I implore you!   4500

MARGARETA [turning towards him]
             And is it really you? How can this be?

FAUST   It is! Come with me, now!

MARGARETA   You have unlocked the chain,
             And now you want to take me in your arms again.
             How is it that you don't recoil from me?
             Do you know who it is, my friend, you have set free? 4505

FAUST   Come with me! It will soon be dawn!

MARGARETA I killed my mother in the early hours,
             I drowned my child when it was scarcely born.
             That child was ours,
             Your child, and mine. It's you! I can't believe it yet.   4510
             Give me your hand! This is no dream –
             It is your own dear hand! But what is this? It's wet!
             There's blood upon it, too.
             Oh, wash it clean!
             Dear God, what have you done?   4515
             Oh, put your sword away,
             I beg of you!

FAUST   The past is past, it's done and gone.
             Your grief will be the death of me.

MARGARETA No! You must stay,   4520
             For you must tend the graves, you see.
             I'll show you how it is to be –
             Tomorrow you must start.

The best plot shall be for my mother,
Beside her then will be my brother.   4525
Put me a little way apart,
But not too far.
My child, and no one else, shall rest
With me, just here, at my right breast.
To lie with you, my love, was such sweet bliss,   4530
There never was such happiness as this!
But now it is as if you would
Be gone from me, as if you shrink away;
I have to force myself on you and make you stay,
And yet it's you, it is your face, so kind and good.   4535

FAUST   If that is what you feel, then come with me!
MARGARETA   Out there? Oh, no!
FAUST   You will be free!
MARGARETA   Yes! If the grave is out there, then I would
               Be free. If death is waiting, then I'd gladly go   4540
               To my eternal rest – not one step further, though!
               I would come with you, Heinrich, if I could.
FAUST   You can! You must! The door is open, see!
MARGARETA   I cannot come with you; what use is it to flee?
               There is no hope out there, they lie in wait for me. 4545
               A beggar's life is such a wretched fate –
               Far more when you're pursued by guilt and hate.
               To go from door to door, from town to town –
               And in the end, I know, they'll hunt me down.
FAUST   I'll stay with you.   4550
MARGARETA   No, you cannot stay –
               Save your poor child, it's not too late,
               Quick, quick! Away!
               Up the stream and through the gate,
               Over the bridge   4555
               And into the wood,
               Left at the fence,
               There, in the pond,
               Quick! Take hold of it!
               It's struggling, you see –   4560
               It's wriggling still!
               Save it! Save it!

FAUST	Be calm! Listen to me!
	One step, and you're free! You'll be mine!
MARGARETA	If only we were past that hill!
	My mother's sitting there on a stone –
	An icy shiver runs up my spine!
	My mother's sitting there all alone,
	Her head's too heavy, it's lolling about,
	She cannot wave or nod, she can't call out.
	She slept so we could be happy, you and I;
	She slept so long, she'll never wake again.
	Those were such happy times. We were together then.
FAUST	If all my pleading fails, then I must try
	To take you up and carry you away with me.
MARGARETA	I'll not put up with force! No, let me be,
	How could you be so brutal? Let me go!
	I always did your bidding, for I loved you so.
FAUST	My love! My love! It is already light!
MARGARETA	Day! Yes, it's day! My last day – my last dawn.
	It was to be my wedding day –
	Tell no one that you were with me tonight.
	Alas, my wreath is torn
	And thrown away.
	We'll meet again, I know –
	We shan't be dancing, though.
	The people press around,
	But make no sound.
	They fill the streets and pack
	Into the market square.
	The bell tolls, and the staff breaks with a crack.[18]
	They seize me, tie me, drag me to the chair.
	The sword sweeps. Every neck can feel
	The sharpness of that biting steel.
	The world is silent as the tomb.
FAUST	I wish I never had been born!
MEPHISTO.	[appears outside]
	Come! Or you will surely meet your doom.
	Morning is here! It is the dawn!
	Stop all this useless talk and come away,
	My horses shake and stamp, they will not stay!

4565

4570

4575

4580

4585

4590

4595

4600

MARGARETA What is that rising from the ground below?
                  It's him! It's him! Tell him to go!
                  What is he doing in this holy place?
                  He wants me!
FAUST   No, you shall live!
MARGARETA   Lord, hear my cry!
                  Thy judgement be upon me. Give me Thy grace.   4605
MEPHISTO. [to Faust] Come! Come, or I'll leave you both to die.
MARGARETA Father, I am yours. Do not reject me now!
                  You angels, all you hosts of heaven, I pray,
                  Surround me and protect me now!
                  You horrify me, Heinrich, more than I can say.   4610
MEPHISTO. She is condemned!
A VOICE [from above]   Redeemed!
MEPHISTO. [to Faust]   Here, to me! Away!
                                      [he disappears with Faust
VOICE   [from within, dying away] Heinrich! Heinrich!

THE SECOND PART
OF THE TRAGEDY
in Five Acts

ACT ONE

A PLEASANT LANDSCAPE

FAUST, *lying in a flower-strewn meadow, weary,*
restless, seeking sleep.

Dusk.
Spirits, small graceful creatures, hover in a circle round him.

ARIEL *sings, accompanied by Aeolian harps* [19]

When the springtime blossom blowing
Drifts in showers on the earth,
When the bright green pastures glowing   4615
Bless all creatures with new birth,
Elves with spirit powers of healing
Haste to help now where they can,
Be he good or evil, feeling
Pity for this wretched man.   4620

Dancing in airy circles now surround him,
And weave your noble elfin spells around him;
Assuage the angry passions in his heart,
And purge from deep within the burning dart
Of self-reproach and bitter suffering.   4625
Through the four watches of the night then sing,
Fill out the hours with your healing art.
On a cool pillow rest his fevered head,
Let Lethe's dew bathe memories away;
Through rigid limbs relaxing sleep will spread   4630
And give him strength to greet the coming day.
Fulfil your highest task tonight:
Restore him to the sacred light.

CHORUS OF ELVES, *alternately solo, in pairs, and in chorus.*

When soft breezes gently hover
Round about the green-fringed glade,   4635
Veils of mist at twilight cover
All with sweetly fragrant shade.
Whisper softly, sweetly singing,
Rock his wounded heart to rest;
Close the gates of daylight, bringing   4640
Peace into this weary breast.

Now the darkness has descended,
Star is joining sacred star,
Great and small, like sparks ascended
Glister near and glint afar,   4645
In the lake reflected gleaming,
Glistening in the spangled night;
Seal of deepest peace, the beaming
Moon now floods the sky with light.

Soon the hours of night have vanished,   4650
Joy and grief are bathed away;
Feel new hope! Your pain is banished;
Trust the light of this new day.
Valleys green and hills emerging
From the peaceful shade of dawn;   4655
In the silent fields are surging
Silver waves of ripening corn.

See, the eastern sky is shining!
Every wish you can fulfil
If you throw off that confining   4660
Husk of sleep that binds you still.
Now be resolute! The milling
Feckless crowd you must not heed;
Swift in thought and deed, fulfilling
All a noble mind can need.   4665

A tremendous tumult heralds the approach of the sun.

ARIEL   Listen! Hear the hours storming!
                 Now on spirit ears the morning

Breaks with mighty tumult dawning.
Rocky portals burst asunder,
Phoebus' wheels like rolling thunder;   4670
With what clamour comes the light!
Horns are blown and trumpets sounded,
Eyes are dazzled, ears astounded:
From unheard-of sound take flight.
Hide in flowerheads, and nestle   4675
Deep beneath each sheltering petal,
Under rocks and leaves, for fear
Deafness strike you if you hear.

FAUST   The pulse of life now quickens, as before me
Ethereal light of dawn from night emerges.   4680
You, Earth, were constant through the dark hours
                                        for me;
Beneath my feet new life within you surges.
I feel such joy in your embrace, deriving
New strength that with fresh resolution urges
My spirit on to ever higher striving.   4685
Upon a stirring world the light is breaking,
A thousand voices in the woods reviving;
Along the valleys trails of mist are snaking,
But from the depths the darkness has receded.
Refreshed, the boughs and twigs below are waking   4690
In dusky hollows where they slept unheeded,
And colours brighten as the air is clearing.
With trembling dewdrops flowers and leaves
                                        are beaded:
A paradise around me is appearing.

Look, where above the giant summits glowing   4695
Announce that the most solemn hour is nearing,
And soon into these shaded valleys flowing
Eternal light will spread its blessing, bringing
New splendour to the world, fresh green bestowing
Upon the meadows to the hillsides clinging.   4700
Now downward step by step it is returning:
The sun appears! – But blinded, from its stinging
Glare I turn, my eyes with fire burning.

And so it is, when from the night that bound us
We near the goal of our most hopeful yearning;   4705
Fulfilment's gates stand open all around us,
Then from eternal heaven's remotest spaces
A mighty flood of flame bursts to confound us.
Life's torch we would have lit to guide our paces –
Engulfed by such a torrid conflagration,   4710
We burn with love, with hate in its embraces,
Feel pain and joy in fearful alternation;
Then we look back to earth, and seek its kindly
Youthful veil to bring us consolation.

Henceforth the sun shall always be behind me!   4715
With what delight I watch this torrent roaring
Along the rocky chasm; dashing blindly
From crag to crag, it plunges, headlong pouring,
And then into a thousand streams diverges,
High in the air its spray in showers soaring.   4720
But with what splendour from this storm emerges
The coloured rainbow's constant flux, now brightly
Painted, now with the misty shadows merges.
A cooling haze around it gathers lightly;
It shows us that our striving for perfection   4725
Must fail. But then we pause, and see more rightly:
Our life is in that colourful reflection.

THRONE ROOM OF THE IMPERIAL PALACE

COUNCIL OF STATE, *awaiting the Emperor.*
Trumpets.
COURTIERS *of all ranks, splendidly dressed, take their places.*
THE EMPEROR *ascends the throne, the* ASTROLOGER *at his right hand.*

EMPEROR   Greetings to all from far and wide,
          Dear loyal subjects gathered here;
          I see the wise man at my side –   4730
          Why does my jester not appear?
NOBLEMAN Hard on your heels the fat-gut fell
          And sprawled his length upon the stair.

They dragged him off and left him there,
Drunk, or dead – they couldn't tell.   4735
SECOND NOBLEMAN But in a flash – it's very queer –
We saw another fool appear,
In splendid clothes, but so bizarre –
I wouldn't trust him very far.
With halberds crossed, the guardsmen bar   4740
His way, Sire, you need have no fear.
But what impertinence! He's here!
MEPHISTOPHELES [*kneeling before the throne*]
What is accursed and yet accepted?
What is desired and yet refused?
What is constantly protected,   4745
And yet upbraided and abused?
Whom may you never bid come near?
Whose name are all men glad to hear?
Who dares approach your throne today?
And who has sent himself away?   4750
EMPEROR Enough of words! Can you not see
Your riddles are no use to me;
These gentlemen have plenty more –
It's answers that we're looking for.
My old fool went a step too far, I fear –   4755
Come, take his place and stand beside me here.

MEPHISTOPHELES *climbs the steps and stands at the Emperor's left hand.*

CROWD [*muttering*] Another fool – Oh, what a bore! –
Where is he from? – Who let him in? –
The old one's done for – that's for sure –
He was too fat – This one's too thin.   4760
EMPEROR And so, my loyal friends, I greet
You all who come from near or far.
Good fortune beckons, for we meet
Beneath a most auspicious star.
But tell me, why it is today,   4765
When we would rather be at play,
And laughing all our cares away
With masquerades and celebrations,
We plague ourselves with these deliberations?

But since you all appear to see it   4770
Otherwise, I must assent – so be it.
LORD CHANCELLOR[20] The highest virtue, like a halo, shines
About the Emperor's head; and only he
May exercise it lawfully.
Justice! – What all humanity enshrines   4775
Within its heart, what all desire, demand,
Is yours alone to grant, yours to command.
But all our wisdom cannot help us when
Good will is banished from the heart of men,
When a wild fever rages out of hand   4780
And daily spreads new ills throughout the land.
Whoever looks down from this height will seem
To see the realm as in an ugly dream,
Where monstrous shapes and apparitions teem.
The very laws the lawless mob protect,   4785
And error spreads across the world unchecked.

Cattle are taken, sisters, wives,
Churches are stripped of priceless treasure;
The thieves go free, and spend their lives
Enjoying the fruits of crime at leisure.   4790
Plaintiffs throng the courts with pleas,
The judges sit in pampered ease,
And meanwhile in a swelling flood
Sedition seethes and bays for blood.
For those who flaunt their evil deeds,   4795
Accomplices will twist the law;
But any innocent who pleads
For justice is condemned for sure.
And so the country falls to pieces,
And decency is put to flight;   4800
Where shall we find, when justice ceases,
A sense of what is good and right?
An honest man will turn in time
To those who flatter, bribe, degrade;
A judge who cannot punish crime   4805
Will join the villain in his trade.
It is a sombre scene; I would
Veil it more darkly if I could.   [*pause*]

Sire, bold decisions must be taken;
The royal throne itself is shaken 4810
In such anarchic times as these.

COMMANDER OF THE IMPERIAL ARMY

A furious rage has seized the land,
The bloodshed has got out of hand.
The soldiers do just as they please,
The townsfolk bar the city gate; 4815
Behind his castle wall the knight
Conspires with them to sit and wait
And keeps his forces out of sight.
Our mercenary troops are growing
More impatient by the day, 4820
And if their wages were not owing,
Then every man would melt away.
Deny them what they want, and we
Would stir a hornets' nest; you'd see
The realm we pay them to defend 4825
Reduced to ashes in the end.
We let them rage and pillage here
Till half the world is overrun;
There are still kings out there, but none
Can see why he should interfere. 4830

LORD TREASURER Who wants such allies anyway?
The subsidies they pledged to pay
Have dried up like a well in drought.
What's more, possession of your lands
Has fallen into others' hands. 4835
New owners buy the country out;
They live like independent knights,
And answer to themselves alone,
While we have given up so many rights
We have no right to call the land our own. 4840
You cannot trust the parties nowadays,
They are indifferent to our fate;
Whether they voice their blame or praise,
They show us neither love nor hate.
Even the Ghibelline and the Guelph[21] 4845
Have tired of their perpetual war;

Who helps his neighbour any more?
Each one cares only for himself.
The wealthy keep their riches stored,
They scrape and save and guard their hoard –   4850
Our source of revenue runs dry.

IMPERIAL STEWARD I too have troubles by the score!
We ought to save, but though we try,
Each day we're spending more and more,
And every day I get no peace.   4855
The cooks are well provided for;
Hares and venison, wild boar,
Turkeys and chickens, ducks and geese –
These things are always paid in kind,
They still come in – but then we find   4860
Our stocks of wine have finally run dry.
The cellars used to be piled high
With barrels of the best that we could buy;
But when they drink, they never seem to stop –
The noble lords have swallowed every drop.   4865
The City Council raid their cellars, too;
They fill their glasses, bar the door,
And drink until they hit the floor –
And I'm supposed to pay the wages.
I'm at the mercy of the Jew;   4870
He gives advances, but it will take ages
To pay back everything he's due.
The pigs are killed before they're fat,
We've pawned the pillows on the bed,
And all we have to eat is borrowed bread.   4875

EMPEROR [*after some thought, to Mephistopheles*]
Well, Fool – can you add any more to that?

MEPHISTO. Indeed not, Sire! This radiance, this light
Surrounding you and yours – how can trust fail
Where might and sovereign majesty prevail,
Prepared to put your enemies to flight,   4880
Where wisdom and good will go hand in hand,
And thousands toil for you throughout the land?
How could misfortune visit such a realm,
Or darkness such effulgence overwhelm?

CROWD [*muttering*] That one's a rogue – I know his style –   4885
              He'll lie his way in – for a while –
              A box of tricks – and then what next?
              Some scheme or other, I expect.

MEPHISTO. There's always something that we lack; it's clear
           It's only money that is lacking here.   4890
           Of course, you can't just pick it off the floor;
           But those endowed with wisdom's secret lore
           Will know, beneath old walls or underground,
           Where coins and seams of gold are to be found.
           Who has this gift? – The man who has combined   4895
           The power of nature with the human mind.

CHANCELLOR Nature – and mind? What godless words are these?
           We have burned atheists for such heresies.
           Nature is sinful, and the mind
           By Satan's promptings is defiled.   4900
           The issue of the two combined
           Is doubt, their misbegotten child.
           No more of that! For two estates alone
           Have governed in this ancient land
           And guarded the imperial throne: 4905
           The clergy and the knights withstand
           The raging storms with one accord,
           And Church and State are their reward.
           But muddled wits sow disaffection,
           Incite the common herd to insurrection,   4910
           And sorcerers and heretics conspire
           To ravage every town and every shire.
           Such creatures now you seek to smuggle in
           To these high circles with your brazen arts,
           To work your mischief in corrupted hearts,   4915
           For they and fools are next of kin.

MEPHISTO. Ah, now the learned man begins to preach!
           What you can't touch is quite beyond your reach,
           What you can't grasp does not exist for you,
           What you can't calculate cannot be true,   4920
           What you can't weigh cannot have any weight,
           A coin you have not minted must be counterfeit.

EMPEROR All this does nothing to relieve our plight;

How can your sermons help to put things right?
I'm tired of all this endless if and when;   4925
We're short of money – well, provide it, then!

MEPHISTO.   I'll get you all you want, more if you will;
But even simple things require some skill.
The stuff is there; the only snag is – who
Can find it and recover it for you?   4930
Think of those days when armies like a flood
Swept in and drowned the people in their blood,
When some were driven in their panic fear
To hide the treasures that they held most dear.
Since Roman times that always was the way;   4935
It has continued to the present day.
It's down there somewhere, buried out of sight;
The ground is yours, Sire – it belongs to you.

TREASURER   This is no fool, for what he says is true;
That is indeed the Emperor's ancient right.   4940

CHANCELLOR   This is impiety, a golden snare
To trap you; it is Satan's work, beware!

STEWARD   If he can help the court, I've no objection
If things don't quite stand up to close inspection.

COMMANDER   This fool is smart, he can please everyone;   4945
The soldier's not too worried how it's done.

MEPHISTO.   Perhaps you think I'm just out to deceive?
The Astrologer's a man you can believe.
He reads the stars, knows what the heavens say –
So tell us how it looks up there today.   4950

CROWD [*muttering*]   Next to the throne – two rogues together –
The fool and the dreamer – birds of a feather –
A weary tune – I know their ways –
The fool beats time – the wizard plays.

THE ASTROLOGER *speaks;* MEPHISTOPHELES *prompts him.*[22]

The sun is purest gold; swift Mercury,   4955
Our favoured messenger, deserves his fee.
Who would not welcome Venus's embrace?
At dawn and dusk she shows her lovely face.
Chaste Luna's moods are fickle as her light;
Mars may not strike, but threatens with his might,   4960
And Jupiter shines fairer than them all.

                    Saturn is large, but to the eye seems small;
                    His value as a metal is not great,
                    Of little worth, for all its massive weight.
                    If only Sol and Luna are combined,   4965
                    With silver gold, then joy is unconfined.
                    Once we have that, we can enjoy the rest:
                    A palace, park, red cheeks, a maiden's breast.
                    Who can provide all this? The learned man
                    Who will accomplish what no other can.   4970

EMPEROR   Although each word was spoken twice,
                    I'm not convinced it's very sound advice.

CROWD [*muttering*] What was all that? – it's just old hat –
                    Astrology – and alchemy –
                    These horoscopes – just raise your hopes –   4975
                    Who will it be? – Some clown, you'll see.

MEPHISTO.   For them such things are too profound;
                    Look how they stand and gawp around,
                    Drivelling about some magic spell –
                    The mandrake or the hound from hell.   4980
                    They call it sorcery, deceit;
                    Just wait, their wit won't help them when
                    Their soles begin to itch, and then
                    They feel unsteady on their feet.

                    For timeless nature can reveal   4985
                    Her secrets deep beneath the ground;
                    She gives you all the power to feel
                    Where living traces can be found.
                    If all your limbs are full of twitches,
                    Or if your flesh begins to creep –   4990
                    There you can dig for hidden riches,
                    That's where the treasure's hidden deep.

CROWD [*muttering*] My feet feel like two lumps of lead –
                    And I've got cramp – My arm's gone dead –
                    Gout in my toe – I've got a stitch –   4995
                    My back just gave a nasty twitch.
                    These symptoms surely make it clear
                    There's tons of treasure buried here!

EMPEROR   Show us these precious places, then, go to it,
                    And make your fantasies come true;   5000

You won't leave here until you do it.
I'll lay down sword, and sceptre too;
These royal hands will see the project through
If there is any truth in what you say –
If not, these hands will send you down to hell.   5005

MEPHISTOPHELES [*aside*]
I wouldn't need your help to find the way –
But Sire, there is far more to tell
About the unowned wealth still to be found.
The humble peasant ploughing on his land
Unearths a golden goblet from the ground,   5010
Or goes to scratch saltpetre from a wall,
And finds with wonder and delight a haul
Of golden metal in his pauper's hand.
What vaults the treasure-seeker has to blast,
What clefts and passages to struggle through,   5015
Until his knowing instinct leads him to
The threshold of the underworld at last!
In vast and ancient cellars deep below
Are tankards, bowls and plates of purest gold;
He will find chalices that glow   5020
With rubies, row on gleaming row.
And should he wish to use them, close nearby
Are noble vintages so old,
That – take my word for it, this is no lie –
The wooden casks have crumbled into dust;   5025
The wine has been preserved in its own crust.
These things cannot be openly displayed;
Such jewels, such rare essences must be
Concealed in darkness, dread and secrecy.
The wise man seeks them undismayed,   5030
For any fool can see what's in the light –
But mysteries are better veiled in night.

EMPEROR   The dark is not for us; go to it, then,
For buried wealth must see the light of day.
At night all cows are black, all cats are grey,   5035
And who can tell the rogues from honest men?
Sniff out those weighty pots of gold down there,
Then plough them up and let them see the air.

MEPHISTO.	Take pick and spade yourself, and show
	Your greatness in such humble toil;	5040
	A herd of golden calves will grow
	Before your eyes out of the soil.
	Do not delay; and then with what delight
	You can adorn yourself, your lady too –
	For majesty and beauty shine anew	5045
	When dazzling gemstones bathe them both in light.
EMPEROR	At once! At once! We have no time to waste!
ASTROLOGER [as above]	Sire, moderate this too impulsive haste
	Till carnival is past; we must prepare
	With self-restraint, with discipline and care,	5050
	Propitiate the powers above, and show
	That we are worthy of what is below.
	If we seek what is good, let us be good;
	If we seek pleasure, let us calm our blood;
	If we seek wine, ripe grapes we have to tread;	5055
	If miracles, by greater faith be led.[23]
EMPEROR	Then let our time for now be spent in pleasure!
	Ash Wednesday soon will bring us welcome leisure.
	Till then our madcap carnival shall be
	Enjoyed more wildly and more merrily.	5060

[trumpets; exeunt

MEPHISTO.	Merit and fortune travel hand in hand –
	That's what these fools will never understand.
	Give them the stone of wisdom, they'd abuse it –
	They'd never find a wise man who could use it.

SPACIOUS HALL

with side rooms, decorated for the carnival masquerade

HERALD	Do not imagine these are German revels,	5065
	Dances of death, of fools and devils;
	We have a pleasant carnival in store.
	Your Lord, in his Italian campaign,
	The lofty Alps has traversed to secure
	His subjects' pleasure and his kingdom's gain,	5070
	And won for us a realm of grace and light.

There at the Holy Father's feet he sought
Assent to rule this land by right;
And when he claimed the crown, he brought
The motley and the mask for our delight.   5075
In this renascence we are all reborn;
The most sophisticated man has worn
The fool's cap gladly for a day;
Beneath the mask he may indeed be wise,
But he must play the fool in this disguise.   5080
I see the throng of revellers emerging,
In ones and twos they tease and flirt and sway,
Dance in and out, a boisterous parade
Of dashing groups and choruses converging.
The world has always been the same –   5085
An endless farce, an antic game,
A universal masquerade!

FLOWER-GIRLS [*singing to mandolins*]

Dressed to please you, young and pretty,
For your pleasure and delight,
Girls from Florence's fair city   5090
Grace the German court tonight.

Brightly coloured flowers twining
In our flowing chestnut hair;
Silken bows and ribbons shining
In the costumes that we wear.   5095

And we feel it is our duty
To take credit where it's due,
For our silken flowers' beauty
Will not fade the whole year through.

Bits and bobs and coloured pieces,   5100
Frills and flounces made to tease;
You may laugh at our caprices –
But the whole effect will please.

Pretty flower-girls so charming
Capture every youthful heart;   5105
Woman's nature, so disarming,
Is not far removed from art.

HERALD   Let us see the fancy treasure
                In the baskets on your arms,
                So that all can share the pleasure   5110
                Of your artificial charms.
                Decorate the paths and bowers,
                Blooms and sprays in every nook;
                Flower-sellers and their flowers –
                Both are worth a closer look.   5115

FLOWER-GIRLS   Come and see what we can sell you,
                But no haggling, please, today!
                Just a few short words will tell you
                What you'll get for what you pay.

FRUITING OLIVE BRANCH I don't envy flowers their beauty,   5120
                For by nature it's my duty
                To avoid all confrontation.
                I am the life-blood of the land,
                An emblem all can understand,
                A pledge of peace to every nation;   5125
                And I am hopeful that I may
                Adorn a worthy head today.

WREATH OF GOLDEN CORN Ceres' gifts sustain and nourish,
                But they can adorn us too;
                May your grace and beauty flourish   5130
                When this wreath is worn by you.

GARLAND OF FLOWERS Coloured blooms like mallows breaking
                From the moss, a gorgeous show!
                These are not of nature's making –
                Fashion can devise them, though.   5135

BOUQUET OF FLOWERS Theophrastus wouldn't know
                What to call me; even so,
                From you all I hope to see
                Someone who will fancy me,
                Someone who would like to wear   5140
                Pretty flowers in her hair –
                Or, if she were willing, pressed
                Gently, closely to her breast.

ROSEBUDS [*challenging them*] Let these colourful creations
        Set the fashion for today;   5145
        Braid them in your hair, display
        These exotic decorations,
        Golden bells and stems of green,
        Such as nature's never seen! –
        But we hide ourselves from view.   5150
        If you find us freshly growing
        When the summer is still new,
        Blushing rosebuds softly glowing –
        Who would sacrifice such bliss?
        Promise and surrender – this   5155
        Is Flora's realm, she holds us all,
        Eyes and hearts and minds in thrall.

Under leafy arcades the flower-girls daintily set out their wares.

GARDENERS [*singing to theorbos*] Charmingly your flowers grow,
        But your floral wiles are wasted;
        Our fruits are not for show –   5160
        These are pleasures to be tasted.

        Peaches, plums and cherries – buy
        What we sun-tanned lads can sell you,
        For your lips and tongues can tell you
        There's far more than meets the eye.   5165

        Taste the sweet and juicy flavour
        As you eat them; you can write
        Poems to roses – but to savour
        Apples, you must take a bite!

        Let's be neighbours for today,   5170
        And together we'll display
        Our ripest wares with your
        Youthful blooms so fresh and pure.

        In secluded shady bowers
        Bright with garlands all around,   5175
        There at once all can be found:
        Buds and leaves, and fruit and flowers.

Singing in turns, and accompanied by guitars and theorbos,
both groups continue to pile their wares high in
decorative rows and offer them for sale.

MOTHER AND DAUGHTER

MOTHER

My girl, when you first saw the light
I dressed you up with pride;
Such dainty limbs, a face so bright,   5180
And smiling eyes so wide.
I saw you as a woman then,
Admired by all the richest men –
I saw you as a bride.

But now so many years have passed,   5185
And uselessly were spent;
The throng of suitors didn't last,
And soon away they went.
You danced with one, and all the while
You teased another with a smile,   5190
And flirted quite content.

At parties you could take your pick,
But every time you'd fail –
Charades and forfeits, every trick
We tried – to no avail.   5195
Today the fools are on the spree –
Uncross your legs, my dear, and see
If one of them will stick.

The daughter's companions, young and pretty,
join them, gossiping among themselves.

Fishermen and birdcatchers appear with nets, rods, limed sticks and
other equipment, and mingle with the pretty girls. They try to attract
them, trap them and capture them; the girls try to escape, while
pleasant exchanges take place.

Enter WOODCUTTERS, *boisterous and uncouth*

Stand back there, please!
Make room there, hey!   5200
We cut down trees
With a crash and a bump;

If you're in the way,
You'll get a thump.
We may be rough,   5205
But give us our due:
If we didn't do
The heavy stuff,
You couldn't afford
To live like a lord.   5210
So don't forget
That you'd all freeze
If we didn't sweat
To fell the trees.

PULCINELLE [*clumsy and clownish*]

Fools, you were born   5215
Bent and worn.
We haven't ever
Worked, we're too clever.
Caps and bells
Are easy to wear;   5220
We dress like swells
With never a care.
Living at leisure,
Bent on pleasure,
Along the street   5225
On slippered feet
We dance about,
Or stand and shout
And screech out loud,
Then through the crowd   5230
We slip like eels,
Take to our heels,
Causing a rumpus,
Making a fuss –
Like us or lump us,   5235
It doesn't worry us!

SPONGERS [*fawning and leering*]

You sturdy loggers
And worthy sloggers,

Without your timber,
Charcoal and tinder   5240
All our prating,
Equivocating,
Fawning and chattering,
Two-faced flattering,
Coaxing and wheedling,   5245
Scheming and needling
Would all be in vain.
If fire should rain
From heaven on high,
It would do no good   5250
Without your supply
Of charcoal and wood
To keep the pot
And oven hot
For seething and boiling   5255
And roasting and broiling.
A proper glutton
Is always able
To smell the mutton
And sniff the fish   5260
On every dish
At his patron's table.

DRUNKARD [*fuddled*] Everything's all right today!
Not a worry, bright and breezy,
Make your own fun, that's the way,   5265
Laughing, singing, free and easy.
So I'm going to go on drinking,
Drink, and set the glasses clinking!
You there, come on, let's go to it –
Drink up, that's the way to do it.   5270

My poor wife was really staggered
When she saw my fancy breeks;
Didn't like it when I swaggered –
Dummy in a mask! she shrieks.
Still, I'm going to go on drinking,   5275
Cheers, let's hear the glasses clinking!

All you dummies, let's drink to it –
Bottoms up! That's how to do it.

Don't tell me I've lost my senses –
I'm all right, I feel just great;   5280
If I can't pay my expenses,
They can chalk it on the slate.
I shall always go on drinking,
All together, glasses clinking!
Drink to each and every one –   5285
Down the hatch, and then we're done.

I don't care what happens when I
Really go out on a spree;
Leave me where I'm lying when my
Legs give way, and let me be.   5290

CHORUS   Brothers, let's all go on drinking,
Quick, a toast, with glasses clinking!
Hold tight to the bench, or you
Will slide under the table too.

*The Herald announces various poets: pastoral poets, poets of chivalry
and romance, sentimental poets, and bardic poets. In the crush of
competing candidates, none will let the others have their say.
One slinks past, muttering a few words.*

SATIRICAL POET   It would give me great delight   5295
And crown my poetic career,
If only I could write
What no one would wish to hear.

*The night and graveyard poets make their excuses, because they are
engaged in an interesting conversation with a freshly resurrected vampire,
from which a new genre of poetry might develop. The Herald lets them
have their way, and meanwhile summons the figures of Greek mythology
who, even in a modern guise, retain their character and charm.*

THE GRACES

AGLAIA   Grace we bring to all your living;
Be as gracious in your giving.   5300
HEGEMONE   When sweet wishes are achieved,
Be they graciously received.

| EUPHROSYNE | And in days of quietude, |
| | Show with grace your gratitude. |

THE FATES

ATROPOS	I, the oldest, for today	5305
	Hold the spindle in my hand;
	There are many thoughts to weigh
	As I spin life's fragile strand.

From the choicest fibres winding
Threads so supple, soft and fine,   5310
Skilful fingers twisting, binding,
Tease a smooth and even line.

If today your merrymaking
Should get out of hand, beware!
For that thread is close to breaking –   5315
You are lost if it should tear.

CLOTHO	Recently the shears of fate
	From the oldest I've acquired,
	For her practices of late
	Left a lot to be desired.	5320

Worthless lives would be extended
When she gave them light and breath;
Early hope and promise ended,
When she cut the thread, in death.

Even I in younger years   5325
Didn't always do things right;
So today I keep the shears
In their case well out of sight.

Gladly I restrict my powers,
For I wish your revels well.   5330
Celebrate these hectic hours
Free from fate's oppressive spell.

LACHESIS	Of the three the most discerning,
	I collect the flowing strand
	On my bobbin, ever turning,
	With a sure and steady hand.	5335

Every thread is caught and wound,
Each is guided on its way
As the reel is driven round –
And not one may go astray.   5340

If my winding ever faltered,
Then all life would be in vain;
Hours and years cannot be altered,
And the weaver takes the skein.

HERALD   Those who come next you will not recognise,   5345
However many ancient texts you know.
They bring us so much ill – but even so,
You'd bid them welcome in their present guise.

They are the Furies – who would believe it, though?
They're pretty, shapely, friendly, and so young;   5350
But get involved with them, and you'll soon know
These cooing doves speak with a serpent's tongue.

They are malicious, but today they feel,
When fools proclaim their failings far and wide,
They should not pose as angels, but reveal   5355
Themselves as plagues on town and countryside.

THE FURIES

ALECTO   That will not help, you'll trust us all the same,
For we are pretty kittens, sweet and fickle;
If someone has a sweetheart, then we'll tickle
Him behind the ears until he's tame –   5360

And then it's time to tell him, face to face,
That she's been playing him a double game;
That she's deformed and stupid, bent and lame,
Not fit to be his bride in any case.

We go to his fiancée, too, and say: 5365
He told a certain girl the other day
He couldn't stand the sight of you – and though
They make it up, some mud will stick, we know.

MEGAERA   That is child's play! For once they've tied the knot,
I come along and really start the rot.   5370

I can turn any happy marriage sour
With whims that change with every passing hour.

No sooner has he won his heart's desire,
But he must hanker after something new;
He leaves behind the happiness he knew   5375
To melt fresh ice with some of his old fire.

With subtle guile I manage these affairs.
My trusty demon Asmodeus knows
Just what to do; the mischief that he sows
Helps me destroy the human race in pairs.   5380

TISIPHONE   Not just gossip – I prepare
               Sword and poison for the traitor.
               If you're fickle, now or later,
               Retribution waits – beware!

               Even sweetest things will pall,   5385
               Turn to venom and to gall;
               Pleas or protests no one heeds –
               He must answer for his deeds!

               Here forgiveness has no place;
               To the rocks I plead my case.   5390
               Vengeance! echoes the reply –
               He was faithless, he must die.

HERALD   Stand back now, please! For what approaches you
          Is something unfamiliar and new.
          You see a mountain plodding through the throng, 5395
          Its flanks with gorgeous tapestries are hung:
          A snaking trunk, long tusks of ivory –
          A mystery to which I hold the key.
          Upon its neck a dainty woman rides,
          And with a slender rod its footsteps guides;   5400
          Enthroned in splendour on that lofty height,
          Another proudly stands in dazzling light.
          Two noble women at each side appear
          In fetters, one serene, one full of fear.
          The one feels free, one longs for liberty;   5405
          Let each one say who she may be.

FEAR
Reeking lamps and torches light
This confused and festive night,
All around false faces leer;
Bound in fetters, I am Fear.   5410

Foolish grinning masks, they fill me
With suspicion, dread and fright;
Those who seek to harm or kill me
Come to harry me tonight.

Here's a friend who came to hate me –   5415
Yes, his mask gives him away.
That man planned my murder lately;
Now I've seen him, he'll not stay.

On all sides the wide world beckons,
Gladly I would take my flight;   5420
But out there destruction threatens,
Keeps me here in dread and night.

HOPE
Greetings, dearest sisters, who
For two days now have paraded
In disguise and masqueraded;   5425
I know well, tomorrow you
Will all reveal yourselves again.
Though we may not feel at ease
In the torches' flickering light,
Sunlit days are coming, when   5430
We shall wander as we please,
Singly or together stray
Through the woods and meadows bright,
Free to work or rest or play,
All our cares behind us leaving,   5435
All our hearts' desires achieving;
And wherever we may go,
Each will be a welcome guest.
Somewhere, sisters, this I know –
All will turn out for the best.   5440

PRUDENCE
Chained, I bring you Hope and Fear,
Human scourges, held at bay.

These two cannot harm you here;
You are safe from them, make way!

This colossal beast I guide,   5445
On its back a castle sways,
Unperturbed, with placid stride
Pacing out the steepest ways.

There with outspread wings on high
Stands the goddess over all,   5450
Ever ready, swift to fly
When she hears the clarion call.

Glorious, radiant deity!
All around her splendour rises,
For her name is Victory,   5455
Goddess of all enterprises.

ZOILO–THERSITES[24]   Huh! So I've come in just on cue;
You're worthless, every one of you;
But she's the one I love to hate –
Dame Victory, who sits in state   5460
With those white wings of hers, so regal,
She's perched up there just like an eagle,
And thinks wherever she turns her face
She's queen of all the human race.
But when I hear hurrahs or cheering,   5465
Then it's my job to do the jeering:
Exalt the low, put down the great,
Make straight the crooked, twist the straight.
That's all just food and drink to me –
That's how I want the world to be.   5470
HERALD   I'll punish your impiety –
You'll feel my sacred staff, you hound!
Yes, now you'll squirm and writhe around!
The dwarfish hybrid starts to change
Into a loathsome lump – how strange!   5475
The lump becomes an egg, and then
The egg begins to swell again.
It cracks in two, and from the shell
Emerge two creatures, twins from hell:

An adder, on its belly sliding,   5480
A bat, around the rafters gliding.
They'll meet outside; I wouldn't care
To join the two of them out there.

VOICES FROM THE CROWD

They're dancing over there, come on! –
No, no, I think we'd best be gone –   5485
Can't you feel a ghostly spell,
Those creepy creatures everywhere? –
Something brushed against my hair –
I felt it on my foot as well –
None of us is hurt, I know –   5490
We're all afraid of something, though –
They've simply ruined all the fun –
That's what those ghastly beasts have done.

HERALD   Since as Herald I was made
Master of the Masquerade,   5495
I have stood on guard today
At the door, unflinching, calm,
So that no one comes to harm
At our revels, come what may.
Through the windows, though, I fear   5500
Airy phantoms now appear;
I confess I cannot say
How to keep these ghosts at bay.
First that horrid dwarf got past –
Now they're coming thick and fast.   5505
I'm supposed to introduce
These apparitions; what's the use,
When I've not the least idea
What is happening in here?
Help me, please, to understand!   5510
What's this floating through the throng?
It's a chariot, drawn along
By a spanking four-in-hand;
Through the crowd it seems to glide,
No one needs to move aside;   5515
Lights that glitter far and wide,
Floating stars and coloured flashes,

Like a magic lantern show –
Snorting, storming, on it dashes.
Stand back! It's uncanny!

BOY CHARIOTEER   Whoa!   5520
Dragons, hold your flight and stand!
Obey your master's guiding hand.
Curb your mettle, as I teach you,
Storm away when I unleash you –
To these halls show our respect!   5525
See, the eager crowds collect
In admiring circles round.
Herald! You are duty bound
To decipher what is meant
By our allegories – so   5530
Reveal our names before we go,
Saying what we represent.

HERALD   What your name is, I don't know;
I think I could describe you, though.

BOY CHARIOTEER   Go on, then.

HERALD   Well, to look at you,   5535
You're young, and you're good-looking, too;
You're still a boy, but when you've grown some more,
The women will be glad to look you over.
You're going to be a ladies' man, I'm sure –
In fact, a proper little Casanova.   5540

BOY CHARIOTEER   That's what I like to hear! Now try
To solve the riddle: who am I?

HERALD   Dark flashing eyes, and curls as black as night,
A jewelled headband glittering in the light;
In graceful folds your garments flow   5545
All edged with purple, head to toe.
With all your sparkling finery,
You have a girlish look – but still,
I'm sure you could give quite a thrill
To any girl who has a will   5550
To help you learn the ABC.

BOY CHARIOTEER   And who is this who sits in state
Upon this chariot of mine?

HERALD   A monarch, wealthy and benign,

Who wants for nothing; fortunate   5555
Are those he favours with his grace;
Where there is need, he turns his face,
And giving of his copious treasure
His greatest joy, his purest pleasure.

BOY CHARIOTEER Do not neglect your herald's task;   5560
A full account is what we ask.

HERALD   Such dignity's beyond all praise;
His moon-like face that shines with health,
His rounded lips, his cheeks that glow
Beneath the jewelled turban's show,   5565
His noble bearing, sovereign gaze,
His sumptuous garments – all proclaim
A king, a man of power and wealth.

BOY CHARIOTEER Plutus, the god of wealth, his name!
He comes in all his pomp to heed   5570
The Emperor's call in time of need.

HERALD   And you yourself, who might you be?

BOY CHARIOTEER I am Extravagance, I am Poetry.
I am the poet who fulfils himself
By giving freely of his inner wealth.   5575
Like Plutus, I am rich beyond compare,
I am his equal, and I am his pride;
To grace his feasts and pageants I am there –
Whatever he may lack I can provide.

HERALD   Such boasting suits you well, I have to say; 5580
But can you demonstrate your arts today?

BOY CHARIOTEER I simply snap my fingers, and the air
Is full of sparks and flashes everywhere.
Look, over there a string of pearls appears!
[he continues to snap his fingers]
A golden necklace, rubies for your ears,   5585
And here are combs and coronets, all set
With flawless jewels, rings more precious yet!
I can make flames as well, if you require;
You never know where you can start a fire.

HERALD   See how they snatch and grab and rush –   5590
They'll overwhelm him in the crush!
He scatters jewels everywhere,

And they all grasp the empty air.
But he has other tricks to play:
However greedily they snatch,   5595
They only find their precious catch
Has sprouted wings and flown away.
One finds his pearls have melted, and
Feels beetles wriggling in his hand;
The poor fool shakes them off – instead   5600
They come back, buzzing round his head.
The other tries to grab a prize,
And only grasps at butterflies.
For all the tales this rascal told,
He offers trash instead of gold!   5605

BOY CHARIOTEER You can announce us, but it's not your task
As Herald to this court to try
To see the truth concealed beneath the mask,
For that requires a more perceptive eye.
Let us not quarrel, though; if you would learn   5610
The truth, then to my master we must turn.
[he turns to Plutus]
Did you not entrust to me, to ride
The storm, this four-spanned chariot I guide?
Do I not go where you might lead me?
Am I not there when you might need me?   5615
On fearless wings have I not sought
The victor's palm for your renown?
For you how many battles have I fought,
How often have I won the day?
And when your head was garlanded with bay,   5620
It was my hand, my art, that wove the crown.

PLUTUS   Gladly I will pay this tribute to you,
For you are spirit of my spirit; do you
Not always act according to my will?
You are as rich as I am, richer still.   5625
You work to shape the laurel wreath I prize
Far more than all the royal crowns I've won,
And I affirm this truth before all eyes:
I am well pleased in you, beloved son.

BOY CHARIOTEER [to the crowd] Now I have scattered everywhere   5630

The greatest gifts I can bestow –
And see! Some heads already glow
With flames I kindled in the air.
They skip from head to head, on some they stay
A while, from others quickly slip away;   5635
But only rarely does the flame leap higher
And burst into a shining tongue of fire.
For most, too soon, before they realise,
It flickers dismally, burns out, and dies.

WOMEN [*chattering*] That one who holds the reins, I swear,   5640
    Is just a charlatan, a fake;
    And crouching right behind him there
    That skinny clown, thin as a rake,
    A bag of bones – give him a pinch,
    I don't suppose he'd even flinch.   5645

MEPHISTOPHELES [*emaciated, as* AVARICE]
    You ghastly brood of females, let me be!
    I know you've always hated me.
    When women kept house for their men,
    I was called Avarice – and then
    The home was peaceful and content,   5650
    For much was saved, and little spent.
    My purse was full, all was provided;
    Such thrift would even be derided
    And thought a vice – but nowadays
    The womenfolk have changed their ways.   5655
    They'd rather borrow now than save,
    Or do without the things they crave –
    So everywhere the husband goes,
    He finds another debt he owes;
    And anything she earns, she'll spend   5660
    It on herself, or on her friend.
    She eats far better, drinks far more,
    And has admirers by the score.
    I worship gold, on gold I feed;
    Now I'm a male – my name is Greed!   5665

LEADER OF THE WOMEN
    You miser, get back to your dragon's den!
    This is all lies and empty bluff!

He's only winding up the men –
And they're already bad enough.

CROWD OF WOMEN   The scarecrow! Just give him a clout!   5670
What does that skeleton think he's about,
Trying to give us all a scare?
Those dragons are made of wood and board –
Come on, let's go for him, the fraud!

HERALD   Now, by my staff! Just calm down there!   5675
But I don't need to help at all:
Each fearsome beast unfolds a pair
Of scaly wings to clear the way.
Enraged, the dragons snarl and spray
A stream of fire throughout the hall   5680
That threatens to engulf the place;
The crowd flees, and we have some space.
[*Plutus dismounts*]
Now he steps down, how like a king!
He gives a sign, at his behest
The dragons from the chariot bring   5685
The miser and the golden chest.
Now at his feet the treasure lies:
A miracle, performed before our eyes.

PLUTUS [*to the Charioteer*]
Now from this tiresome burden you are free;
Away to your own element, and flee   5690
This wild and tangled circle of confusion,
Of motley figures and bizarre illusion,
To where clear eyes can see a clearer light,
The good, the beautiful is your delight,
Where to yourself alone you can be true –   5695
In solitude create your world anew!

BOY CHARIOTEER   To be your worthy envoy is my pride,
I love you as my nearest; you provide
Abundance all around, while I bestow
My precious gifts wherever I may go.   5700
And some in life's confusion think it best
To choose your way, while others come with me.
Your servants live in ease and luxury;
But those who follow me can never rest.

I do not work in secret or by stealth –   5705
I only breathe, and I reveal myself.
You grant the happiness for which I yearn;
Farewell! But whisper, and I will return.

                                    [he leaves as he came

PLUTUS   Now it is time to set these treasures free.
The Herald's staff will break the locks – and see!   5710
They spring apart, in brazen vessels glows
A swirling mass that seethes like golden blood;
Among the crowns and chains and rings it flows
As though to drown them in a molten flood.

SHOUTS FROM THE CROWD

See how the liquid gold is growing,   5715
It fills the chest to overflowing. –
Golden cups are melting down,
Minted coins are tumbling round. –
Ducats dancing, gleaming bright,
It makes my heart leap at the sight. –   5720
You simply couldn't ask for more,
Look how they roll across the floor!
We'll all be rich, it's lying there,
Just pick it up and take your share. –
We'll let you grovel for the rest,   5725
Quick as a flash, we'll take the chest.

HERALD   What's this? You fools are all the same;
It's just a masquerade, a game.
Tonight you've everything you need,
This gold's not real, control your greed;   5730
Counters made of tin or wood
For dolts like you are much too good.
This make-believe, this fantasy
You treat as crude reality.
What's truth to you? In your confusion   5735
You've fallen into blind delusion.
Oh Plutus, master of our revels,
Please rid us of these silly devils.

PLUTUS   Your staff is just the thing for me;
I'll take it for a while – now see!   5740
I dip it in the fiery brew –

You masks, take care now, all of you!
The staff is glowing in the fire,
The sparks are spitting, spraying higher,
And anyone who comes too near   5745
Will feel its searing heat – stand clear!
I'll draw a circle round about.

CROWD [*shouting and struggling*]
　　　　We're done for! Help! Quick, let us out! –
　　　　Run, if you can! Come on, make way! –
　　　　You there behind, get back, I say! –   5750
　　　　The staff is spitting in my face. –
　　　　It's burning me, I need more space. –
　　　　We're finished, help! We're going to die. –
　　　　You mob of masks, just let us through! –
　　　　Get back, make way, you mindless crew! –   5755
　　　　If only I had wings to fly! –

PLUTUS　　Now you have room, I've cleared a way –
　　　　And no one has been burned, I'd say.
　　　　This restive crowd
　　　　Is tamed and cowed;   5760
　　　　But to ensure good order – there!
　　　　I draw a circle in the air.

HERALD　　Your wise and powerful gifts have won
　　　　My thanks for this great work you've done.

PLUTUS　　We still need patience, noble friend;   5765
　　　　More chaos threatens to descend.

AVARICE　　And now one can enjoy the pleasure
　　　　Of studying this crowd at leisure.
　　　　If there's a feast, a party or a show,
　　　　The womenfolk are quicker on their feet.   5770
　　　　I'm not completely past it yet, you know –
　　　　For me a pretty face is still a treat,
　　　　And since today it costs me nothing here,
　　　　I'll see what I can pick up on the way.
　　　　But in this overcrowded hall, I fear   5775
　　　　That most of them won't hear a word I say;
　　　　I think I'd better stage a little play,
　　　　A pantomime to make myself quite clear.
　　　　But hands and feet alone won't do the trick –

I know a better lark. I'll take this gold   5780
And fashion it like clay – for you can mould
This metal – well, to any shape you like.[25]

HERALD Now what's that bag of bones about –
Is this some joke, you skinny lout?
He's kneading all that gold as though   5785
It were as soft as baker's dough.
He's squeezing it into a ball,
But still it has no shape at all.
He's turning to the women; they
All shriek and try to run away.   5790
They're covering their eyes in shame –
He's up to mischief, that's his game;
He's at his happiest when he
Is flouting public decency.
I can't just let him run about –   5795
Give me my staff, I'll chase him out.

PLUTUS He's no idea what danger still remains,
Just let him get on with his silly games.
He'll have no chance to fool around much longer;
The law is strong, but dire need is stronger.   5800

BOISTEROUS SINGING The Wild Hunt marches on its way;
From woods and hills in full array
They sweep, an overwhelming horde,
To praise Great Pan, their sovereign lord.[26]
No one knows their secret lore;   5805
Into the empty ring they pour.

PLUTUS I know your Great God Pan, I know you too,
And the intrepid deeds that you have done;
I know what is not known to everyone,
And open up the circle that I drew.   5810
May fortune smile on them! I fear
The strangest things can happen here;
All unawares, they blindly go
Upon a path they do not know.

WILD SINGING What gaudy faces, tinselled trash!   5815
We're rough and raw, we're coarse and brash,
We leap and run with lusty pride,
We come with vigour in our stride.

FAUNS	We fauns can prance
	A merry dance,	5820
	Oak leaves we wear
	In tousled hair,
	And from a mop of curls appears
	A pair of sharply pointed ears.
	The face is broad, the nose is flat –	5825
	But women rather fancy that.
	And when a faun holds out a paw,
	The prettiest one will take the floor.

SATYR   The goat-foot satyr skips along,
His scrawny limbs are tough and strong.   5830
On lean and nimble legs he seeks
The solitude of rocky peaks,
And like the mountain goat he thrills
To breathe the freedom of the hills,
And scorns contented valley folk   5835
Who live their lives all unaware
Among the murk and reek of smoke,
While in the pure and tranquil air
He's master of his world up there.

GNOMES   The little folk, a tiny band,   5840
Come tripping in, not hand in hand,
But dashing about with much ado,
For all of us have work to do.
With moss-green coats and lanterns bright,
We swarm like glow-worms in the night,   5845
We hurry and scurry to and fro,
And busily to work we go.

To helpful dwarfs we are related,
As surgeons we are celebrated;
We bleed the rocks, and from the veins   5850
Of mountains precious liquid drains.
We stack the hoard of metal high,
And 'Get back safe!' the miners cry.
We're kindly folk, we'll not offend you;
If you're good people, we'll befriend you.   5855
But if the gold that we reveal
Is used to pimp and cheat and steal,

We also have the iron that will
Make men the weapons that can kill.
If three commandments are ignored,   5860
The rest will soon go by the board;
All that's no fault of ours, so you
Must just have patience, as we do.

GIANTS   We are the Wild Men from the Harz,
And well known in those mountain parts;   5865
In we stride, each one a giant,
Naked as nature, strong, defiant.
Each in his hand a pine trunk grips,
A bulging belt around his hips,
All roughly wound with twigs and leaves –   5870
No Pope has bodyguards like these!

CHORUS OF NYMPHS, *surrounding the Great God Pan*
Great Pan draws near:
The one we call
Supreme in all
The world is here!   5875
You smiling nymphs, surround him now,
Light-footed dance around him now;
For he is stern, yet he is kind,
And bids our joy be unconfined.
Beneath the blue vault of the sky   5880
He'd gladly watch with open eye;
But then, by gentle winds caressed,
The rippling streams sing him to rest.
And when he sleeps, lest he awake,
No leaf may stir, no bough may shake,   5885
And fragrant herbs will fill the calm
Of noonday with their healing balm.
No nymph will dare to break the spell,
And where they stand, they sleep as well.
Then suddenly his voice will ring   5890
Like rolling thunder echoing,
Or like the ocean's roar – not one
Knows whether she should stay or run;
The bravest army's put to flight,
The boldest hero shakes with fright.   5895

All honour to our leader who
Has brought us here, all hail to you!

DEPUTATION OF GNOMES, *addressing Great Pan*

With our knowing arts divining
Where the precious metals spread
Through the rocky fissures, shining   5900
Like a labyrinthine thread,

There like troglodytes we measure
Out our vaults deep underground,
And your grace bestows our treasure
Here above on all around.   5905

Now a source appears before us
Of a truly wondrous kind;
Here is gold provided for us,
Such as we could scarcely find.

Sire, to you it is confided,   5910
Use it as a monarch should;
In your hands, by wisdom guided,
Any wealth can work for good.

PLUTUS [*to the Herald*] With calm composure and with high resource
We must allow what comes to take its course.   5915
Be bold and resolute, as you have been;
A dreadful spectacle will now unfold
That no one will believe when it is told –
So write a faithful record of the scene.

HERALD [*grasping the staff that Plutus still holds*][27]
By the dwarfs Great Pan is gently led   5920
To where the fiery source is glowing red;
It seethes up from the depths, and then
It sinks to the abyss again.
The gloomy mouth is gaping wide;
It floods back in a molten tide.   5925
All undismayed, with sheer delight
Great Pan observes this wondrous sight;
All round him sparks cascade in showers –
How can he trust such baleful powers?
He bends to see the fire within –   5930

Ah! Now his beard has fallen in!
Whose is this smooth unshaven chin?
His hand conceals his face from me –
But now, what dire catastrophe:
His beard's alight, the flames have spread,   5935
His chest, the wreath upon his head
Are burning, joy has turned to dread.
All rush to douse the flames, but none
Escapes, they're burning, every one;
They beat and slap themselves in vain –   5940
The flames burst into life again.
Trapped in an incandescent maze,
Our revellers are all ablaze.

And now, what dreadful news I hear
From mouth to mouth, from ear to ear!   5945
Oh, evermore unhappy night,
That brought us to this sorry plight!
Tomorrow we'll be told, I fear,
What none of us would wish to hear.
All round I hear cries of alarm: 5950
'The Emperor has come to harm.'
Oh, how I wish it were not true!
He's burning, all his fellows too.
A curse on those who made him wear
Those twigs of resin in his hair!   5955
That raucous frenzied mob has brought
Destruction down on all the court!
Impulsive youth, when will you ever
Temper pleasure with restraint?
All-powerful monarchs, will you never   5960
Rule with wisdom and constraint?

The forest now is all on fire,
Sharp tongues of flame are leaping higher
Towards the ceiling's wooden beams,
And total conflagration seems   5965
To threaten wholesale misery.
And who can save us? We shall see
Imperial glory, wealth and might

Reduced to ashes overnight.

PLUTUS Fear and terror now be banned, 5970
Ready help is here at hand!
Sacred staff, your power will make
The ground beneath us groan and shake!
Cooling haze will fill the air,
Spreading freshness everywhere. 5975
Vapour-bearing mists, appear,
Drifting, billowing, hover near;
Clouds of moisture, wafting, curling,
Damp this fiery chaos, swirling,
Softly flowing, drizzling, drenching, 5980
All these glowing embers quenching.
Spread your soothing showers here,
So these flames are no more frightening
Than the distant summer lightning.
Magic's power will disarm 5985
Spirits that would do us harm.

A PLEASURE GARDEN

Morning Sunlight

THE EMPEROR, COURTIERS; FAUST, MEPHISTOPHELES,
dressed properly in sober clothes, both kneeling.

FAUST You will forgive our fiery pageant, Sire?
EMPEROR [*motioning them to rise*]
Of such amusements I could never tire.
I saw myself within a glowing sphere,
It was as if I ruled as Pluto here. 5990
Deep in a coal-black chasm burned a fire,
And from its fissures, swirling ever higher,
A thousand raging tongues of flame emerged,
And to a single vault of fire merged.
It formed a lofty dome of blazing flame 5995
That, as it died, renewed itself again.
Among the twisting fiery columns then

I saw in rank and file my fellow men,
The throng of nations gathering to pay
Their homage to me in their wonted way;   6000
My courtiers, too – it seemed I was adored
By countless salamanders as their lord.

MEPHISTO.   You are that, Sire! For majesty holds all
The elements in undisputed thrall.
You have tamed fire to your sovereign will;   6005
Now plunge into the raging sea, until
You tread its rocky bed, all strewn with pearls –
A splendid world around you here unfurls.
Green wavelets, edged with purple, gently swell,
And in this ocean palace you will dwell,   6010
The centre of that realm; those sea-green halls
Move with you as you go, their very walls
Alive, a myriad teeming creatures playing,
As swift as arrows, darting, turning, swaying.
Lured by its gentle gleam, leviathans appear –   6015
They would intrude, but none may enter here;
Gold-spangled dragons all around you play,
You mock the gaping shark, he turns away.
With joyous pride your court now worships you –
But such a throng as this you never knew.   6020
Nor will you want for lovely creatures here:
For Nereids, inquisitive, swim near
Your palace on that cool eternal strand,
The youngest shy and wanton as the fish,
The older prudent. Thetis has her wish:[28]   6025
A second Peleus shall have her hand,
And on Olympus share her bed and throne –

EMPEROR   Enough! For all too soon we shall ascend
Into those airy regions at our end.

MEPHISTO.   And Sire, the earth already is your own!   6030

EMPEROR   What happy chance has brought you to delight
Us with your tales of an Arabian Night?[29]
If you can match Sheherezade in skill,
I'll grant you every favour if you will
Be ready to beguile the hours away   6035
When I am sickened by the cares of day.

IMPERIAL STEWARD *enters hurriedly*

    Your Highness, in my life I never thought
    To bear such happy news as I have brought,
    Or have such pleasure that I may
    In your most gracious presence say: 6040
    Full settlement has now been made
    Of all our debts, the userers paid.
    Free from their hellish claws – what bliss!
    Can heaven hold such joy as this?

COMMANDER OF THE ARMY *follows him*

    We've paid advances to the men;   6045
    They've all signed up with us again.
    The troops are looking much more snappy –
    The landlords and the whores are happy.

EMPEROR   You all look much more cheerful now,
    There's not a single furrowed brow –   6050
    You all come running, one by one!

LORD TREASURER *enters*

    These two will tell you how the thing was done.

FAUST   That should be for the Chancellor to say.

LORD CHANCELLOR, *entering slowly*

    That I should live to see this happy day!
    See this momentous paper in my hand   6055
    That has turned ill to good throughout the land.[30]
    [*he reads*]
    'Let it be known to all who would be told:
    This note is worth a thousand crowns in gold,
    Secured by buried treasure to be found
    In the Imperial lands beneath the ground.   6060
    Those riches, once recovered, shall be deemed
    As full equivalent to be redeemed.'

EMPEROR   But this is folly, criminal deceit!
    Who wrote my signature in counterfeit?
    Was no one punished for this forgery?   6065

TREASURER   Remember, Sire! You signed the note for me
    Last night, when you appeared as mighty Pan.
    The Chancellor and I explained the plan:
    'To crown the pleasure of this celebration,
    A few strokes of the pen will save the nation.'   6070

You signed your name, and by mysterious skills
It was reprinted on a thousand bills.
We issued the whole series right away,
So all could share this benefit today;
Tens, thirties, fifties, hundreds are to hand,   6075
And happiness has spread through all the land.
Your city, once so ravaged with decay –
It teems with joy and life again today.
Although your name has long inspired devotion,
I never heard it praised with such emotion.   6080
We need no further alphabet than this –
That sign alone fills every heart with bliss.

EMPEROR   And they accept these notes as gold, you say?
The court, the army take them as full pay?
So be it, then – but still, it puzzles me.   6085

STEWARD   We couldn't call them back, they fluttered free,
They were in circulation in a flash.
The money-changers honour them for cash –
Silver or gold; they're open night and day.
There's always a commission, though, to pay.   6090
The money goes on wine and bread and meat,
And half the world just wants to drink and eat.
The other half wants nothing but new clothes;
The draper cuts the cloth, the tailor sews.
In all the inns they gorge on stews and roasts,   6095
And drink your health with cheers and hearty toasts.

MEPHISTO.   You saunter through the park alone, and see
A beauty dressed in all her finery;
One eye peeps out behind a peacock fan –
She smiles, and then, provided that you can   6100
Produce a banknote, takes you in her arms
And favours you with all her loving charms.
No purse or moneybag to weigh her down –
She tucks it in her bosom safe and sound,
Along with all her other billets-doux.   6105
The priest can slip it in his prayerbook, too;
The soldier's belt is lighter, so he's free
More swiftly to dispatch the enemy.
Forgive me, Sire, that I thus trivialize

	The noble purpose of this enterprise.	6110
FAUST	The mass of treasure lies deep underground,	
	Inert, unused, still waiting to be found.	
	No thought has scope enough to comprehend	
	Such magnitude of riches without end.	
	The highest flight of fantasy would strain	6115
	To grasp the limits of such wealth in vain;	
	But minds endowed with boundless faith can see	
	To probe the depths of that infinity.	
MEPHISTO.	These notes are more convenient than gold	
	Or pearls, because they don't have to be sold.	6120
	No need to haggle for a price; you may	
	Want wine or women – all you do is pay.	
	If you want cash, the money-changer's bound	
	To help – and if he can't, you dig around,	
	Sell off a goblet or a golden chain –	6125
	And you've redeemed your banknote once again.	
	Soon everyone will want to do the same,	
	And those who doubt or mock be put to shame.	
	Henceforth you'll find throughout your land	
	Sufficient gold and jewels and notes to hand.	6130
EMPEROR	We owe this great prosperity to you;	
	For such high service, high reward is due.	
	To you who know where treasure can be found	
	We now entrust our wealth beneath the ground,	
	And place that hidden hoard in your protection,	6135
	To be recovered at your sole direction.	
	Come, work as one, you guardians of our treasure;	
	Discharge your worthy offices with pleasure,	
	In which the world above, the world below	
	In joyful harmony together go.	6140
TREASURER	We are united in our common mission;	
	I welcome my new colleague, the magician.	

[exit with Faust

| EMPEROR | I now bestow a gift on each of you, | |
| | And you shall say what use you'll put it to. | |

[they each receive their gifts]

| 1 PAGE | I'll live a merry life of carefree bliss. | 6145 |
| 2 PAGE | I'll buy my girl some jewellery with this. | |

1 CHAMBERLAIN	I'll buy the best wines – never mind the price.	
2 CHAMBERLAIN	I feel my fingers itch to roll the dice.	
1 KNIGHT [*thoughtfully*]	I'll clear my castle and estate from debt.	
2 KNIGHT	I'll save it up, I'll be a rich man yet.	6150
EMPEROR	I hoped you'd show new zest, bold enterprise –	
	But knowing you, it comes as no surprise;	
	For all your show of affluence, I see	
	You're still exactly as you used to be.	
FOOL [*approaching*]	You're giving presents – are there any more?	6155
EMPEROR	You've come to life! You'd drink it all, for sure.	
FOOL	These magic notes – I don't know how to use them.	
EMPEROR	I can believe it – you would just abuse them.	
FOOL	They're dropping from the sky; what do I do?	
EMPEROR	Just catch them as they fall – they're all for you.	6160

[*exit*

FOOL	But that's five thousand crowns that I've collected!	
MEPHISTO.	You walking wineskin! Are you resurrected?	
FOOL	I never woke to such good news before.	
MEPHISTO.	You're sweating happiness from every pore.	
FOOL	This paper – I can spend it just like gold?	6165
MEPHISTO.	On all the food and drink that you can hold.	
FOOL	And I can buy a house, a farm with land?	
MEPHISTO.	Why, yes! Just make an offer, cash in hand.	
FOOL	Or an estate with fish and game?	
MEPHISTO.	Of course!	
	I'd like to see your lordship on his horse.	6170
FOOL	Tonight I'll own the castle of my dreams! [*exit*	
MEPHISTO. [*alone*]	Our Fool is not as foolish as he seems.	

GLOOMY GALLERY

FAUST, MEPHISTOPHELES

MEPHISTO.	Why have you brought me to this gloomy den?	
	There's no fun to be had out here – we ought	
	To join the hurly-burly of the court	6175
	And play some tricks on them again.	
FAUST	Don't give me any more of that cheap stuff!	

You've done it all before, I've had enough.
You're just prevaricating so that you
Can wriggle out of what you have to do.   6180
This is an order that I can't resist;
The Steward and the Chamberlain insist –
The Emperor commands it as my duty
To show him the ideal of human beauty.
The living images, distinct and clear   6185
Of Helen and of Paris must appear.
So quick, to work! I must not break my word.

MEPHISTO.   To promise such a thing was quite absurd.

FAUST   My friend, you did not bear in mind
Just where your tricks were leading you.   6190
We made him rich, and now we find
We have to entertain him, too.

MEPHISTO.   It's not so simply done; we stand before
A steeper slope by far. You must explore
The strangest sphere you have encountered yet;   6195
Such recklessness will only bring new debt.
You think you can make Helen just appear
Like all that phantom money? I can show
You witches' tricks, or ghosts and ghouls galore,
Or dwarfish changelings by the score;   6200
The Devil's sweethearts have their charms, I know –
But they won't pass as heroines, I fear.

FAUST   You're grinding out the same old tune again!
You wallow in obscurity, and then
You always put some hindrance in the way;   6205
For all your schemes there is a price to pay.
Just mutter a few words into the air –
Before we know it, she'll be standing there.

MEPHISTO.   These heathens are best left alone;
They have a hell all of their own.   6210
It can be done, though.

FAUST   Tell me, right away!

MEPHISTO.   Such secrets I'm reluctant to betray –
Enthroned in solitude, remote, sublime,
Are deities beyond all space or time.
Their name will make you quail when I reveal it: 6215

They are the Mothers!

FAUST   Mothers!

MEPHISTO.   Do you feel it?

FAUST   The Mothers! – Mothers! – Yes, it sounds so strange.

MEPHISTO.   These goddesses exist beyond the range
             Of mortals; even we avoid their name.
             To find them, you must fathom the abyss –   6220
             And if we need them now, you are to blame.

FAUST   Show me the way!

MEPHISTO.   There is no way to this
             Untrodden void where none may tread, this sphere
             Where none has asked, and none may ask to go.
             Are you prepared? No locks or bolts are here;   6225
             You are adrift, alone. Can you conceive
             What solitude and desolation mean?

FAUST   You don't impress me with such make-believe;
             It all reminds me of that dismal scene
             Inside the witch's kitchen long ago.   6230
             Was my whole life not burdened and constricted?
             Was it not emptiness I learned and taught?
             And if I spoke with reason, as I thought,
             Then all the louder I was contradicted.
             Was I not vilely harried and pursued?   6235
             Into the wilderness alone I fled,
             And to escape that barren solitude
             I fell into the Devil's hands instead.

MEPHISTO.   If you had swum across the furthest ocean,
             And seen the vastness of infinity,   6240
             Though dread of death might seize you, you'd still see
             The rolling waves in never-ceasing motion.
             You would *see something*: schools of dolphins swimming,
             Across the green and placid waters skimming,
             The clouds, the sun and moon, stars overhead. –   6245
             You will see nothing in that void all round,
             You will not hear your footstep where you tread,
             Beneath your feet you'll feel no solid ground.

FAUST   You talk like those old mystagogues, deceivers
             Of all their neophytes and true believers;   6250
             You send me to the void where I'll acquire

More potent arts, but you are using me
Just like the monkey used the cat to haul
The chestnuts for him from the glowing fire.
Come then! I will explore this mystery,   6255
And in your Nothing hope to find my All.

MEPHISTO. Congratulations to you! I can tell
You've got to know the Devil very well.
Here is a key, now take it, hold it tight;
Respect its power, and you will understand.   6260

FAUST This tiny thing? Ah, but it glows with light!
It flashes now, it's growing in my hand!

MEPHISTO. That key will sense the way that you must go,
And lead you to the Mothers far below.

FAUST [*shuddering*] The Mothers! Still it strikes me like a blow!   6265
Why do I shudder when I hear that word?

MEPHISTO. You're bothered by a word you do not know?
You'd only hear what you've already heard?
Don't let the sound of it disturb you – for
You've seen and heard the strangest things before.   6270

FAUST I shall gain nothing if I'm numb with fear;
Our highest self is in our sense of awe.
Though in the world our feelings cost us dear,
Such dread can move us to our inmost core.

MEPHISTO. Descend – or rise, it's all the same – but flee   6275
Beyond the extant world into the free
Untethered realms of forms unfashioned, see
And marvel at what long since ceased to be.
Like clouds they'll drift around you on your way –
Hold out the key to keep the wraiths at bay.   6280

FAUST [*with enthusiasm*] Ah yes! I grasp it, and within my breast
I feel new strength to go on this great quest.

MEPHISTO. You'll see a burning tripod, and you'll know
You've reached the deepest of the depths below.
The Mothers are reflected in its glow;   6285
Some sit, some stand, while others come and go
Just as they please. Formation, transformation:
Eternal thought's eternal recreation.
The forms of all created things drift near;
They cannot see you, all they see is mere   6290

	Abstraction. But the danger here is such,	
	You must be bold: you take the key and touch	
	The tripod with it!	
FAUST	[*strikes a resolute and imperious pose with the key*]	
MEPHISTO.	[*watching him*] That's exactly how!	
	It follows you, you are its master now.	
	Good fortune buoys you up, you calmly rise,	6295
	And bring it back before they realise.	
	Then from the deepest night you can retrieve	
	The hero Paris, and fair Helen too –	
	And you have had the courage to achieve	
	What none before has ever dared to do.	6300
	A cloud of incense then, by magic art,	
	Will form the shapes of gods to play their part.	
FAUST	What now?	
MEPHISTO.	Downward your destination lies;	
	Stamp, and you'll sink, and stamping you will rise.	

FAUST *stamps his foot and sinks from view.*

MEPHISTO.	I hope the key protects him down below!	6305
	Will he come back? – That's what I'd like to know.	

BRIGHTLY LIT ROOMS

EMPEROR, NOBLES, COURTIERS. *Much coming and going.*

CHAMBERLAIN	[*to Mephistopheles*]	
	You promised to put on a spirit show;	
	Our master is impatient, it is late.	
IMPERIAL STEWARD	When will it start? His Highness wants to know;	
	It is disgraceful that he has to wait.	6310
MEPHISTO.	My friend is even now attending to	
	The task that only he can do.	
	Alone, secluded, underground	
	He'll labour till the treasure's found;	
	For such a quest, where beauty is the prize,	6315
	Needs magic arts known only to the wise.	
STEWARD	What kind of arts you use is by the way;	
	The Emperor is waiting, don't delay.	

A BLONDE [to Mephistopheles]
    Oh Sir! My face is clear and white,
    But in the summertime it looks a fright!   6320
    It is so tiresome, I come out in freckles;
    My lovely skin is covered in brown speckles.
    Give me a cure!
MEPHISTO.   Ah, what a shame! It's hard:
    In May such beauty, spotted like the pard.
    Take frogspawn, tongues of toad, and mix them, then 6325
    Distil it when the moon is full, and when
    It wanes, apply it smoothly to your face –
    In spring the spots are gone without a trace.
BRUNETTE They all mob you for favours, so I've come
    To ask you for a cure. My foot is numb –   6330
    It makes me walk and dance so clumsily,
    And I can't even curtsey properly.
MEPHISTO. Of course – but you must let me tread on you.
BRUNETTE Well, that's the sort of thing that lovers do.
MEPHISTO. My child, a kick from me means rather more: 6335
    Foot will heal foot, there is no better cure.
    Like's cured by like, whatever it may be;[31]
    Be careful, though – you must not stamp on me.
BRUNETTE [shrieks] Ow! Ow! It hurts! That was a savage blow,
    Just like a horse's hoof.
MEPHISTO.   You're cured; now go 6340
    And dance the hours away – and you'll be able
    To stroke your lover's foot beneath the table.
A LADY [pushing through the crowd]
    Please let me through! Oh Sir, my heart is aching,
    It's burning deep inside me, nearly breaking.
    Before, he's always told me he adores me – 6345
    But now he talks to her and just ignores me.
MEPHISTO. That's serious; now listen well to me.
    Steal softly up to him – don't let him see –
    Then take this piece of charcoal, draw a line
    Upon his coat, his shoulder or his sleeve;   6350
    With bitter-sweet remorse his heart will grieve.
    The charcoal you must swallow – let no wine
    Or water pass your lips. You can be sure:

	Tonight he'll sigh with love outside your door.	
LADY	It isn't poison?	
MEPHISTO.	[*indignantly*] Respect where it is due!	6355

MEPHISTO. [*indignantly*]   Respect where it is due!   6355
             You don't find such good quality today;
             It's from a fire, a great auto–da–fé –
             But they don't have them like they used to do.

PAGE   I am in love, they think I'm immature.

MEPHISTO.   [*aside*] I don't know which of them to listen to.   6360
             [*to the Page*] You mustn't chase the youngest ones –
                                                          I'm sure
             The more experienced will fancy you.
             [*others jostle for attention*]
             Yet more requests! They're coming thick and fast;
             I'll have to fall back on the truth at last –
             And that won't help. This is too much for me: 6365
             Oh Mothers, Mothers! Please let Faust go free!
             [*he looks around him*]
             Inside the gloomy hall the lights burn low;
             And now I see the court process in slow
             And solemn order, moving by degrees
             Through corridors and distant galleries.   6370
             So! They're assembled in the ancient hall –
             This spacious room can scarcely hold them all.
             Around the walls the tapestries are spread,
             And armour fills up every nook and cranny.
             No need for magic spells – it's so uncanny   6375
             The ghosts will find their own way here instead.

GREAT HALL, *dimly lit*.

THE EMPEROR *and* COURT *are already present*.

HERALD   It is my office to announce the play
             And to explain its meaning; but today
             The phantoms are in charge, all is illusion,
             And I can make no sense of this confusion.   6380
             The stools and chairs are set out in the hall,
             The Emperor is seated, he can see

Before him tapestries upon the wall
Depicting scenes of war and chivalry.
He and his court are all assembled now,   6385
Behind them stretch the benches row on row,
And lovers in the corners of the room
Sit close together in the ghostly gloom.
Now all have found their proper places here,
Let us begin: the spirits can appear!   6390

Trumpets

ASTROLOGER Our Lord commands; the spectacle can start.
Now let the curtained walls be opened wide!
All things are possible through magic art;
The woven tapestries are rolled aside,
The wall divides, swings back, and has become   6395
A deep and spacious stage. A spectral sheen
Sheds a mysterious light across the scene;
I mount the steps to the proscenium.

MEPHISTOPHELES [*pops up in the prompt box*]
From here I hope to merit your good will –
For prompting is the Devil's special skill.   6400
[*to the Astrologer*]
You know the rhythm of the stars, so you
Will understand me when I give the cue.

ASTROLOGER Here by a miracle, before your very eyes,
You see a massive ancient temple rise.
Like Atlas, he who once held up the sky,   6405
Stand rows of sturdy columns, straight and high
To bear its mighty roof – though two alone
Would be sufficient for that weight of stone.

ARCHITECT That's ancient, is it? Well, it's not my style;
It strikes me as a crude and clumsy pile.   6410
They call it great and noble, but it's raw.
Give me slim pillars, soaring to the sky,
The pointed arch that lifts the spirit high –
Such buildings edify us so much more.

ASTROLOGER With reverence welcome this propitious hour;   6415
Let reason be in thrall to magic's power,
And boldly set imagination free

Into a world of splendid fantasy.
You sought what is impossible, so you
Must now believe that what you see is true.   6420

FAUST *rises to view on the other side of the proscenium.*

ASTROLOGER With priestly robe and wreath, this magus can
Complete the task he fearlessly began.
A tripod rises from the vault below,
And from its bowl sweet clouds of incense blow.
His solemn work now nears its consecration;   6425
Good fortune will attend its consummation.

FAUST [*grandiloquently*] O Mothers, you who rule in boundless state,
Communing, yet eternally alone:
The images of life, inanimate
Yet ever active, hover round your throne.   6430
All that once was, and shone with radiant light,
Moves there, for it would be eternal. You,
Almighty powers, can restore it to
The canopy of day, the vault of night.
While some are caught up in life's pleasant course,   6435
Others the magus seeks out at the source,
And then with bold assurance, lavishly
Reveals his miracles for all to see.

ASTROLOGER The glowing key has touched the bowl – a pall
Of misty vapour spreads throughout the hall;   6440
It swirls about in billowing clouds, it glides
And flows, it gathers, merges and divides.
And now, a spirit masterpiece! All round
The drifting clouds give out a haunting sound,
And as they move, spread music everywhere,   6445
Ethereal melodies that fill the air.
Every column, every triglyph rings –
It seems to me that all the temple sings.
The hazy mist subsides, and as it clears,
With measured steps a handsome youth appears.   6450
I need not name him; you will recognise
The lovely Paris, here before your eyes!

PARIS *appears*

A LADY   The bloom of youthful radiance in the flesh!

2 LADY	Just like a peach, so juicy and so fresh!	
3 LADY	So delicate, that sweetly swelling lip!	6455
4 LADY	Yes – I dare say you'd like to take a sip.	
5 LADY	He's very handsome, but not quite refined.	
6 LADY	He moves a little awkwardly, I find.	
A KNIGHT	He's still the shepherd boy he used to be –	
	No manners and no breeding, you can see.	6460
2 KNIGHT	The lad's quite handsome when he's half undressed;	
	In armour, though, he wouldn't look his best.	
LADY	Now he sits down, so gently, gracefully.	
KNIGHT	No doubt you'd rather be there on his knee.	
ANOTHER LADY	How charmingly his arm rests on his head.	6465
CHAMBERLAIN	That's inexcusable! He's so ill-bred!	
LADY	You men find fault in everything you see.	
CHAMBERLAIN	To sprawl like that before his Majesty!	
LADY	He's acting, and he thinks he's all alone.	
CHAMBERLAIN	Even a play should keep the proper tone.	6470
LADY	Sleep overcomes him. Ah, what sweet repose!	
CHAMBERLAIN	How true to life; he'll snore now, I suppose.	

YOUNG LADY [*with delight*]

        Those clouds of incense hold some fragrant balm
        That soothes my heart with such refreshing calm.

OLDER LADY One breath of it can fill the heart with joy;   6475
        It comes from him!

STILL OLDER LADY   Indeed, it is that boy
        Who spreads his youthful fragrance everywhere,
        A sweet ambrosia that fills the air.

HELEN appears

MEPHISTO. So that's her, then! She's pretty, I agree;
        But I'd be safe enough, she's not for me.   6480

ASTROLOGER I must confess I can perform my duty
        No longer in the presence of such beauty;
        That beauty through the ages could inspire
        The poets – ah, if I had tongues of fire!
        Those who see her are at once possessed;   6485
        Those who possessed her were too richly blessed.

FAUST   Have I still eyes? Or can the mind record
        The source of beauty flowing in full spate?

My fearful quest has brought sublime reward!
How empty was the world, how desolate,   6490
Before my priestly mission! How alluring
Now, how firmly founded and enduring!
If I should weary of your company,
Then may I breathe my last and cease to be. –
That lovely form that once enchanted me   6495
Within the magic mirror, that reflection
Was but a fleeting glimpse of such perfection!
I pledge to you all strength that stirs in me,
The passion deep within me, my affection,
My love, the worship of my frenzied soul!   6500

MEPHISTOPHELES [*from the prompt box*]
    Pull yourself together! Stick to your role!
OLDER LADY She's tall and shapely – but her head's too small.
YOUNG LADY Look at her feet – no proper shape at all.
DIPLOMAT Like some princesses that I used to know –
    Beauties, all of them, from head to toe.   6505
COURTIER She steals up softly to the sleeping youth.
LADY So young and pure, he makes her look uncouth.
POET Her beauty bathes him in a radiant light.
LADY Endymion and Luna! Lovely sight!
POET Indeed! As if from heaven she descends,   6510
    She seems to want to drink his breath; she bends –
    A kiss! His cup is full, the lucky lad!
DUENNA In front of everyone! This is too bad!
FAUST To lavish favours on that boy!
MEPHISTO.   Be still!
    Keep quiet, let the ghost do what it will.   6515
COURTIER She slips away as he begins to stir.
LADY And now she's looking back, the little tease!
COURTIER He thinks it is a miracle he sees.
LADY He might – but it's no miracle to her.
COURTIER She turns to him, so gracious, so demure.   6520
LADY Yes, I can see she's taking him in hand.
    Men are so stupid, they don't understand;
    He'll think that he's the first she's had, for sure.
KNIGHT Oh come, be fair! She's regal, so refined.
LADY She's nothing but a common tart, I find.   6525

PAGE	If I were in his place, I wouldn't mind.
COURTIER	Who wouldn't want to walk into that snare!
LADY	That jewel's been through several hands; the gold
	Has worn a little thinner here and there.
ANOTHER LADY	She's been no good since she was ten years old. 6530
KNIGHT	Sometimes you take the best that you can get;
	What's left of her is good enough for me.
A SCHOLAR	She's standing there as large as life – and yet
	I'm not sure it's the real one I see.
	You cannot judge things properly by looks; 6535
	I'll stick to what is written in the books.
	They tell us that she brought especial joy
	To all the aged citizens of Troy.
	That seems to fit the picture perfectly:
	I'm not a young man, and she pleases me. 6540
ASTROLOGER	A boy no more, a hero now, his arms
	Are round her, she can scarce resist his charms.
	He lifts her in his powerful embrace –
	Is he abducting her, perhaps?
FAUST	Disgrace!
	Rash fool, that is enough! How dare you! No! 6545
MEPHISTO.	It's *you* that's putting on this phantom show!
ASTROLOGER	I've one thing more to add: I name this play
	The Rape of Helen, as performed today.
FAUST	How, rape? Am I not here, and in my hand
	Do I not hold this key that guided me 6550
	Across the fearsome waste, the surging sea
	Of solitude, and brought me safe to land?
	This is reality; my spirit dares
	To struggle with these spirits, and prepares
	To claim the double kingdom as its prize. 6555
	She was so far, now here before my eyes!
	I'll save her, she'll be mine in doubled bliss;
	Oh Mothers, Mothers! You must grant me this!
	Who sees her can no longer live without her.
ASTROLOGER	Faust, what is this? He throws his arms about her, 6560
	He seizes her, the figure fades, now he
	Has turned towards the youth, and with the key
	He touches him. Ah, what calamity!

Explosion. Faust falls to the ground. The spirits disappear in smoke.

MEPHISTO. [*taking Faust on his shoulder*]
>   To have to carry fools like this around
>   Can even break the Devil's back, I've found.   6565

Darkness. Confusion.

ACT TWO

HIGH–VAULTED NARROW GOTHIC ROOM, FORMERLY FAUST'S STUDY, UNCHANGED

MEPHISTOPHELES *appears from behind a curtain. As he lifts it and looks back,* FAUST *is seen stretched out on an old-fashioned bed.*

MEPHISTO. Poor wretch! Lie down and rest in here,
You hopelessly besotted lover!
If Helen's knocked you out, I fear
Your wits won't easily recover.
[*he looks around*
It's just the same here; everywhere I look   6570
Nothing has altered, not a single book.
The coloured panes are duller now, I think –
More spiders' webs, too, than there used to be.
This paper's yellowed, and the ink
Has dried, but all's in order still –   6575
And this must be the very quill
Faust used when he assigned himself to me.
Yes! Inside there a drop of blood's congealed
With which the Devil's document was sealed.
It ought to be put on display –   6580
A real collector's piece, I'd say.
And this old fur still hanging on the door
Reminds me how I fooled that student, taught
Him things he'd never known before;
I think I gave him food enough for thought.   6585
In fact, I have a fancy to put on
This reeking gown again – I might
Be able to show off and play the don,
Convinced that everything I say is right,

As scholars always are – although   6590
The Devil lost the knack some time ago.

He takes down the fur gown and shakes it. Crickets,
beetles and moths swarm out.

CHORUS OF INSECTS We hail you and greet you,
Our father and lord!
We swarm out to meet you,
Your long-legged horde.   6595
You laid us in secret
And hid us away,
And now in our thousands
We come out to play.
You'll never discover   6600
The thoughts of a villain;
The lice in his coat are
Less easily hidden.

MEPHISTO. How glad I am to meet my youthful progeny!
We sow, not knowing what we'll reap one day.   6605
I'll give this ancient fleece another shake, and see –
Yet more emerge and flutter on their way.
My little darlings, hurry now and hide;
There are a hundred thousand nooks
In these old boxes. Burrow deep inside   6610
The yellowed parchments and the tattered books,
In pots and jars, in all those dusty pockets,
Or in that old skull's dry and empty sockets.
A scholar's whims, like moths, will always need
Some mould and mustiness in which to breed.   6615
[*he slips on the gown*]
Come, let me wrap myself in you again!
Today I am once more the Head of College;
But what's the use of such a title, when
There's no one to impress with my great knowledge?

He pulls the bell, which rings with a deafening, penetrating sound.
The building shakes and doors fly open.

FAMULUS [*stumbling along the long dark corridor*]
What a clanging! What a shaking!   6620
Stairs are swaying, walls are quaking!

Through the coloured windows flashing
Bolts of lightning, thunder crashing.
Floors are splitting, plaster peeling,
Rubble falling from the ceiling.   6625
Burst wide open stands the door
So securely locked before.
Look! In Faust's old gown, I swear
I see a giant standing there.
How he stares! It makes me freeze –   6630
I feel like falling on my knees.
Shall I stay, or shall I flee?
Oh, what will become of me?

MEPHISTO. [*beckons him*] Come in! You're Nicodemus, I've heard say.

FAMULUS   I am, most Reverend Father. Let us pray.   6635

MEPHISTO. Let's not.

FAMULUS   I am so pleased you know my name.

MEPHISTO. Oh yes! No youngster, but a student all the same.
Even the greatest mind, my moss-grown friend,
Must go on learning to the bitter end.
We build our modest house of cards, but none   6640
Will ever finish what he has begun.
Your master, though – all men revere his name;
Who has not heard of Doctor Wagner's fame?
He is the leading scholar of his day,
The single pillar of the world of learning,   6645
Who treads the path of truth and lights the way.
Alone he keeps the torch of knowledge burning,
Disciples gather at his feet to hear
His teachings, students flock from far and near.
He holds Saint Peter's keys, the power to know   6650
All things in heaven above and here below.
His reputation glitters, and his fame
Outshines all others we have ever known,
Obscuring even Faust's illustrious name;
Of all inventive minds, he stands alone.   6655

FAMULUS   Oh, Reverend Sir, forgive me if I dare
To contradict. My master does not care
At all for fame or reputation;
With pious modesty he follows his vocation.

The great man's sudden disappearance left   6660
Him quite inconsolable and bereft;
His only comfort is to hope and yearn,
And count the days to Doctor Faust's return.
No one has touched his study since the day
He was mysteriously called away;   6665
I scarcely dare to put my foot inside.
Perhaps the hour of destiny is near;
The very walls appeared to quake with fear,
The locks were shattered, doors burst open wide –
Or you yourself would not be sitting here.   6670

MEPHISTO.   Your master is the man I came to see;
So take me to him, or bring him to me.

FAMULUS   But Sir, I would not dare to break my word;
He gave strict orders not to be disturbed.
He's lived for months in absolute seclusion,   6675
And toils to bring the Great Work to conclusion.
This gentlest of scholars labours there
Just like a charcoal-burner; as he blows
The fire, his eyes are reddened from the glare,
His face is black with soot from ears to nose.   6680
He craves the moment consummation nears;
The clattering tongs are music to his ears.

MEPHISTO.   Then surely he will see me; I'm the man
To help him out, if anybody can.

*The Famulus leaves; Mephistopheles seats himself
with solemn dignity.*

I've scarcely settled in my chair,   6685
I see a well-known figure over there.
But how he's changed in such a little while!
So infinitely bumptious – it's the latest style.

GRADUATE [*rushing down the corridor*]
Doors wide open! Let us hope
No one's here to sit and mope   6690
In this festering decay,
Getting feebler by the day
Like the living dead, for whom
Life leads only to the tomb.

These old walls are crumbling fast;   6695
Soon the end will come at last.
If we don't escape, we'll all
Perish with them when they fall.
I fear nothing – but I fear
They can teach me nothing here.   6700

This all looks familiar, though:
Was it here, so long ago,
I arrived in my first year,
Timid, nearly numb with fear,
Took those fossils at their word,   6705
Swallowed all the rot I heard?

All the lies they taught, they took
From some mouldering old book,
Knew quite well it wasn't true –
Wasted my life, and theirs too.   6710
Look! In the corner of the room
One's still sitting in the gloom.

That's astonishing! I swear
It's the same one in that chair,
In the same old gown as when   6715
I left him: nothing's changed since then.
He was so clever then, I thought –
Now I know the tricks he taught.
But he won't fool me today –
Let's up and at him right away!   6720

Most ancient Sir, if Lethe's turgid stream
Has not benumbed your venerable brain,
You see your grateful student here again,
Freed from the disciplines of academe.
It seems I find you as you ever were –   6725
But *I* am quite another person, Sir.

MEPHISTO.   I'm glad the bell has summoned you to me.
You were a bright young man, my hopes were high;
For in the grub, the chrysalis, we see
The future gorgeous butterfly.   6730
So like a child you were; your eager face

	Was framed with curls, your collar fringed with lace,	
	For pigtails then, I think, were hardly worn –	
	Today I see you're fashionably shorn.	
	You look so resolute, unwavering;	6735
	Don't go bald-headed, though, at everything.	
GRADUATE	I see that nothing's altered here a bit.	
	But times have changed; we have no patience for	
	Your clever puns or your ironic wit –	
	These tricks do not impress us any more.	6740
	You teased the simple boy who trusted you;	
	Old men find that an easy thing to do –	
	You'd never get away with it today.	
MEPHISTO.	You try to teach these lads the honest truth,	
	But that just doesn't suit our callow youth.	6745
	Then, after years of trying, when they gain	
	Some inkling of it in their clumsy way –	
	They think it sprang straight out of their own brain;	
	That teacher was an awful fool, they say.	
GRADUATE	A rogue, more like! Does any teacher speak	6750
	The plain unvarnished truth his students seek?	
	With light or heavy hand his subtle skill	
	Manipulates their tender minds at will.	
MEPHISTO.	To learn, they say, can take us many years;	
	But you can teach already, it appears.	6755
	In all your lengthy studies, I dare say	
	You've picked up some experience on the way?	
GRADUATE	Experience! That's so much ballyhoo	
	Compared with what the human mind can do.	
	All we have ever known, you must admit,	6760
	Is simply not worth knowing, none of it.	
MEPHISTO. [after a pause]		
	I've long suspected it; and I regret	
	I was so dim and foolish in the past.	
GRADUATE	I'm glad to hear some proper sense at last! –	
	The only sensible old man I've met!	6765
MEPHISTO.	I looked for treasure hidden underground,	
	And worthless dross was all I ever found.	
GRADUATE	Admit it, then: your wits have grown so dull,	
	Your head is emptier than that old skull.	

MEPHISTO. [*good-naturedly*]
        My friend, such rudeness isn't really right.   6770
GRADUATE In German only liars are polite.
MEPHISTO. [*rolling his wheelchair closer to the front of the stage, addressing*
        the pit] He takes my breath away! I need more air;
        Can some of you make room for me down there?
GRADUATE It is presumptuous for anyone
        To think he's needed when his day has gone.   6775
        Our lives are lived in blood, and only here,
        In youthful veins, does blood run fast and clear:
        New strength, new blood that freshly circulates
        And with new energy new life creates.
        While you all sleep, great things are being done;   6780
        The weak go to the wall, the stronger man
        Takes charge, and half the world's already won.
        What were you doing? Dreaming up some plan,
        And when that failed, dreamed up another one.
        Old age is like a fever, it's a blight   6785
        That numbs the wits and freezes up the mind.
        And once you're over thirty, then you might
        As well be dead; it would be kind
        To put you down before it is too late.
MEPHISTO. What can the Devil add to this debate?   6790
GRADUATE Without my will, the Devil isn't there.
MEPHISTO. [*aside*] He'll catch you bending yet, young man: take care.
GRADUATE This is youth's loftiest vocation!
        The world around me is my own creation;
        Out of the sea I caused the sun to rise,   6795
        And set the changing moon across the skies.
        The green earth flourished in the light of day,
        And blossomed for me as I went my way.
        It was at my command in that first night
        The stars revealed their glory to my sight.   6800
        And it was only I who set you free
        From narrow philistine banality.
        But I am free to let the spirit lead
        Me onwards, guided by my inner light;
        In self-delighted rapture I proceed,   6805
        The day before me, and behind me night.   [*exit*]

MEPHISTO.   Farewell, young genius, in all your glory!
It would be cruel to tell you the old story:
There's nothing foolish, nothing wise we know
That was not thought of centuries ago.   6810
But such absurdity can't really harm us;
In just a few years he will toe the line.
This furious fermentation may alarm us –
But in the end it makes a decent wine.
[*to the younger section of the audience, who are not applauding*]
I see my words of wisdom leave you cold;   6815
I'm not upset, dear children, if they do.
The Devil, don't forget, is very old –
When you are old, you'll understand him too.

LABORATORY

*in medieval style, filled with cumbersome apparatus
for weird experiments.*

WAGNER [*at the kiln*]
The bell tolls out its awful chime,
And echoes through the sooty walls.   6820
The weary and uncertain time
Is over, and fulfilment calls.
The brightness in the glass is growing,
And deep inside the phial gazing,
I see a point of light, a glowing   6825
Flame, like coal, like jewels blazing:
A brilliant shaft, a pure white spark
That shines and flashes in the dark.
This time I shall not fail, for sure –
Oh God! Who's rattling at the door?   6830

MEPHISTOPHELES *enters*
Greetings! Good will and friendship bring me here.
WAGNER [*anxiously*] Welcome! The hour of destiny is near.
[*softly*] But hold your breath, I beg you, say no more;
This glorious project must not be delayed.
MEPHISTO. [*more softly*] What is it, then?
WAGNER [*more softly still*]   A man is being made.   6835

MEPHISTO.   A man? So have you got some amorous pair
            Sealed in the chimney-flue up there?

WAGNER   No, God forbid! Such crude and foolish passion
            Is now completely out of fashion.
            The tender spot from which life first began,   6840
            And welled up from within, that gentle force
            That took and gave, ordained by nature's plan
            To shape itself, first from its ambient source,
            And then from others – that has had its day,
            And only beasts will procreate that way.   6845
            Mankind with all its gifts is surely worth
            A far superior, nobler form of birth.
            [*he turns to the kiln*]
            It's glowing! Look! That is a hopeful sign;
            For when so many substances combine,
             And if they have been fully integrated,   6850
            Then human tissue has coagulated.
            And if it's sealed within a flask
            And properly distilled, the task
            Is done, and life has been created!
            [*turning back to the kiln*]
            It lives, it moves! The substance clears and flows,   6855
            And every moment my conviction grows.
            Though nature's works were hid in mystery,
            Our scientific skills have found the key;
            What her organic processes devised
            Is now synthetically crystallized.   6860

MEPHISTO.   If you live long enough, like me,
            You learn there's nothing new under the sun.
            When I was on my travels once, I saw
            Crystallized humans – it's been done before.[32]

WAGNER [*still gazing intently at the phial*]
            It's rising, flashing, swelling more and more;   6865
            Another moment, and it will be done.
            At first a major project seems insane,
            But chance one day will be eliminated;
            I see a future when a powerful brain
            By some great intellect will be created.   6870
            [*he gazes into the phial with delight*]

The glass rings loudly with a pleasant tone;
Again it's growing cloudy – but it clears.
It's worked at last! A tiny shape has grown,
And now a dainty little man appears.
What higher aspiration can there be?   6875
The mystery is there for all to see;
And if we listen to the sound, we hear
It turn into a voice that speaks out clear.

HOMUNCULUS [*in the phial, to Wagner*]
Well, Daddy dear, it was for real – I'm here.
How are you? Give me a hug – but very lightly;   6880
The glass will shatter if you squeeze too tightly.
That's how it is – the world's too small, I fear,
For creatures of a natural kind;
What's artificial needs to be confined.
[*to Mephistopheles*]
So you're here, cousin – at the right time, too,   6885
You clever rogue; I'm much obliged to you.
It was most fortunate you came today;
Now I exist, I must find things to do.
I'd like to get to work without delay –
You're just the one to help me on my way.   6890

WAGNER   Please, just a word! It does embarrass me
When people of all ages harass me
With questions such as this: how can it be
That soul and body are both integrated
So closely that they can't be separated,   6895
And yet they plague each other constantly?
What's more –

MEPHISTO.   Enough! I'd rather want to know
Why man and wife must always quarrel so –
That's what we'll never have the answer to.
Let's give the little man something to do!   6900

HOMUNCULUS What's to be done?

MEPHISTO. [*pointing to a side door*]   It's here, behind the door.

WAGNER [*still gazing into the phial*]
You are a darling little boy, for sure!

The side door opens. FAUST *is seen stretched out on the bed.*

HOMUNCULUS [*astonished*] Remarkable!

The phial slips out of Wagner's hands, and floats above Faust,
shedding light on him.

A lovely scene! I see
Clear waters, bushes, women who undress –
It's getting better! Ah, what loveliness!   6905
But one shines out above them all, for she
Must be divine, or of heroic blood.
Into the limpid stream she dips her feet,
And cools her noble body's living heat
Within the softly yielding crystal flood.   6910
But now the rapid beat of wings is heard;
What frantic dashing, splashing has disturbed
The placid pools? The women flee, the queen
Alone looks calmly on the hectic scene,
And with a woman's pride she smiles to see   6915
The prince of swans who nestles at her knee,
So tame, and yet persistent as a lover.
He settles to her now; but mists arise,
And with impenetrable veils they cover
The loveliest of visions from our eyes.[33]   6920

MEPHISTO.   This is pure fantasy! You may be small,
But all these tales you tell are pretty tall.
I can't see anything –

HOMUNCULUS.   That's no surprise;
You're from the north, you grew up in a pall
Of monkish gloom and chivalry; your eyes   6925
Are not accustomed to the light –
You only feel at home in fog and night.
[*he looks around him*]
This grimy, mouldering, repellent masonry,
These Gothic arches, all this florid tracery –
It's so debased! If he wakes up, he'll not   6930
Survive, he'll drop dead on the spot.
His mind is haunted by auspicious dreams
Of naked beauties, swans and woodland streams.
This is no place for him; I'm pretty easy,
But I can't stand it here, it makes me queasy.   6935

We must get him away!

MEPHISTO.   Indeed – but how?

HOMUNCULUS If you invite a young girl dancing, or
                You give a soldier orders in the war,
                The thing's no sooner said than done. Well, now:
                Today's the date, if memory serves me right,   6940
                Of Classical Walpurgis Night.
                We simply couldn't find a better cure –
                That is his proper element, for sure.

MEPHISTO.   What's that? I don't believe a word of it.

HOMUNCULUS How could you possibly have heard of it?   6945
                Romantic ghosts and ghouls are all you know –
                Classical phantoms are the real ones, though.

MEPHISTO.   Where do we go? I'm not too keen to see
                Colleagues from classical antiquity.

HOMUNCULUS You haunt the north-west, Satan – but today   6950
                It's to the south-east we must make our way.
                Past cool secluded bays and bushy banks
                All fringed with trees, Peneus wanders through
                A mighty plain; Pharsalus, old and new,
                Stands high upon the mountain's craggy flanks.   6955

MEPHISTO.   Oh, no, forget it! All that history
                Of slaves and tyrants doesn't interest me.
                They fight it out among themselves, and then
                They can't agree and start it all again –
                And none of them can see that they're in thrall   6960
                To Asmodeus, who's behind it all.
                They say it's freedom that they're fighting for;
                It's slaves versus slaves, like any other war.

HOMUNCULUS These are the wilful ways of humankind;
                Each must defend himself as best he can   6965
                From boyhood onwards till he is a man.
                A cure for *him* is what we have to find,
                So tell us if you know a remedy –
                If not, you'd better leave the thing to me.

MEPHISTO.   Some Brocken tricks might do it, I suppose;   6970
                I just don't understand these heathens, though.
                I never liked the Greeks. Oh yes, I know
                They dazzle you with beauty, and entice

Your senses with the most beguiling vice;
Our sins are very dull compared with those.   6975
What now, then?
HOMUNCULUS   You're not usually so shy;
Thessalian witches should appeal to you –
I think you know what I'm referring to.
MEPHISTO. [*lecherously*] Thessalian witches! Yes, that's worth a try!
I've often thought I'd like to meet a few.   6980
Mind you, I wouldn't want to spend
Too many nights with them – but still,
A flying visit might just fit the bill.
HOMUNCULUS Then wrap your cloak around our sleeping friend,
As you have done before, and it will bear   6985
You both upon your journey through the air.
I'll light the way.
WAGNER [*anxiously*]   Am I not coming too?
HOMUNCULUS You must stay here; you have great work to do.
Look out the ancient manuscripts; collect
Life's building blocks in order, one by one,   6990
Assemble them with caution, and reflect
On what to do – but more on *how* it's done,
While I go out into the world, and try
To find the dot to put upon the i.
Such effort will bring rich reward to those   6995
Who can succeed in such a lofty aim:
Good health, long life, with honour, wealth and fame –
Knowledge and virtue too, perhaps – who knows?
Goodbye!
WAGNER [*sadly*]   Dear boy, farewell! My heart is heavy, for
I fear I may not see you any more.   7000
MEPHISTO. To the Peneus, then, away from here!
My little cousin has the right idea.
[*to the audience*] That's how it is, you see; we all depend
On creatures we've created in the end.

CLASSICAL WALPURGIS NIGHT

Pharsalian Fields[34]
Darkness

ERICHTHO   How often to this gruesome festival tonight   7005
Have I, Erichtho, sombre witch of graveyards, come –
Though not so loathsome as the poets' slanderous
Exaggerations.[35] Wretched brood! They never cease
To carp or flatter. – Now it seems a pallid sea
Of ghostly tents has bleached the vastness of the plain,   7010
Recurrent vision of that dread and sorry night.
How many times has it returned! It will return
Through all eternity – for none will yield the realm
To any other, none give way to those who win
And rule by might. For every man who cannot rule   7015
His inner self is all too ready to usurp
His neighbour's will to satisfy his swelling pride.
A great example was fought out upon this field
Of force encountering an even greater force,
How freedom's sweet and many-flowered wreath
                                                  was torn,   7020
And how the barren laurel crowned the victor's brow.
Here Pompey dreamed of early glory blossoming;
There Caesar watched the wavering finger of the scales.
The balance swings; and all the world knows well
                                               who won.

The flames of burning watchfires spread their
                                    reddish gleam,   7025
The soil exhales the flush of blood spilt long ago;
Lured by the strange enchantment of the shining night,
The legions of Hellenic legend gather round.
Among the fires they drift uncertainly, or sit
At ease, the fabled creatures of the ancient world.   7030
The rising moon is on the wane, but brightly still
It shines, and casts a gentle sheen across the plain;
The phantom tents have vanished, fires are burning blue.

Above me, though, what unexpected meteor?
The shining sphere illuminates a human form.   7035
I sense a living presence, but it ill becomes
Me to approach, I am the bane of all that lives;
It profits nothing, brings me only ill repute.
The sphere descends; discretion bids me to be gone.

[*she moves off*

THE AERONAUTS, *above*

HOMUNCULUS   One more time we circle round   7040
              High above the plain below;
              Ghostly fires on the ground
              Cast an eerie spectral glow.

MEPHISTO.   In the gloomy north I've seen
              Many ghastly phantoms roam;   7045
              Looking at this dismal scene,
              I feel perfectly at home.

HOMUNCULUS   Look! A tall shape, over there,
              Hurries off with rapid strides.

MEPHISTO.   When she saw us in the air,   7050
              She took fright, and now she hides.

HOMUNCULUS   Let her go! Our friend must stand
              With his feet upon the plain.
              In this fabled wonderland
              He'll soon come to life again.   7055

FAUST [*as he touches the ground*] Where is she?

HOMUNCULUS   That I couldn't say,
              But someone here should know the way.
              You still have time enough to go
              Among these flames before it's day.
              You dared to face the Mothers, so   7060
              You'll not be daunted here, I know.

MEPHISTO.   I too have things to do, so I suggest
              That for each one of us it would be best
              To wander through the flames tonight,
              And seek our own adventures where we can.   7065
              And then, to summon us, the little man
              Should ring his glass and guide us with his light.

HOMUNCULUS This is how I'll flash, that's how I'll ring.

The glass hums and shines brightly.

Let's see what marvels this strange night will bring!

[they leave

FAUST [*alone*] Where is she? Do you need to ask for more?   7070
Though this is not the land where she was young,
Nor this the wave that broke upon her shore,
It is the air that spoke her mother tongue.
What miracle has brought me here to stand
Upon the soil of Greece, her native land?   7075
I woke refreshed, Antaeus-like I found
My strength returning as I touched the ground.[36]
This labyrinth of flames I shall explore,
And see what prodigies it has in store.

[he moves off

ON THE UPPER PENEUS

MEPHISTO. [*prying around*] I'm ill at ease among this maze of flame;   7080
The creatures here are practically nude!
It's scandalous! The sphinxes have no shame,
The gryphons are impertinently rude.
Inspect them from the front or from behind,
They've very little on but fur or feather;   7085
We're thoroughly indecent, but I find
Antiquity too lifelike altogether.
We cover things with fig-leaves nowadays
To hide such details from the public gaze.
Disgusting! Still, don't let it bother you;   7090
Greet them politely, as a guest should do –
Greetings, lovely ladies, learned grey 'uns.
GRYPHON [*snarling*] Not grey 'uns! Gryphons! No one wants to be
Called old and grey. In every word we say,
The sound betrays its etymology –   7095
Like grumpy, graveyard, grisly, grim or grey.
They have a common derivation – we
Derive no pleasure from it.
MEPHISTO.   All the same,
The 'grip' in 'gryphon' makes a splendid name.

GRYPHON [*still snarling*] Of course! There is a close affinity;   7100
    It does us credit, though we get some blame.
    You grasp a woman, grab a crown, or gold –
    And if you grip them tight, your luck will hold.

ANTS *of the colossal kind*
    You talk of gold; we had a massive hoard
    Concealed in caves and fissures in the rock.   7105
    The Arimaspians found where it was stored;
    They stole it from us, now they sit and mock.

GRYPHONS Don't worry, we'll soon bring them to account.

ARIMASPIANS But not tonight! We're free to celebrate
    The festival – and then you'll be too late.   7110
    Tomorrow we'll have spent the whole amount.

MEPHISTO. [*who has meanwhile seated himself between the sphinxes*]
    I find I'm quickly getting used to you –
    And I can understand your language, too.

SPHINX We breathe our spirit tones; your ear
    Lends its own meaning to the sounds you hear.   7115
    We do not know you yet; what is your name?

MEPHISTO. I am called many things – such is my fame.
    Are any Britons here? A restless race;
    They look for battlefields and waterfalls,
    Obscure and ancient sites with crumbling walls –   7120
    They would be quite delighted with this place.
    In mystery plays they had a part for me;
    They used to call me Old Iniquity.

SPHINX Why did they call you that?

MEPHISTO.   I couldn't say.

SPHINX Maybe. Do you know your astrology?   7125
    What do the signs portend for us today?

MEPHISTO. [*looks upwards*]
    A shower of stars, the waning moon shines clear;
    I feel so snug and comfortable here.
    Your fur is warm; it would be most unwise
    To reach beyond ourselves into the skies.   7130
    Let's have a riddle, a charade or two.

SPHINX The riddle here is no one else but you.
    Decipher your own nature if you can:
    'A fencing-bodice for the pious man

To practise his ascetic discipline;   7135
A wild companion for a life of sin –
For his amusement Zeus devised this plan.'[37]

FIRST GRYPHON [*snarling*] I don't like him.

SECOND GRYPHON [*snarling even louder*]   He's got a nasty face.

TOGETHER   What does he think he's doing in this place?

MEPHISTO. [*fiercely*] You should remember that a stranger's claws   7140
Can scratch as well; they're quite as sharp as yours.
Just try it!

SPHINX [*mildly*]   If you wish to, you can stay;
But your own urge will soon drive you away.
In your own land you may command respect,
But you are ill at ease here, I suspect.   7145

MEPHISTO.   On top, I must admit, you look delicious;
But down below the lion's claws are vicious.

SPHINX   You scoundrel, you will live to rue your cheek;
Our claws are healthy, sound and strong.
Your withered horse's hoof is nature's freak –[38]   7150
In company like ours you don't belong.

SIRENS *sing a prelude above.*

MEPHISTO.   What are those birds that come to nest
Among the poplars by the river there?

SPHINX   Be on your guard; the noblest and the best
Have fallen for their siren song. Take care!   7155

SIRENS   What unworthy spell has bound you
To those ugly beasts around you!
Let our melodies surround you.
Hear the Sirens sweetly singing,
High among the branches clinging.   7160

SPHINXES [*mocking them to the same tune*]
Make them come down and reveal
What the twigs and leaves conceal;
Vicious claws will savage you
If you pause to listen to
What the Sirens sing to you.   7165

SIRENS   No more envy! No more hate!
All the purest joys await

Those who follow us today;
On the water, on the land,
We extend a gracious hand   7170
To the guests who come our way.

MEPHISTO.   These new-fangled sounds just bore me.
Flowing melodies combining,
Notes and voices intertwining –
All that noise does nothing for me.   7175
I hear them warbling, but their art
Doesn't really move my heart.

SPHINXES   Your heart, indeed! What vanity!
A shrivelled leather bag would be
More suited to a face so tart.   7180

FAUST [*approaches*] What wonders here! It lifts my heart to see
Such greatness in these monstrous forms impressed!
I feel good fortune will attend my quest;
This solemn spectacle entrances me.
     [*turning to the Sphinxes*]
Once Oedipus encountered such as these.   7185
     [*turning to the Sirens*]
Their song bewitched the bound and writhing Ulysses.
     [*turning to the Ants*]
These harvested the richest treasure-hoard.
     [*turning to the Gryphons*]
These faithfully kept watch where it was stored.
I feel fresh life, new spirit through me surging,
In these great forms, great memories emerging.   7190

MEPHISTO.   You would have scorned such beasts before,
But I can see you've changed your mind;
Now it's a lover you are looking for,
You welcome every monster you can find.

FAUST [*to the Sphinxes*] Now answer me, for you are women too: 7195
Was Helen ever seen by one of you?

SPHINXES   We did not live to see such times as these;
The last of us was slain by Hercules.
You should ask Chiron; he will surely know.
On nights like this he gallops to and fro;   7200
You will do well if you can stop him, though.

SIRENS   You'll not fail, you can be sure!
                Ulysses once paused to hear us,
                Such a hero did not fear us;
                We'll confide to you today   7205
                All the things he heard and saw,
                If you join us by the shore
                Of our green Aegean bay.

SPHINX   Noble friend, ignore their pleas,
                Do not be bound like Ulysses;   7210
                Let us guide you on your way.
                Find great Chiron, he will know
                How to help you. Quickly, go!

                        Faust moves away.

MEPHISTO. [*irritably*] What are those birds with raucous cry
                That chase each other through the sky   7215
                So quickly they deceive the sight,
                Too swift for any hunter's eye?
SPHINX   These are the swift Stymphalides;
                Wild as the winter winds they fly.
                Even the darts of Hercules   7220
                Could hardly reach them in full flight.
                They screech a lot; you needn't fear
                Their vulture's beaks – they want to be
                Made welcome in our family.
MEPHISTO. [*nervously*] Something just whistled past my ear. 7225
SPHINX   Those are the heads of the Lernaean Snake,
                Chopped off by Hercules. You mustn't take
                Them seriously – they think they still exist.
                But now what has got into you?
                What's making you so agitated, though?   7230
                What is it? Ah, I see you can't resist
                The beauty chorus over there; you'll screw
                Your neck off very soon. Well, go
                And see those lovely creatures for a while.
                The Lamiae are a lascivious crew,   7235
                With brazen looks and an alluring smile.
                They suit the satyrs perfectly, so you
                Should find them most accommodating too.

MEPHISTO.   But will you still be here when I come back?

SPHINXES   Yes; go and join that flighty pack.   7240
            Since ancient Egypt our unblinking gaze
            Has measured out the seasons in the sky.
            We sit and watch millennia go by,
            And count the solar and the lunar days,
                By the Pyramids forever,   7245
                At the councils of the nations;
                Flood or war or peace could never
                Shake us from our sure foundations.

ON THE LOWER PENEUS [39]

PENEUS, *surrounded by tributary streams, and* NYMPHS

PENEUS   Reeds and rushes, slender sisters,
            Softly breathe your sighing whispers,   7250
            Rustling willow branches, quiver,
            Lisping poplars, lightly shiver,
            And restore my broken dream.
            What is this mysterious shaking?
            All around a fearful quaking   7255
            Has disturbed my placid stream.

FAUST [*approaching the river*]
            From the tangled shrubs and sedges
            Swaying by the river's edges,
            In the air I seem to hear
            Human voices calling near.   7260
            Ripples laughing, breezes playing –
            Can I tell what they are saying?

NYMPHS [*to Faust*] Among the cool shallows
                Tired limbs will recover,
                Beneath the tall sallows   7265
                Lie down and discover
                The peace that eludes you,
                The sleep of the blest;
                Our whispers will soothe you
                And lull you to rest.   7270

FAUST This is not sleep! Oh, hold them there,
These forms, sublime beyond compare,
Before my waking eyes once more!
What is this strange and joyous yearning,
What dreams, what memories returning?   7275
Such ecstasy was yours before!
The stream meanders through a glade
Of tangled shrubs and leafy shade
With scarce a murmur, smooth and slow.
From every side into a cool   7280
And gently sloping limpid pool
A hundred sparkling freshets flow.
Young women, lithe of limb and supple,
Reflected in the pool – a double
Vision to entrance my eyes.   7285
In playful groups I watch them bathing;
Boldly swimming, shyly wading,
They chase and splash with noisy cries.
I should be quite content to find
Fulfilment here, but still my mind   7290
Compels my gaze towards that green
And leafy canopy beside
The stream, whose foliage must hide
The noble figure of the queen.

What new marvels! Swans converging,[40]   7295
From secluded bays emerging;
With such regal grace they glide,
Calmly sailing, gentle, caring,
Yet how dignified of bearing,
Holding high their heads with pride. –   7300
One, supreme among the others,
Nobler, bolder than his brothers,
Swims ahead with urgent pace;
Feathers swelling, never slowing,
Like a wave he rides the flowing   7305
Ripples to that holy place. –
With shining plumage on the brimming
Stream the rest are calmly swimming.

But they clash; a lively fight
Is joined, and now each timid beauty,   7310
Heedless of her sacred duty,
Seeks to save herself in flight.

NYMPHS   Lay your ear upon the ground,
                Sisters, for I seem to hear
                Distant hooves; it is the sound   7315
                Of a horseman drawing near.
                Who is this, we ask, who might
                Bring such urgent news tonight?

FAUST   Do I hear the earth resounding
            With a horse's rapid pounding?   7320
                What do I see
                Over there; can it be
                Some happy chance has brought
                The miracle I sought?
            It is a horseman coming near,   7325
            Endowed with wisdom, without fear,
            His shining mount as white as snow –
            I see him now; can it be true?
            It is Philyra's son, I know!
            Stop, Chiron, stop! I have to speak to you.   7330

CHIRON   What is it?

FAUST   Curb your speed, I beg you, stay!

CHIRON   I do not rest.

FAUST   Please! Help me on my way.

CHIRON   Climb on my back! And tell me as we ride
            Where you would go. Don't stand there on the bank;
            I'll gladly take you to the other side.   7335

FAUST [climbs on to his back] No matter where! For ever I will thank
            The great and noble pedagogue, the same
            Who raised a race of heroes to his glory:
            The band of Argonauts, and all whose fame
            The poets celebrate in song and story.   7340

CHIRON   Let's not go into that! No teacher's word,
            No, not Athene's wisdom earns their praise;
            They still behave as if they'd never heard,
            And stubbornly pursue their wilful ways.

FAUST	The great physician whose resource and skill	7345
	Finds healing roots and herbs for every ill,	
	Who cures the sick, and soothes their pain and fear –	
	With mind and body I embrace you here!	
CHIRON	I'd help a wounded hero or a friend,	
	And comfort them as only I knew how;	7350
	But then I left my knowledge in the end	
	To priests and witches – they're the healers now.	
FAUST	A man of such humility	
	Is shown in his true greatness, when	
	He modestly pretends to be	7355
	No better than his fellow men.	
CHIRON	You choose your compliments most cleverly;	
	I see you have a gift for flattery.	
FAUST	You will not contradict me when I say	
	You knew the finest heroes of your day –	7360
	A demigod who sought to emulate	
	The noblest enterprises of the great.	
	But say: of all the heroes taught by you,	
	Which was the very worthiest you knew?	
CHIRON	Among the glorious Argonauts, I'd say	7365
	That each was eminent in his own way,	
	And each would use his given talent to	
	Accomplish what another could not do.	
	The Dioscuri would be to the fore	
	Whenever youth and beauty counted more;	7370
	If swift decisive action was required,	
	The selfless Boreades never tired;	
	Beloved of women, shrewd in thought and deed,	
	Astute in counsel, Jason took the lead;	
	When gentle, pensive Orpheus touched his strings,	7375
	He was the lord of all created things;	
	The sacred vessel safely made its way	
	With keen-eyed Lynceus watching night and day.	
	Companionship in danger stands the test;	
	What one achieves, wins praises from the rest.	7380
FAUST	You make no mention of great Hercules?	
CHIRON	Oh, do not wake such memories for me!	
	Apollo, Hermes, Ares – these	

	I never knew, but suddenly	
	I saw what all would recognise	7385
	As godlike, there before my eyes.	
	That splendid youth was born to be	
	A king of men, but loyally	
	He served his brother as his due –	
	And served the loveliest women, too.	7390
	Earth will not bear his like again,	
	Nor Hebe raise to share her throne;	
	Their feeble songs are all in vain,	
	In vain they batter at the stone.	
FAUST	For all their boasts, no sculptor can	7395
	Bring him to life, or truly show	
	The stature of the finest man.	
	What of the finest woman, though?	
CHIRON	A woman's beauty is a pose,	
	Too often just a lifeless face;	7400
	But I reserve my praise for those	
	Whose lives are filled with joy and grace.	
	For beauty is aloof, apart,	
	While grace alone can move the heart –	
	As Helen did the time I bore	7405
	Her on my back.	
FAUST	This very seat!	
	I was confused enough before,	
	But now my rapture is complete!	
CHIRON	She grasped my hair and held it tight,	
	Just as you do.	
FAUST	What sheer delight!	7410
	Oh, I am lost beyond recall;	
	She is my sole desire, my all.	
	But tell me how you carried her, and where.	
CHIRON	It was the time when that intrepid pair,	
	The Dioscuri, set their sister free	7415
	From her abductors. But these men,	
	Who were resolved to capture her again,	
	Pursued them wildly as they tried to flee.	
	Now when they came to Eleusis, they found	
	Their flight was hindered by the swampy ground;	7420

The brothers waded, Helen sat astride
My back, we struggled to the other side.
She stroked my mane, caressed my dripping flanks,
And with sweet words she whispered gracious thanks;
So lovely, young, an old man's joy!

FAUST   And she   7425
Was only ten years old!

CHIRON   Ah, I can see
The scholars with their muddled speculation
Have quite confused you. In mythology,
A woman is the poet's free creation:
Always youthful, ageing never,   7430
Keeping her enticing shape for ever,
Abducted young, still courted in her prime –
The poet cannot be constrained by time.

FAUST   Then no constraint of time shall ever bind her!
Like Achilles on Pherae let me find her,[41]   7435
Beyond all time. What bliss it then would be
To win her love, defying destiny!
Why should my passionate desire not seek
To draw back into life the most unique,
Immortal creature, born to be divine,   7440
In whom proud grandeur and sweet grace combine?
You saw her once; today I saw her too –
Such charm, such beauty as I never knew.
She holds my thoughts, my very self in thrall;
Without her now I cannot live at all.   7445

CHIRON   Such rapture makes a man seem quite estranged;
We spirits, though, would say you are deranged.
But as it happens, you're in luck today;
For every year for just a while I pay
A visit to the Sibyl Manto, daughter   7450
Of Asclepius, who spends her days
Communing with her father as she prays
To him to make the doctors change their ways,
And save the patients from their reckless slaughter.
Of all the Sibyls' guild I like her best,   7455
She's good and kind, not crazy like the rest –
And if you spend some time with her, I'm sure

	Her potions will provide a thorough cure.	
FAUST	I'll not be healed with treatment of that kind,	
	It would demean me: I am sound of mind!	7460
CHIRON	The healing spring is what you need, it seems;	
	Dismount, don't miss your chance, we are quite near.	
FAUST	But will you tell me to what distant shore	
	We've come this haunted night through gravel streams?	
CHIRON	Between Olympus and Peneus – here[42]	7465
	The Greeks and Romans fought their bitter war.	
	The greatest empire sinks into the sands,	
	The people triumph, and the king must flee.	
	Look yonder! Bathed in solemn moonlight, see	
	The place where the eternal temple stands.	7470

MANTO [*dreaming within*] The threshold rings
                    With horses' hooves; what brings
                    These demigods so near?

CHIRON	Indeed!	
	Awake! See who is here!	7475

MANTO [*waking*] Welcome! You have returned, I see.

CHIRON	As long as your temple stands, I will.	
MANTO	Are you still roaming tirelessly?	
CHIRON	Around you all is calm and still,	
	But I prefer to wander free.	7480
MANTO	I sit, while time encircles me.	
	Who's this?	
CHIRON	The wild night's swirling tide	
	Has swept this madman to your side.	
	Helen has set his heart on fire,	
	Helen is his sole desire.	7485
	He's lost, and looking for a guide;	
	He badly needs your help.	
MANTO	I love those best	
	Who make what is impossible their quest.	

CHIRON *is already far away*

MANTO	Be glad, rash lover! This dark gallery	
	Will lead us downwards to Persephone,	7490
	Where in Olympus' hollow caverns hidden	
	She waits for those who seek what is forbidden.	

I smuggled Orpheus down here long ago;
Take heart! Don't waste your chance as he did, though.

[*they descend*

ON THE UPPER PENEUS, *as before*

SIRENS   Plunge into Peneus' flood!   7495
              Splash among the ripples, singing
              Your alluring songs, and bringing
              Joy to this unhappy brood.
              Haste to the Aegean shore!
              Water is our true salvation,   7500
              Join our festive celebration,
              Where all pleasures lie in store.

                            Earthquake

              Foaming waves roll back and force
              The river from its placid course;
              Streams are blocked, the ground is shaking,   7505
              Gravel bed and banks are breaking.
              Come away! This wondrous roar
              Profits no one, let us flee.

              Noble guests, we'll welcome you
              To our pageant by the sea.   7510
              Glittering waves in gentle motion
              Shivering, lap the rocky shore;
              Luna, mirrored in the ocean,
              Bathes us in her sacred dew.
              If you follow us, you'll find   7515
              Fluid forms in rich profusion;
              Here is nothing but confusion –
              Leave this fearful place behind.

SEISMOS [*rumbling and thumping underground*]
              One more effort with your shoulders,
              Shove aside the rocks and boulders!   7520
              That's the way to get up there;
              Let them stop us if they dare.

SPHINXES What a rumbling! What revolting
 Shocks and tremors, horrid jolting!
 All around the earth is quaking, 7525
 Swaying to and fro and shaking,
 What upheaval everywhere!
 Let all hell break loose – we stay
 In our places, come what may.

 Now before our wondering eyes, 7530
 See a vaulted arch arise;
 That same giant, it was he,
 Grizzled, ancient as the earth,
 Who raised Delos from the sea
 For a mother to give birth.[43] 7535
 Now with straining arms he lifts
 Soil and pebbles, clay and boulders
 Like an Atlas on his shoulders,
 Bends his back and heaves, and shifts
 Sand and gravel, grass and sedge 7540
 From our peaceful river's edge,
 And a great abyss he tears
 In our quiet valley's bed,
 Still half-buried in the ground,
 With colossal stonework crowned; 7545
 Caryatid-like he bears
 Fearful loads upon his head.
 But we shall not be disturbed;
 Sphinxes sit here unperturbed.

SEISMOS This is my own unaided making; 7550
 Without my shovelling and shaking,
 You must admit this world would never be
 So beautiful if it were not for me.
 If I'd not thrust your mountains high
 Into the pure and azure sky, 7555
 How could you marvel when you see
 Such grandeur, such sublimity?
 My forbears, Night and Chaos, saw
 Me join the Titans in their furious war.
 Ossa and Pelion like balls we threw 7560

    In youthful madness, till we grew
    So weary of our sport, we ceased to fight
    And impudently set those mountains down
    Upon Parnassus' lofty height,
    So it could wear them as a double crown;   7565
    And now Apollo joins the blessed choir
    Of Muses there, to charm them with his lyre.
    For Jupiter himself I raised the throne
    From which his dreaded thunderbolts are thrown;
    So now I heave myself with all my might   7570
    Up from the very depths towards the light,
    And summon into life a joyful band
    Of creatures who will populate the land.

SPHINXES   If we hadn't seen this mound
    Squeeze itself out of the ground,   7575
    We would be forced to concede
    That it's very old indeed.
    A leafy forest spreads across its face,
    And still the rocks are settling into place.
    But come what may, a Sphinx will not retreat;   7580
    We'll not be shaken from our holy seat.

GRYPHONS   Gold that gleams and gold that glimmers –
       Through the crevices it shimmers;
       Ants, don't let this treasure go –
       Scrape it out, and don't be slow.   7585

CHORUS OF ANTS   Giants have lifted it
       Out of the ground;
       Soon we'll have shifted it –
       Scrabble around!
       Through the cracks in the earth   7590
       Swarming and creeping,
       Every last speck is worth
       Taking and keeping.
       Even the smallest crumb
       Must be collected,   7595
       In every corner some
       Can be detected.
       Dig out what you can find,
       Scurry and scratch about;

	Leave all the dross behind –	7600
	Just get the gold out!	
GRYPHONS	Bring the gold for us to keep!	
	Pile it up in one great heap.	
	Between our claws the richest hoard	
	Is safely and securely stored.	7605
PYGMIES	Here we are and here we stay,	
	How it happened isn't clear;	
	Where we're from we couldn't say –	
	All we know is, we are here.	
	If we like the look of it,	7610
	Any land for us will do;	
	Any rocky cleft or split –	
	You will find a dwarf there too.	
	Male and female, in a trice	
	Working busily together,	7615
	Every pair – we wonder whether	
	It was so in paradise.	
	Still, we like it where we are,	
	So we thank our lucky star.	
	East or west, old Mother Earth	7620
	Gladly brings new life to birth.	
DACTYLS	If in a single night	
	She brought these dwarfs to light,	
	She can also beget	
	Tinier creatures yet.	7625
PYGMY LEADERS	Quick, to your places!	
	Find the best spaces.	
	Strength you don't need –	
	Strength is in speed.	
	Peace still affords	7630
	Time to be busy;	
	Forge in your smithy	
	Arms for our hordes!	
	Soon we'll have war;	
	Ants by the score,	7635
	Dig out the ore!	
	Even the small	
	Dactyls must haul	

Wood for the fire.
Each one in turn   7640
Pile the sticks higher;
We shall require
Charcoal to burn.

GENERALISSIMO   With bows and arrows,
Off to the wars!   7645
Down in the shallows,
Herons in scores,
Lordly and arrogant,
Haughty, extravagant:
Slaughter them there,   7650
Every last one,
So we can wear
The plumes we have won.

ANTS AND DACTYLS   Now who can save us?
Iron we fetch to make   7655
Chains that enslave us.
It is not time to break
Free from our present fate,
So we submit – and wait.

THE CRANES OF IBYCUS[44]

Murderous shouts and deathly cries,   7660
Frantic fluttering of wings!
From below what panic brings
To our ears such groans and sighs?
All have perished in the slaughter,
Red with blood the placid water.   7665
Greedily the crests they tear
From the herons' noble brow;
Paunchy bow-legged villains wear
Plumes upon their helmets now.
Comrades of our migrant band,   7670
Wanderers by sea and land,
For our cousins' sake, all swear
Neither strength nor blood you'll spare
To avenge this sorry deed
And destroy this pygmy breed!   7675

[with raucous cries they scatter into the sky

MEPHISTOPHELES [*in the plain*]

> I handle northern witches as I please,
> But I can't cope with foreign ghosts like these.
> The Brocken's a much better stamping-ground,
> Where you can always find your way around.
> Frau Ilse keeps a look-out from her stone,[45]   7680
> And Heinrich's happy up there on his own,
> The Snorers snorting into Elend's ears –
> There, nothing changes in a thousand years.
> But here you can't be sure; you never know
> What might erupt out of the ground below.   7685
> I'm walking down a smooth and level track
> Along the valley, when behind my back
> A mountain suddenly appears – and how
> Am I to find my friends the Sphinxes now?
> But there are fires still burning all around;   7690
> Who knows what new adventures might be found?
> [*he catches sight of the Lamiae*]
> Alluring shapes that sway as they advance –
> A wicked chorus in a teasing dance.
> Tread softly now! You've had such treats before;
> There's always something that's worth looking for.   7695

LAMIAE [*luring Mephistopheles on*]

> Quickly now, run!
> Quick, come away!
> Then we can stay a while,
> Chatter and play a while.
> It's very pleasing   7700
> Taunting and teasing
> This old roué,
> Leading him on.
> Put him to shame!
> Here he comes, hobbling,   7705
> Stumbling and wobbling –
> One of his feet
> Is frozen and lame;
> Time to retreat!

MEPHISTO. [*stops*] Since Adam men have been traduced,   7710
> Deceived, bamboozled and seduced!

   Old age makes us no wiser – you're
   More stupid than you were before!

  I know they're worthless, with their painted faces,
  Their bodies corseted with stays and laces,   7715
  Unwholesome, too – whichever part you touch,
  That sagging flesh is flaccid to the touch.
  You know, you feel it, see it clear as day –
  But still you dance the tune these bitches play.

LAMIAE [*pausing*] Wait! He's not sure, he can't make up his mind; 7720
  Stay within reach, don't let him lag behind!

MEPHISTO. [*following them*]
  Don't let these doubts discourage you,
  Go on and join their crazy revel –
  For if there were no witches, who
  The hell would want to be a devil?   7725

LAMIAE [*seductively*] Round and round this hero wind!
  Surely in his heart we'll find
  Love for one of us tonight.

MEPHISTO. This uncertain light, it's true,
  Makes you quite a pretty sight;   7730
  I might fancy one of you.

EMPUSA [*intruding*] Why not try your luck with me?
  Let me join the company.

LAMIAE Oh no, not her! This ugly dame
  Always tries to spoil our game.   7735

EMPUSA [*to Mephistopheles*] Empusa greets you with elation!
  I have an ass's foot, my dear –
  So with your horse's hoof, it's clear
  You're really quite a close relation.

MEPHISTO. I thought they were all strangers here, 7740
  But they're my cousins, I can see;
  From Hellas to the Harz, I fear
  We're all just one big family.

EMPUSA I don't believe in standing still,
  I can transform myself at will;   7745
  And so, to honour you today,
  My ass's head is on display.

MEPHISTO. The ties of kith and kin appear

	To mean a lot to people here;	
	But even if they're family,	7750
	The ass's head is not for me.	
LAMIAE	Leave that old hag, she only drives	
	Away our pleasure and delight,	
	And all that's beautiful takes fright	
	And vanishes when she arrives.	7755
MEPHISTO.	These slim and dainty cousins, too –	
	I'd watch your step if I were you;	
	Those rosy cheeks could quickly change	
	Into something very strange.	
LAMIAE	There's lots of us – just have a go	7760
	And try your luck; you never know	
	What hidden charms you might discover.	
	For all your talk and all your leering,	
	All your swaggering and sneering,	
	You are a lamentable lover!	7765
	He's coming now – when he gets near,	
	Take off your masks and let him see	
	Just how attractive we can be.	
MEPHISTO.	I'll take the prettiest one here –	
	[*seizing her*] A skinny broomstick! What a sight!	7770
	[*he seizes another one*]	
	And this one – ugh! She looks a fright!	
LAMIAE	You randy devil – serves you right!	
MEPHISTO.	That little lizard over there,	
	Smooth as a snake, with glossy hair –	
	She's wriggled through my hands! Maybe	7775
	This lanky one will fancy me –	
	I've grabbed a thyrsus wand instead,	
	That's got a pine-cone for a head!	
	Whatever next? This fat one might	
	Arouse my jaded appetite.	7780
	One last try: what a fleshy beast!	
	All squishy, squashy! My, she's loaded!	
	She'd fetch a good price in the East –	
	A puffball! Damn! Now she's exploded.	
LAMIAE	Now scatter, sway and glide around,	7785
	With wings as black as night surround	

This interloping son of hell,
Confuse him with a fearful spell,
Like whispering bats. We'll make him pay
For his adventures here today.   7790

MEPHISTO. [*shaking himself*]

It seems I am no wiser than before;
I find these southern spirits as bizarre
As any of our northern phantoms are,
People and poets rotten to the core.
These masquerades are all the same –   7795
Just some kind of licentious game.
Those lovely masks were a delusion,
Loathsome creatures, horrid, vile;
I'd gladly fall for their illusion
If they weren't quite so volatile.   7800

He wanders among the rocks.

Where am I? How shall I get back?
This used to be a level track,
And now there's just a pile of scree,
A wilderness in front of me.
I scramble up and down – but how   7805
Shall I ever find my Sphinxes now?
A whole new mountain has appeared
In just one night – it's very weird.
The witches here work fast – they've grown
A Blocksberg of their very own.   7810

OREAD [*from the natural rocks*]

Up here! Come, if you want to climb
A mountain that's as old as time.
Respect these steep and rocky banks,
The last of Pindus' spreading flanks.
I stood when Pompey took his flight   7815
Across my never-changing brow;
That phantom vision of the night
Will vanish at the first cock-crow.
I've often seen such fictions rise, and then
They just as quickly disappear again.   7820

MEPHISTO.   I hail the worthy head that's crowned
With noble oak trees all around.

The very brightest moonlight could
Not penetrate this sombre wood.
But in the bushes there I see   7825
A light that glimmers modestly.
What happy chance has guided us –
It is indeed Homunculus!
Well, little man, where are you bound?

HOMUNCULUS I float about and hover round.   7830
I'd like to break the confines of my jar,
So in the truest sense I can exist;
But everything I've seen so far
Has made it all too easy to resist.
Between ourselves, I overheard   7835
These two philosophers, who seemed to be
Discussing nature; Nature! was the word.
And now I mustn't let them go;
They surely know about the world – maybe
They'll finally enable me   7840
To find out what I want to know.

MEPHISTO. Why not do it your own way, though?
Philosophers are only needed when
The place is full of phantoms – then they will
Invent a dozen more to show their skill;   7845
That's how they all impress their fellow men.
You'll make mistakes, but still you should persist;
Your own way's best if you want to exist.

HOMUNCULUS But they might have some good advice for me.

MEPHISTO. Well, off you go and ask them. We shall see.   7850

                                        [they separate

ANAXAGORAS [to Thales]
Will nothing ever change your stubborn mind?
What further reasons do I have to find?

THALES   To wind the wave will offer no resistance,
But from the jagged rock it keeps its distance.

ANAXAGORAS This rock exists through incandescent force.   7855

THALES   Of all life water is the primal source.

HOMUNCULUS [between the two]
Please let me go along with you;
I'm seeking an existence, too.

ANAXAGORAS Have you, O Thales, ever raised a height
                    Like that from mud and slime in just one night?   7860
THALES   We cannot count in days or nights or hours
                    The steady course of nature's living powers.
                    There is no violence; to great and small,
                    Her gentle laws give shape and form to all.
ANAXAGORAS But here there was! Plutonic fire broke through   7865
                    The earth's old crust, a vast explosion blew
                    Aeolian gases high into the air,
                    So that a mountain was created there.
THALES   But what is all this argument about?
                    The mountain's there, that is beyond all doubt.   7870
                    It's just a waste of time, a waste of breath
                    That bores a patient listener to death.
ANAXAGORAS Now all at once the mountain swarms
                    With countless busy little forms;
                    From every crack and fissure pour   7875
                    Ants, dactyls, pygmies by the score.
                    [*to Homunculus*]
                    You've led a sheltered life, it's true,
                    And never aimed for great reward;
                    But if you wish, I'll sponsor you
                    As king of all this tiny horde.   7880
HOMUNCULUS What do you say, my Thales?
THALES   No:
                    From small things only small things grow,
                    But great deeds make the smallest great.
                    Look there! A dark and threatening cloud
                    Of cranes attacks the milling crowd –   7885
                    Their king would also share their fate.
                    With beaks and claws they stab and tear
                    The tiny creatures; from the air
                    Like bolts of lightning doom descends.
                    The peaceful herons in the reeds   7890
                    Were cruelly murdered; for their deeds
                    The pygmies' blood will make amends.
                    The cranes take furious revenge;
                    With ruthless slaughter they avenge
                    Their cousins on those bloody fields.   7895

What use are helmets, spears and shields,
Those waving plumes, the herons' pride?
In vain the ants and dactyls hide –
The pygmies flee, their army yields.

ANAXAGORAS [*after a pause, solemnly*]

Till now the powers below have heard my praise,   7900
But here to those above my voice I raise. –
O ever ageless deity on high,
Threefold in name and shape, I cry
To you to spare my people's agony:
Diana, Luna, Hecate, hear my plea![46]   7905
Opener of hearts, profound and pensive light,
Serenely shining, armed with inner might,
Now show your ancient power, and reveal
The fearful chasms that your shades conceal!
[*pause*]

    Was I too quickly heard?   7910
    Through my cry
    To those on high
    Has nature's order been disturbed?
Now large and ever larger grows the sphere;
The goddess's encircled throne draws near.   7915
A monstrous spectacle of dread!
Its fire darkens, glowing red –
No closer, awful disc! Your fall
Will wipe out land and sea, destroy us all!

So it is true then what the ancients tell: 7920
Thessalian women sang their wicked spell
And drew you down from your predestined course
To work their mischief through your magic force.
The bright orb darkens, now it splits asunder,
It flares and blazes, sparkling, flashing: 7925
What a hissing, what a crashing,
Shrieking wind and roaring thunder!
Before your throne I humbly plead
Forgiveness for my reckless deed.
[*he prostrates himself*]

THALES   The things he thinks he heard and saw!   7930
What happened then, I'm not quite sure –

But it was not how he imagined it.
These are mad times, one must admit,
But Luna's calm and placid face
Still shines down from its normal place.   7935

HOMUNCULUS The pygmies' hill has changed its shape somehow;
The top was rounded, but it's pointed now.
I felt a sudden violent shock —
It was as if a monstrous rock
Fell from the moon, and friend and foe   7940
Were flattened by a single blow.
One must admire such forces, though,
That from above and from below
Created this impressive sight
And made a mountain overnight.   7945

THALES It was imagined, everything!
That horrid brood, it serves them right —
It's just as well you weren't their king.
Come to the pleasant pageant by the shore!
Who knows what sights and wonders lie in store.   7950

[*they move off*

MEPHISTO. [*climbing up the other side*]
Up steep and stony pathways stumbling and tripping,
On roots of ancient oak trees sliding and slipping!
In my own Harz the firs give off a smell
Of resin, just like pitch — I like it well,
And sulphur, too; but here in Greece you find   7955
No whiff of brimstone — so what kind
Of fuel do they use, I'd like to know,
To stoke their fires in Hades down below?

DRYAD In your own land your native wit might do,
But foreign places seem to baffle you.   7960
So put away all thoughts of home; revere
The grove of sacred oaks you've entered here.

MEPHISTO. When we're away from home, we're all inclined
To think we left a paradise behind.
But in the dim light of that cavern there   7965
I see three huddled figures; what are these?

DRYAD The Phorkyads! Approach them if you dare,
And speak to them — but mind, your blood may freeze.

MEPHISTO.   Why not? Oh, what a sight! It takes your breath away!
              I thought I'd seen it all, but I must say   7970
              I've never seen the like of these before –
              They're even worse than mandrakes, that's for sure.
              The vilest sin could never be
              One half as ugly as the three
              In this unwholesome trinity.   7975
              We wouldn't even let them dwell
              In the ghastliest corner of our hell.
              Here in this ancient land of beauty, we
              Can still find relics of antiquity.
              They stir, they sense my presence, pipe and squeak   7980
              Like vampire bats; now they begin to speak.

ONE OF THE PHORKYADS Sisters, give me the eye, so it can see
              Who dares to trespass on our sanctuary.

MEPHISTO.   Permit me, honoured ladies, to draw near;
              To ask your threefold blessing I am here.   7985
              Although we've not been introduced before,
              We share a distant kinship, I am sure.
              I've met such venerable deities
              As Ops and Rhea, worshipped such as these;
              The Fates, sisters to Chaos – and to you –   7990
              A day or two ago I saw them too.
              But creatures such as you I never saw;
              I stand here speechless with delight and awe.

PHORKYADS This spirit seems to talk quite sensibly.

MEPHISTO.   How is it that no poet ever thought   7995
              To sing your praise, no artist ever wrought
              Your noble features for posterity?
              Why carve a Juno, Pallas, Venus too,
              When they could fashion images of you?

PHORKYADS We three sit plunged in solitude, confined   8000
              In night; such thoughts have never crossed our mind.

MEPHISTO.   Of course! You live apart, in your own sphere,
              And no one sees you, you see no one here.
              You should be living in another land,
              Where art and splendour share a common throne,   8005
              Where every day the sculptor's busy hand
              Carves out another hero from the stone,

Where —

PHORKYADS   Hold your tongue, and do not make us long
For what can never be — why tempt us so?
In darkness born, to darkness we belong,   8010
Unknown to all; ourselves we scarcely know.

MEPHISTO.   It can be done, if you find someone who
Is keen to take on your identity.
One eye, one tooth's enough for three of you,
So three could be united into two —   8015
Such things can happen in mythology —
And then the third could lend her shape to me,
Just for a while.

ONE OF THE PHORKYADS   I don't know; shall we try?

THE OTHERS Why not? But we must keep the tooth and eye.

MEPHISTO.   But that deprives me of the best effect!   8020
The image would not be at all correct.

ONE OF THE PHORKYADS It's very simple; all you have to do
Is close an eye and bare a fang, and you
Would have a perfect profile - it would be
As if you were one of the family.   8025

MEPHISTO. How flattering! Let's try it.

PHORKYADS   There! It's done!

MEPHISTO. [as Phorkyas, in profile]
So here I stand — old Chaos' favourite son!

PHORKYADS We're Chaos' daughters, too, beyond a doubt.

MEPHISTO.   I'm a hermaphrodite: I have come out!

PHORKYADS Now what a beautiful new trinity: 8030
Two eyes, two teeth to share between the three!

MEPHISTO.   I'll have to go and hide in hell; this sight
Would give the fiends down there a dreadful fright.

[exit

ROCKY BAYS OF THE AEGEAN SEA

The moon remains at the zenith throughout

SIRENS [grouped on the rocks, playing pipes and singing]
Once Thessalian witches sought you,
With their wicked magic brought you   8035

Down to earth at dead of night;
Bathe us now in peaceful light,
Gently sparkling, softly gleaming
On the ocean's rippling surges,
And illuminate the teeming   8040
Throng that from the waves emerges.
Lovely Luna, turn your face
Upon us, bless us with your grace!

NEREIDS AND TRITONS [*marine prodigies*]

Louder, clearer let your singing
Fill the bay with music, bringing   8045
Creatures of the deep to hear!
Fleeing from the raging ocean,
From the furious storm's commotion,
Your sweet songs have drawn us near.

See with what delight and pleasure   8050
We have harvested your treasure,
Crowns and girdles bright with spangles,
Golden chains and jewelled bangles,
To adorn ourselves today.
Your song lured the ships that shattered   8055
On the reefs, their riches scattered,
Demons of our rocky bay.

SIRENS

Fish live happily, we know,
In the cooling depths below us,
Where they love to glide and play;   8060
For this festive pageant, though,
Teeming shoals of creatures, show us
That you're more than fish today.

NEREIDS AND TRITONS We had that in mind before
We set out for this rocky shore.   8065
Brothers, sisters, let us go;
We shall find, not far away,
Everything we need to show
That we're more than fish today.

[*they swim off*

SIRENS   Over the surf they race,   8070
                 Heading straight for Samothrace,
                 Borne on a following breeze.
                 What mission do they pursue
                 In the realm of the lofty Cabiri? These
                 Are gods so strange and so bizarre,   8075
                 Forever begetting themselves anew,
                 But never knowing what they are.[47]

                 Linger overhead, we pray,
                 Gracious Luna, through the night,
                 For we fade in the light   8080
                 At the dawn of the day!

THALES [*on the shore, to Homunculus*]
                 I'd gladly take you to old Nereus –
                 His cave is just ahead in front of us;
                 But he's a proper misery,
                 As sour and grumpy as can be.   8085
                 There's nothing that all humankind
                 Can do that's right to that old grouch's mind;
                 But since he has the gift to tell
                 The future, he's respected, too.
                 He's done some people good; you would do well 8090
                 To show him deference – he might help you.

HOMUNCULUS No harm in calling on him, anyway –
                 My glass and flame are safe, I'm sure.

NEREUS   Do I hear human voices at my door?
                 That's put me in a bad mood right away.   8095
                 These creatures strive to be like gods, but they
                 Are doomed to be themselves for evermore.
                 I lived at godlike ease for many years,
                 But I could help great men, so I believed,
                 To do great things; and what have they achieved? 8100
                 It's clear my words have fallen on deaf ears.

THALES   But still they trust you, Old Man of the Sea,
                 You are so wise; please don't turn us away!
                 This flame looks human, it is true, but he
                 Needs your advice – he'll do just what you say.   8105

NEREUS   Advice! What human being ever heard

Advice! They never listen to a word.
Whatever dreadful fate might lie in store,
They're still as wilful as they were before.
Did I not warn young Paris when he tried   8110
With eager lust to snare another's bride?
As he stood boldly on the Grecian shore,
I told him of the vision that I saw:
The reeking skies, the rafters blazing red,
The slaughter and the heaps of Trojan dead,   8115
The dreadful story of the city's fall,
Forever set in verse, well known to all.
The shameless youth, inflamed with passion, spurned
An old man's warning words, and Ilium burned –
A huge and rigid corpse whose long ordeal   8120
Gave Pindus' eagles many a welcome meal.
And Ulysses! Did I not warn him, too,
Of Circe's wiles, the Cyclops' rage – but then
All his delays, the folly of his men,
Led them astray, so what good did it do?   8125
Till after years the kindly ocean bore
His battered vessel to a friendly shore.

THALES   It pains a wise man when his words aren't heeded;
A good man, though, gives help when it is needed.
A modicum of thanks will compensate   8130
For such ingratitude, however great.
This young lad seeks your counsel and assistance
To find the best way to a real existence.

NEREUS   Don't try to spoil this rare good mood for me!
I've other things to think about today.   8135
My daughters are all due to come this way –
They are the Dorids, Graces of the sea.
Upon Olympus' heights, upon your earth
Such dainty beauty never came to birth.
From the sea-dragons' scaly backs they leap   8140
To Neptune's horses with such graceful motion,
So tenderly united with the ocean
They seem to ride the foam across the deep.
On Aphrodite's opalescent shell
They carry fairest Galatea, for   8145

Since Venus went from us, she came to dwell
In Paphos as the goddess we adore;[48]
And so the lovely nymph claims as her own
The sacred temple and the scallop throne.

Away! No hateful words or thoughts should sour   8150
A father's joy at such a magic hour.
Ask Proteus; that mystery man will know
How to be born and be transformed. Now go!
                    [*he moves off towards the sea*

THALES   We've made no progress; even if we find
Old Proteus, he simply melts away.   8155
And if we found him, what he'd have to say
Would make no sense and just confuse your mind.
Still, that sort of advice is what you need;
Let's try this way – who knows where it might lead?
                    [*they move off*

SIRENS [*on the cliffs above*] What is it we see riding   8160
                    The waves in graceful motion,
                    As if the breeze were guiding
                    White sails across the ocean? –
                    The sea's transfigured daughters,
                    That shine upon the waters.   8165
                    Climb down! The bay is ringing
                    With their triumphant singing.

NEREIDS AND TRITONS We bring a precious treasure
                    For your delight and pleasure;
                    Chelone's shell[49] now bears   8170
                    Resplendent shapes: austere
                    High gods we should revere
                    With songs and solemn prayers.

SIRENS   Of stature slight,
                    But great in might,   8175
                    Rescuing those they can,
                    Worshipped since time began.

NEREIDS AND TRITONS The great Cabiri's powers
                    Will bless our festive hours;
                    For Neptune smiles when these   8180
                    Preside upon the seas.

SIRENS   We give you your due:
                       Undaunted you save
                       The shipwrecked crew
                       From the threatening wave.   8185

NEREIDS AND TRITONS We only brought the three;
                       The other wouldn't come, you see.
                       He said he was the best of them,
                       Who thought for all the rest of them.

SIRENS   One god can ridicule   8190
                       Another god; but as a rule
                       You should revere them,
                       Honour and fear them.

NEREIDS AND TRITONS Seven there should be.

SIRENS   Where are the other three?   8195

NEREIDS AND TRITONS That we couldn't swear to;
                       Ask on Olympus – they should know.
                       The eighth one might be there, too –
                       No one's thought of him, though.
                       Creatures of good will,   8200
                       But all imperfect still,
                       These beings are unique,
                       Their striving unrestrained;
                       Yearning, hungering, they seek
                       What cannot be attained.   8205

SIRENS   We also pray
                       To sun or to moon,
                       At midnight or noon –
                       It's sure to pay.

NEREIDS AND TRITONS We lead this festival; our fame   8210
                       Will surely shine more clearly!

SIRENS   The heroes of Greece
                       Are put to shame,
                       Your fame will shine more clearly;
                       They brought home the Golden Fleece,   8215
                       But you brought the Cabiri!

[repeat, in chorus]   They brought home the Golden Fleece,
                       ⎰We ⎱ brought the Cabiri!
                       ⎱You⎰

                                          [the Nereids and Tritons move on

HOMUNCULUS They look to me like pots of clay,
     Misshapen, crude, and battered;   8220
     Now scholars rack their brains all day
     Until their wits are scattered.
THALES That's what they value most: a coin that's just
     Been dug up, with a coat of grime and rust.
PROTEUS [*unseen*] I like a yarn myself – the more bizarre 8225
     And strange, the more acceptable they are.
THALES Where are you, Proteus?
PROTEUS [*like a ventriloquist, first close, then distant*]
         Here! And there!
THALES Up to your tricks again, old friend, I see.
     But I don't mind, you can't bamboozle me;
     I know that you can speak from anywhere. 8230
PROTEUS [*from far away*] Goodbye!
THALES [*sotto voce to Homunculus*] He's very close. Now shine your light!
     He's curious as a fish; if he comes near
     A flame, he can't resist the sight.
     Whatever shape he's in, he will appear.
HOMUNCULUS I'll start to shine, but modestly; I fear 8235
     My glass will shatter if it gets too bright.
PROTEUS [*in the form of a giant turtle*]
     What's that with such a lovely glow?
THALES [*covering up Homunculus*]
     Well, come and see it if you want to know.
     And if you take the trouble to appear
     On two feet in a human shape, then we 8240
     Will willingly consent to let you see
     Just what it is that we have hidden here.
PROTEUS [*appearing in a noble form*]
     I see you can still play a trick or two.
THALES And changing shape – that still appeals to you.
     [*he uncovers Homunculus*]
PROTEUS [*amazed*] A luminescent dwarf! Now what on earth – 8245
THALES He wants you to advise him if you can.
     It's most peculiar; he says his birth
     Was incomplete – he's only half a man.
     He has a mind of great lucidity,
     But lacks the physical solidity.   8250

He has this glass instead of flesh and bone,
But now he wants a body of his own.

PROTEUS You really are a spinster's son:
You came before you should have done.

THALES [*sotto voce*] There's something else that's not quite right – 8255
I think he's a hermaphrodite.

PROTEUS That means he'll have a better chance;
He can adapt to any circumstance.
The answer's obvious, it seems to me –
You'll have to start your new life in the sea. 8260
At first you live with smaller fry,
Which you devour, and by and by
You grow and grow, and then with due persistence
You reach a higher level of existence.

HOMUNCULUS I like this gentle breeze, it has a smell 8265
So fresh and green; it suits me very well.

PROTEUS I can believe it, dearest boy!
And further out there's far more to enjoy.
Upon that spit of sand the atmosphere
Is infinitely pleasanter than here. 8270
Here comes the great marine procession –
From there we'll have a closer view.
Come on with me!

THALES   I'm coming too.

HOMUNCULUS Triply momentous spiritual progression!

TELCHINES *from Rhodes*[50]
on sea-horses and sea-dragons, carrying Neptune's trident

CHORUS OF TELCHINES

We fashioned this trident with skill and devotion 8275
For Neptune to calm the rebellious ocean.
When Zeus rips the gathering storm clouds asunder,
Poseidon responds to the roars of his thunder,
And when from the heavens the lightning is flashing,
The billows below he sets foaming and crashing; 8280
The raging abyss of the deep will devour
All those who are caught in their furious power.
He lends us his sceptre today, so the breeze
Will carry us lightly on untroubled seas.

SIRENS   Votaries of Helios, you who   8285
                Worship his diurnal light,
                Priests of day, we welcome you to
                Luna's festival tonight.

TELCHINES   O loveliest goddess enthroned on your height,
            The praise of your brother you hear with delight.   8290
            On Rhodes' blessed island a chorus of voices
            United in hymns to Apollo rejoices.
            Each day on his fiery course through the sky
            He gazes upon us with radiant eye.
            The god looks with pleasure on all he surveys,   8295
            The mountains, the cities, the sea and the bays.
            No layer of mist can obscure what he sees;
            It melts in his rays, swept away by the breeze.
            In countless creations his image we raise,
            As youth, as colossus; we honour and praise   8300
            His greatness, his mildness, for we first began
            To shape the divine in the likeness of man.

PROTEUS   Just let them boast – they always do!
                Such lifeless works mean nothing to
                The sacred radiance of the sun.   8305
                They carve and mould and forge, and when
                They've cast a form in bronze, why then
                They're mighty pleased with what they've done.
                But their achievements are in vain;
                The gods that once stood proud and tall,   8310
                An earthquake has destroyed them all –
                They've long been melted down again.

                On land there's nothing but commotion,
                There's only strife and misery.
                But life can flourish in the ocean;   8315
                You would do best to come with me.
                Just let old Proteus be your guide,
                [*he transforms himself into a dolphin*]
                And all will turn out happily;
                Upon a dolphin's back you'll ride
                Towards your marriage with the sea!   8320

THALES   Give way to laudable temptation!
            Start at the source of all creation,

Be swift to follow nature's plan;
Progressing through a myriad forms
According to eternal norms –   8325
In time you could become a man.

Homunculus mounts the dolphin Proteus

PROTEUS   Now let your spirit merge with me
Into the vast and liquid sea,
And roam at will; but as you do,
Don't strive to reach a higher state.   8330
Once you become a man, your fate
Is sealed, and that's the end of you.
THALES   That all depends; a certain fame
In one's own day and age is no great shame.
PROTEUS [*to Thales*] Someone like you, you mean to say?   8335
You've lasted well enough, it's true –
Because for centuries I've noticed you
Among the pallid ghosts that come this way.

SIRENS [*on the cliffs*] See how flocks of clouds are forming
Round the moon in shining rings: 8340
Birds inflamed with passion, swarming
White as light on gleaming wings.
Ardent doves from Paphos, Grecian
Aphrodite's envoys here,
Mark our festival's completion: 8345
Joy and rapture, full and clear!

NEREUS [*joining Thales*] To a traveller in the night
Such a halo would be merely
Mist and haze, a play of light.
But we spirits see more clearly: 8350
They are doves in congregation
Round my daughter's scallop throne;
In mysterious migration
Thus for ages they have flown.
THALES   It's the best thing we can do,   8355
If within our hearts we treasure
Something sacred, something true –
That can give a good man pleasure.

PSYLLI AND MARSI [*on marine bulls, calves and rams*]⁵¹

    In rugged Cyprian caves below,
    Where Neptune cannot wake us   8360
    And Seismos cannot shake us,
    Where timeless breezes blow,
    In peaceful contentment we've hidden,
    And as in the days long ago
    We've guarded the chariot of Venus.   8365
    No new generation has seen us;
    Through the rippling weft of the waters
    In the whispering nights we have ridden
    To bring you the loveliest of daughters.
    No worldly dominions or powers   8370
    Can disturb our industrious hours;
    Undeterred by the menace
    Of wars ever-present,
    The struggles incessant
    Of cross or of crescent,   8375
    Roman eagle or lion of Venice –
    With tireless devotion
    We bring you the loveliest mistress of ocean.

SIRENS
    Lightly round the chariot riding,
    Circling with unruffled haste,   8380
    Now in coiling patterns gliding,
    Sinuously interlaced,
    Nimble Nereids, come near,
    Lusty women, lithe and wild,
    Gentle Dorids, bring us here   8385
    Galatea, your mother's child.
    Grave and godlike every feature,
    Blessed with immortality –
    Yet the fairest human creature
    Is not lovelier than she.   8390

DORIDS [*in chorus, riding on dolphins past Nereus*]
    Radiant light and shady cover
    Lend us, Luna, shining clear;
    Each has brought a youthful lover
    For our father's blessing here.
[*to Nereus*] Young lads, rescued from the dreaded   8395

	Breakers of the ocean's maw,	
	Then on moss and rushes bedded,	
	Warmed to light and life once more.	
	Now to kisses sweet and tender	
	They must willingly surrender;	8400
	Greet them kindly, we implore!	
NEREUS	You profit twice from your recovered treasure:	
	You show compassion and enjoy your pleasure.	
DORIDS	If you favour our endeavour,	
	Father, you will grant us this:	8405
	To embrace these lads, forever	
	Youthful in eternal bliss.	
NEREUS	Enjoy your catches while you can,	
	And teach each youth to be a man;	
	But I could never give to you	8410
	What only mighty Zeus can do.	
	The flowing wave's your element,	
	Where even love cannot endure,	
	So soon your passion will be spent;	
	Then guide them gently back to shore.	8415
DORIDS	Dear lads, we have grown so fond of you,	
	But alas, we must let you go;	
	We wished that we could be forever true –	
	The gods will not let it be so.	
THE YOUNG MEN	It's a sailor lad's idea of bliss,	8420
	Your tender loving care;	
	We've never had it as good as this –	
	And it couldn't get better, we swear.	

GALATEA *approaches in her scallop-shell chariot.*

NEREUS	Beloved, you're here!	
GALATEA	It's my father! He calls me!	
	Stay, dolphins! The joy of this moment enthralls me!	8425
NEREUS	Already they're gone and lost from view,	
	In wide-swept circles wheeling.	
	They spare no thought for my heart's inmost feeling;	
	How I wish they would take me too!	
	And yet one single glance will do	8430
	To comfort me the whole year through.	

THALES   Hail! And hail again!
          My joy flows unrestrained,
          For truth and beauty are made plain:
          In water all things have their source,   8435
          By water all things are sustained,
          The ocean eternally governs their course.
          Without the clouds it sends us,
          The gushing springs it lends us,
          The flowing streams converging,   8440
          To mighty rivers merging,
          The plains and the mountains, the earth could not be.
          The freshness of life is sustained by the sea!

ECHO [*the whole company in chorus*]
          The freshness of life has its source in the sea.

NEREUS   Far off they wheel and turn again,   8445
          The eye no longer sees them plain.
          In widening circles gliding,
          In winding columns riding,
          The festive company sweeps along.
          But now, and now again, I see   8450
          The scallop shell of Galatea;
          It shines like a star
          Among the throng.
          My beloved daughter shines for me!
          And though so far,   8455
          Glistens bright and clear,
          Forever true, forever near.

HOMUNCULUS   This scene my light's revealing –
              So moist and so appealing,
              Such beauty all around!   8460

PROTEUS   This moistness, life-creating,
              Will set your light pulsating
              With such a splendid sound.

NEREUS   What new revelation amidst the commotion
          Appears to our eyes from afar on the ocean?   8465
          Around Galatea's shell chariot what's burning,
          Now tenderly glowing, now blazing with yearning,
          As if driven on by the pulse of desire?

THALES   It's Homunculus! Proteus has kindled his fire.

I sense the imperious longing that cries 8470
In this anguish of passion, these groans and these sighs.
His glass will be smashed on the glittering shell;
A torrent of flame pours out into the swell.

SIRENS What fiery wonder transfigures the waves,
And sets all the crests of the breakers ablaze? 8475
It flickers and flashes, and bathes in its light
The bodies that glow as they ride through the night,
And all is aflame in a vast conflagration;
All hail then to Eros, the lord of creation!
Hail to the waves, the surging tide, 8480
By this fire sanctified!
Hail to fire! Hail the sea!
Hail this sacred mystery!

CHORUS [*tutti*] Hail the winds that softly blow!
Secret caverns deep below! 8485
To you all our hymns be raised:
All four elements be praised!

ACT THREE

BEFORE THE PALACE OF MENELAUS IN SPARTA

Enter HELEN *and a chorus of captive Trojan women.*
PANTHALIS *leads the chorus.*

HELEN

So much admired, so much reviled, I, Helen, come
From that same strand where only now we
                                        stepped ashore,
Still swaying with the unsteady rocking of the waves   8490
That bore us on their swelling crests from Phrygia's
                                        plain
By Euros' strength[52] and by Poseidon's grace, at last
To safety in the shelter of our native bays.
Down there King Menelaus and his bravest men,
Rejoicing, celebrate the warriors' safe return.   8495
But I would crave a welcome from this noble house
My father Tyndareus built among the hills
When he returned home from Athene's sacred mount;
No house in Sparta was so splendidly adorned.
I grew up with my sister Clytemnestra here,   8500
With Castor and with Pollux played our happy games.
My greetings to you, double doors of massive bronze!
One day these hospitable gates, flung open wide,
Received a suitor, chosen from so many men,
When glorious Menelaus claimed me as his bride.   8505
Now open once again, that as a loyal wife
I may fulfil the urgent orders of the king.
Let me come in, and let me leave behind the storms
Of fate that hitherto have raged about my head.
For since I left this threshold free of care to do   8510
My sacred duty at the shrine of Cythera,

But where the Phrygian pirate ravished me, since then
So much has happened that so many far and wide
Have loved to tell, but cannot please the ear of one
Whose story was spun out into fantastic tales.   8515

CHORUS   O splendid woman, do not disdain
                The highest gift that honour bestows!
                For the greatest fortune is granted to you:
                The fame of beauty, surpassing all else.
                The hero's name rings proud in his ears,   8520
                And proudly he walks;
                But even the most unyielding of men
                Will submit to beauty's all-conquering might.

HELEN   Enough! I sailed together with my husband here,
            And to his city now he sends me on ahead;   8525
            But what he may intend for me I cannot say.
            Do I come as a wife? Do I come as a queen?
            Or as a sacrifice for all his bitter hurt,
            And for the long-endured misfortunes of the Greeks?
            I am his conquest; but his captive, too, perhaps!   8530
            For fate and reputation, beauty's ominous
            Companions, the immortals have decreed for me
            Obscurely; at this very threshold here they stand,
            A menacing and gloomy presence at my side.
            When we were in the hollow ship my husband
                                                looked   8535
            At me but rarely, and he spoke no word of cheer;
            As if he brooded mischief, there he sat in thought.
            But when we sailed into Eurotas' deep-cleft bays,
            The leading vessels' prows had scarcely kissed
                                                the shore,
            It was as if a god had prompted him to speak: 8540
            'My warriors shall disembark in order here;
            I will review their ranks drawn up along the shore.
            But you shall go ahead, and make your way along
            Eurotas' sacred banks among the fruitful groves,
            And lead your horses through the meadows lush
                                                and bright   8545
            With flowers until you reach the lovely Spartan plain,

Where Lacedaemon, once a broad and fertile field,
Was built among the stern and close-encircling hills.
And entering the lofty-towered royal house,
Assemble all the serving-maids I left behind,   8550
Together with the wise and aged stewardess,
And bid her show you that rich store of treasure which,
Bequeathed by your own father, I myself have made
Far richer still with all the spoils of peace and war.
You will find everything in proper order, for   8555
It is the ruler's privilege, when he returns
To his own home, that he should find that all is still
In its appointed place just as he left it there.
These things no servant has authority to change.'

CHORUS   Now let this treasure, ever-increased,   8560
                Regale your eyes and gladden your heart!
                For those burnished chains, those glittering crowns,
                They lie there idly with insolent pride;
                But if you boldly challenge their worth,
                Then they will take arms.   8565
                I love to see beauty measure its might
                Against gold and pearls and the richest of gems.

HELEN   And as my lord spoke further, he commanded me:
          'When you have made account and ordered everything,
          Then take such instruments you think will be required 8570
          For sacrifice, the tripods and the vessels, that
          The sacred ritual may properly proceed.
          And take the bellied pots, the bowls, the shallow dish;
          The tallest jars shall hold the purest water from
          The sacred spring, and further hold in readiness   8575
          The driest wood that quickly feeds the hungry flames.
          Above all, do not fail to take a keen-edged knife;
          What else may be required, I leave to your good care.'
          These words he spoke, and pressed me to depart;
                                                      but still
          His careful plans made mention of no living thing   8580
          For sacrifice to honour the Olympian gods.
          This troubles me; but I will put it from my thoughts,
          And let the gods on high dispose these things as they

Are minded to accomplish them. It matters not
That men may count their purposes as evil or   8585
As good; that is the lot as mortals we must bear.
There have been times the consecrated axe was raised
Above the tethered victim's head, when all at once
An enemy or else a god has intervened
To stay the consummation of the sacrifice.   8590

CHORUS
What the future holds, you cannot divine;
Majesty, go your way,
Bold of heart!
Good and evil come
Unforeseen; even if we   8595
Are forewarned, we do not believe.
Troy was ablaze, and did we not see
Death all round, ignominious death?
And are we not here,
At your side, glad to serve you,   8600
Under the radiant sun in the heavens,
With the fairest of creatures,
Gracious fount of our happiness?

HELEN
Then come what may; whatever lies in store, I must
Go up without delay into the royal house,   8605
So sorely missed, so longed for and so nearly lost,
That stands, I know not how, before my eyes once
                                                                more.
Less boldly, though, my feet will carry me than when
With childish leaps I lightly climbed these lofty steps.
                                                        [*exit*

CHORUS
Sisters, who suffered in   8610
Dismal captivity,
Cast aside all your troubles.
Share the queen's happiness,
Share Helen's happiness,
Who to her father's house and hearth   8615
Has returned; with belated but
All the more sure and resolute
Steps she joyfully enters.

Praise to the holy gods,
For they protect us and   8620
Lead us homewards to safety.
Those set at liberty
Soar as on wings aloft
Over the roughest paths, while those
Who are languishing still must grieve,   8625
Yearning and reaching with outstretched arms
From the towers that hold them.

But a god delivered her
From her exile;
From the ruins of Troy   8630
Seized her and carried her back
To her ancestors' newly furbished,
Ancient house.
After sorrows and
Joys beyond telling,   8635
Days of youth recalled
To new life will restore her.

PANTHALIS [as leader of the Chorus]

I beg you, sisters, leave the joyous path of song
And turn your eyes towards the portals of the house!
What is this that I see? Does not the queen return   8640
Distraught, with agitation in her hasty steps?
Great queen, what terrible encounter could it be
That so disturbed you when you stepped inside
                                        your house,
Expecting loyal greetings? For you cannot hide
The horror and revulsion written on your brow,   8645
Where noble anger struggles with astonishment.

HELEN [who has left the doors open, speaks with agitation]

Base fear does not become the daughter of great Zeus,
She is not touched by panic's light and fleeting hand;
But horror that emerges from the primal womb
Of ancient night, that in a myriad shapes rolls forth 8650
Like glowing clouds that billow from the fiery pit,
Strikes dread and terror even in a hero's heart.
Today the Stygian powers have set so hideous

A mark upon the threshold of the house that I
Would gladly, like a guest departing, shun these steps   8655
My feet so often trod, for which I yearned so long.
But no! You powers that drove me back into the light,
Whoever you may be, I shall retreat no more.
Through consecration I will purify the hearth,
Whose warmth shall welcome back the master
                                                and his wife.   8660

PANTHALIS It is our honour to support you, noble queen;
Reveal to your devoted servants what you saw.

HELEN   Your eyes shall witness for themselves that fearful shape,
Unless primaeval night has swallowed it again
To hide it in the depths of its prodigious womb.   8665
But I will tell you what I saw in my own words:
As, mindful of my duty and with solemn tread
I stepped into the courtyard of the royal house,
I wondered at the silence of the empty halls.
No sound of swift and busy footsteps reached my ears,   8670
Nor did I see the household hurrying to their tasks;
No maid, no stewardess appeared to offer me
The friendly greetings every stranger used to hear.
But then as I approached more closely to the hearth,
The cooling embers cast their dying glow upon   8675
A woman, tall and veiled, who sat beside the fire,
Not sleeping, so it seemed, but musing deep in thought.
I ordered her to be about her household tasks,
Assuming her to be the stewardess who had
Been left in charge before my husband went away,   8680
But still the shrouded figure sat there motionless.
At last, in answer to my threats, she raised her arm,
As if she would dismiss me from my hearth and home.
I turned away in anger, and I strode towards
The staircase leading to the richly-furnished rooms,   8685
The bridal chamber and, nearby, the treasure-house.
At once the apparition scrambled to its feet,
Imperiously it barred the way and showed itself:
A tall and haggard form, with sunken bloodshot look,
So strange that it confused the eye, disturbed the mind.   8690
But all my words are wasted, and I speak in vain,

For words cannot construct or re-create such forms.
Now there she is! She ventures out into the light!
But we rule here, until our royal master comes.
The beauty-loving Phoebus drives the horrid spawn   8695
Of night back to their caves, they must submit to·him.

PHORKYAS *appears at the threshold between the doorposts.*

CHORUS   Much have I seen, although the dark ringlets
Youthfully tumble over my temples!
Many the dreadful things I have witnessed,
Horrors of war, and Ilium's night   8700
When it fell.

Through all the dust-filled clouds of advancing
Warriors I heard the gods as their fearful
Voices were calling, heard as the conflict
Raged and the brazen shouts as they rang   8705
From the walls.

Still the ramparts of Troy stood fast;
But already the blazing flames,
Swiftly leaping from house to house,
Spread destruction at dead of night   8710
Through the city here and there,
Fanned by the blast of the fire-storm.

As I fled through the fire and smoke,
Through the swirling of flames I saw
Angry gods in their awful rage,   8715
Wondrous figures of giant shape,
Striding through the reeking dark,
Lit by the glow of the raging fire.

Did I see these things, or did
Panic fear create in my mind   8720
Such a confusion? I cannot say;
But I know for sure that this
Hideous shape before my eyes –
This I can see for certain.
Could I not touch it with my hands,   8725
If the fear of its threatening
Menace did not repel me?

Which one are you of
Phorkys's daughters?
For I can see you are   8730
One of these creatures.
Are you perhaps a sibling of the
Grey-born sisters who share in turn
One sole eye and one sole tooth:
Are you one of the Graiae?   8735

Monster, how dare you
Stand before beauty?
Phoebus' discerning eye
Would be offended.
Still, come out if you will; Apollo   8740
Sees no ugliness such as yours,
For his sacred eye sees not
What is hidden in shadow.

But we mortals, alas, must yield
To our sorrowful fate; our eyes   8745
Have to endure the unspeakable pain
Lovers of beauty must feel at the sight of so
Vile and loathsome a shape as this.

Hear us, then, as you bar our way
With such insolence, hear our curse,   8750
Our anathema, hear the scorn
Menacing you from the mouths of the fortunate
Fashioned by the eternal gods.

PHORKYAS   An ancient saying, but it holds a lasting truth:
           That modesty and beauty never have been known   8755
           To walk the earth's green path together hand in hand.
           For deep within them both an ancient hatred dwells,
           And should they ever meet along the way, the one
           Will always turn its back upon its enemy;
           Then each will hurry on unheeding, modesty   8760
           Downcast and blushing, beauty insolent and bold,
           Until the yawning night of Orcus swallows it,
           Unless old age long since has tamed its sullen pride.
           Now here I find you brazen creatures pouring in

From foreign parts, so bold and shameless, like a flock   8765
Of noisy cranes that sweep with hoarse and croaking
                                                    cries
In trailing clouds above our heads, a raucous sound
That makes the silent traveller look up to watch
Their passage; but they go their way across the sky,
While he goes his – and so it soon shall be with us.   8770

Who are you, then, to storm about the royal house
Like frenzied Maenads, as if you were flown with wine?
Who are you that you rail against the stewardess,
Like dogs that vent their fury howling at the moon?
You think I do not know the race from which you
                                                sprang,   8775
You war-begotten, battle-nurtured youthful brood?
Man-hungry all of you, seducing and seduced,
Enfeebling warriors and citizens alike.
To see you flock together is to see a swarm
Of locusts settle on a field of tender crops.   8780
You parasites who feed from others' toil! You browse
The growing shoots, destroy the land's prosperity!
You spoils of war, you peddled wares, you bartered
                                                goods!

HELEN   To scold the servants in the presence of the queen
Is to impugn the mistress's authority;   8785
Hers is the right alone to praise what merits praise,
And hers to punish what is reprehensible.
But I am well content with all the services
They rendered to me when the might of Ilium
Was under siege, and when the city fell; no less,   8790
When we endured together all the suffering
Of that long voyage, still they served me selflessly.
Here too, I hope, these lively girls will do the same;
A servant's judged by what he does, not who he is.
So hold your tongue and cease your sneers and
                                                mockery.   8795
If in the absence of the mistress you have kept
The royal house in proper order, praise is due;
But now she has returned, and you must stand aside,
Or else expect reproof instead of well-earned thanks.

PHORKYAS	To chide the household servants is a privilege	8800
	The noble consort of a heaven-blessed ruler earns	
	By dint of many years of prudent governance;	
	I here acknowledge you as mistress and as queen.	
	Since you have once again assumed your former place,	
	Now seize the reins that have so long hung slack,	
	and rule:	8805
	Take up the treasure which, like all of us, is yours.	
	But most of all protect me, aged as I am,	
	From this loud rabble, who beside your swan-like grace	
	Are nothing but a shabby flock of cackling geese.	
PANTHALIS	How hideous next to beauty is such ugliness.	8810
PHORKYAS	How foolish next to wisdom is such ignorance.	

The members of the Chorus step forward and reply one by one.

CHORUS 1	Speak of your father Erebus, your mother Night.	
PHORKYAS	Speak of your sister Scylla, your true flesh and blood.	
CHORUS 2	How many monsters are there in your pedigree!	
PHORKYAS	Go down to Hades if you wish to find your kin.	8815
CHORUS 3	Down there is no one who is half as old as you.	
PHORKYAS	Try your seductive wiles on old Tiresias.	
CHORUS 4	Orion's nursemaid surely was your grandson's child.	
PHORKYAS	The Harpies must have raised and nurtured you in filth.	
CHORUS 5	What food sustains a figure so cadaverous?	8820
PHORKYAS	Well, not the blood that whets your lustful appetites.	
CHORUS 6	You crave the flesh of corpses, loathsome corpse yourself.	
PHORKYAS	Your shameless mouth reveals the flash of vampire's teeth.	
CHORUS 7	It would close yours if I should tell you who you are.	
PHORKYAS	Then first tell me your name; the riddle will be	
	solved.	8825
HELEN	In sorrow, not in anger, I must intervene	
	To put a stop to this exchange of wild abuse!	
	There's nothing hurts the master of a household more	
	Than loyal servants falling out among themselves,	
	For then his orders find no echo, no accord	8830
	That his instructions will be swiftly carried out,	
	Instead he hears a raging storm of stubborn wills;	
	Distraught, he may rebuke them, but to no avail.	
	Not only that; in your unseemly quarrel you	
	Have conjured up such dismal images of dread	8835

That crowd into my mind and seem to drag me down
To Orcus, though I stand among the fields of home.
Do I remember, or do I delude myself?
Was I all this? And am I? Shall I always be
That nightmare spectre who brings ruin to the towns?   8840
My women shudder, only you, the oldest, stand
Unmoved; I turn to you for words of wise advice.

PHORKYAS   To those on whom good fortune smiles for many years,
The highest favours of the gods seem but a dream.
But you, extravagantly favoured as you were,   8845
Your whole life long saw only men inflamed with love,
And all on fire for reckless deeds of every kind.
The lustful Theseus was first to ravish you,
A man of splendid stature, strong as Hercules.

HELEN   He took me as a slender fawn, just ten years old,   8850
And held me in Aphidnus' fort in Attica.

PHORKYAS   But Castor soon with Pollux liberated you,
And all the noblest heroes vied to win your hand.

HELEN   I will confess quite freely that Patroclus was
My secret choice, Achilles' friend and counterpart.   8855

PHORKYAS   But then, according to your father's wish, you wed
Seafaring Menelaus, guardian of this house.

HELEN   To him he gave his daughter and his kingdom too,
And from that union Hermione was born.

PHORKYAS   But while he claimed his heritage in distant Crete,   8860
His lonely wife received an all too handsome guest.

HELEN   Why must you now recall that semi-widowhood,
And the appalling ruin that it brought on me?

PHORKYAS   I am a free-born Cretan; but that voyage led
To my captivity, long years of slavery.   8865

HELEN   He brought you here as stewardess, entrusted you
With many things: the house, the treasure boldly won.

PHORKYAS   Which you relinquished for the towers of Ilium,
And all the inexhaustible delights of love.

HELEN   Do not speak of delights! My heart and head were
filled   8870
With an infinitude of all too bitter grief.

PHORKYAS   But it is said that you appeared in double shape,
That you were seen in Egypt and in Ilium.[53]

HELEN	Do not add more confusion to my muddled wits,	
	For even now I am not certain which I am.	8875
PHORKYAS	They say that from the shadows of the underworld	
	Impassioned Achilles returned to be with you,	
	For he had loved you once, defying fate's decree.[54]	
HELEN	I was a phantom, with his phantom I was joined;	
	It was a dream, the very words must tell you so.	8880
	I swoon; I have become a phantom to myself.	

[*she sinks into the arms of the semichorus*]

CHORUS   Silence! Silence!
            Ill-favoured of face, evil of tongue!
            From those single-toothed, odious
            Lips, what stench of vileness   8885
            Breathes from such a disgusting maw!

            For such malevolence, that poses as kindness,
            Wolfish rage in a sheep's woollen fleece,
            Terrifies me more than the jaws of the
            Three-headed hound of Hades.   8890
            Fearfully we wait to hear
            When, how, where it will break out,
            Monstrous malice,
            Lurking there in the depths of spite.

            Why now, instead of kind words that bring
                                           comfort,   8895
            Words that help to forget, words that console,
            Drag from the past all that is sorrowful,
            Nothing of good, but evil,
            Overshadowing the light
            Of her present happiness   8900
            And the future's
            Gently glimmering ray of hope?

            Silence! Silence!
            Let the spirit of Helen,
            Ready to vanish away,   8905
            Still hold fast and not leave us,
            For the sun never has seen a
            Lovelier form, surpassing all forms.

HELEN *has recovered and again takes the centre of the stage.*

PHORKYAS	Out of fleeting clouds appearing,
	noble sun of this our day,
	If when veiled you were entrancing,
	now you reign in dazzling light. 8910
	See, the world beneath unfolds its
	glory to your gracious gaze;
	Though I am reviled as ugly,
	I know well where beauty lies.
HELEN	With unsteady steps emerging
	from the darkness of my swoon,
	I would gladly rest awhile, so
	heavy are my weary limbs;
	But for rulers it is fitting,
	as indeed it is for all, 8915
	To stand firm and with composure
	face whatever threat may rise.
PHORKYAS	Now before us in your greatness,
	in your beauty now you stand;
	Regally your eye compels us;
	tell us, what is your command?
HELEN	Do the duty that your quarrel
	shamelessly so long delayed;
	Hurry, as the king has ordered,
	to prepare the sacrifice. 8920
PHORKYAS	All is ready in the palace,
	bowl and tripod, sharpened blade,
	Water, incense; you must tell us
	what the offering shall be.
HELEN	But the king gave no instructions.
PHORKYAS	He did not? Oh, misery!
HELEN	What is this dismay that grips you?
PHORKYAS	Queen, that offering is you!
HELEN	I?
PHORKYAS	And these.
CHORUS	And us? Oh, pity!
PHORKYAS	You shall fall beneath the axe. 8925
HELEN	Horror! But not unexpected.
PHORKYAS	There is no escape, I fear.

CHORUS	What of us? What is to happen?
PHORKYAS	She will die a noble death;

You will dangle from the rafters
        that support the gabled roof,
Strung up in a row like thrushes
        twitching in the hunter's snare.

HELEN *and the* CHORUS *stand, shocked and fearful,*
in a striking, carefully arranged group.

PHORKYAS   You spectres! Petrified, like statues there you stand,   8930
Afraid to leave a life on which you have no claim.
For mortals, phantoms all like you, will always be
Reluctant to forsake the glorious light of day.
No plea, no help can save them from the bitter end;
Though all may know it, few are glad to take
        their leave.   8935
Enough! You are all lost! So quickly now to work.

She claps her hands, and masked dwarfish figures appear in the
doorway, who promptly carry out the orders as they are given.

To me, you gloomy spherical monstrosities!
Come rolling over here, there's mischief to be done.
Bring on the gold-horned altar, set it in its place,
And lay the gleaming axe along its silver edge;   8940
Then fill the jars with water that will wash away
The horrid stains and traces of the blackened blood.
Spread out the precious carpet here among the dust,
So that the victim regally may kneel and then,
Enshrouded, though the head be severed from
        its rump,   8945
Be buried decently with all due dignity.

PANTHALIS   The queen stands to one side alone and deep in thought,
The women wilt like meadow grass when freshly mown;
My sacred duty as the oldest is, it seems,
To seek a word with you, most ancient of us all.   8950
Experienced and wise, you seem to wish us well,
Although these foolish creatures have misjudged
        your worth.
So tell us if you know how we might yet be saved.

PHORKYAS   That is quite simple; it is for the queen alone

	To save herself and you, her underlings, as well;	8955
	But firm resolve and swiftest action is required.	
CHORUS	We implore you, wisest Sibyl,	
	most revered of all the Fates,	
	Stay your golden shears and tell us	
	how our lives may still be spared;	
	For our tender limbs already	
	feel a ghastly swinging, swaying,	
	Limbs that rather would be moving	
	in a graceful dance, or resting	8960
	In a lover's fond embrace.	
HELEN	It is not fear I feel, like these, but rather pain;	
	Yet if you can protect us, you shall have our thanks.	
	What seems impossible can often be achieved	
	By those with wisdom and discernment. Tell us, then.	8965
CHORUS	Speak, and tell us, tell us quickly,	
	how can we escape the gruesome	
	Menace of the noose that threatens,	
	like a cheap and tawdry necklace,	
	Soon to tighten round our throats? Poor	
	wretches, we can feel already	
	Choking, breathless suffocation,	
	if you do not show compassion,	
	Rhea, mother of all gods.	8970
PHORKYAS	Have you the patience to be still and listen to	
	My long-drawn-out account? For there is much to tell.	
CHORUS	Yes, quite enough! For while we listen, we shall live.	
PHORKYAS	The man who guards his house and all its treasures safe	
	And keeps the lofty walls of home in good repair,	8975
	His roof secure from the assaults of storm and rain –	
	He will enjoy prosperity for all his days.	
	But those who lightly stray with restless feet beyond	
	The sacred limits of the threshold of the house	
	Will find, when they return to that familiar place,	8980
	That everything has changed, or even been destroyed.	
HELEN	What is the purpose of these well-worn adages?	
	Leave such distressing thoughts aside, and tell your tale.	
PHORKYAS	It is the simple truth, and no reproach is meant.	
	The pirate Menelaus sailed from bay to bay,	8985

	And pillaged every shore and island that he found,	
	Returning with the booty that now fills his house.	
	For ten long years he sat before the walls of Troy;	
	How long it took him to return, I do not know.	
	But what became of Tyndareus' noble house,	8990
	And of the kingdom he established all around?	
HELEN	Are you so ill-disposed by nature, that abuse	
	And blame is all that ever issues from your lips?	
PHORKYAS	The mountain valleys rising steeply to the north	
	Of Sparta stood deserted for so many years,	8995
	Where from Taygetos[55] a dashing stream descends	
	To swell Eurotas as it flows between the reeds	
	And spreads along the valley where it feeds your swans.	
	But to these mountain valleys came a hardy race	
	From deep Cimmerian night to occupy the land;	9000
	A fortress, lofty and impregnable, was raised,	
	From which they plague the land and people as they please.	
HELEN	How could they do all this? It seems impossible.	
PHORKYAS	But they had nearly twenty years; that's time enough.	
HELEN	Are they a band of robbers? Are they leaderless?	9005
PHORKYAS	They are not robbers; one man leads them as their lord.	
	I speak no ill of him, though he has plagued me too.	
	He could have pillaged everything, but was content	
	To take not tribute, but some freely-offered gifts.	
HELEN	And his appearance?	
PHORKYAS	Fine enough! I like him well.	9010
	A man of spirit and of handsome stature, bold –	
	And such intelligence is rare among the Greeks.	
	They call these folk barbarians, but none of them,	
	I think, would be as cruel as some heroes who	
	Behaved like cannibals before the walls of Troy;	9015
	The man's nobility commands respect and trust.	
	And then his fortress! You should see it for yourself![56]	
	That is quite different from the clumsy masonry	
	Your forebears piled up anyhow without a thought,	
	Cyclopic as the Cyclops, throwing rough-hewn stones	9020
	On other rough-hewn stones; up there, however, all	

Is regular and measured out by rule and line.
Seen from outside, it soars and reaches to the sky,
So true and well-aligned, and smooth as polished steel;
To climb those walls – why, even thought can find
                                            no hold.   9025
Inside are many spacious courtyards, all enclosed
And built around in every kind of form and style.
You can see pillars, vaults and arches, balconies
And galleries from which to see – or to be seen.
And coats of arms –

CHORUS   Why, what are they?
PHORKYAS   You will have seen   9030
Upon the shield of Ajax serpents intertwined;
The Seven against Thebes all carried on their shields
Devices, images of rich significance:
The moon and stars, resplendent in the sky at night,
Or goddesses and heroes, ladders, torches, swords,   9035
And weapons that a noble city sees with dread.
Such images our heroes have inherited;
They bear the shining colours of their ancestors.
You will see lions, eagles, beak and talons too,
Or bisons' horns, or wings and roses, peacocks' tails,   9040
And stripes of gold and black and silver, blue and red.
All these devices hang like banners, row on row,
In halls immeasurable as the world itself;
And you can dance there!

CHORUS   Are there dancing-partners too?
PHORKYAS   The finest! Scores of lads, fair-haired, and in the
                                            bloom   9045
Of fragrant youth! Such fragrance only Paris had,
The day he came too close to Sparta's queen.

HELEN   Your words
Are out of place. Now finish what you have to say.
PHORKYAS   It is for you to give your solemn word; say yes,
I will at once surround you with those walls.

CHORUS   O speak   9050
That simple word, and save yourself, save all of us!
HELEN   What? Should I fear that Menelaus, that the king
Should act so cruelly and seek to do me harm?

PHORKYAS   Have you forgotten how he mutilated your
Deiphobus, the brother of dead Paris, so   9055
Atrociously, when he with stubborn force took you,
The widow, as his mistress? He cut off his ears,
His nose – and much besides; it was a gruesome sight.

HELEN   What he did to that man, he did because of me.

PHORKYAS   Because of him he now will do the same to you.   9060
Beauty is indivisible; who once possessed
It whole, destroys it rather than be cursed to share.

Trumpets sound in the distance; the CHORUS *start in terror.*

PHORKYAS   The strident trumpets' blast can rend the ears and grip
The bowels; so the claws of jealousy can grasp
And tear the heart of one who never can forget   9065
What once he had and now has lost and has no more.

CHORUS   Can you hear the trumpets blaring?
        Can you see the glint of arms?

PHORKYAS   You are welcome, king and master!
        I will gladly give account.

CHORUS   What of us?

PHORKYAS   You see it clearly,
        see her death before your eyes.
There inside your own awaits you;
        no, there is no help for you.   9070
[*pause*]

HELEN   I have reflected on the course I dare to take.
You are a hostile demon, that I feel quite plain,
And fear you may turn good to evil ends. For now,
However, to that fortress I will follow you.
What other thoughts I have, I know; but what the
                                 queen   9075
May hide within the secret places of her heart
Shall be revealed to none. Old woman, lead the way!

CHORUS   Oh what glad, swift-footed steps
      Hurry us onwards!
      Death at our back,   9080
      There in front of us
      Rises a fortress
      With impregnable walls.

May they protect us as well
As did the ramparts of Troy,   9085
Which succumbed at last
To contemptible guile alone.

Mists rise, obscuring the background and foreground.

Ah, what is this?
Sisters, look around!
Was it not glorious day?   9090
Mist is rising, drifting in bands
From Eurotas' sacred stream;
See how its beautiful
Reed-girt banks have vanished from sight,
And the swans, proud and free,   9095
Gently gliding, rejoicing
As they swim together,
I can see no more!

Yet I can hear
How they call to us,   9100
Call in hoarse tones from afar!
That, men say, presages death.
Let it not be meant for us,
Let our promised salvation not
Be instead a message of doom;   9105
Woe to us, swanlike ones,
Long-white-throated ones, and woe
To our swan-begotten
Mistress, woe, woe!

All around us is now   9110
Cloaked in smothering mist,
Each to the other lost from view.
What is this? Do we walk,
Or do we float,
Dancing and tripping over the ground?   9115
Can you see? Is not Hermes there,[57]
Leading us on? Is that his golden staff
I can see gleaming, conducting us back
To that mournful, dismally grey twilight world

Filled with insubstantial phantoms,   9120
Overflowing, ever empty Hades?

Yes, a sudden gloom has fallen,
                and the pallid mist has lifted,
Brown as stone, devoid of lustre.
                Now our eyes can see no further
Than the walls that rise around us.
                What is this? A moat, a courtyard?
Either one would make me shudder.
                Sisters, ah, we are imprisoned,   9125
More than ever captives now!

INNER COURTYARD OF A CASTLE

surrounded by ornate and fantastic medieval buildings

PANTHALIS You rash and foolish creatures, women that you are!
The playthings of the moment, fickle as the wind;
Come fortune or misfortune, neither can you bear
With calm or fortitude. Each one must contradict   9130
The other furiously, and then be crossed in turn;
In pain and joy alone you wail and laugh as one.
Be silent now! and wait to hear your noble queen
Say what she has decided for herself and us.

HELEN Where are you, ancient Sibyl, whoever you may be? 9135
Come out from the vaulted chambers of this gloomy fort.
If you have gone to tell this wondrous warrior lord
Of my arrival here, and bid him welcome me,
Accept my thanks and lead me in without delay;
I long to end this wandering, all I want is rest.   9140

PANTHALIS In vain, my queen, you look around on every side;
That horrid shape has vanished, now perhaps it lurks
Among the mist that swallowed us and brought us here,
I know not how, so soon without a single step.
Perhaps she strays uncertainly within the maze   9145
Of this strange castle merged from many into one,
And seeks for you a royal welcome from its lord.

But look, above us there already I can see
A host of servants hurrying to and fro in all
The windows, doorways, galleries; this promises   9150
A dignified reception for a royal guest.

CHORUS   This gladdens my heart! O see, over there,
They descend with unhurried and decorous tread,
Such beautiful youths, how stately their steps
In well-ordered ranks. Who commanded

                                                them here,   9155

To assemble so soon in such noble array,
These splendid young men in the flower of youth?
What impresses me most? That they walk with

                                                such grace?

Or is it those rich curls round their luminous brows?
Is it perhaps those cheeks that are red as a peach,   9160
On which the skin is so downy and soft?
I long for a taste, but it fills me with dread;
For I fear if I do, my mouth might be filled,
I shudder to say it, with ashes.

Now they approach us,   9165
These fairest of youths;
What are they bringing?
Steps to the throne,
Carpets and seats,
Curtains, a rich   9170
Canopied roof;
High above it billows,
Like a garland of clouds
Over the head of the queen.
Now she is bidden   9175
To ascend the sumptuous throne.
Gather around,
Lining the steps in
Solemn array.
Blessings, blessings, threefold blessings   9180
On this gracious reception be poured!

*Everything has been carried out in order
as described by the Chorus.*

*When the pages and squires have made their way down in a long pro-
cession,* FAUST *appears at the head of the staircase in the courtly costume
of a medieval knight. He descends with slow and dignified steps.*

PANTHALIS [*observing him carefully*]
      Unless the gods have granted, as they often do,
      For but a passing moment such outstanding gifts
      As this man has, a figure so magnificent,
      Such captivating grace, a bearing so sublime,   9185
      His triumph is assured, whether in manly war,
      Or in the battle for the loveliest woman's heart.
      He is desirable above so many men
      My eyes have seen, and who were also much admired.
      With slow and solemn measured steps, respectfully   9190
      The prince approaches us; now turn, my queen,
                              and see!

FAUST [*approaches, a man in chains at his side*]
      No courteous greeting, as would be more fitting,
      No ceremonious welcome do I bring;
      Instead, I offer you this fettered slave,
      Who failed his duty, robbing me of mine.   9195
      Before this noble lady kneel, and make
      A full confession of your guilt to her.
      This man, exalted queen, is set to watch
      Upon the highest tower, from there to search
      With eyes of rare and penetrating sight   9200
      The vault of heaven and the wide-spread earth,
      And see whatever stirs from far and near,
      From the encircling hills, across the plain
      To this sure fortress; whether grazing herds,
      Which we protect, or armies on the march,   9205
      Which we must meet. Today, what carelessness!
      He failed to signal your approach, and so
      An honourable welcome was denied
      Our noble guest. Such frivolous neglect
      Demands his death; already he should lie   9210
      In his own blood, but, lady, you alone
      Shall punish or show mercy, as you please.

HELEN   Since you have granted me such privilege

As judge and ruler, though I may suspect
That it is meant to try me, I will do   9215
A judge's foremost duty, and will hear
What the accused might have to say. So speak.

LYNCEUS THE WATCHMAN Let me kneel and let me gaze,
    Let me die or let me live;
    All my heart and soul I give   9220
    To this god-sent lady's praise.

    Watching for the sun at morning,
    To the east I turned my eyes,
    Suddenly, a wondrous dawning:
    In the south I saw it rise.   9225

    Southwards then my gaze directing,
    Blind to valleys, mountain peaks,
    Heavens and earth alike neglecting,
    Her alone my vision seeks.

    Keenest eyesight I was granted,   9230
    Like the lynx its searching beam;
    Now it dimmed as if enchanted
    By a deep and torpid dream.

    All around me shapes were shifting,
    Towers and ramparts disappeared;   9235
    But the swirling mists were lifting
    As this lovely goddess neared.

    On her gentle radiance gazing,
    Heart and eyes were filled with light;
    But such beauty, brightly blazing,   9240
    Dazzled, robbed me of my sight.

    I forgot my watchman's duty,
    Failed to sound the horn's alarm.
    Death may threaten me, but beauty
    Tames all rage, and shields from harm.   9245

HELEN I cannot punish wrong that I myself
Have brought. Alas! What iron destiny
Pursues me everywhere, so to bewitch

The hearts of men that they will sacrifice
Themselves and any worthy cause. Seduced,   9250
Abducted, fought for, carried here and there
By demigods and heroes, gods and spirits,
Who led me in distraction to and fro –
One Helen brought confusion to the world,
And two still more; now three and fourfold is   9255
The grief I bring. Let this good man go free;
No shame shall come to those the gods delude.

FAUST   O queen, I marvel how unerringly
You aimed the shaft that pierced your victim's heart;
The arrow has returned to wound the one   9260
Who loosed it from his bow. Now thick and fast
Your arrows strike me; in a feathered swarm
They fill my castle's passages and halls.
What am I now? For all at once you turn
My vassals into rebels, and my walls   9265
Cannot protect me. My most trusted men
Obey this conquering, unconquered queen.
What can I do but offer up myself,
And all that I had thought was mine, to you?
Now let me kneel and freely pledge myself   9270
To you as queen; no sooner were you here,
Than all my kingdom and my throne were yours.

LYNCEUS [*with a treasure-chest, followed by men bearing others*]
I have returned, my gracious queen!
The richest man who once has seen
Your face, must feel his poverty;   9275
And yet no prince is rich as he.

What was I once? What am I still?
What can I do? What is my will?
My vision cannot penetrate
The glory of your throne and state.   9280

We came out of the east;[58] our horde
Soon put the west to fire and sword.
The peoples rolled in waves so vast,
The first knew nothing of the last.

One fell, another took his stand;   9285
A third stood ready, sword in hand;
Each reinforced a hundredfold,
For each a thousand died untold.

We surged on in a furious band,
We were the lords of every land;   9290
And where I ruled supreme today,
Tomorrow was another's prey.

We took whatever met our eyes;
The fairest women were our prize,
The sturdy cattle from the stall,   9295
The horses too – we took them all.

But I looked out for something more,
The rarest things you ever saw;
For me, what other men might own
Is withered grass that has been mown.   9300

With piercing eyes I hunted round
Wherever treasure could be found;
Each purse lay open to my quest,
Transparent every treasure-chest.

Great heaps of gold I made my own,   9305
And many a splendid precious stone;
But only emeralds should rest
Next to your heart, upon your breast.

Pearls from the deepest ocean bed
Shall hang about your face; the red   9310
Of rubies would grow pale and weak
Against the crimson of your cheek.

So here before you I have brought
The richest treasure that I sought,
And at your gracious feet I lay   9315
The spoils of many a bloody fray.

I bring you coffers, iron-bound;
I know where others can be found.
If I may serve you, many more
Shall fill up every treasure-store.   9320

You scarce ascended to the throne,
When all acknowledged you alone;
The wise, the rich, the mighty bow
To you, the peerless figure, now.

All this was mine, I held it fast;   9325
To you I set it free at last.
For what I thought the greatest prize
Is now as nothing in my eyes.

All I possessed has passed away,
Is withered like the new-mown hay;   9330
One smiling look, and you'll restore
Its value to the full once more.

FAUST   Remove this weighty treasure boldly won.
You go unpunished; seek for no reward.
Already all this castle holds is hers;   9335
To offer her some special part of it
Is futile. Go and set those riches out
In order, so that splendours yet unseen
Appear in glorious display! The vaults
Shall shine like newly furbished skies; create   9340
Rich paradises here of lifeless life,
Unroll the carpets bright with flowers beneath her feet,
So that she walks upon the softest ground,
And let her see such radiance all around
That dazzles all but the immortals' eyes.   9345

LYNCEUS   Sire, the service that you ask
Is a light and joyful task;
For such beauty holds us all,
Wealth and health and life in thrall.
All our warriors grow tame,   9350
All their weapons blunt and lame;
A form so luminous, so bright,
Robs the sun of warmth and light,
And a countenance so fair
Makes the whole world bleak and bare.   9355

[*exit*

HELEN [*to Faust*] I wish to speak with you, but you must sit
        Beside me here! This empty place awaits
        Its master, who will make my own secure.

FAUST   First let me kneel and pledge myself to you,
        Most noble lady; let me kiss the hand   9360
        That is held out to raise me to your side.
        Confirm me as co-regent of your realm
        That knows no bounds, and let me be at once
        Your guardian, your admirer, and your slave.

HELEN   I see and hear so many wonders here;   9365
        I am amazed, I wish to ask so much.
        But first explain to me why this man's speech
        Had such a strange, a strange but friendly tone.
        One sound appeared companion to the other,
        And if one word is pleasing to the ear,   9370
        Another follows to caress the first.

FAUST   If you find pleasure in our people's tongue,
        Their song will surely charm you too, and soothe
        Your ears and senses to the very depths.
        Let us rehearse it now; one sound calls forth   9375
        Its answering echo as we speak in turn.

HELEN   So tell me then, how can I learn this art?

FAUST   It is quite simple; it comes from the heart.
        And when our hearts are filled with joy like this,
        We look around and ask –

HELEN   Who shares our bliss.   9380

FAUST   We see no past nor future, but confess
        That here and now is all –

HELEN   Our happiness.

FAUST   This is our wealth, our treasure, all we own;
        And what will seal this pledge?

HELEN   My hand alone.

CHORUS   Who would dare reproach our princess,   9385
        If she grants this castle's lord
        Gracious signs of friendship?
        For we are, let us admit it,
        Captives all, as we often have been
        Since the infamous fall of Troy,   9390

And the grief we have suffered
In the labyrinth of our flight.

Women who are used to wooing
Cannot have their choice of men,
But are skilled in loving.   9395
It may be golden-haired shepherds,
Or fauns, black-bearded and bristling,
Or whatever may chance their way;
Equally all will be granted
Rights to shapely, voluptuous limbs.   9400

Closer and closer see how they sit,
Leaning one on the other.
Shoulder to shoulder, knee to knee,
Hand in hand as they recline
High on the throne's   9405
Softly cushioned magnificence.
Majesty does not seek to hide
Intimate pleasures,
But may joyfully flaunt them
For the eyes of the people to see.   9410

HELEN   I feel so far away, and yet so near,
And all I wish to say is: I am here!

FAUST   I scarcely seem to breathe, no words I find;
It is a dream, the world is left behind.

HELEN   My life seemed done, and yet I feel so new;   9415
Now, stranger, we are one, I live for you.

FAUST   Do not ask how or why of fate, but seek
To live for now; this moment is unique.

PHORKYAS [*bursts in*] Spelling out your love-sick pleasure,
Cooing to your lovers' measure,   9420
Idly wooing at your leisure –
But you have no time to spare.
Can you hear a muffled pounding?
Can you hear the trumpets sounding? –
Danger threatens everywhere.   9425
Menelaus will surround you,[59]
Hordes of people all around you,
Call your men to arms, prepare!

     If his warriors can tame you,
     Like Deiphobus he'll maim you,   9430
     Penance for your love-affair.
     They'll be strung up from the ceiling,
     At the altar she'll be kneeling,
     Waiting for the axe. Beware!

FAUST   This insolent intrusion is importunate!   9435
     For even in danger I detest such mindless haste.
     The fairest envoy is made ugly by bad news,
     And you, the ugliest, take pleasure in the worst.
     But this time you shall fail; you waste your breath
                  and shake
     The air with idle words. There is no danger here, 9440
     And even danger would be but an empty threat.

   Signals, explosions from the towers, horns and trumpets,
    martial music. A mighty army marches past.

FAUST   A band of heroes, none are braver,
     You'll see assembled, row on row;
     No man deserves a woman's favour
     Who cannot shield her from the foe.   9445

     [*to the commmanders, as they step out of the ranks*
      and come forward]
     With calm resolve unleash your furious
     Rage, and victory is yours,
     You bloom of northern youth, you glorious
     Flower of our eastern shores.

     The mighty steel-clad host advances,   9450
     And empires fall beneath their sway;
     The lightning flashes from their lances,
     The thunder speeds them on their way.

     It was at Pylos that we landed,
     Where ancient Nestor lived and died;   9455
     The petty kings against us banded
     Were overwhelmed and swept aside.

     Now from these walls unleash your thunder,
     Drive Menelaus to the sea.

There let the pirate roam and plunder;   9460
That is his chosen destiny.

As overlords I nominate you;
This is your royal queen's decree.
The spoils of victory await you;
Protect her land, and keep it free.   9465

With walls and ramparts, German legions,
The bays of Corinth fortify;
And in Achaia's rugged regions
The Goths all comers shall defy.

In Elis, Franks shall guard the beaches;   9470
Messenia is the Saxons' prize.
You Normans, sweep the ocean's reaches;
Great Argolis again shall rise.

Then each shall found his habitation,
By force of arms protect his own;   9475
In Sparta, chief of every nation,
Your queen shall claim her ancient throne.

To land with plenty overflowing
She grants each one a sovereign right,
Upon you all her gifts bestowing,   9480
The fount of justice and of light.

*Faust descends, the overlords gather round to hear his
further commands and dispositions.*

CHORUS   Who desires the fairest of all,
Let him show himself worthy;
He would be wise to arm himself well.
Though sweet words have won for him   9485
All that earth has to offer,
His possession is not secure.
Prowling rivals will lure her away,
Robbers brazenly carry her off;
Let him take care to protect what is his.   9490

Therefore we commend our prince,
Praise him over all others;

Boldly and wisely choosing his men,
So the strongest await his word,
Ever ready to serve him.   9495
They will obey his every command;
Each of them fights for his own gain
And the duty he owes to his lord,
Sharing the glory of victories won.

For who can capture her now   9500
From her powerful protector?
She is his, and he worthy of her.
Doubly we grant him this; does he
Not also guard us with impregnable ramparts,
And a great army beyond those walls?   9505

FAUST   And so we grant to every nation
A gift of rich and fruitful land.
Let each now occupy his station;[59]
We hold the centre, here we stand.

By these competing tribes protected,   9510
Our wave-lapped shores are safe again,
This demi-isle, by gentle hills connected
To Europe's last, remotest mountain chain.

This shining land pours out its blessing
For evermore on every race,   9515
Where now my queen rules, repossessing
The land that first looked on her face

When once she broke the shell confining
Her, where sweet Eurotas plays,
Her eyes in radiance outshining   9520
Her mother's and her siblings' gaze.

This land on you in dedication
Bestows its gifts from far and near.
This is your country, this your nation;
Above all others hold it dear.   9525

While on its jagged crests the sunlight blazes
With frosty shafts that pierce the mountain air,

The goat upon the greening hillside grazes
And seeks among the rocks its meagre share.

The springs and streams united flow in fountains,   9530
And soon the meadows, slopes and clefts are green;
Upon the pastures of a hundred mountains
The scattered flocks of fleecy sheep are seen.

The cattle move with footsteps sure and steady
Along the chasm's steeply rugged face;   9535
Among the cliffs they find a shelter ready –
A hundred caves provide for each a place.

There Pan protects them, while in moist crevasses
Are nymphs who dwell in cool and leafy shade,
And branching trees in densely crowded masses   9540
Rise heavenward from each thickly-wooded glade.

Primaeval woods! The stubborn oak tree braces
Its massive boughs in jagged symmetry;
Replete with sweetest sap, the maple graces
The forest with its airy canopy.   9545

In shaded groves warm mother's milk is flowing,
The suckling child, the lamb contented sips,
While in the vale the mellow fruit is growing,
And from the hollow tree the honey drips.

Contentment is a birthright here, a blessing   9550
That shines in every creature's face;
Such bliss, such health and happiness possessing,
Each is immortal in its place.

And so we watch the comely infant growing
To fatherhood in this pure sphere,   9555
And still we wonder at it, scarcely knowing
If these are gods or mortals here.

The shepherd boys who with Apollo tended
Their flocks, were no less fair than he;
Where nature rules, all worlds as one are blended   9560
Into a perfect harmony.

[*he sits beside her*]

In us that primal state is consummated.
The past is done, acknowledge as your own
The highest god by whom you were created;
To that first world you now belong alone.   9565

No castle walls, no fortress shall surround us,
For we shall dwell where bliss is unconfined.
Eternal youth still burgeons all around us;
In Sparta, here, Arcadia we'll find.

Lured to this blessed place by fateful powers,   9570
You fled to this most happy destiny.
Now let our thrones be leafy bowers,
Our joy Arcadian and free!

*The scene is completely transformed. In front of a series of rocky caves
are enclosed arbours. A shady grove extends to the surrounding cliffs.
Faust and Helen are not to be seen. The women of the Chorus
lie scattered about the stage, asleep.*

PHORKYAS   How long these girls have been asleep, I cannot say;
And whether they have dreamed the things that
                                          I have seen   9575
So clear and plain before my eyes, I do not know.
I'll wake them, then. These youngsters shall be quite
                                                    amazed;
You too, you greybeards, who sit waiting there below
To see these truthful miracles explained at last.
Wake up! Come, shake your tousled heads and rub
                                          the sleep   9580
Out of your eyes! Stop blinking, I have tales to tell.

CHORUS   Speak and tell us then, what wonders
                          came to pass while we were sleeping!
Most of all we like to hear of
                          things that are beyond believing,
For these dreary rocks are boring,
                          we are tired of looking at them.

PHORKYAS   Are you bored already, children,
                          when you've only just awoken?   9585
Listen, then: these very caverns,
                          grottoes, bowers have provided

Shelter and secure protection,
    a secluded lovers' idyll
For our master and our mistress.

CHORUS   What, in these?

PHORKYAS   In isolation
From the world they called upon me
    to perform my silent duty.
I was honoured to attend them;
    but I kept my gaze averted,   9590
As befits a trusted servant.
    Searching here and there, I gathered
Healing roots and barks and mosses,
    for I know their secret powers,
So that they were left alone.

CHORUS   You would have us think these grottoes
    held a whole wide world inside them,
Woods and meadows, lakes and rivers;
    what fantastic tales you tell!   9595

PHORKYAS   Why, of course, you callow creatures!
    These are depths you cannot fathom:
Flights of rooms and spacious courtyards,
    I explored them, deep in thought.
Suddenly a burst of laughter
    echoes through the empty spaces;
From a woman's lap an infant
    leaps into his father's arms,
From the father to the mother,
    such a hugging, such a cuddling,   9600
Fond caresses, playful teasing,
    shouts of joy and peals of laughter
Deafen me with all their noise.

Naked, like a wingless cherub,
    faunish, though a human creature,
On the floor he jumps and tumbles,
    from the solid ground rebounding,
Bounces upwards ever higher,
    and again he springs until he   9605
Soars to touch the vaulted roof.

Now his anxious mother cautions:
        leap as much as you may wish to,
But beware of flying freely,
        you must curb the urge to fly.
Thus his father fondly warns him:
        in the very earth's resilience
Is the force that drives you upwards;
        though you touch the ground but lightly,   9610
Like the son of earth Antaeus,
        you will find new strength at once.
So among the rocks he skips,
        rebounding from the dizzy edges
Of these massive crags, and bounces
        back and forward like a ball.
All at once he disappears
        into the rugged gorge's crevice,
He is lost, it seems; the father
        comforts the distracted mother.   9615
I look on with anxious gestures;
        but now, what an apparition!
Has he found a hidden treasure?
        He is dressed in flowered garments
Worthy of his dignity.

From his arms hang coloured tassels,
        round his chest silk ribbons flutter,
In his hand a golden lyre,
        truly like a young Apollo,   9620
Stepping blithely on the clifftop's
        very edge. We stand astonished;
With delight and joy the parents
        fall into each other's arms.
Round his head, a shining glory!
        Is it gold that glows so brightly,
Or the spirit flame that blazes
        in the all-creative mind?
In his bearing, in his gestures,
        thus the child proclaims the future   9625
Master of all grace and beauty,
        through whose very limbs eternal

Melodies will flow unceasing;
      you yourselves shall shortly hear him,
You yourselves shall see a wonder
      such as you have never known.

CHORUS   You, from the isle of Crete,
Call this a wonder?   9630
Have you never been told
Tales that the poets taught us?
Never heard before the stories
Of Ionia or Hellas,
Rich legends that our ancient   9635
Forebears sang of gods and heroes?

All that the present day
Ever can offer
Is a sad echo of those
Days of ancestral glory.   9640
What you tell us cannot ever
Match that loveliest of fables,
More credible than truth is,
Sung about the son of Maia.[60]

When this infant was newly born,   9645
Strong but dainty in stature,
Wrapped in the softest, purest down,
Bound in the finest of swaddling clothes,
Heedless his nurses turned their backs
While they gossiped and chattered.   9650
Soon though, the little rascal stirs,
Twists and wriggles his supple limbs,
Then he cunningly slips them
Out of the wraps that confine him,
Calmly leaving the irksome   9655
Purple covering where he lay,
As the fully-grown butterfly
From its rigid chrysalis
Rapidly slips and unfolds its wings,
Flutters at will and boldly soars   9660
Into the radiant ether.

So this nimble and clever child
Proved himself as the favoured
Patron of rogues and thieves, and all
Those who profit from knavery,   9665
Demonstrating his artful skills
In his earliest exploits.
First the lord of the sea was robbed
Of his own trident, and Ares' sword
Slyly filched from its scabbard;   9670
Phoebus' bow and arrows he stole,
And the tongs of Hephaestus.
Even Zeus' thunderbolts
He'd have taken, but feared their fire;
When he fought with Eros, he   9675
Tripped and wrestled him to the ground.
From the bosom of Venus he stole,
As she caressed him, her girdle.

*The alluring and tuneful sound of a stringed instrument is
heard from the cave. All listen carefully and appear deeply
moved. There is a full musical accompaniment from
this point until the pause indicated below.*

PHORKYAS   All these fables must be banished!
                Hear these lovely sounds, and know   9680
                That your ancient gods have vanished
                In the past, so let them go.

                No one knows what they betoken,
                We demand a higher art;
                From the heart it must be spoken,   9685
                If it is to move the heart.
                                    [*she withdraws towards the cliffs*

CHORUS   If these sounds are so appealing,
                Fearful creature, to your ears,
                We, restored to youthful feeling,
                Cannot but be moved to tears.   9690

                Though the sun by clouds be covered,
                In the soul a light can rise;
                In our hearts can be discovered
                What the sullen world denies.

HELEN, FAUST; EUPHORION *in the costume described above.*[61]

EUPHORION	Parents share in childish pleasure	9695
	When they hear an infant's voice;	
	When you see me dance a measure,	
	Let your loving hearts rejoice.	
HELEN	When two hearts in love are plighted,	
	Mortals feel what bliss can be;	9700
	But three hearts in love united	
	Know divine felicity.	
FAUST	Here we stand, for love has bound us,	
	Me to you and you to me;	
	All we ever sought has found us –	9705
	This was surely meant to be!	
CHORUS	They shall find in love's reflection	
	Shining from this gentle boy	
	Many years of deep affection;	
	All our hearts are moved to joy!	9710
EUPHORION	Let me go springing	
	Higher and higher!	
	Heavenward winging,	
	All I desire!	
	Drawing me upward,	9715
	Driving me on.	
FAUST	Take care, take care, though!	
	Curb your ambition,	
	Or you will surely	
	Fall to perdition,	9720
	And we shall lose our	
	Beloved son!	
EUPHORION	Earth shall no longer	
	Bind or retain me;	
	Let me go, do not	9725
	Try to restrain me!	
	Nothing can hold me –	
	I must go on!	
HELEN	Think, we implore you,	
	How it would grieve us,	9730
	Those who adore you,	
	If you should leave us,	

	If you bring ruin to	
	All we have won.	
CHORUS	I fear this bond will	9735
	Soon be undone.	
HELEN AND FAUST	For our sake, moderate	
	Such wild desire;	
	Curb this intemperate	
	Urge to soar higher!	9740
	Stay, we implore you,	
	Here in the plain.	
EUPHORION	All my love for you	
	Bids me remain.	
	[*he weaves among the Chorus,*	
	drawing them into the dance]	
	Join in the dance with me,	9745
	Keep the step light.	
	Is this the melody,	
	Have I the movement right?	
HELEN	Lead these fair girls about,	
	Weave and sway in and out –	9750
	That is well done.	
FAUST	All this frivolity	
	Has no appeal for me.	
	Would they were gone!	

Euphorion and the Chorus, dancing and singing,
move in intricate patterns.

CHORUS	Moving your arms, you make	9755
	Charming caresses;	
	Tossing your head, you shake	
	Glistening tresses;	
	Over the ground you go,	
	Gliding with nimble feet;	9760
	Supple limbs to and fro	
	Move to the rhythm's beat.	
	You have achieved your goal;	
	You have beguiled	
	All of us, heart and soul,	9765
	Loveliest child.	

Pause.

EUPHORION
 Light-footed deer, I'll
 Harry and chase you;
 Through wood and mere I'll
 Quickly outpace you!   9770
 I am the hunter,
 I lead the chase.

CHORUS
 You need not hurry,
 We shall soon tire;
 We are your quarry,   9775
 All we desire,
 Loveliest hunter,
 Is your embrace!

EUPHORION
 By grove and fountain,
 Forest and mountain!   9780
 Easy prey I despise,
 Won without fight;
 Only the hard-won prize
 Gives me delight!

HELEN AND FAUST
 What a furious altercation,   9785
 What unbridled agitation!
 All around us perturbation,
 Horns through woods and valleys blaring,
 What confusion, shouts and cries!

CHORUS [*entering hastily, one by one*]
 He disdained us, and refusing   9790
 All our charms, ran on uncaring,
 Seized the wildest of us, choosing
 Her as his most favoured prize.

EUPHORION [*carrying a young girl*] [62]
 Now I've caught this sturdy treasure,
 I shall force her to my pleasure;   9795
 I'll subdue her, tame her, pressed
 Close to her unwilling breast.
 Though she struggles, yet she must
 Satisfy my wilful lust.

THE GIRL
 Let me go! You shall not take me,   9800
 While I've strength and courage still
 In this body, you'll not make me

Bend to your imperious will.
Do you think I am defenceless?
Do not trust your strength too much!   9805
Hold me tighter then, you senseless
Fool, and feel my burning touch.
[*she bursts into flames and flies into the air*]
Seek me in the air, or follow
Me to caverns dark and hollow –
I have fled beyond your clutch!   9810

EUPHORION [*shaking off the last flames*]

Cliffs that rise tall and sheer,
Thickets that bar my way;
Why stay imprisoned here,
Wasting my youth away?
Waves breaking on the shore,   9815
And the wind's distant roar –
I hear them calling me,
There I must be!
[*he leaps higher and higher up the cliffs*]

HELEN, FAUST AND THE CHORUS

Chamois-like he clambers higher,
We must watch with dread and fear.   9820

EUPHORION   To the summits I aspire,
Where the view is wide and clear.
Now I know where I stand;
I am in Pelops' land.
This is my island home,   9825
Rimmed by the ocean's foam.

CHORUS   But we would rather you
Stayed here at leisure,
And we would gather you
Fruits for your pleasure;   9830
Figs from the plain below,
Grapes from the hills above.
Stay in this land you know,
This land you love!

EUPHORION   You dream of peace? Then stay,   9835
Dreaming of peace one day.
War! is the call for me,

Onward to victory! [63]

CHORUS   If you banish
Peace for the sake of war,   9840
Joy and hope vanish
For evermore.

EUPHORION   Sons that this country bore,
Bloodshed and danger saw,
Undaunting, free and brave,   9845
Gladly their lives they gave,
Never their glorious
Spirit shall fail –
May these victorious
Warriors prevail!   9850

CHORUS   See him climbing ever higher,
Yet in stature still he grows;
Victory his one desire,
Bright his burnished armour glows.

EUPHORION   Let no castle walls surround us,   9855
Self-reliance is our shield;
We shall need no fortress round us –
Iron hearts will never yield.
If you would live undefeated,
Arm yourselves, and you will see   9860
All your sons as heroes greeted:
Amazons your wives shall be.

CHORUS   Heavenly poetry,
Sacred word of the free!
Rise to the distant sky,   9865
Radiant star on high;
Echoing far and near,
Your voice will reach us here,
And never die.

EUPHORION   Not as a helpless child appearing,   9870
A warrior youth in arms you see;
In spirit willing, strong, unfearing,
Companion of the bold and free.
Away!
The day   9875
Leads on to fame and victory.

HELEN AND FAUST Scarce to light and life emerging,
                    Must we plead with you in vain?
                    Why obey these voices urging
                    You to suffering and pain?   9880
                    Are we three
                    Doomed to be
                    But a dream that fades again?
EUPHORION   The ocean roars, from every valley
                    The thunder echoes far and near;   9885
                    On land and sea the armies rally,
                    They will not flinch, they know no fear.
                    On to die!
                    Is the cry;
                    Death is the command they hear.   9890
HELEN, FAUST, CHORUS Dread and horror, mind-appalling!
                    Must you follow fate's decree?
EUPHORION   Shall I stay when they are calling
                    Me to share their destiny?
HELEN, FAUST, CHORUS Perilous pride that brings   9895
                    Death and despair!
EUPHORION   See – I unfold my wings,
                    Trust to the air!
                    I must be with them – thus
                    Let me fly free!   9900

*He hurls himself into the air, his robes bear him up for a moment,
his head shines, he leaves a trail of light behind him.*

CHORUS   Icarus! Icarus!
                    What misery.

*A handsome youth falls dead at his parents' feet. We seem to recognise
a familiar figure; but his bodily form quickly vanishes, the halo rises like
a comet to the sky. His robe and lyre remain on the ground.*

HELEN AND FAUST Bliss must give way to pain;
                    All joy has flown.
EUPHORION'S VOICE [*from below*]
                    Mother, must I remain   9905
                    Here in the dark alone?
                        Pause.

CHORUS [*threnody*] You are not alone! for though you
                    Fled the light so soon, wherever
                    You may dwell, we seem to know you;
                    In our hearts you live for ever.   9910
                    We can scarcely mourn you; sadness
                    Yields to envy of your fate,
                    For in days of grief or gladness,
                    All you sang was brave and great.

                    Born to highest rank, to power   9915
                    And to fortune, soon you strayed
                    From your path, and soon the flower
                    Of your youth was doomed to fade.
                    You derided worldly fashion,
                    But all hearts to you were known;   9920
                    Women yielded to your passion,
                    And your song was yours alone.

                    Heedless on you rushed, defying
                    Every snare along the way,
                    Scorning every law, denying   9925
                    All conventions of the day.
                    Then at last a brave ambition
                    Spurred your spirit on to gain
                    Glory in a noble mission;
                    But your valour was in vain.   9930

                    Who can bring that liberation?
                    Shrouded fate makes no reply
                    In those days of desolation
                    When the people bleed and die.
                    But new songs shall lift them, bringing   9935
                    Hope renewed, though crushed to earth;
                    Songs that flow forever, springing
                    From the soil that gave them birth.

                    Complete pause. The music stops.

HELEN [*to Faust*] Alas! An ancient saying proves its truth in me:
                    That happiness and beauty form no lasting bond.   9940
                    The ties of life and love alike are severed now;
                    Lamenting both, I bid farewell to you in grief,

And one last time I throw myself into your arms.
And now, Persephone, receive my son and me!

*She embraces Faust, her bodily form vanishes,
leaving her robe and her veil in his arms.*

PHORKYAS [*to Faust*] Hold fast to all that she has left behind.   9945
Do not let go the robe! Already demons
Are tugging at its corners, and would like
To drag it down to Hades. So hold fast!
It is no more the goddess that you lost,
But it is still divine. Now use this rare   9950
And priceless gift to bear yourself aloft;
If you endure, it will convey you through
The ether, high above the commonplace.
Far, far from here we two shall meet again.

*Helen's robes dissolve into clouds which surround
Faust, lift him upwards and carry him away.*

PHORKYAS   [*picks up Euphorion's costume and lyre, advances into
the proscenium, holds up the exuviae,[64] and speaks*]
Now there's a lucky find for you!   9955
The vital flame is out, it's true,
But never mind; there's plenty here to start
A guild of poets with its petty rifts
And jealousies, all in the name of art.
I can't endow them with poetic gifts –   9960
But with these clothes, at least they'll look
the part.

[*she sits at the foot of a pillar in the proscenium*]

PANTHALIS   Now hurry, girls! At last we're rid of sorcery,
Free from the foolish spell of that Thessalian crone,
From all that twanging and tinkling that confused
our ears,
Befuddling the mind with its alluring sounds.   9965
Away to Hades! For with swift and solemn tread
Our queen has gone before; so in her footsteps now,
As faithful servants, we are bound to follow her
To the throne of the inscrutable Persephone.

CHORUS   Queens may be content, indeed, wherever
                                              they are;   9970
                       Even in Hades, standing above the rest
                       In the company of their peers,
                       Favourites at Persephone's court.
                       We though are forever hidden
                       Deep in fields of asphodel,   9975
                       Only scrawny poplars
                       Round us, and the barren willow-trees.
                       What amusement is there for us?
                       Squeaking like bats, we twitter
                       In dismal whispers, cheerless and ghostly.   9980

PANTHALIS Whoever did not strive for noble deeds, and those
           Who won no fame, shall to the elements be gone.
           I yearn to join my queen; for not through worth alone,
           Through loyalty we live on for posterity.   [*exit*

CHORUS   Once more we are restored to the light of day;   9985
                       We are persons no more,
                       We feel it, we know full well.
                       But we shall never return to Hades;
                       Nature, the ever-living, claims
                       Us as her spirits,   9990
                       Just as we lay claim to her fullness.

A SECTION OF THE CHORUS[65]
                       Where a thousand branches whisper,
                                    quiver rustling in the treetops,
                       Cradled here we play, enticing
                                    from the roots the living juices
                       Gently upwards, till the leaves and
                                    blossoms burgeon in abundance;
                       Then we deck our hair with flowers,
                                    thriving in the airy spaces.   9995
                       When the ripened fruit has fallen,
                                    beasts and people flock together
                       Joyfully to taste and gather,
                                    eager to bring in the harvest,
                       Bending low as if to worship
                                    early gods from ancient times.

A SECOND SECTION

From afar the polished mirror
        of the rock face shines and glistens;
Here we nestle, fondly clinging
        to the cliffs in gentle waves,   10000
Here we listen for the notes of
        birdsong or the reed-pipes fluting,
Even Pan's dread voice will find us
        ready to return his sound.
Murmurs we reflect in murmurs,
        to the thunder-crash our echoes
Thunder back with doubled fury,
        threefold, tenfold in reply.

A THIRD SECTION

Sisters, we are restless spirits,
        with the streams we hurry onwards,   10005
Tempted by the rich abundance
        of the distant slopes that beckon,
Ever downwards, ever deeper
        we meander; so we water
Mountain pastures, river meadows,
        and the gardens round the house.
Where above the banks and rippling
        waves the slender cypress rises
Skyward high above the landscape,
        there we leave our fertile traces.   10010

A FOURTH SECTION

Wander where your fancy takes you;
        round the hillsides we will gather,
Where the slopes are closely planted,
        where the tethered vines are grown;
Every hour of every day the
        vintner toils with dedication,
Never sure that he will reap a
        full reward for all his care.
Here he labours, always digging,
        raking, hoeing, pruning, tying;   10015
Prays to all the gods to help him,
        to the sun-god most of all.

Pampered Bacchus does not listen,
        does not heed his faithful servant,
Sleeps in arbours, sprawls in grottoes,
        babbling to the youngest faun.
All he needs for half-befuddled
        reveries is ever-present,
Kept for him in gourds and wineskins,
        long preserved in jars and vessels   10020
Deep within the coolest caverns,
        stored for all eternity.
But the gods have blessed the vineyard,
        Helios above all others;
Breezes, moisture, warmth and sunlight
        swell the grapes to luscious fullness.
Where the silent vintner laboured,
        all at once a lively bustle
Swarms among the rustling trellis,
        shakes the bunches on the vine.   10025
Baskets creak and buckets clatter,
        till the groaning tubs are filled,
All goes to the mighty winepress
        for the treaders' sturdy dance;
So the pure and sacred ripeness
        of unblemished fruit is trodden,
Rudely crushed, it foams and bubbles,
        vilely squashed into a pulp.
Now the ear is pierced by brazen
        gongs and cymbals loudly clashing;   10030
From these mysteries the wine-god
        Dionysus is revealed,
With his goat-foot satyrs, goat-foot
        women slung across their shoulders,
In their midst the raucous braying
        of Silenus' long-eared beast.
Licence reigns; decorum, manners,
        under cloven hooves are trampled,
Senses reel in giddy turmoil,
        ears are deafened by the noise,   10035

Drunkards grope towards the pitchers,
           heads and bellies overloaded;
One or two urge moderation,
           only to increase the tumult –
For old wineskins must be emptied,
           so the new wine can be stored!

The curtain falls.

*In the proscenium, the huge figure of Phorkyas rises,
but she steps down from her buskins, removes her mask
and veil, and reveals herself as Mephistopheles, who
in an epilogue delivers such commentary on
the play as may be necessary.*

ACT FOUR

HIGH MOUNTAINS
Forbidding, jagged peaks

A cloud drifts by, clings to the rock, and sinks onto a projecting ledge. It parts, and FAUST *steps out.*

FAUST   Profoundest desolation yawns beneath my feet;
With care I tread the margins of this lofty peak,   10040
And quit the chariot of cloud that carried me
Gently through sunlit skies, and over land and sea.
It drifts away from me, but yet does not disperse,
And moves, a dense and gathered mass, towards the east.
Amazed and marvelling, the eye pursues its course;   10045
It parts and billows, shifts in ever-changing shapes,
Yet seeks a form. Ah yes, my eyes are not deceived:
In sunlit splendour, pillowed on a cloudy bed,
Reclines a massive, yet a godlike woman's shape,
Like Juno, Leda, Helen – yes, I see it now!   10050
Majestic, beautiful, it floats before my eyes,
But soon disperses; shapeless, broad, it towers and hangs
Like distant snow-clad summits in the east, and there
Reflects the dazzling greatness of ephemeral days.

But round me floats a bright and gentle wraith of mist;   10055
Its fond caresses cool my brow and cheer my heart.
It rises lightly, wavers; climbing higher still,
It takes a shape. Is this a dream from my first youth,
Of highest bliss I knew and lost so long ago?
The deepest treasures of the heart come welling up: 10060
This airy image adumbrates the dawn of love,
That first glance, quickly felt but scarcely understood,
A gift beyond all others, had I held it fast.

In its ethereal beauty now that lovely form
Does not disperse, but rises skyward; as it climbs,   10065
It draws with it what I hold dearest in my heart.

A seven-league boot lumbers onto the stage. Another follows it at once.
MEPHISTOPHELES steps down. The boots stride off rapidly.[66]

MEPHISTO.   Now that's the way to get around!
             But why land here, all on your own?
             What is this ghastly place you've found,
             These yawning rocks and piles of stone?   10070
             It wasn't always here; I know it well –
             It used to be the very floor of hell.

FAUST   You're always ready with some foolish story,
             So once again you have to come and bore me.

MEPHISTO. [*seriously*]
             When the Lord God – for reasons I well know –   10075
             Expelled us from the regions of the air
             To that abyss where central fires glow,
             And where eternal flames burn everywhere,
             We found ourselves, among that blazing light,
             Squashed close together in a sorry plight.   10080
             So all at once the cooped-up devils started
             To belch and sneeze; they spluttered and they farted,
             Until the sulphur fumes began to swell
             Into a gas that filled the pit of hell.
             And very soon, there was no holding it,   10085
             The level earth's thick crust just had to split.
             It turned the whole thing topsy-turvy – so
             These mountain peaks were once deep down below.
             On this they base their doctrines, showing how
             The lowest have become the highest now;   10090
             We rule as princes of the air, you see,
             Since we escaped that torrid slavery.
             An open secret that was well concealed,
             And only later to the world revealed. [Ephesians 6: 12][67]

FAUST   These mountains are of no concern to me,   10095
             I don't ask how or why they came to be.
             When nature in and by itself was founded,
             It made this globe, complete and purely rounded,

Formed peaks and chasms for its own delight,
Arranging rock on rock and height on height, 10100
And then it smoothed the gentle hills that flow
And slope towards the valleys there below;
Rejoicing in their green fertility,
She needs no turbulent nativity.

MEPHISTO. That's what you say! You think it's all so clear; 10105
But I know how it was, for I was here
When down below the deep abysses boiled
And seethed and flowed, a flaming molten tide,
When Moloch with his mighty hammer toiled
To forge the rocks and fling them far and wide. 10110
Those massive stones still strewn about the land –
Who can explain the force that hurled them there?
This no philosopher can understand;
To think about it drives them to despair –
The rocks are there, there they must let them stand. 10115
The common sense of simple folk alone
Can grasp the truth about these blocks of stone,
And in their wisdom they have long since said it:
Such miracles are all to Satan's credit,
And so they trudge in faithful pilgrimage 10120
Up to the Devil's Rock or Devil's Bridge.

FAUST It's quite remarkable to see the way
That devils look at nature, I must say.

MEPHISTO. Leave nature how it is! Why should I care?
You have the Devil's word, for he was there. 10125
We are the ones who forged our grand designs
Through turmoil, force and chaos – read the signs!
But let me put it plainly: has there been
Nothing that pleases you in all you've seen?
The kingdoms of the world stretched out before you 10130
And all their glory I can conquer for you. [Matthew 4]
Would you, who are so hard to please,
Not even be content with these?

FAUST I have great things in mind – but you
Must guess.

MEPHISTO.   Well, that's not hard to do. 10135
I'd find myself a city where

They squash into the market square
To buy the food to meet their needs,
Their onions, cabbages and swedes –
All narrow streets and pointed gables,   10140
With fly-blown meat laid out on tables.
At any time of day you'll find
A stinking mass of humankind;
But further out, it's much more gracious –
The streets are broad, the squares are spacious,   10145
And then, beyond the city wall,
For miles the endless suburbs sprawl.
I'd watch the coaches bowl along,
Enjoy the crowds, the noisy throng,
And see the swarms of people go   10150
Like ants, forever to and fro.
And if I drove or rode, you'd see
Me lionised by thousands at
The centre of society.

FAUST   I'd never be content with that.   10155
One's pleased to see the population
Increase and feed itself, and even spend
Some time in learning – but your education
Only makes rebels of them in the end.

MEPHISTO. Then in some pleasant spot I'd build myself   10160
A splendid palace to show off my wealth.
With woods and hills and meadows I'd create
A gorgeous garden out of my estate –
Green hedges, velvet lawns, straight avenues
With artful shadows to enhance the views,   10165
Where rocky cataracts flow unconfined
To fountains and cascades of every kind;
The noble column soars, but to the side
It spurts and squirts and pisses far and wide.
I'd build some cosy cottages, designed   10170
To house the loveliest women I could find;
Secluded there, I'd spend eternity
In their most pleasurable company.
That's women in the plural – for, you see,
I find one beauty's not enough for me.   10175

FAUST	A modern Sardanapalus! What vulgarity![68]
MEPHISTO.	And might one guess what you were striving for?
	No doubt it was sublime and brave.
	You've sailed close to the moon – I'm sure
	It's something like the moon you really crave. 10180
FAUST	No, not at all! This planet still
	Has room for noble deeds. I will
	Astound the world; I feel new energy,
	A bold ambition has inspired me.
MEPHISTO.	So fame is what you want? It's clear to me 10185
	You've had a heroine for company.
FAUST	I'll rule in territories I can call
	My own; fame's nothing, but the deed is all.
MEPHISTO.	There will be poets, all the same,
	Whose foolish stories will proclaim 10190
	To all posterity your glorious name.
FAUST	How can you know the things that fire
	Men's hearts and kindle their desire?
	Your mind, where bitter malice breeds –
	What can it know of human needs? 10195
MEPHISTO.	Your will be done; perhaps you'll let me know
	What mighty project takes your fancy, though?
FAUST	Towards the open sea I turned my eyes;
	I saw the swelling ocean surge and rise,
	Until the towering billows broke to pour 10200
	In rolling waves along the level shore.
	And I was vexed, as any mind that's free,
	That holds all rights and law in due respect,
	Must feel disturbed when furious anarchy
	Unleashes passions that cannot be checked. 10205
	I thought it was mere chance, but looked again:
	The tide had turned, the waves rolled back, and then
	From its proud goal the sea withdrew defeated,
	And in due time the struggle was repeated.
MEPHISTO. [*aside, to the audience*]	
	That's nothing new! I can't believe my ears: 10210
	I've known that for a hundred thousand years.
FAUST [*continues passionately*]	
	The sterile sea creeps into every bay,

And spreads sterility along its way;
It surges, and the rolling breakers pour
Across the dismal wasteland of the shore.   10215
There for a time the waves rule unrestrained,
But they recede, and nothing has been gained.
That aimless play of elemental might
Dismays me, it could drive me to despair!
My spirit soars beyond itself; to fight   10220
And tame that ebb and flow is what I dare.[69]

It can be done! The rising tide flows round
Each hill and elevation of the ground;
Though it advances with imperious force,
The slightest height will proudly check its course,   10225
The slightest depth will drain it instantly.
At once my plans were formed: what could give more
Sweet satisfaction than to tame the sea,
To hold the lordly flood back from the shore,
To set the ocean's limits far and wide,   10230
And turn back on itself the surging tide?
So step by step I've planned with thought and care;
That is my wish – now help me if you dare!

*To the right, behind the audience, the sound of drums
and martial music is heard in the distance.*

MEPHISTO.	That's easy! Can you hear those distant drums?	
FAUST	More war! The wise man shudders when it comes.	10235
MEPHISTO.	Whether it's war or peace, a clever man	
	Will find some profit in it if he can.	
	Watch carefully, take any chance you see;	
	Come, Faust, and seize your opportunity!	
FAUST	Spare me your riddles, and instead explain	10240
	Yourself. What is this all about? Speak plain!	
MEPHISTO.	During my travels I became aware	
	Our friend the Emperor is in despair.	
	You know him well enough; when we amused him	
	With dreams of bogus wealth, it so confused him	10245
	He thought the whole wide world was his to own.	
	He was so young when he came to the throne,	

	He fancied – wrongly, as it seems to me –	
	It would be most desirable if he	
	Could reconcile his duty and his pleasure,	10250
	That is, to rule and still enjoy his leisure.	
FAUST	A great mistake. A ruler must fulfil	
	His duty, and find joy in that alone.	
	Within his heart he guards his sovereign will;	
	What he himself desires must not be known.	10255
	His lightest word is instantly obeyed,	
	His will is done for all the world to see;	
	He reigns supreme, his power will never fade –	
	Mere pleasure robs him of his dignity.	
MEPHISTO.	That's not his style. He took his pleasure, and	10260
	Soon anarchy was rife throughout the land.	
	The lords and commons fell upon each other,	
	They banished, murdered, brother fought with brother,	
	Castle warred with castle, city with city,	
	The guilds and nobles feuded without pity,	10265
	Bishops with flock and chapter locked in fight –	
	All men, it seemed, were enemies on sight.	
	The churches ran with blood, beyond the city gate	
	Travellers and merchants met a gruesome fate.	
	They all grew bold; they knew that if you meant	10270
	To live, you had to fight. That's how things went.	
FAUST	They fell apart! They stumbled, tripped, and then	
	They got up and went headlong once again.	
MEPHISTO.	But no one stopped it – they just didn't care,	
	And all of them were eager for a share.	10275
	The lowest strove to emulate the rest,	
	Until it got too much; and so the best	
	And ablest took a stand. Whoever can	
	Establish peace, they said, shall be our man.	
	The Emperor has failed; let us elect	10280
	Another who'll revive the realm, restore	
	Security and order, self-respect,	
	Create a new world and secure	
	Justice and peace for evermore.	
FAUST	How very pious.	
MEPHISTO.	Yes, the priests were there	10285

To fill their bloated paunches with a share.
They were involved far more than others, too,
And blessed the insurrection as it grew.
The ruler we amused approaches fast
To fight a battle that could be his last.   10290

FAUST   I'm sorry; he was honest, good and kind.
MEPHISTO. Where there's life, there's hope; if he can find
A way out of this narrow valley, he
Could live to fight a thousand times again.
You never know how lucky he might be –   10295
And if he wins, he'll not be short of men.

They cross the foothills and observe the position of the army in the valley.
The sound of drums and martial music is heard from below.

MEPHISTO. It's quite a good position that he's in –
And if we join him, he'll be sure to win.
FAUST   What help can we provide, I'd like to know –
Deceit and magic tricks, all empty show!   10300
MEPHISTO. Battles are won by craft and guile;
Be mindful of your great ambition, while
You plan the tactics to achieve your aim.
If we can help the Emperor reclaim
His throne and country, he'll confer on you   10305
The title to the boundless shore in feu.
FAUST   You've done a lot of things, it must be said,
So you can win a battle; go ahead!
MEPHISTO. No, you'll do that – this time, you see,
You'll be the general in command, not me.   10310
FAUST   You want me to give orders when
I've no idea how to? Think again!
MEPHISTO. You leave that to your General Staff;
Being Field Marshall's just a laugh.
I knew this war was coming, so   10315
I hired my fighters long ago;
Primaeval toughs from mountains old
As time. They're worth their weight in gold.
FAUST   Who's that I see in arms? Three men –
You've raised your brigands from the mountains,

                                          then? 10320

MEPHISTO.   Not quite! Like Peter Quince, I chose for you
             The very essence of that motley crew.

             Enter the THREE MIGHTY MEN [II Samuel 23: 8]

MEPHISTO.   Here come my bully boys! All three
             Are different ages, as you see.
             Their clothes and armour vary, too –   10325
             You won't do badly if they fight for you.
             [*aside*] These days the children like historical
             Accounts of knights in arms and chivalry;[70]
             And since these oafs are allegorical,
             They should suit everyone just perfectly.   10330
BASHER [*young, lightly armed, colourfully dressed*]
             If anybody dares to look at me,
             I'll smash him in the teeth, and when
             Some feeble coward tries to turn and flee,
             I grab his hair and drag him back again.
SNATCHER [*a grown man, well armed, richly dressed*]
             These brawls are pointless, just a farce,   10335
             A waste of time and energy;
             Grab what you can and shift your arse –
             Don't wait to ask, just do it, see?
GRASPER [*older, heavily armed, scantily dressed*]
             That's not much good to anyone!
             The richest fortune is soon gone,   10340
             The stream of life will carry it away.
             Just take my word for it, I'm old and grey:
             It's good to take, but keep it safe, and then
             You'll never have to part with it again.
                          [*they all go down into the valley together*

IN THE FOOTHILLS

             Drums and martial music from below.
             EMPEROR, COMMANDER IN CHIEF, GUARDS
COMMANDER   The plan seems well advised: to concentrate   10345
             Our forces all together on the floor

           Of this secluded valley, and to wait.

           It is a prudent move, I'm sure.

EMPEROR   Well, we must see; I'm sorry we retreated

           As if we'd fled, already half-defeated.   10350

COMMANDER My Prince, our right flank holds the higher
                                      ground!

           No better disposition could be found:

           A rising hill protects us at the back,

           Far simpler to defend than to attack.

           And we're half-hidden by that sloping bank;   10355

           No cavalry would dare to charge that flank.

EMPEROR   I must approve your admirable plan;

           So let strong arms, stout hearts do what they can.

COMMANDER Our phalanx, drawn up in the centre field,

           All eager for the fray, will never yield.   10360

           See, through the mist still hanging in the air,

           Their pikes are flashing in the morning sun,

           In thousands packed into a mighty square,

           With hearts on fire for glory, every one!

           That dark and swaying mass, I guarantee,   10365

           Is strong enough to break the enemy.

EMPEROR   As fine a sight as ever met my eyes –

           It is as if our army's twice the size.

COMMANDER There's nothing I need say about our left.

           Our bravest fighters guard that rocky cleft;   10370

           Those cliffs protect the vital pass, and there

           You see the glint of weapons everywhere.

           We'll catch them unawares; here I foresee

           The bloody slaughter of our enemy.

EMPEROR   And here they come, those false relations who   10375

           Would call me uncle, cousin, brother too,

           Who, with such insolent ambition flown,

           Robbed of respect the sceptre and the throne.

           Their wars destroyed the realm; now they unite

           In arms against me to dispute my right.   10380

           The fickle crowd will follow them, and go

           With the drifting stream wherever it may flow.

COMMANDER A trusted scout runs down that rocky slope;

           We sent him out to spy. Good news, I hope!

FIRST SCOUT   It was a most successful mission;   10385
                      With a bold and cunning ruse
                      We infiltrated their position,
                      But we bring no happy news.
                      Many swear their dedication,
                      Promise to support your cause –   10390
                      But excuse their hesitation
                      In the turmoil of these wars.

EMPEROR   Their selfish counsels teach them self-protection,
             Not grateful duty, honour or affection.
             Do you not know, when your account is due,   10395
             Your neighbour's fire will spread to your house too?

COMMANDER   Our second scout! In every limb he shakes –
             And see what weary, leaden steps he takes.

SECOND SCOUT   We were pleased when we detected
                      Wild disorder everywhere;   10400
                      Suddenly, all unexpected,
                      A new emperor was there.
                      Now the mob prepares for battle,
                      Stirred to action by his lies,
                      Following like sheep and cattle   10405
                      Where the rebel banner flies.

EMPEROR   I welcome this new rival; only he
             Could show me what an emperor must be.
             I have borne arms, but never in the wars;
             Now I shall bear them in a higher cause.   10410
             For all the splendour of my feasts at court,
             They lacked one thing: the danger that I sought.
             I tilted at the ring, but though my heart
             Longed for the lists, I could not play my part.
             If you had let me go to war, my name   10415
             Would now shine brightly with a hero's fame.
             My bosom swelled with pride when I was seen
             Reflected in that fiery realm below,
             Surrounded by those dreadful flames; although
             It was not real, it was a noble scene.   10420
             My fame, my conquests, were an idle dream;
             Such frivolous neglect I will redeem.

The Heralds are dispatched to challenge the rival emperor

FAUST, *in armour, with half-closed visor.*
The THREE MIGHTY MEN, *armed and dressed as before.*

FAUST   We hope you will accept our help; it's wise
          To be prepared in times of peace or war.
          The mountain folk appear in any guise,   10425
          They read the stones and study nature's lore.
          Long since these spirits left the plain below
          To live among the rugged hills; they know
          The labyrinthine fissures, where they sense
          The noble gas of precious elements.   10430
          By sifting, testing, blending, to invent
          Some unknown substance is their sole intent.
          With patient spirit skills they have perfected
          Transparent shapes of crystal purity,
          In whose eternal silence they can see   10435
          The image of the world above reflected.

EMPEROR   I've heard of them, and credit what you say;
          But my good man, what use to us are they?

FAUST   The Sabine necromant of Norcia, Sire,[71]
          Is your devoted servant and your friend.   10440
          He well remembers what a hideous end
          Awaited him upon the burning pyre;
          The faggots blazed, the tongues of flame leapt higher,
          Twigs mixed with pitch and sulphur fed the fire.
          No devil, man or god could spare his pains;   10445
          You, Sire, alone could break his glowing chains
          That day in Rome. Indebted still, he cares
          And watches over you and your affairs.
          Since then he serves your interests, not his own;
          Consults the heavens, the earth, for you alone.   10450
          Most urgently he charged us to stand fast
          In your support. The mountain's power is vast,
          Where nature works and rules supreme and free –
          Dull-witted priests see only sorcery.

EMPEROR   We welcome guests who come from far and near   10455
          To celebrate our feasts and bring good cheer;
          We love to see a crush of people pour
          Into our halls until they hold no more.

How much more welcome is an honest man,
Who comes to offer us what help he can   10460
This sombre morning hour when we await
The fickle judgment of the scales of fate.
And yet we beg you, sheathe your sword, and stay
Your willing hand on this most solemn day;
Respect the hour when thousands come as friend   10465
Or foe to fight and die. I must defend
My honour, I must prove that I alone
Am truly worthy of my crown and throne.
This phantom emperor, this upstart thief,
Who would usurp our titles and our lands,   10470
Be first of all our lords, our army's chief,
I shall dispatch to hell with my own hands.

FAUST   However great your cause, it is not wise
To risk your life in such an enterprise.
That royal helmet, with its plume and crest,   10475
Protects your head, gives courage to the rest.
Without the head, what can the body do?
For if it fails, the limbs are useless too.
If it is injured, every member feels
The wound, but will recover when it heals.   10480
In swift defence the strong and ready arm
Will raise the shield to save the skull from harm;
The sword will do its duty, as it must –
To parry, and at once return the thrust.
Stamped on the victim's neck triumphantly,   10485
The sturdy foot then shares the victory.

EMPEROR   Just so! My anger urges me to treat
His proud head as a footstool for my feet.

HERALDS [*returning*] With scant honour we were treated
On our diplomatic mission,   10490
And our noble terms were greeted
With contemptuous derision.
'Gone is your imperial glory,
Like an echo far away
From a half-forgotten story: 10495
Once upon a time, they say.'

FAUST   This turns out, for the loyal men who stand

	Beside you, Sire, just as they would have planned.	
	The foe comes on, your troops will not hold back:	
	Now is the time to order the attack.	10500
EMPEROR	From this point I shall give no more commands,	
	[to the Commander in Chief]	
	And lay this duty, Prince, into your hands.	
COMMANDER	Our right wing shall deploy and take the field!	
	Their left is moving to attack the height;	
	Before they reach it, they will be in flight –	10505
	Our true and trusted youth will never yield.	
FAUST	Permit this lively hero straight away	
	To be recruited to your ranks today;	
	If he joins forces with you, you will see	
	Just what a powerful ally he can be.	10510
	[he points to the right]	
BASHER [steps forward]	Whoever shows his face to me, before	
	He turns around he gets a fractured jaw;	
	Or if he turns his back on me, I smash	
	His head and neck into a grisly hash.	
	And if your men can fight like me	10515
	With mace and sword and tooth and claw,	
	Then to a man the enemy	
	Will drown in their own blood and gore. [exit	
COMMANDER	Now move the central phalanx to attack;	
	A well-directed thrust will drive them back.	10520
	Already to the right a fierce display	
	Of force has put their plan in disarray.	
FAUST [pointing to the second Mighty Man]		
	Then let this nimble fellow join the fray;	
	He'll sweep up everything that's in his way.	
SNATCHER [steps forward]		
	Our troops will fight like heroes – all the more	10525
	When driven by the thirst for spoils of war.	
	The rival emperor's tent shall be	
	The rich reward for victory.	
	His pride will soon be overthrown;	
	I'll lead the phalanx, and we'll have his throne.	10530
QUICKLOOT [vivandière, clinging to him]	I may not be his wife, but he	
	Has always been the man for me.	

And what rich pickings lie in store!
A woman's pitiless in war,
She robs and plunders ruthlessly;   10535
So no holds barred, and on to victory!   [*they both leave*

COMMANDER   Their right flank has attacked, as we expected;
Our left wing, though, is heavily protected.
They will resist the onslaught, and defend
That narrow mountain pass right to the end.   10540

FAUST   [*pointing to the left*]
Add this man to your strength, Sir, if you will;
It does no harm if you are stronger still.

GRASPER [*steps forward*] The left flank will be well secured!
If I am there, possession is assured.
You can rely on me, I'm old –   10545
No thunderbolt can shatter what I hold.

MEPHISTO.   [*coming down from the hill*]
Now look! Above and to the rear,
How scores of men in arms appear
From every craggy gorge to block
The narrow pathways through the rock.   10550
With helmet, armour, sword and shield
They form a wall that will not yield,
And wait, all ready for the fray.
[*sotto voce, conspiratorially*]
Just where they're from, I shouldn't say;
But I've been busy looking round.   10555
In ancient armouries I found
Them all, on horseback or on foot, as though
They ruled the earth as they did long ago.
They were kings, knights, or emperors before –
But now they're empty snail-shells, nothing more.   10560
Inside, a lot of phantoms have survived:
The Middle Ages here have been revived.
Whatever devil animates them now,
They should be quite effective, anyhow.
[*aloud*] Just listen to that tinny rattle –   10565
You know they're simply itching for a battle!
Their tattered banners and threadbare flags
Want a fresh breeze to stir their rags;

You see an ancient nation ready for
The call to action in a modern war.   10570

A fearsome blast of trumpets from above.
Clear signs of disarray in the enemy ranks.

FAUST   The distant skyline has gone dark,
             But here and there you see a spark,
             An ominous and ruddy glow.
             Blood-red the weapons flash and gleam;
             The woods, the rocks, the heavens seem   10575
             To share the bloody scene below.

MEPHISTO.   Our strong right flank is holding out,
             And in the middle of the fray
             Our bold Jack Basher goes about
             His business in his usual way.   10580

EMPEROR   An arm was raised – and then I saw
             Where there was one, a dozen more.
             It is not natural, I say.

FAUST   Have you not heard of mists that drift
             Around Sicilian coasts by day?[72]   10585
             They swirl and glisten, then they lift
             Until they hang suspended, where
             Reflected in the gauzy air
             The strangest visions come and go.
             Great cities shimmer to and fro,   10590
             And gardens float before your eyes;
             A myriad shapes pervade the skies.

EMPEROR   I am uneasy, all the same;
             Our spears all shine with ghostly flame,
             And nimble tongues of fire dance   10595
             About the tip of every lance.
             It is too weird.

FAUST   This glow is cast
             By spirit beings from the past.
             It is the Dioscuri, Sire,
             Reflected in Saint Elmo's Fire;   10600
             The twins to whom the sailors pray
             Have mustered all their strength today.

EMPEROR   To whom are we indebted, say,

	That nature lends her strangest powers	
	To help us in this cause of ours?	10605
FAUST	None other than the Master; he	
	Is guardian of your destiny.	
	He sees your enemies conspire	
	Against you, and his sole desire	
	Is to protect you; he would give	10610
	His own life so that you might live.	

FAUST   None other than the Master; he
               Is guardian of your destiny.
               He sees your enemies conspire
               Against you, and his sole desire
               Is to protect you; he would give   10610
               His own life so that you might live.

EMPEROR   They feted me with pomp and jubilation;
               I felt my power, and sought its confirmation –
               So I was minded on a whim to free
               The greybeard from his fiery agony.   10615
               But I had spoilt the clergy's sport, and they
               Have shown no favours to me since that day.
               Now after many years, am I to see
               The boon of that glad deed repaid to me?

FAUST   A generous act brings rich rewards.   10620
               But now, Sire, lift your eyes towards
               The heavens; the Master sends a sign
               Whose meaning we shall soon divine.

EMPEROR   An eagle wheeling in the sky,
               A gryphon following close by.   10625

FAUST   Take heed! This portent favours us.
               The gryphon's a chimaera; thus
               It cannot hope to match in flight
               The eagle's true, authentic might.

EMPEROR   On outspread wings they wheel and float   10630
               In distant circles through the air;
               Now each attacks to rip and tear
               With savage claws the other's throat.

FAUST   The worthless gryphon's power is shattered,
               See how it tumbles, mauled and battered;   10635
               Its lion's tail is limp, it flees
               To hide among the crags and trees.

EMPEROR   I am amazed, and trust that we
               Shall soon fulfil this prophecy.

MEPHISTO. [looking to the right]
               From our constantly repeated   10640
               Fierce attacks they have retreated;

Now they seek to take the fight
In confusion to the right.
Their main force, in disarray
On the left, must soon give way.   10645
Now our phalanx, rank on rank,
Strikes like lightning, in a flash
Charging at their weakest flank.
Matching force with force they clash,
Wave on foaming wave converging,   10650
Both in savage combat merging.
Never was there such a glorious
Sight as this: we are victorious!

EMPEROR [*on the left, to Faust*] I am still not reassured.
    Look! Our men have not secured   10655
Their defences; not one stone,
Not one missile has been thrown.
Those above have all forsaken
Their positions, and the foe
Swarms up through the rocks below;   10660
Soon the pass will have been taken.
So your godless strategy
Brings defeat, not victory.

Pause

MEPHISTO. Here come my ravens; let us hear
    What message they have brought. I fear   10665
That things may not be going well.

EMPEROR Those dismal birds! Whatever brings
    Them sailing here on tarry wings
From that fierce battle on the fell?

MEPHISTO. [*to the ravens*] Sit close, and whisper in my ear,   10670
    For your advice is wise and clear,
And those you guard are guarded well.

FAUST [*to the Emperor*] You've heard of pigeons, I dare say,
    That fly from countries far away,
Returning home to feed and nest.   10675
In peace by pigeon post they bore
Our messages; in time of war
This raven post will serve us best.

MEPHISTO.   I fear the news they bring is dire;
            See where our heroes struggle, Sire,   10680
            Among the rocks. A sudden raid
            Has overrun the lower slopes;
            And if they take the pass, our hopes
            Of victory must surely fade.

EMPEROR   So finally I am betrayed,   10685
            Entangled in the snare you laid;
            I shudder as you draw it tight.

MEPHISTO.   Have courage! We can put things right
            With guile and patience. Now stand fast!
            The fight is fiercest at the last.   10690
            I trust my ravens; if you let
            Me take command, we'll triumph yet.

COMMANDER IN CHIEF [who has approached in the meantime]
            No good can come of sorcery;
            For long, Sire, it has troubled me
            To see these men at your right hand.   10695
            I see no way out; if they can,
            Let them complete what they began.
            I must relinquish my command.
            [he offers his baton to the Emperor]

EMPEROR   No, keep your staff till fortune sends
            Us better times than these today.   10700
            This fellow with his raven friends
            Fills me with horror and dismay.
            [to Mephistopheles]
            I cannot hand the staff to you,
            It would not be the proper thing to do.
            But take command, and come what may,   10705
            Do what you can to save the day.
                [he retires to his tent with the Commander in Chief

MEPHISTO.   That staff's no use to anyone.
            He's welcome to it – I could swear
            It had a cross on it somewhere.

FAUST   So what do we do now?

MEPHISTO.   It's done!   10710
            Now, my black cousins, fly to the waters
            Of the great lake. My greetings to its daughters;

Ask them to conjure up a flood for me.[73]
These nymphs have women's arts to cast a spell
So subtle and confusing, none can tell   10715
The false appearance from reality.

Pause.

FAUST   Our ravens' arts of flattery, it seems,
Have charmed the water-maidens; tiny streams
Already have begun to flow,
And from the dry and rocky mountainside   10720
The gushing springs unite into a tide
That threatens to engulf the foe.

MEPHISTO.   This strange reception has confused them all;
Their boldest climbers lose their hold and fall.

FAUST   One torrent joins with others; they converge,   10725
And with redoubled force from clefts emerge,
Then headlong in a falling arc they flow
To dash against the rocks, where they divide
In foaming cataracts on either side,
Cascading to the valley down below.   10730
However valiantly they struggle, they
Are swallowed by the flood and swept away,
And even I must shudder at their plight.

MEPHISTO.   I can see nothing of these watery lies –
They only work their spell on human eyes;   10735
But I can still enjoy this wondrous sight.
In droves they turn and run, they slide and sprawl,
The fools are on dry land, but shout and bawl
As if they're drowning; round and round they crawl
With silly swimming motions. It is all   10740
Complete confusion; they are in full flight.

The ravens have returned.

I will commend you to the Master by and by;
But show yourselves as masters now, and fly
To where the dwarfs, who never tire,
Strike from the forge's glowing fire   10745
Bright sparks with metal and with stone.
And ask them, as you sing their praises,
For fire that flashes, spits and blazes,

In which their highest arts are shown.
Sheet lightning flickering in the distant sky,   10750
Stars falling in the twinkling of an eye,
We see in any summer's night;
But lightning in the bushes all around,
Or stars that hiss and fizz along the ground –
That is a less familiar sight.   10755
They can do this, there's nothing to it:
Ask first, then order them to do it.

The ravens fly off. Events take place as described.

Now let the pitch-black darkness fall,
And bring confusion to them all;
Then sparks and flashes everywhere,   10760
To blind them in the sudden glare.
That's excellent! But now some dire
And fearful sound's what we require.

FAUST   The empty suits of armour that survived
In cobwebbed halls, the fresh air has revived;   10765
They clank and rattle as they lumber round –
A strangely false, discordant sound.

MEPHISTO. They cannot wait to take the field,
Exchanging blows with lance and shield,
As knights did in the days of yore.   10770
Those arms and legs encased in tin
Like Guelphs and Ghibellines begin
To fight their endless feud once more;
No hope of reconciliation –
It runs through every generation;   10775
All round I hear the battle's roar.
The Devil likes to celebrate
When feuding parties, full of hate,
Commit the vilest horrors, till
The valleys ring with their satanic   10780
Screams of strident fear and panic
Re-echoing from every hill.

Tumultuous warlike music in the orchestra,
finally giving way to lively martial tunes.

THE RIVAL EMPEROR'S TENT

Throne, rich furnishings.

SNATCHER. QUICKLOOT.

QUICKLOOT Look! We're the first ones here.

SNATCHER   Indeed!
          No raven matches us for speed.

QUICKLOOT It's filled with loot right to the top!   10785
          Where shall I start? When shall I stop?

SNATCHER   It's stuffed with treasure, fit to burst!
          I don't know what to pick up first.

QUICKLOOT This carpet's just the thing for me –
          I need a bit of luxury.   10790

SNATCHER   And here's an iron mace with spikes;
          Exactly what a fighter likes.

QUICKLOOT A scarlet cloak with golden seams –
          The sort of thing you wear in dreams.

SNATCHER [*takes the weapon*] With this you only need one blow   10795
          To kill a man, and on you go.
          [*to Quickloot*] You've grabbed at everything you could,
          But what you've got is not much good.
          Just leave that rubbish where it lies –
          This chest is a much bigger prize.   10800
          Inside it is the army's pay,
          It's all pure gold – take that away.

QUICKLOOT It's such a weight, I'll never shift it.
          It's murder! I can't even lift it.

SNATCHER   Bend down! Bend lower! That'll do;   10805
          I'll hoist it on your back for you.

QUICKLOOT Oh God, you've really done it now!
          My back is breaking! Help me! Ow!

          The chest falls and bursts open, scattering the gold.

SNATCHER   You've spilt it everywhere. Come on,
          Quick, scoop it up and let's be gone.   10810

QUICKLOOT [*crouches down*] Just fill my apron with the stuff!
          There's plenty here, we'll have enough.

SNATCHER   Get on with it! [*she stands up*] Oh no, it's split!
          Your apron's got a hole in it.

You're spilling it all on the floor –   10815
With every step you're dropping more.

OUR EMPEROR'S GUARDS This is the Emperor's treasure. Who
Are you, and what are you up to?

SNATCHER We risked our lives. We want a share
Of all this loot – that's only fair.   10820
These are the spoils of war, they're due
To us by right; we're soldiers, too.

GUARDS That's not the proper thing to do;
We don't want thieving scum like you,
But honest men to fight our wars,   10825
Who won't disgrace the Emperor's cause.

SNATCHER We know you and your honest dealing;
It's just another form of stealing.
It's reparations, so you claim –
It means 'Hand over' just the same.   10830
[to Quickloot] Come on, take what you can. It's clear
The two of us aren't welcome here.   [they leave

1 GUARD Why didn't you give him a clout?
He's got away, the cheeky lout.

2 GUARD I felt so weak just then; I swear   10835
There's something weird about that pair.

3 GUARD I couldn't see, my eyes went dim;
He flickered when I looked at him.

4 GUARD There's something strange, I don't know what.
The whole day through it's been so hot,   10840
So sultry and oppressive, too.
Some stood, some fell, you never knew
Where you were going, but the foe
Fell dead with every single blow.
Before your eyes there was a mist,   10845
And in your ears it buzzed and hissed.
That's how it carried on all day;
How we got here, I couldn't say.

> *Enter* THE EMPEROR *with four Princes.*
> *The Guards withdraw.*

EMPEROR Let that be as it may! The enemy is shattered,
His troops across the plain in headlong flight are
                                                    scattered. 10850

Here stands the empty throne, rich tapestries surround
The traitor's treasure hoard that fills the space around.
Protected by our guards, we graciously await
The nations' envoys here in honourable state.
We hear the joyful news pour in from every side;   10855
The Empire is restored, the people pacified.
Some trickery there was, but when all's said and done,
It was by us alone this victory was won.
For chance can often play a part in any fight –
A shower of stones or blood that puts the foe
                                           to flight;   10860
Sounds echo from the caves, a wondrous noise we hear
That spurs us on, but fills the enemy with fear.
Despised by all, he now lies humbled in the dust;
The victor praises God, in whom he put his trust.
'Te deum laudamus' – a million voices rise   10865
In glad spontaneous song that reaches to the skies.
And yet the highest praise comes from the pious heart;
Neglected duty calls on me to play my part.
A young and carefree prince may lightly spend his days,
But with the passing years he learns to mend his ways.   10870
With you four worthy lords united I shall stand
To serve my house, my court, my empire and my land.
[to the first] To your command, O Prince, the army
                                           was confided,
And by your valiant deeds to victory was guided;
But other duties call in peacetime. I create   10875
You Lord High Marshal; you shall bear the sword
                                           of state.[74]

LORD HIGH MARSHAL

The troops who in these wars their loyalty have shown
Will keep your borders safe, defend your life and throne.
We beg, then, that to us the privilege may fall
To guard you at the feasts in your ancestral hall.   10880
Before you I will bear this sword, and as a sign
Of highest majesty forever it shall shine.

EMPEROR [to the second]

A man who is both brave and courteous I ask
To be Lord Chamberlain. It is no easy task;

You are appointed head of all our household here.   10885
When servants are at odds, they serve us ill, I fear;
Let your example be an honourable guide
To those who serve their lord and all his court
                with pride.

LORD CHAMBERLAIN It is an honour, Sire, to do your sovereign will,
To serve the best aright, and do the worst no ill,   10890
Be open without guile, and calm without deceit;
If you but know my heart, my joy will be complete.
And at the feasts to come, then let the task be mine
To reach the golden bowl to you before you dine.
And I will hold your rings, that on these festive days   10895
Your hands may be refreshed, as I am by your gaze.

EMPEROR At such a solemn time our burdens seem too great
For feasting; but we shall have time to celebrate.
[to the third] You are Lord Seneschal, and you shall
                oversee
Poultry and game, my farms and my estates for me.   10900
In season you'll provide the very choicest dishes,
And see they are prepared according to my wishes.

LORD SENESCHAL Then let my duty be to fast until I'm able
To set a tasty dish upon my master's table.
Your kitchen staff shall help me to anticipate   10905
The seasons, and to bring rare produce to your plate;
With much exotic fare your banquet shall be graced –
Though plain and wholesome food, I know, is to
                your taste.

EMPEROR [to the fourth] With banqueting, it seems, we are
                preoccupied,
And so to you, young knight, this office we confide: 10910
As Lord Cupbearer you are charged by us to see
Our cellars stocked with wines of finest quality.
Yourself be moderate, resisting the temptation
To share too freely in our festive celebration.

LORD CUPBEARER The youth to whom his lord entrusts such
                honour can,   10915
Before you are aware, grow up to be a man.
At that great feast I see myself with loving care
Adorn your royal board with rich and precious ware,

With vessels of pure gold, the finest silver too.
The loveliest cup of all I shall seek out for you: 10920
A pure Venetian glass, in which contentment sits,
Lends flavour to the wine, but never dulls the wits.
This wondrous gift has led so many to temptation;
But you, Sire, put your faith in prudent moderation.

EMPEROR In trust you have received the honours I conferred   10925
At this most solemn time upon my given word.
As Emperor my word is absolute and sure;
And yet each privilege must still be made secure
By seal and signature. The man who has the power
To formalise these gifts comes at this timely hour.   10930

The ARCHBISHOP–LORD CHANCELLOR *enters.*

EMPEROR When in a vault at last the keystone is secured,
For ages still to come its structure is ensured.
You see four princes here; thus far we only sought
To order what concerns our household and our court.
But now the governance of our whole realm shall be   10935
Assigned to five of you with full authority.
Your territories shall outshine all other lands;
So I extend their bounds, and give into your hands
The heritage of those who have betrayed the throne.
You, loyal friends, shall call their forfeit lands

your own, 10940

Together with the right to add to your possession
By purchase or exchange, reversion or succession.
I further grant to you all powers that may pertain
To you as sovereign lords within your own domain.
Supreme judicial power your highest courts shall

wield; 10945

Their judgments shall not be contested or repealed.
All taxes, rents and tithes, all tolls and levies due,
Coinage and mineral rights, shall be assigned to you.
So that my gratitude to you be fully shown,
Your station has been raised to rank next to my own.   10950

ARCHBISHOP–LORD CHANCELLOR

You have our deepest thanks, we speak with one accord.
You make us strong; thereby your own strength is assured.

EMPEROR   A higher honour still to you five lords I give.
             Most gladly I shall rule my country while I live;
             And yet a noble line of forbears calls to mind,   10955
             Amid our urgent plans, the fate of all mankind.
             One day I too shall bid my dearest friends adieu;
             The choice of my successor then shall fall on you.
             Crown him and raise him high upon the altar; may
             Peace reign, without the storms we have endured
                                                          today.   10960

LORD CHANCELLOR With fervent pride, and yet with deep humility,
             Your highest princes kneel before Your Majesty.
             Until the loyal blood within these veins is still,
             We are the body that is guided by your will.

EMPEROR   And finally, what we have hitherto debated   10965
             By writ and signature shall be perpetuated.
             As sovereign princes you are free to rule, provided
             One thing alone: your realm shall never be divided.
             Whatever further land you may in time acquire,
             You shall bequeath it to your eldest son entire.   10970

LORD CHANCELLOR Most willingly I will record in my own hand
             This statute that will bring great blessings on our land.
             In chancery the script and seal shall be prepared,
             And by your signature as law shall be declared.

EMPEROR   I give you leave to go, that each of you now may   10975
             In quietude reflect on this momentous day.

                              [*the secular princes withdraw*

ARCHBISHOP [*stays behind and speaks with great feeling*]
             The Chancellor has left, the Bishop lingers here.
             An urgent sense of doom warns him to seek your ear;
             His father's heart is filled with sorrow and despair.

EMPEROR   On such a joyful day, what cause have you for care?   10980

ARCHBISHOP   What bitter pain it is to find, this very hour,
             Your Sacred Majesty in thrall to Satan's power!
             Your throne is safe, it seems, and yet, alas, you still
             Hold God to scorn and mock the Holy Father's will,
             Who, when he hears of this, will swiftly overwhelm   10985
             And with his sacred bolts destroy your sinful realm.
             He still recalls how you, when newly crowned, decreed
             That at the final hour the sorcerer be freed.

All Christians took offence when on that cursed head
Fell the first ray of grace your diadem had shed.   10990
But if to Mother Church you prove yourself contrite,
And of your ill-won gains give up some modest mite:
That slope on which you set your tent, and where
                                         you made
Your pact with evil powers that hastened to your aid,
Where to the Prince of Lies you lent a willing ear –   10995
Endow with pious heart a sacred precinct here,
The woods that clad the hills as far as can be seen,
The lush green pastures where the flocks may graze
                                         serene,
Clear lakes that teem with fish, the countless streams
                                         that flow
In winding cataracts down to the vale below,   11000
The speading valley too, its hollows, dells and meads –
Such penance will atone for all your sinful deeds.

EMPEROR   With dread and fear I own my grievous fault; so let
            The Church decree how far these limits shall be set.

ARCHBISHOP Then first, that place that was so foully desecrated   11005
            Shall to the service of Our Lord be dedicated.
            Already in my mind I see the walls rise higher;[75]
            The morning sunlight gleams upon the lofty choir,
            A crossing then is joined, and to complete the whole
            The soaring nave brings joy to every Christian soul.   11010
            With pious fervour through the noble porch they
                                         crowd,
            And over hill and dale the bells ring clear and loud;
            The lofty towers that rise to heaven send out the sound,
            And new-born penitents flock in from all around.
            Then soon, we trust, to mark the day of consecration,   11015
            Your presence, Sire, will grace our joyful celebration.

EMPEROR   Then let this holy task our sacred will proclaim:
            To praise the Lord our God, and purge me of my
                                         shame.
            Enough! My soul exults, I feel myself inspired.

ARCHBISHOP A final deed and covenant is still required.   11020

EMPEROR   Prepare the documents that formally convey
            These rights; I'll gladly sign the deeds without delay.

ARCHBISHOP [*makes to leave, but turns back at the last moment*]
        You will besides assign to us the revenue
        From these estates, the tithes and rents that shall
                                  accrue –
        In perpetuity; for to administrate   11025
        And properly maintain it all, the costs are great.
        A portion of the spoils of war will expedite
        The building of our church on this deserted site.
        Much timber, lime, and slate, and other things beside
        From many distant parts must also be supplied.   11030
        The people will provide for transport; they are taught
        The Church will bless all those who toil in her support.
                           [*he makes to leave*

EMPEROR   The sins I have incurred are surely very great;
        These sorcerers have brought me to a sorry state.

ARCHBISHOP [*turns back once more, and bows deeply*]
        Your pardon, Sire! This ill-famed man was granted all   11035
        The Empire's shore in feu. Anathema must fall
        Upon his head unless the Church receives its due
        Of privileges, tithes – and other income, too.

EMPEROR [*with irritation*]
        The land is not yet there! It lies beneath the sea.

ARCHBISHOP With patience, time will bring its just reward.
                         Then we   11040
        May take your word for all you promised us today?
                              [*exit*

EMPEROR [*alone*] At this rate my whole realm will soon be
                            signed away.

ACT FIVE

OPEN COUNTRY

TRAVELLER Yes, these are the trees I know!
Though I was away so long,
Still these shady lindens grow,   11045
Older now, but tall and strong.
Here I see the dunes once more,
Where that day the raging sea
Cast me on that lonely shore,
And the hut that sheltered me.   11050
And my hosts, who came to save me –
Blessings on that kindly pair!
Old they were, but still they gave me
Shelter, warmth and loving care.
All their pleasure was in giving   11055
Help to those who came that way;
Are those pious folk still living?
Shall I meet them here today?

BAUCIS [*a little woman, very old*]⁷⁶ Softly, stranger, do not wake him!
For my husband's sleeping sound.   11060
He is old, his rest will make him
Stronger for the daily round.

TRAVELLER Mother, I am not a stranger;
Did you both not rescue me
When I was a youth, in danger   11065
From the fury of the sea?
Baucis, you who fought to save me,
Warmed me back to life once more?

The husband approaches.

You, Philemon, who so bravely

Brought my treasure safe to shore? 11070
By the fire you swiftly lighted,
And the tolling of your bell,
In dire peril I was guided
Safely through the stormy swell.
Let me gaze upon the ocean 11075
In its boundlessness, and there
I shall kneel, and with devotion
Ease my burdened heart in prayer.
[*he walks out onto the dune*]

PHILEMON [*to Baucis*] Hurry now, and set the table
In the garden by the trees; 11080
He will be alarmed, unable
To believe the things he sees.
[*he stands beside the Traveller*]
Look: the foaming sea that treated
You so cruelly, has been tamed.
Gardens bloom where it retreated; 11085
Paradise has been reclaimed.
I was old by then, and ailing,
Found no work that I could do;
Just as my own strength was failing,
So the tide was ebbing too. 11090
Clever masters gave instructions
Carried out by toiling slaves;
Dykes and ditches – their constructions
Made them masters of the waves.
See the lush green pastures growing, 11095
Gardens, villages, and trees;
But now come, the sun is going,
Let us eat and take our ease.
Sails on the horizon yonder
Into harbour make their way; 11100
Birds, however far they wander,
Seek their nests at close of day.
Now the sea is but a gleaming
Seam of blue, a distant band;
In its place you see a teeming, 11105
Densely populated land.

All three sit at a table in the garden.

BAUCIS	Friend, your appetite is meagre,
	And you've spoken not a word.
PHILEMON	Tell him then, since you're so eager,
	How these miracles occurred.

11110

BAUCIS	Miracles they were! They leave me
	Still uneasy to this day.
	What has happened here, believe me,
	Was not done the proper way.
PHILEMON	But the Emperor ordained it,

11115

Made him lord of all the shore;
Has a herald not proclaimed it
His according to the law?
Tents and huts they first erected
Near our dunes, beside the wood;

11120

Suddenly, all unexpected,
In their place a palace stood.

BAUCIS	In the daytime workmen laboured,
	All to no avail; but where
	Ghostly flames at night had wavered,

11125

By the dawn a dyke was there.
Every night we heard the screaming –
Human sacrifice, they say –
Molten rivers, seaward streaming,
Turned to a canal next day.

11130

All he wants is to acquire
Our hut and grove, I fear.
Godless man! His sole desire
Is to be the master here.

PHILEMON	But he offered us a favour –

11135

	Fine new property instead!
BAUCIS	Higher ground is always safer;
	Do not trust the ocean bed!
PHILEMON	The sun is setting fast; we must
	Go to the chapel now, and there

11140

Toll the bell, and kneel in prayer
To the old God in whom we trust.

A PALACE

A spacious pleasure-garden beside a broad, straight canal.
FAUST, *in extreme old age, walks to and fro in thought.*

LYNCEUS [*speaks through a megaphone from his watchtower*][77]

 How gladly those last ships are steering
 For harbour with the setting sun;
 Close by on the canal is nearing   11145
 A laden ship, its journey done.
 How cheerfully the boatman raises
 The coloured pennants on the mast!
 With joyful heart he sings your praises;
 Good fortune favours you at last.   11150

 The chapel bell rings out from the dune.

FAUST [*enraged*] Accursed bell! That sound behind me
 Is like a dagger in my back.
 Why must its mocking chime remind me
 Not what I have, but what I lack?
 Out there no boundaries confine   11155
 My vast estates, except the seas;
 But here that dingy hut, those trees,
 That crumbling chapel, are not mine,
 So I can never rest at leisure.
 The shadow that they cast, I fear,   11160
 Would chill me, rob me of all pleasure.
 If only I were far from here!

LYNCEUS [*as above*] Towards us on the evening tide
 A gaily painted vessel sails,
 Its deck piled high on every side   11165
 With chests and boxes, crates and bales.

A splendid ship, richly laden with exotic products from all parts.
MEPHISTOPHELES. THE THREE MIGHTY MEN.

CHORUS   We're back on land,
      She's tied up fast.
      Ahoy there, Master!
      Home at last.   11170

They come ashore. The cargo is unloaded.

MEPHISTO. We've all worked hard, stuck to the task;
    Our master's praise is all we ask.
    We set out with two ships; we've brought
    Another twenty back to port.
    We've earned our laurels, every one –   11175
    The cargo shows how well we've done.
    The open sea frees up the mind –
    All scruples can be left behind;
    Whether it's ships or fish you catch,
    It's best to make a sudden snatch.   11180
    You start with two, you grab one more;
    It's easy then to make it four.
    The fifth one won't put up a fight,
    It's all quite simple: might is right.
    It's what you get, not how it's done,   11185
    That matters when you're out at sea;
    War, piracy and trade are one
    Inseparable trinity.

THE THREE MIGHTY MEN We haven't heard
    A single word   11190
    Of thanks from him!
    We've got a hoard
    Of loot on board,
    But he looks grim,
    As if he thinks   11195
    Our cargo stinks!

MEPHISTO. There's no more pay
    For you today.
    Each one of you
    Has had his due.   11200

THE THREE MEN That's just small beer,
    A pittance! We're
    Still owed a share,
    That's only fair.

MEPHISTO. Take our haul   11205
    Inside, unpack it,
    And then stack it
    Wall to wall;

And when he's seen
His treasure hoard   11210
With his own eyes,
He won't be mean.
He'll realise
He can afford
To give the fleet   11215
A royal treat!
Tomorrow — I give you my word —
Each man will have a pretty bird.

The cargo is removed.

MEPHISTO. [*to Faust*] Good fortune smiles upon you now,
So why this frown, this furrowed brow?   11220
Your wisdom has been crowned, for sea
And land are now in harmony.
Your vessels set out from the quay,
And quickly reach the open sea —
So from your palace here the whole   11225
Wide world is under your control.
It all began here; on this land
Were your first huts. Here, where we stand,
You dug the trenches where today
Your busy ships go on their way.   11230
Your vision, and our industry,
Gave you command of land and sea.
From here —

FAUST   A curse on *here*! It preys
Upon my mind and sours my days.
Since you're so well informed, I will   11235
Confess I cannot bear the pain
That stabs me to the heart — but still
I blush to have to speak it plain:
That aged couple must give way!
Those lindens shall be mine alone;   11240
Those few trees taunt me day by day,
Pollute my joy in all I own.
There I shall build among the boughs
An airy platform that allows

My eager gaze to wander free,   11245
And from that viewpoint I shall see
With one glance all that I have done:
A triumph of the human mind
That with resource and skill has won
New habitations for mankind.   11250

The richest man will always grieve
For what his wealth cannot achieve.
That clanging bell, those trees in bloom,
Are like the shadow of the tomb;
That sandy hillock can confound   11255
The freedom of my sovereign will.
How can I halt that mocking sound?
I rage, and yet I hear it still.

MEPHISTO.   Yes, such a nuisance, I can see,
Must make your life a misery.   11260
A horrid noise like that, it's clear,
Must grate on any noble ear.
That ding-dong-ding can cast a gloom
Across the peaceful evening sky,
And everyone is haunted by   11265
That dismal sound from font to tomb,
As if each life were just a long
Forgotten dream from ding to dong.

FAUST   Their wilful stubbornness can blight
All joy in my supreme success,   11270
That in my anguish, my distress,
I tire of doing what is right.

MEPHISTO.   I don't know why you're agonising –
You're long since used to colonising.

FAUST   Then get them both out of my sight!   11275
You know the little cottage where
I meant to house the aged pair.

MEPHISTO.   We'll move them out, and soon they'll be
Resettled very happily;
And even if we must persuade them,   11280
Their lovely home will compensate them.

He gives a shrill whistle. The Three appear.

You heard his orders; when it's done,
There'll be a feast for everyone.

THE THREE   He gave us a frosty reception; the least
He can do is give us a proper feast.   11285

[*they leave*

MEPHISTO. [*aside, to the audience*]
This kind of thing has happened before;
You've heard of Naboth's vineyard, I'm sure. [I Kings 21]

DEAD OF NIGHT

LYNCEUS THE WATCHMAN [*sings from the palace tower*]
To watch is the duty
Entrusted to me,
And my joy is the beauty   11290
Of all that I see.
I see what is far,
And I see what is near:
The moon and a star,
The woods and the deer.   11295
I see everywhere
The eternal design,
And rejoice that a share
Of its beauty is mine.
So be as it might,   11300
How blessed I have been
To find such delight
In all I have seen!

Pause

Not for joy alone was I
Set to watch up here so high;   11305
What appalling horrors loom
Out of the surrounding gloom!
In the darkness there a fire
Burns among the linden trees.
Sparks and flames are leaping higher,   11310
Fanned to fury by the breeze,
And the little hut that stood

Damp and moss-grown in the wood,
Is in flames; will no one heed
The call for those in direst need?   11315
If not, that old and kindly pair
Who used to tend their hearth with care
Must soon be overwhelmed and choke
In that infernal pall of smoke.
Now the mossy timber frame   11320
Is all ablaze; if only they
Could save themselves! – There is no way
To flee that hell of raging flame.
Swirling tongues are leaping higher,
Leaves and twigs are all on fire,   11325
Burning branches break and go
Crashing to the ground below.
Why was I gifted with such sight
To see these horrors in the night?
Alas! the little chapel now,   11330
Crushed beneath a falling bough,
Is on fire. Throughout the wood
Flickering tongues of flame have spread;
Where the linden trees once stood,
Hollow trunks glow fiery red. –   11335
[after a long pause, he sings]
That vision that delighted me,
For evermore has ceased to be.

FAUST [on the balcony, looking towards the dunes]

What whimpering song comes to my ears?
Too late now for regret or tears.
My watchman wails; it vexes me   11340
That it was done so hastily.
The lindens are destroyed, each tree
A charred and blackened stump; but here
I'll build a lofty belvedere
To gaze into infinity.   11345
From there the dwelling I shall see
Where that old pair can end their days
In quiet happiness, and praise
Their fortune and my charity.

MEPHISTOPHELES and THE THREE [*below*]

	We came as quickly as we could;	11350
	The news, we fear, is not too good.	
	We knocked and rattled, all in vain –	
	No one replied. We tried again,	
	We pounded louder than before –	
	And then we battered in the door.	11355

We came as quickly as we could;   11350
The news, we fear, is not too good.
We knocked and rattled, all in vain –
No one replied. We tried again,
We pounded louder than before –
And then we battered in the door.   11355
We shouted, threatened them, but still
They didn't answer us at all.
It's often like that when we call;
They just don't listen, never will.
We didn't want to hang about –   11360
Our orders were to get them out.
The old ones didn't suffer a lot,
They died of fright right on the spot.
There was a stranger hiding there
Who drew his sword, so we took care   11365
Of him. But he put up a fight;
Some coals got scattered from the fire,
And set a pile of straw alight,
Which turned into their funeral pyre.

FAUST   Were you quite deaf to what I said?   11370
             I wanted them removed, not dead.
             A curse upon you all, and on
             Your wild and mindless tricks. Begone!

CHORUS   An ancient proverb we've heard tell:
             Give way to force, for if you choose   11375
             To stand and fight, then you could lose
             Your house and home – your life as well.

                                                   [*exeunt*

FAUST [*on the balcony*] The stars have gone, the darkness grows,
             The flames have died, the fire glows.
             A drifting pall of smoke is fanned   11380
             Upon the breeze to where I stand.
             Rash words, too soon obeyed, I fear! –
             What ghostly shadows hover near?

MIDNIGHT

Four grey women appear.

1 WOMAN	My name is Want.
2 WOMAN	And mine is Debt.
3 WOMAN	My name is Need.
4 WOMAN	And mine is Care. 11385
THE FIRST THREE	The door is locked fast, we cannot get in;
	A rich man lives here, we've no hold over him.
WANT	I fade to a shadow.
DEBT	And I cease to be.
NEED	The pampered and wealthy pay no heed to me.
CARE	My sisters, you three cannot enter, but Care 11390
	Can slip through the keyhole, so let him beware!

CARE *disappears.*

WANT	Then come, my grey sisters, for we cannot stay.
DEBT	Lead on, I will be at your side all the way.
NEED	And close on your heels will be Need, never fear.
ALL THREE	Dark clouds are obscuring the sky; every star 11395
	Hides its light. But look yonder! Who comes from afar?
	It is Death, he is coming, our brother draws near.

[exeunt

FAUST *in the palace*

FAUST	I saw four figures come, but only three
	Have gone. Their words made little sense to me.
	I thought they spoke of need, of want and debt, 11400
	And then I heard a dismal echo – death;
	It was a hollow sound, a ghostly breath.
	I have not fought my way to freedom yet;
	If I could banish magic, and disown
	The spells and incantations binding me, 11405
	Stand face to face with nature all alone,
	My life would be worthwhile: I would be free.
	I was a free man once, before I first
	Sought out the dark forbidden ways and cursed
	Myself and all the world. But now the air 11410

Is full of ghosts; I hear them everywhere.
Though day dispels unreason with its light,
Those phantoms come to haunt us in the night.
We may return from meadows in full bloom,
But then we hear the raven croak of doom,   11415
For superstitions constantly surround us,
We see their signs and omens all around us.
We stand alone, in trembling and in fear;
A door will creak – but no one will appear.
[*alarmed*] Is someone there?

CARE   Yes; I am here.   11420

FAUST   Who are you?

CARE   It is I, as you can see.

FAUST   Begone!

CARE   I am where I am meant to be.

FAUST [*at first angry, then calmly, to himself*]
          Take heed, and speak no word of sorcery.

CARE   Though no ear may ever hear me,
                            In their hearts all men must fear me;   11425
                            In an ever-changing guise
                            Baleful power I exercise.
                            All their lives, by land or sea,
                            They dread my fearful company.
                            Never sought, but always near,   11430
                            Cursed and flattered, I am here.
          Do you not know me? I am Care.

FAUST   I have rushed through the world, and everywhere
          I went I seized each pleasure by the hair.
          What did not satisfy me, I would let   11435
          It go without the least regret.
          What I desired I have achieved, and then
          I thirsted for desire again.
          At first a wild and stormy life I led;
          More wisely now, more cautiously I tread.   11440
          This world I know quite well enough; what lies
          Beyond, our eyes will never penetrate,
          And only fools endeavour to create
          Some likeness of themselves above the skies.
          This world has much to give an able man   11445

Who will stand firm, achieving what he can;
He need not search eternity to find
What lies within the compass of his mind.
So let him journey on through joy and pain;
When phantoms haunt him, let him go his way,   11450
Press on regardless – but let him remain
Dissatisfied each moment of the day!

CARE   Any man whom I possess
          Finds the whole world profitless;
          Dwelling in perpetual night   11455
          Where the sun can shed no light,
          Though his senses may be whole,
          Darkness will enshroud his soul.
          All the treasures he has known
          He can never call his own;   11460
          All his feelings turn to whim,
          And no food can nourish him.
          Joy or sadness, bliss or sorrow,
          Never can be his today;
          Ever mindful of tomorrow,   11465
          He must fret his life away.

FAUST   Enough! I will not listen to this kind
          Of nonsense, it has no effect on me.
          Begone! Your dismal litany
          Could drive the wisest man out of his mind.   11470

CARE   Should he go or should he stay?
          Always he will hesitate,
          Even on the smoothest way
          Lurching with unsteady gait.
          Ever more withdrawn, askance   11475
          He views the world with sullen glance.
          Gasping for his breath, he smothers
          All his joy, and burdens others.
          Breathing still, but not reviving,
          Not despairing, still surviving,   11480
          Liberated and oppressed,
          Fitful sleep brings him no rest.
          Unremitting obligation,
          Unrelenting abnegation,

| | Bind him like a baleful spell, | 11485 |
| | And prepare his way to hell. | |

FAUST   Unholy spectres! Time and time again
You come to plague and harry mortal men.
On the most humdrum day you can ensnare
Them in a fearful tangle of despair.   11490
Demons, I know, are with us everywhere;
That stubborn spirit bond we cannot sever,
Or rid ourselves of them – but I will never
Recognise the creeping power of Care!

CARE   But you shall feel it yet before I go,   11495
For I leave you my curse behind:
Most men are blind throughout their lives, and so
You, Faust, shall at the last be blind!

             [*she breathes on him, and leaves*

FAUST [*blinded*] Now darker, ever darker seems the night,
Yet deep within me shines a burning light.   11500
I hasten to fulfil my master plan;
At my command alone it can be done.
Now rouse yourselves, my workers, every one,
To finish the brave scheme that I began!
The ground is marked, the measurements are made,   11505
So set to work at once with pick and spade!
We can achieve the very highest prize
Through discipline and toil; to realise
My great work for the sake of humankind,
A thousand hands need but a single mind.   11510

GREAT FORECOURT OF THE PALACE

Torches

MEPHISTOPHELES [*as overseer, leading*]

     Come on, Lemures, come on in,
You shambling patched-up dummies,
You scraps of sinew, bone and skin,
Half-dead, half-living mummies.

CHORUS OF LEMURES[78] We come at once at your command;   11515
Did we get the impression

That there's a vacant piece of land
For us to take possession?

We've chains to measure out the plot,
And stakes to mark it clear;   11520
But if you ask us, we forgot
Why we were summoned here.

MEPHISTO. No special skills are needed; come,
Just measure up by rule of thumb –
The tallest one lies on the ground,   11525
The others cut the turf all round.
That's where our fathers lie asleep –
A simple trench, just six feet deep.
Straight from a palace to this narrow bed;
A silly way to end, it must be said.   11530

LEMURES [digging with mocking gestures]
In youth when I did live and love,
It was my sweetest pleasure
Wherever merry music played
To dance a lively measure.

Now old age trips me with his crutch,   11535
I stagger and I stumble;
The grave is open wide – just one
More step, and in I tumble.

FAUST [comes out of the palace, feeling his way to the doorpost]
What joy to hear the clang of spades! My band
Of workmen toil to reconcile the land   11540
With its own borders, to confine the sea
Within a stern unyielding boundary,
And set a limit to the surging tide.

MEPHISTO. [aside] Your labours are in vain; these slaves
Who build your dykes and groynes are on our side.   11545
The water-devil Neptune rules the waves,
And you are lost. Your futile schemes prepare
A royal feast for him; here, everywhere,
The elements conspire with us to send
Your efforts to oblivion in the end.   11550

FAUST   Overseer!

MEPHISTO.   Here!

FAUST   By any means you can
Recruit more workers, summon every man.
Encourage them with threat or promise, use
Persuasion, force, or bribe them with more pay,
Whatever will work best, and bring me news   11555
Of how my dyke progresses every day.

MEPHISTO. [*sotto voce*] That isn't what I heard; it was more like
A grave that they were digging, not a dyke.

FAUST   A swamp extends along the mountainside,
And spreads disease across the land I've gained;   11560
But if that filthy marshland could be drained,
In that last deed I'd take the greatest pride.
For millions then new land I could provide
To live, not safe perhaps, but free to toil,
Both man and beast, contented side by side   11565
In green and fertile fields on virgin soil.
Within the shelter of the banks erected
By tireless labour, they shall live protected,
And though the sea may rage at will outside,
A paradise shall flourish here. The tide   11570
May gnaw and batter at the dykes, but each
And every one will rush to close the breach.
This is the vision that inspires me,
This is my wisdom's final word: that they
Who must defend their freedom every day   11575
Deserve to live lives that are truly free.
So here, beset by danger, each shall spend
A life of honest effort to the end.
A happy throng! If only I could see
Upon free land a people truly free,   11580
Then to the passing moment I might say:
You are so beautiful, I bid you stay!
The traces of my life can never be
Effaced from human memory.
As I anticipate my vision, this   11585
Is now the moment of my highest bliss.

Faust sinks back; the Lemures seize him and lay him on the ground.

MEPHISTO.   This man no joy or pleasure satisfied.
              He snatched at every changing shape, and tried
              To seize the fleeting moment as it passed;
              But that sad, empty moment was his last.   11590
              That old man struggled to resist my power;
              He lies here in the sand, and time has won.
              The clock stands –

LEMURES [*chorus*]   Silent as the midnight hour.
              The hand falls.

MEPHISTO.   It is finished. All is done.

CHORUS   It is all over.

MEPHISTO.   Over? Stupid word!   11595
              Why over? The expression is absurd.
              What's over is just nothing, it's all one.
              Why else are we eternally employed
              To drag what has been made into the void?
              All's over – what is that supposed to mean?   11600
              Over! It might as well have never been,
              But still it runs around as if it were –
              Eternal emptiness I'd much prefer.

INTERMENT

LEMUR [*solo*]   Who was it built this house so ill
                      With shovel and with spade?   11605

LEMURES [*chorus*]   For you, poor guest in hempen coat,
                      It is far too well made.

LEMUR [*solo*]   No furniture is in the hall,
                      No chairs or table set.

LEMURES [*chorus*]   His lease will not be long at all –   11610
                      He was too much in debt.

MEPHISTO.   There lies the body; should the spirit flee,
              I'll soon show it the deed it signed for me
              In blood. They have so many ways today
              To cheat the Devil of his rightful prey;   11615
              They take offence at the old-fashioned ways,
              The new ones haven't been accepted yet.

I used to do it on my own; these days
I take on all the helpers I can get.

We have to work in terrible conditions!   11620
Time-honoured customs, all the old traditions –
You can't rely on these things any more.
It used to exit when they breathed their last;
I'd lie in wait, and snap! out came a claw
As quick as any mouse – I'd have it fast.   11625
But now it hangs about and stays inside
The foetid corpse, a horrid, gloomy place;
The elements start fighting for more space
And drive it out – it's so undignified.
I rack my brains each hour of every day: 11630
How, when – and *where*? Impossible to say.
You can't be certain *whether* nowadays —
Old Death is less decisive in his ways.
I've often leered at rigid limbs, but then
It's all a sham – they start to twitch again.   11635
[*he summons his troops with elaborate and exaggerated gestures*]
Come on now, double quick, you motley crew,
Old-fashioned devils of the proper kind,
With crooked horns or straight ones, I don't mind –
But bring the gaping jaws of hell with you.
It's true that hell has many jaws, for all   11640
According to their rank or status – yet
In future, at the final curtain call,
They won't insist on too much etiquette.

The fearsome jaws of hell open left.

Hell bares its fangs, vast streams of fire flow
In fury from the yawning vault below.   11645
Down there among the seething fumes I see
The city of flame that burns eternally.
A red wave surges from the pit beneath,
Upon it swim the damned, who crave salvation;
But crushed in the hyena's mighty teeth   11650
They are swept back into the conflagration.
The furthest nooks and corners still conceal
So many horrors in the depths below;

You do your best to frighten sinners – though
They still don't think the flames of hell are real.   11655
[*to the fat devils with short straight horns*]
Pot-bellied rascals, with your sweaty faces
Still burning from the brimstone fires below,
You bull-necked blockheads, down here take your places,
And if you see a phosphorescent glow –
That is the soul, winged Psyche as it's called;   11660
If you tear off its wings, it's just a bald
And horrid grub. I'll stamp my mark on it,
Then fling it down into the blazing pit!

You bloated bladders, get to work,
And guard the nether regions well;   11665
It's very difficult to tell
If that's where it prefers to lurk.
It likes the navel – so take care
It doesn't slip away from you down there.
[*to the thin devils with long curly horns*]
You gangling fools, you giant semaphores,   11670
Stand tall and wave your spindly arms about!
Hold them out straight, and spread your claws
To grab it as it tries to flutter out.
It doesn't like its old abode, I'm sure –
And genius will always want to soar.   11675

Radiance from above right

THE HEAVENLY HOST   Heaven is sending
Angels descending
On wings from above;
Hovering, wheeling,
Soaring, revealing   11680
Mercy unending.
Dust shall be shriven,
Sinners forgiven
Through heavenly love.

MEPHISTO.   From that unwelcome cloud of light a jingling,   11685
A horrid dissonance grates on my ear;
Those winsome girlish choirboy voices mingling
Are what the prim and pious love to hear.

You know we plotted, when we fell from grace,
To bring destruction on the human race;   11690
We found the very vilest of our notions
Was just the thing they need for their devotions.[79]

Now here they come, the wily pharisees!
They've cheated us of many a juicy prize.
They know our methods, and they use them – these   11695
Are devils too, but devils in disguise.
To lose to them would shame us all for ever:
Stand by the grave, and hold your ranks together!

CHORUS OF ANGELS [*scattering roses*] Roses in showers,
                    Balm-fragrant flowers,   11700
                    Floating and drifting,
                    Shining, uplifting,
                    Slender twigs holding
                    Blossoms unfolding,
                    Burgeon apace.   11705

                    Spring colours, glowing
                    Red and green, showing
                    This sleeper the grace
                    Of heaven's embrace.

MEPHISTOPHELES [*to the devils*]
                    You flinch and wince! Is that all hell can do?   11710
Just let them throw their roses, stand your ground,
Stay at your posts, you ninnies, all of you!
They think that simply scattering flowers around
Will douse your brimstone like a fall of snow.
One puff from you will shrivel them, so blow,   11715
You windbags, blow! – Enough! Don't overdo it –
Your torrid breath has scorched their swarm of roses;
We'll all be lost if you set fire to it.
You've blown too hard, so shut your mouths and noses –
You don't know when to stop! When will you learn? – 11720
They're turning brown, now they begin to burn.
A shower of caustic flame rains down. Hold fast!
Close up your ranks, resist them to the last!
The devils weaken, their morale is low;
They seem to sense a strange, alluring glow.   11725

CHORUS OF ANGELS Blessed are the blooms of spring,
                  Joyful the flames we bring,
                  Blissfully scattering
                  Love that will conquer wrong,
                  All hearts delight.   11730
                  True words of charity,
                  Heavenly clarity;
                  For the eternal throng
                  All shall be light.

MEPHISTO. A curse on you, for shame, you useless dolts –   11735
           The devils are all doing somersaults!
           Head over heels, arse over tip, pell-mell
           The clumsy oafs all tumble down to hell.
           A good hot bath is what you all deserve!
           But I shall stand my ground and hold my nerve.   11740
           [*he beats off the roses floating around him*]
           Get off me, jack o' lanterns! Once you're caught,
           Your light goes out, you turn in to a sort
           Of horrid slime that sticks to me like glue,
           And burns like pitch and brimstone. Off with you!

CHORUS OF ANGELS What is not yours to win,   11745
                  You may not share it;
                  What pains you deep within,
                  You cannot bear it.
                  If it has taken root,
                  We must be resolute;   11750
                  Those who love, those alone
                  Love will lead in!

MEPHISTO. My head's on fire, my heart and liver burn!
           This element hurts more infernally
           Than hell's own fires that burn eternally.   11755
           So that's why unrequited lovers sigh
           So mournfully, and why they twist and turn
           Their necks to see their mistress passing by.

           Me too! What turns my head in that direction?
           They are the enemy, we are at war –   11760
           I couldn't stand the sight of them before!

Have I succumbed to some unknown infection?
They are such lovely lads, it's quite alarming:
I ought to curse them – but they're just too charming.
If I let these erotic stirrings rule   11765
My head, I shall forever feel a fool.
Confound the boys, I should abominate them;
They're just too beautiful – how can I hate them?

You lovely children, it's as if you were
Direct descendants of great Lucifer.   11770
You're all so pretty I would like to kiss you –
And I'm delighted that I didn't miss you.
I feel a warm and comfortable glow,
As if I'd seen you all before; you're so
Desirable, and cuddly as a kitten –   11775
The more I look at you, the more I'm smitten.
Come closer, give me just one tender glance!

ANGELS   We're here – but you retreat as we advance.
We're getting nearer; stay there if you can.

The Angels hover round him, filling the stage.

MEPHISTOPHELES [*forced out into the proscenium*]
You call us fiends, damned spirits come from hell –   11780
But you're the real sorcerers; no man
Or woman's safe from your seductive spell.
To hell with this accursed game!
Can this be love? My body's all aflame;
It hurts so much that I can scarcely tell   11785
Where those damned roses burned my neck as well.
Stop floating to and fro! Come down and sway
Your lovely limbs in a more worldly way.
That grave and sober look is just your style –
But still, what would I give to see you smile!   11790
For me that would be never-ending bliss;
I mean the sort of look that lovers share –
Just give your mouth a little twitch, like this.
That tall one there – it's you that I prefer;
Why can't you look a little lewd, at least –   11795
That solemn face makes you look like a priest.
You'd all look well with fewer clothes, I'm sure;

Those flowing robes are simply too demure.
And now they're turning round – ah, but I find
The rascals so delicious from behind!   11800

CHORUS OF ANGELS Turn, flames of love, to
                  Radiance, revealing
                  Truth from above to
                  Bring sinners healing.
                  So from the snares of hell   11805
                  They shall be free,
                  In our blest company
                  Ever to dwell.

MEPHISTOPHELES [*recovering his composure*]
                  What's this? I'm full of boils, like Job! My hide
                  Is a repulsive sight! But deep inside   11810
                  I've triumphed over love! That pox I caught
                  Has come out on my skin. I always thought
                  I could stand firm, it's in my pedigree;
                  The Devil's noble parts are good as new,
                  Those loathsome flames are out – I'm free   11815
                  To curse you all, the whole celestial crew!

CHORUS OF ANGELS Holy flames glowing,
                  Goodness bestowing
                  On those you touch, giving
                  Bliss to the living.   11820
                  Let us all raise
                  Voices in praise,
                  Let the soul breathe there,
                  Purer the air!

          They rise, bearing off the immortal part of Faust.

MEPHISTOPHELES [*looking around*] Now what? They've disappeared,
                            the whole damned throng!   11825
                  The cheeky rascals caught me by surprise,
                  And now they're off to heaven with their prize.
                  That's why they sniffed about the grave so long!
                  I've lost the greatest treasure there could be;
                  That lofty soul that pledged itself to me,   11830
                  They've snatched away before my very eyes!

Who can I turn to? Who will hear my plea?
Who will restore my rightful property?
You've been deceived, you're in a sorry plight –
And at your age as well; it serves you right.   11835
I've bungled things disgracefully, and so
A huge investment has been squandered, just
Because a devil old enough to know
Succumbed so shamefully to common lust.
If someone so experienced can spend   11840
His time on such a silly childish spree,
It must be folly of a high degree
That took possession of him in the end.

MOUNTAIN GORGES

Woods, Cliffs, Wilderness
Holy anchorites in their cells in clefts at various heights among the cliffs.[80]

CHORUS AND ECHO Branches that bend and sway,
       Massive rocks downward weigh;   11845
       Roots clinging to the ground,
       Trees cluster thickly round;
       Torrents in foaming waves
       Close by the sheltering caves.
       Lions that round them pace   11850
       Silently, peacefully,
       Honour this sacred place,
       Love's holy sanctuary.
PATER ECSTATICUS [*hovering between higher and lower regions*]
       Bliss of eternal fire,
       Glowing chains of desire,   11855
       Searing pains of the breast,
       Joy of those God has blessed.
       Arrows, transfix me, you
       Lances, come pierce me through,
       You cudgels, batter me,   11860
       Thunderbolts, shatter me!

> Let the world's vanity
> Fade so that I may see
> Constant the star above
> Of everlasting love.   11865

PATER PROFUNDUS [*in the lower region*]
> This rocky chasm that below
> On deeper chasms rests its weight,
> These thousand sparkling streams that flow
> To fearful depths in foaming spate;
> These trunks that rise erect and tall   11870
> And thrust towards the skies above,
> Betoken the almighty love
> That shapes and cherishes us all.

> All round I hear a furious roaring
> From cliffs that echo, trees that sway;   11875
> I hear the swollen torrents pouring
> With pleasing thunder on their way
> To irrigate the valley, where
> The jagged bolts of lightning blaze
> To purify the sullen air   11880
> Of poisonous fogs and sultry haze.

> These messengers of love proclaim
> Eternal forces that enfold
> And form all things. May they inflame
> My inner self, confused and cold,   11885
> Where torpid senses vex and bind
> With painful chains my spirit tight.
> Bring peace, Lord, to my troubled mind,
> And to my barren heart bring light!

PATER SERAPHICUS [*in the middle region*]
> Drifting through the swaying trees are   11890
> Misty forms, like clouds at dawn.
> But what dwells within them? These are
> Spirit-children, scarcely born.

CHORUS OF BLESSED BOYS Tell us, kindly Father, tell us,
> Who we are, what place is this,   11895
> How such happiness befell us

In this gentle state of bliss?

PATER SERAPHICUS Blessed boys, at midnight born,[81]
　　　　　　　　Mind and senses half developed,
　　　　　　　　From the arms of parents torn,　　　　　　　11900
　　　　　　　　Soon by angels' wings enveloped;
　　　　　　　　Feel a loving presence flowing
　　　　　　　　All around as you draw near,
　　　　　　　　Happy innocents, not knowing
　　　　　　　　Worldly sorrows, pain or fear.　　　　　　　11905
　　　　　　　　Come, descend into my being;
　　　　　　　　Gazing through my earthly eyes
　　　　　　　　You may look around you, seeing
　　　　　　　　What a world before you lies!
　　　　　　　　[he absorbs them into himself]
　　　　　　　　See these trees, these rocks, these roaring　　11910
　　　　　　　　Waterfalls whose mighty flow
　　　　　　　　Rolls in surging torrents, pouring
　　　　　　　　Steeply to the depths below.

BLESSED BOYS [from within] Such an awesome scene we see,
　　　　　　　　But we quake with dread and fear;　　　　　11915
　　　　　　　　Noble Father, set us free,
　　　　　　　　For it is so gloomy here!

PATER SERAPHICUS Rise to higher regions, growing
　　　　　　　　All unnoticed, purified
　　　　　　　　By God's grace forever flowing,　　　　　　11920
　　　　　　　　By His presence fortified.
　　　　　　　　Spirit nourishment will feed you:
　　　　　　　　Love eternal, manifest
　　　　　　　　In that purest ether, lead you
　　　　　　　　On to dwell among the blest.　　　　　　　11925

CHORUS OF BLESSED BOYS [circling round the highest peaks]
　　　　　　　　Dance in a ring now,
　　　　　　　　Join hands and circle round,
　　　　　　　　Joyfully sing now,
　　　　　　　　Let your hosannas sound!
　　　　　　　　Trust and revere him　　　　　　　　　　11930
　　　　　　　　Whose teaching is sure;
　　　　　　　　Soon you will near Him
　　　　　　　　Whom you adore.

ANGELS   [*hovering in the higher atmosphere, carrying the immortal part
           of Faust*] [82] This noble spirit is released
           From evil and damnation;   11935
           For those whose striving never ceased
           We can lead to salvation. [83]
           And if from highest heaven love
           And mercy should reprieve him,
           Then all the blessed host above   11940
           Will joyfully receive him.

THE YOUNGER ANGELS Loving women gave these flowers,
           Holy sinners whose contrition
           Helped us in our noble mission
           To defeat the Devil's powers   11945
           And snatch that spirit from perdition.
           Evil yielded as we scattered,
           Demons fled, their forces shattered;
           Not by agonies of hell,
           But by pangs of love undone.   11950
           Even ancient Satan fell
           Prey to passion's painful spell.
           All rejoice! for we have won.

THE MORE PERFECTED ANGELS We cannot carry higher
                   These earthly traces   11955
                   That no refiner's fire
                   Ever effaces.
                   Spirit and substance tied
                   So close together –
                   No angel could divide   11960
                   One from the other.
                   When they are fused to one
                   Single duality,
                   Eternal love alone
                   Can set them free.   11965

THE YOUNGER ANGELS I sense a presence near;
                   Drifts of mist, wreathing
                   Round the high summit here –
                   Spirit forms weaving.
                   Now through the clearing cloud   11970
                   I see a lively crowd

                Of blessed boys,
                Freed from the weight of earth,
                All in a ring
                Tasting the joys   11975
                Of their rebirth
                Into celestial spring.
                Let him begin his rise
                Into the purer skies
                Under their wing!   11980

THE BLESSED BOYS Gladly we now receive
                This spirit-chrysalis;
                Thereby we shall achieve
                Pledge of angelic bliss.
                Loosen the threads of earth   11985
                That still impede him!
                Transfigured, to new birth
                We shall soon lead him.

DOCTOR MARIANUS [*in the highest, purest cell*]
                On high the view is clear,
                Spirit-uplifting;   11990
                Women are passing near,
                Heavenward drifting.
                Among them can be seen,
                Glorious in flight,
                Star-crowned, our heavenly queen,   11995
                Radiant with light.

     [*in ecstasy*] Sovereign of the world, on high
     Enthroned, reveal to me
     In the blue vault of the sky
     Your great mystery.   12000
     Grant the man whose loving breast
     Is moved by yearning for you
     May know the rapture of the blest
     And lay his heart before you.

     Pride and courage never fail   12005
     When we do your will;
     Should your gentle love prevail,
     Fiery hearts grow still.

Fairest virgin, pure, serene,
Mother we revere,   12010
Chosen as our heavenly queen,
And of gods the peer.

Small clouds surround her,
Women beneath her
Cluster around her,   12015
Breathing the ether –
Penitents, kneeling,
Beg for the healing
Balm of her grace.

Spotless, pure in every way,   12020
To you the power is given
That those whom sin has led astray
May hope to be forgiven.

Weak they were, and it may be
Hard indeed to save them;   12025
Who unaided may break free
From passions that enslave them?
How easily the feet may slip
Upon the path they tread;
By flattery of eye or lip   12030
How many are misled!

The Mater Gloriosa soars upwards.

CHORUS OF PENITENTS Onward you soar to
Regions eternal,
Peerless, supernal;
Grant, we implore you,   12035
Fullness of grace!
MAGNA PECCATRIX [Luke 7: 36] By the love that bathed the feet
Of your glorious son with tears,
Soothing them with balm so sweet,
Defying pharisaic sneers;   12040
By the alabaster box
That dripped with fragrance rich and rare,
By the softly flowing locks
That dried His sacred limbs with care –

MULIER SAMARITANA [John 4] By the sacred well, where first 12045
       The flocks of Abraham were driven;
       By the jar to cool His thirst
       That to our Saviour's lips was given;
       By the limpid waters ever
       Since from that pure fountain springing, 12050
       Overflowing, failing never,
       To the world salvation bringing –

MARIA AEGYPTIACA [Acta Sanctorum][84]
       By the tomb in which they laid
       The body of our Lord immortal,
       By the arm that once forbade 12055
       Me entry to its sacred portal;
       By the forty years I suffered
       Penance in a distant land,
       By the parting words discovered
       Written in the desert sand – 12060

ALL THREE You have never turned your face
       From those whom grievous sin has stained,
       Who by penance still a place
       In eternity have gained.
       Now for this good soul we pray, 12065
       Unaware of sin or flaw,
       Who but once had gone astray:
       Your forgiveness we implore!

ONE OF THE PENITENT WOMEN, *formerly called Gretchen,*
       approaches, entreating her.

       Matchless in grace,
       Our Lady, incline 12070
       Your radiant face
       Upon this happiness of mine!
       My lover – see,
       Transfigured, he
       Returns to me! 12075

BLESSED BOYS [*circling closer*]
       His powerful limbs have grown
       Too heavy for us;
       For our true care his own
       Gifts will reward us.

We did not live to reach   12080
What life could afford us;
This learned man will teach
What lay before us.

THE PENITENT [*formerly called Gretchen*]

The blessed hosts of heaven surround him;
His spirit still seems scarce aware   12085
Of this new life that dawns around him,
But soon with them he will compare.
He has cast off the husk that shrouded
Him, the bonds of earth are torn,
Clad in ethereal robes, unclouded,   12090
To youthful vigour now reborn.
To new spheres grant that I may guide him,
Still dazzled by celestial day.

MATER GLORIOSA Rise higher, then! With you beside him,
He will not fail to find the way.   12095

DOCTOR MARIANUS [*prostrate in devotion*]

All contrite hearts, behold the face
That is your true salvation,
And thankfully implore the grace
Of blest transfiguration.
May all nobler spirits vie   12100
To serve you, faith confessing;
Virgin, Mother, Queen on high,
Goddess, grant your blessing!

CHORUS MYSTICUS All that is mutable
Is but reflected;   12105
What is inscrutable
Here is effected.
What is not understood,
Here it is done;
Eternal womanhood   12110
Draws us all on.

FINIS

THE UNPUBLISHED SCENARIOS
FOR THE WALPURGIS NIGHT

AFTER THE INTERMEZZO

A lonely, desolate place. Trumpet blasts. Lightning, thunder from above. Pillars of fire, billowing smoke. A rock juts out of it. It is Satan. Large crowd of people all around. Delay. How to get through. Injury. Shouting. Song. They stand in the inner circle. The heat is unbearable. Who is first in the circle. Satan's speech, etc. Presentations. Investitures. Midnight. The apparition sinks. Volcano. Breaks up in disorder. Smashing and raging.

*　　　*　　　*

Fiery fingers of Mephistopheles

*　　　*　　　*

He climbs the hill, see, over there,
Far off the people stand and stare.
The pious bless themselves, for he
Comes on in certain victory.

*　　　*　　　*

*Summit. Night. Fiery colossus. Closest circle.
Crowds. Groups. Speech*

*　　　*　　　*

SATAN She-goats to the left,
The females all smell;
He-goats to the right –
And they stink as well.
But even if he
Should stink even more,
She can't do without him –
That's what he's for.

CHORUS Now fall down and worship

Our master and lord;
All peoples and nations
His teachings applaud.
All nature's deep secrets
His words will convey;
To life everlasting
He'll show you the way.

SATAN   [*turning to the right*]
You worship two things,
You know nothing finer:
The glitter of gold,
And a woman's vagina.
The one it devours,
The other procures;
How happy you'd be then,
If both could be yours!

A VOICE
I'm so far away,
I couldn't quite hear
The wonderful words
Of the master out here.
I'm not any wiser –
The deep mystery
Of life and of nature
Means nothing to me.

SATAN   [*turning to the left*]
Two things are delightful
For you to behold:
A glorious phallus
And glittering gold.
Now listen, you women,
For you must be told
To treasure the phallus
Far more than the gold!

CHORUS
Bow down at his altar,
His voice shall be heard.
How happy are those who
Give ear to his word!

A VOICE   I'm too far away
                          From the altar to hear
                          The comforting words
                          Of the master, I fear.
                          So who will explain
                          The deep mystery
                          Of life everlasting
                          And nature to me?

MEPHISTO.   [*to a young girl*] You're weeping! Why, what
                                    makes you sad, my pretty dear?
             Your tears are surely out of place up here!
             Has all this crush of people been too rough with you?

YOUNG GIRL   Oh, no! I find that gentleman's words so confusing.
             He talks of gold and phallus, gold and vagina, too –
             And all the people seem to find it so amusing.
             But only grown-ups understand these things, it seems.

MEPHISTO.   Don't fret, my child, it's quite clear what the
                                               Devil means;
             And if you want to know, just grope about
             Inside your neighbour's trousers, and you'll soon
                                               find out!

SATAN   [*turning to the front*]
                          You lasses have come here
                          On broomsticks, I see.
                          Now stand in the middle
                          And listen to me.
                          Be swinish by night,
                          And proper by day;
                          Just take my advice,
                          And you'll go a long way!

                          Individual audiences
                          Master of Ceremonies

X   . . . and if within this land his laws
             Will grant me absolute autocracy,
             Although by nature I support democracy,
             Then I will gladly kiss the tyrant's claws.

M.C.   His claws! Dear Sir, you must aspire

	To show your loyalty more eagerly than this!
x	What does the ritual require?
M.C.	It is the master's backside you must kiss.
x	No matter; I am equally inclined

To kiss my liege's front – or his behind.
Your nose above, O Master, would traverse
The heavens to the distant spheres;
But here below a hole appears
That would engulf the universe.
What perfumes waft from this colossal orifice!
In paradise it cannot smell as sweet as this.
That well-constructed entrance, gaping wide,
Arouses the desire to creep inside.
Should I go on?

SATAN   Enough, my vassal good and true!
I grant to you a million souls in fee.
The man who licks the Devil's arse as well as you
Has proved himself supremely skilled in flattery.

*   *   *

APPARITION: EXECUTION

CHORUS   Where human blood flows hot and free,
All magic shuns the light of day;
The brotherhood in black and grey [85]
Is roused to new activity.
For bloody works we offer thanks,
For pious work, blood is the price.
Round fire and blood our solemn ranks
Surround the fiery sacrifice.

A woman's wanton look means blood,
And wine sets drunken minds aglow.
The glance, the drink provokes the flood;
The knife is out, and blood will flow.
Blood cries for blood when it is shed,
One drop can to a fountain grow.
One stream by others will be fed,
And soon in rivers blood will flow.

Crowds. They climb a tree. G.[86] *People talking. On*
burning ground the phantom naked. Its hands behind its
back. Neither the face nor the pudenda covered. Singing.
The head falls off. Blood spurts and puts out the fire.
Night. Roaring. Devil-children chattering.
From which Faust learns that . . .

FAUST. MEPHISTOPHELES

*   *   *

CHORUS OF WITCHES

And as the witches homeward stream
The shoots are yellow, the stubble is green.
No one really cares a bit –
The witches puke and the sows all shit.

MEPHISTO.

To get away from soot and witches,
We'll set our course for southern pitches.
Down there they have quite different beasts –
We'll live with scorpions and priests.

URFAUST

Goethe's Faust *in its Original Form
after the Göchhausen Transcript*

NIGHT

In a high-vaulted narrow Gothic room
FAUST *sits restlessly at his desk.*

FAUST

Medicine, and Law, and Philosophy –
Even, God help you, Theology;
You've worked your way through every school,
And sweated at it like a fool.
Why labour at it any more?   5
You're no wiser now than you were before.
They call you Doctor, nay, Professor,
And for ten long years you've done nothing better
Than lead your students a fearful dance
Through a maze of error and ignorance.   10
And all this misery goes to show
There's nothing we can ever know.
Oh yes, you're brighter than all those relics,
Professors and Doctors, scribblers and clerics;
No doubts or scruples to trouble you,   15
Defying hell, and the Devil too.
But there's no joy in self-delusion;
Your search for truth ends in confusion.
Don't imagine your teaching will ever raise
The minds of men or change their ways.   20
And as for worldly wealth, you've none –
What honour or glory have you won?
A dog could stand this life no more.
And so I've turned to magic lore;
The spirit message of this art   25
Some secret knowledge might impart.
No longer shall I sweat to teach
What always lay beyond my reach;
I'll know what makes the world revolve,
Its inner mysteries resolve,   30
No more in empty words I'll deal –
Creation's wellsprings I'll reveal!

Sweet moonlight, shining full and clear,
Why do you light my torture here?
How often have you seen me toil,   35
Burning last drops of midnight oil.
On books and papers as I read,
My friend, your mournful light you shed.
If only I could flee this den
And walk the mountain-tops again,   40
Through moonlit meadows make my way,
In mountain caves with spirits play –
Released from learning's musty cell,
Your healing dew would make me well!

But no, you're stuck inside this lair,   45
In this accursed dungeon, where
The very light of heaven can pass
But dimly through the painted glass.
Immured behind a pile of books,
Motheaten, dusty, in the reek   50
Of papers stuffed in all these nooks –
This is the wisdom that you seek.
These jars and cases row on row,
Retorts and tubes and taps and gauges,
The useless junk of bygone ages –   55
This is the only world you know!

And still you wonder why this pain
Constricts your heart and hems it in,
Why agonies you can't explain
Sap all life's energies within?   60
When God created us, he founded
His living nature for our home;
But you sit in this gloom, surrounded
By mildewed skull and arid bone.

Escape into a wider sphere!   65
This book of secrets will provide
The magic writings of the Seer;
Let Nostradamus be your guide.

If nature helps us, we can seek
The paths the stars in heaven go; 70
Through her we have the power to know
How spirits unto spirits speak.
Your dusty learning can't expound
The magic symbols written here.
The spirits hover close around: 75
Now answer me, if you can hear!
[*he opens the book and sees the Sign of the Macrocosm*] [87]
Ah, what ecstatic joy at this great sight
I feel at once through all my senses flowing!
What vital happiness, what sheer delight
Through veins and nerves with youthful
                                passion glowing. 80
Was it a god that wrote this sign for me?
The raging in my soul is stilled,
My empty heart with joy is filled,
And through some urgent mystery
All nature's forces are revealed to me. 85
Am I a god? My mind's so clear!
With mystic vision now I see
In these pure signs how nature beckons me. [88]
At last I grasp the message of the Seer:
'The spirit world is with us still, 90
Your mind is closed, your heart is dead.
Up, worldly scholar, drink your fill –
At heaven's gate the dawn is red!'
[*he studies the Sign*]
How all into a wholeness weaves,
Each in the other moves and lives! 95
The powers of heaven ascending and descending,
And to each other golden vessels sending,
With fragrant blessings winging,
From heaven to earth their bounty bringing –
In harmony the universe is ringing! 100

Ah, what a vision! But a vision, and no more.
I do not feel the pulse of nature, nor
Feed at her breasts. The springs of life that nursed

All things, for which creation yearns,
To which the flagging spirit turns,   105
They flow, they suckle still, but I must thirst!
[*disconsolately he turns the pages and sees the Sign
of the Earth Spirit*]
I see more inspiration in this sign!
Earth Spirit, we are of a kind.
I feel new energies, my mind
Now glows as if from new-fermented wine.   110
Now I can dare to face the world again,
To share in all its joy and all its pain.
Into the eye of storms I'll set my sail,
And in the grinding shipwreck I'll not quail.
Clouds gather overhead,   115
The moon conceals its light!
The lamp burns low!
Mist swirls around! Red flashes flicker
About my head. A chill shiver
Blows down from the vault above   120
And grips me!
I feel your presence round me,
You heard my call;
Great Spirit, you have found me –
Reveal yourself! It tears my heart, and all   125
My senses reel
And burn with passions new. I feel
My heart goes out to you, I have no fear;
If it should cost my life, you must appear!
[*he seizes the book and with mysterious words invokes
the Sign of the Earth Spirit. A red flame flickers, the
fearful shape of the Spirit appears in the flame*]

SPIRIT   Who calls me?
FAUST   [*turning away*] A dreadful shape I see!   130
SPIRIT   Your potent spells have brought me here;
          You sought to draw me from my sphere,
          And now –
FAUST   You are too terrible for me!
SPIRIT   With sighs you begged me to appear,
          My voice you would hear and my face you would see; 135

Your mighty pleas have summoned me.
I'm here! But now – what piteous fear
Has seized you, superman? The soul that cried
                                      for me, where
Is it now? The heart that in itself could bear
A whole created world, and in its swollen pride   140
Puffed up, with us, the spirits, would have vied?
Where are you, Faust, whose voice reached to
                                     my sphere,
Who summoned all your powers to draw me here?
You, who have scarcely felt my breath,
You quake as if you go to meet your death,   145
A frightened worm that twists and writhes!

FAUST   Creature of flame, to you I'll not give in;
             I, Faust, I am your equal, am your kin!

SPIRIT   In all life's storms and surging tides
             I ebb and flow   150
             From birth to grave,
             Weave to and fro,
             An endless wave
             In all life's changes.
             On time's humming loom, as I toil at the treads,   155
             For God's living garment I fashion the threads.

FAUST   Industrious spirit, to the world's furthest end
             You rove; how close you seem to me!

SPIRIT   You match the spirit that you comprehend,
             Not me!   [*vanishes* 160

FAUST   [*shattered*] Not you?
             Who then?
             I, made in God's image,
             No match for you?

               A knock at the door

             Oh death! It's my assistant at the door.   165
             To plunge me into worse despair,
             Dissolve these teeming visions into air,
             It only needs that over-eager bore.

    WAGNER *in nightgown and nightcap, holding a lamp.*
        FAUST *reluctantly turns to him.*

WAGNER	Forgive me, but I heard your voice –
	It sounded like a tragedy in Greek.	170
	That is an art that I would learn by choice.
	These days one has to know just how to speak
	One's lines; an actor, people often say, could teach
	A parson in the art of how to preach.
FAUST	Why, surely – if the parson's only acting,	175
	And many times I daresay that's the case.
WAGNER	But all this study I find so distracting;
	One scarcely sees the world beyond this place.
	It's difficult to see how all persuasion's arts
	Can better men or win their hearts.	180
FAUST	If you don't feel, your words will not inspire;
	Unless from deep within you speak sincere,
	And with a charismatic fire
	Compel the hearts of all who hear.
	Oh, you can sit there glueing bits together	185
	Or mixing cold leftovers in a stew,
	Blowing at the ashes, wondering whether
	There's any fire left to warm your brew.
	Yes, fools and children you'll impress –
	If that is really what you want to do;	190
	But you will never know another's heart, unless
	You are prepared to give yours too.
WAGNER	But good delivery can help the speaker's art!
FAUST	Yes – in a puppet-show to speak his part.
	My learned friend, God help you then,	195
	Your foolishness will never end!
	Delivery counts for nothing when
	You say 'I love you' to a friend.
	If with sincerity you speak,
	Why, then for words you need not seek.	200
	The dazzling rhetoric a speaker spins,
	The frills and flourishes with which he weaves
	His spell, are all as barren as the frosty winds
	That play among the arid autumn leaves.
WAGNER	Ah God, but art is long,	205
	And short our life's duration!
	In all my critical deliberation

I often fear the way I chose was wrong.
How hard it is to get the method right
To follow learning to its very source;   210
Before we're even half-way through our course
We'll surely die and never reach the light.

FAUST The manuscripts, are they the sacred springs
From which one drink will slake your thirst for ever?
You'll find no profit in these things   215
Unless you own heart flows with fresh endeavour.

WAGNER Forgive me, but it's such delight
To bring the spirit of the past to light,
To study all the thoughts of history's wisest men –
And marvel at the progress we have made since then.   220

FAUST Oh yes, we've reached the stars! And yet
The past, my friend, by which you set
Such store, is a book with seven seals to us.
It is a mirror that reveals to us
Only the minds of those who seek   225
This spirit of the past of which you speak.
Believe me, all you'll find is bunk,
A lumber-room stuffed full of junk,
At best a blood-and-thunder play
From which most audiences would run away;   230
A catalogue of pompous commonplaces,
A puppet-play that's full of empty phrases.

WAGNER Yes – but the world! The human heart and mind!
We all seek knowledge, surely, in this sphere?

FAUST Why, yes, however knowledge is defined.   235
But who will dare to speak the truth out clear?
The few who anything of truth have learned,
And foolishly did not keep truth concealed,
Their thoughts and visions to the common
                                herd revealed,
Since time began we've crucified and burned.   240
But please, my friend, it's deep into the night,
And I must sleep now – if I can.

WAGNER I'd gladly stay till dawn; it's such delight
Exchanging thoughts with such a learned man.   [exit

FAUST How is it that his mind can take such pleasure,   245

Forever dabbling in these shallow terms.
He digs so avidly for hidden treasure,
And then rejoices when he digs up worms.

MEPHISTOPHELES *in a nightgown,*
wearing a large wig. STUDENT.

STUDENT	I've recently arrived at College	
	In my earnest quest for knowledge;	250
	On you, Sir, with respect I call –	
	You are acclaimed by one and all.	
MEPHISTO.	Well, your politeness pleases me;	
	A man like other men you see.	
	You've had a good look round the place?	255
STUDENT	Please take me on, if you've the space!	
	I'm young and eager, keen to please,	
	And I've enough to pay my fees.	
	My mother was sad to see me go,	
	But there's so much that I want to know.	260
MEPHISTO.	Why, then you've come to the right door.	
STUDENT	But to be frank, I'm not quite sure.	
	There's a drawn look on every face,	
	As if a famine had hit the place.	
MEPHISTO.	I beg you, do not be misled;	265
	The students pay, so we're all well fed.	
	But first, where are you going to live?	
	That's most important!	
STUDENT	Can you give	
	Me guidance where I ought to stay?	
	An innocent young lamb can stray	270
	Into bad ways – though truth to tell,	
	I'd like some fun and freedom as well.	
	I want to study everything	
	And fill my brain up to the brim.	
	Oh Sir, help me to reach my goal	275
	Through learning to improve my soul.	
MEPHISTO.	[*scratches himself*] You have no lodgings yet, you said?	
STUDENT	It hadn't even entered my head.	
	The inn I'm at is not too bad –	
	The girls there think I'm quite a lad.	280

MEPHISTO. Oh, God forbid! You're in a fix:
     Coffee and billiards – leave those tricks!
     These girls are tarts, they'll ruin you;
     They'll waste your time, and waste you too!
     That's why I'd like to see you here   285
     With other students from far and near,
     So once a week, to hear us teach,
     You'll come within your tutor's reach.
     Sit close enough to feel his spray –
     You'll sit at his right hand one day.   290
STUDENT But that's a miserable vocation!
MEPHISTO. It's known as higher education.
     But first, as to your digs, my friend,
     I've nothing better to recommend
     Than Mrs Fizzybeer's splendid place. 295
     I know there's not a lot of space;
     She packs them in just like sardines,
     But treats them well – within her means.
     Noah's Ark was tidier, I'd say –
     But students have always lived that way. 300
     You'll pay what the others paid before
     Who wrote their names on the shithouse door.
STUDENT That's not quite where I want to be –
     It sounds too much like school to me.
MEPHISTO. So – that's your digs; now we must think 305
     Of how you're going to eat and drink.
STUDENT But surely that's not hard to find;
     I thought I'd come to feed my mind!
MEPHISTO. My dear boy! You're so young and green,
     And new to the academic scene.   310
     I'm sure your mother's food was a treat;
     Here, rancid butter is what you'll eat.
     No sweet young shoots or tender beans –
     You'll get stinging-nettles instead of greens.
     They turn your shit to liquid jelly, 315
     Then leave you with an empty belly.
     Mutton or veal, you'll have your say –
     But that's the choice till Judgement Day.
     And you'll be paying through the nose

For the debts your predecessor owes. 320
Look after your money – never lend
A penny, especially to a friend.
But keep some cash behind the dresser
For your landlord, your tailor – and of course,
                                                                    your Professor.

STUDENT For that, Sir, gladly I'll provide. 325
But now, I beg you, be my guide!
In Wisdom's fields I would rejoice
To wander and to take my choice;
But it's so topsy-turvy there,
And at the edges dry and bare. 330
Yet from afar it seemed at first
Like Tempe's Vale to quench my thirst.

MEPHISTO. Well, first of all, it seems to me
You need to choose a Faculty.

STUDENT Medicine's what my parents planned; 335
But I would like to understand
All of nature, heaven and earth below,
And everything there is to know.

MEPHISTO. You've got the right idea – though
You must be careful how you go; 340
And so, young friend, my pedagogic
Judgement is, you start with Logic.
For there your mind is trained aright;
It's clamped in Spanish boots so tight
That henceforth with a clearer head 345
The wary path of thought you'll tread,
And not like Jack o' Lantern go
Hopping and flickering to and fro.
For here with rigour you'll be taught
That things you'd never given a thought, 350
Like eating, drinking and running free,
Must be done in order: one, two, three!
The mind, however, needs more room;
It's like a master-weaver's loom.
A thousand warps move as he treads, 355
The shuttle flies, and to and fro
The fibres into patterns flow –

One stamp combines a thousand threads.
Send for a philosopher, and he
Will prove to you that it must be: 360
The first is thus, the second so,
Ergo: the third and fourth we know.
If first and second were not here,
Then third and fourth would disappear.
The students love it, I believe –   365
But none of them have learned to weave.
To know what nature is about,
First you must drive the spirit out;
And when you've pulled it all apart,
What's missing is the vital spark.   370
'Nature's knack!' the chemists cheer – [89]
But that just means they've no idea.

STUDENT   I'm not quite sure I follow you.

MEPHISTO.   Don't fret, my boy, you'll still get through
            When you've learned the tricks and when you're able   375
            To simplify things and give them a label.

STUDENT   I'm afraid I've simply lost the thread;
            It's like a mill-wheel grinding in my head.

MEPHISTO.   And after logic, what should you do?
            Ah! Metaphysics is the thing for you;   380
            You'll learn without the slightest trouble
            Stuff that would make your brain-cells bubble.
            For notions that won't fit inside your head,
            You'll find a splendid word instead.
            But this first term, whatever you read,   385
            A strict routine is what you need.
            Five hours a day – it's not a lot,
            Be in the classroom on the dot;
            Prepare the texts at home with care,
            And study all the details there –   390
            You'll know without even having to look
            He's reading straight out of the book.
            But write it all down, concentrating
            As if it were the Holy Ghost dictating!

STUDENT   Forgive me if I pester, you're so kind.   395
            But I would much appreciate your view

	Of whether Medicine is the thing to do,	
	For it's a course I also have in mind.	
	Three years can very soon be past,	
	And one must learn it all so fast.	400

Of whether Medicine is the thing to do,
For it's a course I also have in mind.
Three years can very soon be past,
And one must learn it all so fast.   400
They say the course is very tough;
With your advice I'd cope, I know.

MEPHISTO. [*aside*] I've played the Professor long enough;
Now let the Devil have a go.
[*aloud*] It's not too hard to learn a Doctor's skill;   405
You study till there's nothing left to know,
And in the end you let things go
According to God's will.
But all that science doesn't get you very far;
We all learn willy-nilly what we can –   410
But if you learn to seize your chance, you are
The up-and-coming man.
You're well-built, a good-looking chap,
You've got a saucy manner, too;
Self-confidence, that's the secret, that   415
Will give your patients confidence in you.
The women are the ones to make for;
They're always ready to complain
About a little pain –
I'm sure you know the remedy they ache for.   420
And if they think you understand,
You'll have them eating from your hand.
There's nothing like a Doctor's title for
Persuading them they really can respect you,
And in your first examination you'll explore   425
Places that others would take years to get to.
You take her hand to check the pulse is steady,
Look deep into her eyes, and then be ready
To slip your arm about her slender waist,
Just to make sure she's not too tightly laced.   430

STUDENT   That sounds much better than Philosophy!
MEPHISTO. Listen, my friend: the golden tree
Of life is green, all theory is grey.
STUDENT   I never dreamed I'd learn so much today!
I'd like to come along another day   435

	To hear more of your wisdom, if I may.
MEPHISTO.	What I can do, it shall be gladly done.
STUDENT	Just one thing more, and I'll be gone.
	I've got my album here; please could you say
	Some words to help me on my way.

440

MEPHISTO.	Of course. *[he writes and hands back the book*
STUDENT	*[reading]* Eritis sicut Deus, scientes bonum et malum.[90]
	[he shuts the book reverently and takes his leave
MEPHISTO.	'You'll be like God'; my aunt, the serpent, was
	quite right.
	Just heed her words, and one day you'll get such a fright!

AUERBACH'S CELLAR IN LEIPZIG

Drinkers carousing

FROSCH   Come on, drink up, let's have a ball!   445
           What's the matter with you all?
           I've never seen such po-faced gits –
           You'd get on anybody's tits.

BRANDER   Well, you're not much fun, anyway –
           No laughs or filthy jokes today.   450

FROSCH   [*tips a glass of wine over his head*]
           You asked for it!

BRANDER   You fool! You swine!

FROSCH   That's your speciality, not mine.   452

SIEBEL   Hell's bells! Calm down! Pass the jug round, take a
           swig and let's have a song. Come on! Holla la la la!

ALTEN   Cotton wool, quick! He'll burst our eardrums.

SIEBEL   I can't help it if there's such an echo in this place, the
           ceiling's too low. Sing!

FROSCH   Aaaah! Tra la la! Mi mi mi! Right, that's the pitch!
           Now then –

           To the Holy Roman Empire – but whatever,
           I ask you, holds the dear old thing together?

BRANDER   Urgh! What a rotten song! That's a dreadful political
           song. You should thank God the Holy Roman Empire's
           none of your business. Let's see who can sup a jug of
           wine quickest, and we'll make him Pope.

FROSCH   Oh nightingale, fly to my love;
           A thousand kisses for my turtle dove.

SIEBEL   Hell and damnation, I'm not sending mine any kisses.
           Sod the nightingale, I'll send the bitch rat poison baked
           in shit.[91] She dumped me – bag and baggage, threw me
           out like a bucket of slops, and all because – Bloody
           hell! She won't get anything from me except a brick
           through her window!

FROSCH [*banging his jug on the table*] Quiet! Here's a new song, comrades, or an old one if you like! Watch the beat, and join in the chorus. Right, here we go, sing up!

> In a cellar once there was a rat
> Who lived off lard and butter.
> She grew and grew, she got as fat
> As Doctor Martin Luther.
> The cook put poison down the drain,
> And soon she felt an awful pain –
> As if love's dart had stuck her!

CHORUS [*exuberantly*] As if love's dart had stuck her!

FROSCH
> She twitched as if she'd had a fit
> And drank from every puddle,
> She chewed and scratched and gnawed and bit,
> Her wits were in a muddle.
> She jumped till she could jump no more,
> And very soon lay at death's door –
> As if love's dart had stuck her!

CHORUS As if love's dart had stuck her!

FROSCH
> In panic then at break of day
> She ran into the kitchen,
> And by the fireside she lay
> In agony a-twitchin'.
> The cook just laughed and said 'Oh my,
> That rat is surely going to die –
> As if love's dart had stuck her.'

CHORUS As if love's dart had stuck her!

SIEBEL I'd give that cook a good dose of rat-poison in her soup. I'm not soft-hearted, but you'd have to have a heart of stone not to feel sorry for that rat.

BRANDER That's because you're a rat yourself! I'd like to see this bag of guts snuff it in front of the fire just like that rat!

FAUST, MEPHISTOPHELES

MEPHISTO. Now, take a look at this lively lot! If you like, I can provide company like this for you night after night.

FAUST Good evening, gentlemen.

ALL Thank you kindly!

SIEBEL	Who's this cheapjack?
BRANDER	Watch it! They're toffs, they are, travelling incognito. They've got that nasty stuck-up expression on their faces.
SIEBEL	Get away! They're actors, I'll bet you.
MEPHISTO.	[*aside*] You see, these people never notice the Devil, however close he is to them.
FROSCH	I'll sort them out. We'll find out where they're from. Is the road from Rippach so bad that you've had to travel all night to get here?
FAUST	That's not the way we came.
FROSCH	I thought you might have stopped to have lunch with Hans over there. Everybody knows him, he has trouble with his Rs.[92]
FAUST	I've never heard of him. [*the others laugh*
FROSCH	Oh, he's from a very old family. There's a lot of them around here.
MEPHISTO.	And I suppose you're one of his cousins, are you?
BRANDER	[*aside to Frosch*] Watch it! He's rumbled you.
FROSCH	And at Varting it's terrible, sometimes you have to wait hours for the v–v–verry.
FAUST	Really?
SIEBEL	[*aside*] They're from the imperial territories down south, you can tell by the look of 'em. As long as they're cheerful. You like a good drink, do you? Come and join us.
MEPHISTO.	Here's to you. [*they touch glasses and drink*
FROSCH	Now, gentlemen, a little song. For every jug a song, that's the proper way to do it.
MEPHISTO.	I'll sing one for me, another one for my friend, a hundred if you like. We've just come from Spain, where they sing songs at night, as many as the stars in the sky.
BRANDER	I couldn't stand that, I hate all that twanging and jangling, unless I'm really pissed, then I could sleep through Judgement Day. That sort of music's for little girls who can't get to sleep, and spend all their time at the window gawping at the moon.

MEPHISTO.	Once upon a time there was a king, Who had a great big flea!
SIEBEL	Quiet! Listen! Something new! This sounds promising!
MEPHISTO.	Once upon a time there was a king, Who had a great big flea. He loved him more than anything, More than a son did he. He said to his tailor, listen to me, Get busy with tucks and stitches; Just measure him up and make my flea A pair of silken breeches!
SIEBEL	Measure him carefully! [*they burst out laughing*] Make sure there's no creases in 'em!
MEPHISTO.	So soon that flea was kitted out, In finest velvet dressed, With silks and ribbons fitted out, And medals on his chest. They gave him a knighthood, called him Sir – He really was a swell; And all of his relations were Created peers as well. The court was in a dreadful stew, They weren't allowed to fight 'em; The Queen and all her ladies, too – The fleas knew where to bite 'em; They itched and scratched, but not a man Could harm the little blighters. But we can catch 'em if we can, And squash 'em when they bite us.
CHORUS	[*exuberantly*] But we can catch 'em if we can, And squash 'em when they bite us!
ALL	[*together*] Bravo! Bravo! Fine! Splendid! Encore! More wine! More songs!
FAUST	Gentlemen! This wine's so-so – but in Leipzig all the

	wine is only so-so. I'm sure you'll allow me to tap a different barrel for you.
SIEBEL	Have you brought your own wine-cellar with you? Are you wine merchants? Or are you one of those rogues from the Empire?
ALTEN	Hang on a minute! [*he stands up*] I've got a sort of test, to see whether I've had enough. [*he shuts his eyes and stands there for a while*] Eh up! My head's beginning to go round!
SIEBEL	Get away! One bottle! I'll answer for it to God and your wives. Let's see your wine, then.
FAUST	Get me a gimlet.
FROSCH	The landlord's got a basket of tools over there in the corner.
FAUST	[*takes the gimlet*] Right! What sort of wine do you want?
FROSCH	Eh?
FAUST	What sort of wine would you prefer? I'll get it for you!
FROSCH	Well, then I'll have a glass of Hock – real Niersteiner.
FAUST	Right! [*he bores a hole in the table in front of Frosch*] Now get some wax!
ALTEN	Here's the end of a candle.
FAUST	There! [*he plugs the hole*] Leave it now! And you?
SIEBEL	Muscadet! And Spanish, nothing else will do. I just want to see what this is all about.
FAUST	[*bores a hole and plugs it*] What is your request?
ALTEN	Red wine! And French! I can't stand the Frogs, but there's nothing wrong with their wine.
FAUST	[*as before*] Now, what will you have?
BRANDER	Is he trying to take the piss?
FAUST	Quick, think of a wine!
BRANDER	All right, Tokay! Does he think it'll come pouring out of the table?
FAUST	Be quiet, young man! Now, look out! Hold your glasses underneath. Take the plugs out, all of you – but don't spill a drop on the floor, or there'll be trouble!
ALTEN	I'm beginning to feel a bit uneasy. This bloke's uncanny.
FAUST	Draw the plugs! [*they draw the plugs, and each one's glass fills with the wine he asked for*]
FAUST	Plug the holes! And now try it!

SIEBEL	Very good! That's the right stuff!
ALL	Delicious! A royal treat! You're very welcome, Sir!
	[*they drink again and again*]
MEPHISTO.	They're well on the way.
FAUST	Let's go!
MEPHISTO.	Just a moment.
ALL	[*sing*] We're all as pissed as cannibals,
	And happy as pigs in clover!
	[*they drink one glass after another.* SIEBEL *draws his plug and drops it, the wine spills onto the flagstones and bursts into flames in front of him*]
SIEBEL	Hell and damnation!
BRANDER	Sorcery! Witchcraft!
FAUST	Didn't I warn you? [*he plugs the hole and mutters a few words. The flame dies down*]
SIEBEL	In the Devil's name! You think you can worm your way into respectable society and get up to your devilish hocus-pocus here!
FAUST	Quiet, fat-gut!
SIEBEL	Me? Fat-gut? You beanpole! Come on, lads, kick him in! Cut him! [*they draw their knives*] These magicians are fair game – it's the law of the land. [*they rush at* FAUST. *He waves his hand, they all stop and look at each other in astonished delight.*]
SIEBEL	Where am I? It's a vineyard!
BRANDER	Grapes! At this time of year!
ALTEN	Ripe grapes! That's marvellous!
FROSCH	Hang on, that's the nicest bunch!
	[*they seize each other by the nose and lift their knives*]
FAUST	Stop! Go and sleep it off!
	[FAUST *and* MEPHISTOPHELES *leave. The others wake up and let go of each other with loud cries.*]
SIEBEL	My nose! Was that your nose? Is that what the grapes were? Where is he?
BRANDER	Come on, let's go! It was the Devil himself.
FROSCH	I saw him ride out of here on a barrel.
ALTEN	Did you? Then we won't be safe out there, even in the market place. How are we going to get home?

BRANDER	Siebel can go first!
SIEBEL	I'm not so stupid!
FROSCH	I know, we'll wake up the watchmen in the town hall cellar. They'll do their job if you pay them. Come on!
SIEBEL	I wonder if there's any of that wine left? [*he inspects the plugs*]
ALTEN	Don't you believe it! Dry as a bone!
FROSCH	Come on, lads, get going!

[*they all leave*

A COUNTRY ROAD

A crucifix by the wayside, to the right an old castle on a hill,
in the distance a cottage.

FAUST	What's up, Mephisto, what's the hurry?	
	Why do you flinch before a shrine?	
MEPHISTO.	I just can't stand the things, I'm sorry –	455
	It's an old prejudice of mine.	

A STREET

FAUST. MARGARETA *walks by*.

FAUST	Fair lady, you are all alone;	
	May I take your arm and see you home?	
MARGARETA	I'm not a lady, nor am I fair,	
	And I can find my own way there.	460

[she pulls herself away and goes

FAUST	That girl is just so lovely, she	
	Has really captivated me.	
	Demure and virtuous, you can tell –	
	But with an impish look as well.	
	And such red lips and cheeks so bright,	465
	How could you ever forget that sight!	
	The bashful look she had just now,	
	It touched my heart, I can't say how.	
	She sent me packing, and quite right –	
	But that's what gave me such delight!	470

MEPHISTOPHELES *enters*

FAUST	I've got to have that girl, d'you hear?	
MEPHISTO.	Which one?	
FAUST	The one that just went by.	
MEPHISTO.	But she came straight from church! I fear	
	The priest just gave her the all clear.	
	I listened to them on the sly;	475

	She's just too innocent, I guess –	
	She had nothing whatever to confess.	
	I can't touch her, she's far too pure.	
FAUST	But she's over fourteen, that's for sure.	
MEPHISTO.	My, what a lecher we've become!	480
	He thinks he can pick them one by one;	
	His head's so turned by his conceit	
	He thinks they'll all fall at his feet.	
	It's not as simple as all that.	
FAUST	Yes, you can preach and you can scoff,	485
	But spare me all that moral chat,	
	And just you listen carefully:	
	If you can't get that girl for me,	
	And by tonight, I tell you, we	
	Are finished, and the deal is off.	490
MEPHISTO.	Be reasonable, you randy beast.	
	I'll need a good two weeks at least	
	To sniff around and see what's what.	
FAUST	I don't need you to show the way;	
	I'd take about a week, I'd say,	495
	To bed a little girl like that.	
MEPHISTO.	You're getting a bit French, my friend!	
	Why are you so impatient, though?	
	You mustn't rush these things, you know –	
	You'll get your pleasure in the end.	500
	Take time to talk her round to it,	
	Impress her, flatter her a bit.	
	Soften her up with little advances –	
	That's how Italians get their chances.	
FAUST	I can do without all that.	505
MEPHISTO.	But seriously, I tell you flat,	
	You can't just have that girl today;	
	You've got to plan, prepare the way.	
	You'll never get in there by force –	
	We'll think of a more subtle course.	510
FAUST	Get me something of hers to keep,	
	Show me where she lies asleep,	
	Get me a scarf that's touched her breast,	
	A garter, anything she's possessed!	

MEPHISTO.	Well, I'll do everything I can	515
	To help you on your lovesick way.	
	We'll not waste time; I have a plan	
	To take you to her room today.	
FAUST	And shall I see her? Have her?	
MEPHISTO.	No.	
	Tonight she's at a neighbour's, so	520
	For a few minutes you can go	
	And breathe the atmosphere at leisure,	
	And dream about your future pleasure.	
FAUST	Can we go now?	
MEPHISTO.	No, I'll say when.	
FAUST	Get me a present for her, then.	[*exit* 525
MEPHISTO.	Your Highness is in such a fever!	
	If very many more of these	
	Want Lucifer to pay their fees,	
	He'll have to call in the Receiver.	[*exit*

EVENING

A small, tidy room

MARGARETA [*plaiting and tying up her hair*]
    I wonder who that man could be   530
    Who stopped today and spoke to me.
    A handsome gentleman he was,
    A nobleman, I'm sure, because
    He had a certain air, I knew –
    And he was very forward, too.   [*exit* 535

Enter MEPHISTOPHELES *and* FAUST

MEPHISTO. You can come in now, the coast is clear.
FAUST   [*after a pause*] Just leave me for a moment here.
MEPHISTO. [*prying around*] Tidier than most girls are, it
                              would appear. [*exit*
FAUST   [*gazing around him*] The gentle light of evening falls
    Into this sanctuary; within these walls   540
    Love's pangs clutch at your heart, but you
    Must still your cravings with hope's meagre dew.
    This peaceful homestead seems to breathe
    A sense of order and content.
    Such poverty is wealth indeed,   545
    And there is bliss in such imprisonment!
    [*he throws himself into the leather chair by the bed*]
    How many generations has this seat
    Borne through all the years of joy and care!
    Her forebears sat upon this very chair,
    A throng of children playing at their feet.   550
    Perhaps my love, when Christmastime was near
    With pious thanks and childish cheeks so sweet
    Would kiss the feeble hand that rested here.
    Dear child, I sense your presence all around me,
    Integrity and order everywhere.   555
    The traces of your daily tasks surround me;
    The table that you set with loving care,
    The sand you scattered on the flagstones there.

One touch of your dear hand, and in a trice
This humble dwelling is a paradise.   560
And here! [*he raises the curtain round the bed*]
      Ah, what a shiver of delight!
Here I could sit for hours and dwell
On dreaming nature's magic spell
That fashioned that angelic sight.
As she lay here, the glowing surge   565
Of life pulsed in her gentle breast,
And here a pure creative urge
God's image on the child impressed.

And you! What brought you to her door?
What do you want? Why is your heart so sore?   570
What feelings hold you in their sway?
Ah Faust, poor fool, I fear you've lost your way.

Is there some magic spell around me?
I lusted for her, and I find
A dream of love comes to confound me.   575
Are we the playthings of a breath of wind?

And what if she should come while you are here?
You'd answer for your recklessness, and all
Your bold bravado would just disappear –
Abject and sighing at her feet you'd fall.   580

MEPHISTO. Quickly! She just came through the gate.
FAUST   I'll never come back here again. Let's go!
MEPHISTO. Here is a box of jewels – just feel its weight;
I got it from – well, from a place I know.
Put it in this cupboard here; I swear   585
She'll fall into a faint, your little dove.
Some of the things she'll find in there
Would make a princess fall in love.
But then, they're all just kids at heart.
FAUST   I don't know if I should.
MEPHISTO.   Oh please, don't start!   590
D'you want to keep it for yourself? Then,

Lecherous Sir, I beg of you,
Think what you really want to do,
And please don't waste my time again.
I hope you're not a miser, too!   595
I rack my brains and toil away –
[*he puts the casket into the cupboard and locks it up again*]
Now, come with me! –
So you can have your wicked way
With that sweet child, and all I see
Is the sort of miserable expression   600
You wear before you give a lesson,
As if physics and metaphysics too
Were standing there in front of you.
Come on!
                                                  [*exeunt*

MARGARETA [*with a lamp*]
It feels so close and stuffy here,   605
[*she opens the window*]
And yet outside it's not so warm.
I don't know why, I feel so queer –
I wish my mother were at home.
You silly girl, you're shivering –
You really are a timid thing!   610

[*she sings as she undresses*]
In Thule a king was living
Whose love had died, we're told,
Upon her death-bed giving
To him a cup of gold.

He would drink from no other,   615
It was his dearest prize;
Remembering his lover
The tears would fill his eyes.

And on his death-bed lying,
His heirs around him come;   620
Bequeathed his lands, but dying
He gave the cup to none.

And many a faithful vassal
And knight sat by his knee
In his ancestral castle   625
Beside the northern sea.

One last time he drank up then,
His cheeks with wine aglow,
And hurled the sacred cup then
Into the waves below.   630

He watched it falling, sinking
Beneath the ocean deep;
Then he had done with drinking –
His eyes were closed in sleep.

[*she opens the cupboard to put her clothes away,
and sees the casket*]
Whoever put that casket there?   635
I locked the cupboard up, I swear.
Goodness, whatever can it be?
Perhaps it was left as surety,
And mother lent some money for it.
And here's a ribbon with a key –   640
Well, really, I can't just ignore it.
But what is this? Ah, glory be!
I've never seen such jewels before.
All this expensive finery
Was made for some great lady, that's for sure.   645
I wonder how they'd look on me?
But who can it belong to, though?
[*she tries on some jewels and stands in front of the mirror*]
I'd love to have these earrings – oh,
What a different girl you are!
But youth and beauty, what's it worth?   650
It's not your fortune on this earth,
It doesn't get you very far.
They flatter you and call you pretty,
But it's gold they crave,
For gold they slave –   655
And poverty they pity!

AN AVENUE

FAUST *pacing up and down deep in thought, then* MEPHISTOPHELES

MEPHISTO.	By all frustrated love! By all hell's fires, and worse!
	I wish I knew more dreadful things by which to curse!
FAUST	What is it now? What's biting you today?
	I never saw a face as black as yours.

660

MEPHISTO.   I'd go to the Devil right away –
That is, if I weren't one myself, of course.

FAUST   Has something happened to disturb your mind?
This snarling and spitting suits you well, I find.

MEPHISTO.   That box of jewels I got for Margaret –   665
A bloody priest has snaffled it!
I tell you, it just isn't fair,
It's enough to make an angel swear.
Her mother found the jewels last night –
They gave her quite a nasty fright;   670
That woman smells brimstone a mile away,
She's forever kneeling down to pray.
She only needs to sniff a chair
To tell the Devil's been sitting there.
As for our jewels, well, that's clear –   675
She knows there's something fishy here.
'Gretchen,' she says, 'ill-gotten gold
Corrupts the heart, ensnares the soul.
The Blessed Virgin must have this hoard,
And manna from heaven be our reward.'   680
Poor little Gretchen nearly weeps –
She thought her gift horse was for keeps,
And whoever put it in her drawer
Can't be all that bad, for sure.
Her mother summoned up the priest;   685
He'd hardly heard her out, the beast,
When he began his peroration:
'A Christian act! For there's no question
That victory lies in abnegation.
The Church has an excellent digestion;   690

It's gobbled up countries by the score,
But still has room for a little more.
Only the Holy Church, dear ladies,
Can properly digest the Devil's wages.'

FAUST   That's the way it is, it's true –   695
         But Jews and kings can do it too.

MEPHISTO. He raked those rings and bangles in
           As if they were just bits of tin;
           He packed them up and took them away
           As if this happened every day.   700
           'Heaven will surely reward you,' he sighed –
           And they, of course, were greatly edified.

FAUST   And Gretchen?

MEPHISTO.   She's unhappy, too;
           Doesn't know what she ought to do.
           Thinks of her jewels night and day –   705
           But even more, who put them in her way.

FAUST   The darling girl! It's such a shame.
         Well, go and get more of the same;
         The first ones weren't much anyway.

MEPHISTO. Oh yes, to you it's all child's play!   710

FAUST   Now listen, do exactly what I say:
         Get to know her neighbour, act the pimp –
         I never knew the Devil was such a wimp.
         And get more jewels – do it now, today!

MEPHISTO. Your slightest wish is my command, my lord.   715

                                              [exit Faust

           That lovesick fool's completely lost his wits;
           Just in case his girlfriend might get bored,
           He'd blow the sun, the moon and all the stars to bits.

                                              [exit

THE NEIGHBOUR'S HOUSE

MARTHA	May God forgive my husband, he
	Has not done the right thing by me. 720
	He took off one day on his own,
	He left me flat, and all alone.
	I didn't nag, and never took the huff;
	God knows, I loved him well enough.
	[*weeping*] And if he's dead, I'm in a sorry state – 725
	I haven't even got a death certificate!

–   –   –   –   –   –
–   –   –   –   –   –   [93]

MARGARETA	[*enters*] Oh, Martha!
MARTHA	Gretchen, what's the matter, pet?
MARGARETA	Oh, Martha, I'm in such a sweat; 730
	There's another box of jewels for me!
	A lovely box, it's made of ebony,
	Such precious things in it, I swear
	They're even finer than the others were.
MARTHA	Don't show them to your mother, then, 735
	Or else she'll give them to the priest again.
MARGARETA	Look at this necklace, and this ring!
MARTHA	[*dressing her in some jewels*]
	Oh Gretchen, you're a lucky thing!
MARGARETA	I can't wear them in public, that's forbidden,[94]
	Or to church – I'll have to keep them hidden. 740
MARTHA	Just you come over to my place
	Whenever you like, and put your jewels on,
	See yourself in the mirror and do up your face –
	We'll have our little bit of fun.
	Then maybe at a wedding or a party 745
	You gradually start to dress a bit more smartly –
	A gold chain first, then pearl drops in your ear;
	We'll tell your mother that they weren't too dear.
	[*a knock at the door*]
MARGARETA	Oh God! Is that my mother at the door?

| MARTHA | [*peering through the curtain*] |
| | Come in! It's a man I've never seen before. | 750 |

Enter MEPHISTOPHELES

MEPHISTO. May I come in? Oh, please excuse me, Miss.
It's very rude of me to walk straight in like this.
[*he bows respectfully to* MARGARETA]
It's Mrs Martha Schwerdlein that I called to see.

MARTHA How can I help you, Sir? For I am she.

MEPHISTO. [*aside to Martha*]
Ah yes, of course, I could have guessed.   755
But you're entertaining a distinguished guest;
Forgive me, I'll retire right away,
And come again – around noon, shall we say?

MARTHA [*aloud*] Now, child, there's a compliment for you –
This gentleman thinks you're a lady, too!   760

MARGARETA You're quite mistaken, Sir, I fear;
I'm just a girl who lives round here,
And all this finery's not my own.

MEPHISTO. Ah, but it's not the jewels alone;
It's in your bearing, in your gracious smile –   765
How fortunate that I can stay awhile.

MARTHA What is your business, may I ask?

MEPHISTO. I only wish I had a happier task.
I hope the messenger won't get the blame;
Your husband's dead, but greets you all the same.   770

MARTHA He's dead? The dear man's gone, you say?
My husband's dead! Oh, what a dreadful day!

MARGARETA Oh Martha dear, please don't despair.

MEPHISTO. Would you like to hear the tragic story?

MARGARETA I'll never fall in love, I do declare;   775
I'd die of grief if my love died before me.

MEPHISTO. But joy and grief are never far apart.

MARTHA Please tell me of my husband's sad demise.

MEPHISTO. Of course, dear lady. Now, where shall I start?
In Padua at St Anthony's he lies,   780
And in that cool and pleasant spot
He rests for ever in a consecrated plot.

MARTHA And have you nothing else for me?

MEPHISTO.   Oh yes – a serious and solemn plea
             To say three hundred Masses for his soul.   785
             But otherwise I fear, dear lady, that is all.

MARTHA   What! Not a single keepsake, not a ring?
             What every poor apprentice carries in his kit,
             A token of affection, some small thing
             He'd rather starve or beg than part with it?   790

MEPHISTO.   Madam, I have to say with great regret,
             It wasn't trifling sums that got him into debt.
             He saw the error of his ways, it's true –
             But then, he blamed it all on bad luck, too.

MARGARETA   I find it sad that fate is so unkind.   795
             I'll pray for him, say lots of Masses for the Dead.

MEPHISTO.   You are a lovely child, it must be said.
             Have thoughts of marriage never crossed your mind?

MARGARETA   Oh no, Sir, I can't think of such a thing.

MEPHISTO.   If not a husband, what of a lover's charms?   800
             It is the highest gift that heaven can bring
             To hold such a sweet creature in one's arms.

MARGARETA   That's not the custom in these parts, for shame!

MEPHISTO.   Custom or not, it happens all the same.

MARTHA   But tell me about my husband!

MEPHISTO.   Ah yes, I was at his side. 805
             It was as a good Christian, repenting, that he died.
             Confessed his sins as he lay there upon some
                                                filthy straw –
             But then, he had so many he could scarcely keep
                                                the score.
             'Alas!' he cried aloud, 'It is a wicked thing I've done,
             To quit my trade, my home, and leave my poor
                                                wife all alone!   810
             It tortures me to think of it, and now before I die
             I pray that she'll forgive my sin.'

MARTHA   [weeping] The dear man! I've forgiven him.

MEPHISTO.   'But then, God knows,' he told me, 'she was more
                                                to blame than I.'

MARTHA   The liar! What, he lied when he was at death's door? 815

MEPHISTO.   He was delirious at the end, I'm sure;
             I've seen it happen many times before.

'I never had a minute's rest,' he said,
'With her and all her children to be fed,
And always wanting more –   820
I never had the peace to eat my share.'
MARTHA   Had he forgotten all the love and care,
The way I slaved for him by day and night?
MEPHISTO.   Oh no, dear lady, he remembered that all right.
He told me: 'As we left Valletta Bay,   825
I prayed most fervently for wife and children too,
And heaven heard me, for that very day
We took a Turkish vessel, who
Had some of the Great Sultan's wealth on board.
And as I wasn't backward in the fight,   830
When it was over, as was only right,
I got my proper share of the reward.'
MARTHA   Oh, fancy! Did he bury it, d'you think?
MEPHISTO.   Gone with the wind, on women and on drink.
When he was in Naples feeling lonely,   835
A pretty lady took him as a friend,
And she was kind and loving to him, only –
Love left its mark on him right to the end.
MARTHA   The wretch! With children and a wife to feed,
He left us here in poverty and need.   840
Oh, what a shameless life he led!
MEPHISTO.   Well yes, you see – that's why he's dead.
If I were you, if you'll take my advice,
I'd mourn him for a year or so,
And then look round for someone really nice.   845
MARTHA   I'll never find another like him, though,
I'm sure of that, however hard I try.
He was a scamp, but still I liked him fine.
He never could stay put, I don't know why,
And chasing other women too, and all that wine,   850
And gambling everything he earned.
MEPHISTO.   Well, many couples get on well like that.
If he'd been easy-going, if he'd turned
A blind eye to whatever you were at –
Why, I myself, on that condition   855
Might be prepared to make a proposition.

MARTHA	Ah, you will have your little joke with me!
MEPHISTO.	[*aside*] It's time to go; this tough old bird
	Would take the very Devil at his word.
	[*to Gretchen*]
	And you, Miss – all alone and fancy-free? 860
MARGARETA	Sir, what do you mean?
MEPHISTO.	[*aside*] Sweet innocence of youth!
	[*aloud*] Goodbye then, ladies.
MARTHA	Wait! I need some proof!
	I need a death-certificate to show
	How, when and where my loved one passed away.
	I want to put it in the paper too, you know – 865
	One must do these things properly, I always say.
MEPHISTO.	Madam, of course; two witnesses will do
	To prove in law that what they say is true.
	I have a good friend living near –
	He'll tell the magistrate just what you want to hear. 870
	I'll bring him here tonight.
MARTHA	Oh, do!
MEPHISTO.	And this young lady, will she be here too?
	He's a fine lad, well-travelled, very charming;
	The ladies find his manners quite disarming.
MARGARETA	Oh, I would only blush if we should meet. 875
MEPHISTO.	You needn't blush before a king, my sweet.
MARTHA	Until this evening in the garden, then.
	We shall expect you – shall we say, at ten?
	[*they all leave*

FAUST. MEPHISTOPHELES

FAUST	Well, what's the news? Did you get anywhere?	
MEPHISTO.	Ah, bravo! All on fire – that's what I like to see!	880
	Soon Gretchen will be yours, I guarantee.	
	At Martha's place, this evening – she'll be there.	
	That woman's born to be a go-between,	
	By far the finest pimp I've ever seen.	
FAUST	Well, good for her.	
MEPHISTO.	There's a small price to pay;	885
	One good turn deserves another, so	
	We have to swear a solemn oath and say	
	What's left of her late husband here below	
	Now rests in Padua – at least till Judgement Day.	
FAUST	Oh, brilliant! Now we've got to go to Italy.	890
MEPHISTO.	*Sancta simplicitas!* Of course we don't – [95]	
	Just swear, and leave the rest to me.	
FAUST	You want me to commit perjury? I won't!	
MEPHISTO.	Oh, what a Holy Joe! Is that your problem, then?	
	You mean you've never told a lie before?	895
	Was it the truth you told your students, when	
	You spoke of God, the world, the hearts and	
	minds of men,	
	And heaven knows what else that lay beyond	
	your ken,	
	With such authority? You lied with every breath;	
	And if the truth were told, you knew no more	900
	Of all these matters than of Schwerdlein's death.	
FAUST	The Devil always deals in sophistry and lies.	
MEPHISTO.	Oh yes, with you of course it's otherwise.	
	Tomorrow, I suppose, in all sincerity,	
	With all the tricks of the seducer's art	905
	You'll try to capture little Gretchen's heart?	
FAUST	And I shall mean it, too.	
MEPHISTO.	That's as may be.	
	You'll swear undying love and true emotion,	
	Assure her of your passionate devotion –	

| | Will that stand up to closer scrutiny? | 910 |
| FAUST | Indeed it will, for that is truly what I feel. | |

FAUST Indeed it will, for that is truly what I feel.
       If I can't find the phrases to confess
       This fevered love that makes my senses reel,
       And search in vain for ways that would express
       This passion burning deep inside me,   915
       And if I grasp at lofty words to guide me,
       And swear that love's for ever, that it never dies –
       Is that a tawdry pack of Devil's lies?

MEPHISTO. I beg to differ.

FAUST   You always do, of course,
       So hold your tongue and bottle up your spite.   920
       You talk and never stop to listen, so perforce
       You're always right.
       I'm tired of all this talk, I'll spare my voice –
       And you are right, because I have no choice.

A GARDEN

MARGARETA *on* FAUST'S *arm.* MARTHA *strolling to
and fro with* MEPHISTOPHELES

MARGARETA	I feel, Sir, that you only speak to me	925
	So kindly and so condescendingly	
	Because a travelled man like you	
	Believes it is the proper thing to do.	
	My conversation's dull, it is so shaming –	
	I can't think why you find it entertaining.	930
FAUST	One look, one word from you diverts me more	
	Than all the wisdom that the world could store.	

[he kisses her hand

MARGARETA	Oh no, how could you? You embarrass me.	
	My hands are rough, and unattractive, too;	
	It's all the housework that I have to do –	935
	My mother's so particular, you see. *[they walk on*	
MARTHA	And you, Sir – always travelling, I daresay?	
MEPHISTO.	Indeed, we visit many different places.	
	But then business and duty summon us away,	
	And it is sad to leave such friendly faces.	940
MARTHA	Ah yes, for younger men it can be fun	
	To roam the world alone and see its ways;	
	But soon one's years of travelling are done,	
	And as a lonely bachelor to end one's days –	
	Why, that's a dismal thought for anyone.	945
MEPHISTO.	A distant prospect that I dread to contemplate.	
MARTHA	Then make your plans before it is too late. *[they walk on*	
MARGARETA	But out of sight, I'll soon be out of mind.	
	You're very gracious and polite to me,	
	But you have many friends of your own kind	950
	Far cleverer than I could ever be.	
FAUST	Oh dearest, cleverness isn't all, you know;	
	It's often vain and superficial –	
MARGARETA	Oh?	
FAUST	While innocence and sweet simplicity	
	Are rarely valued as they ought to be.	955

Humility and modesty – they
Are the highest gifts that loving nature gave us, when –

MARGARETA If you can think of me just now and then.
I shall have time enough when you're away.

FAUST And are you often on your own?   960

MARGARETA Oh yes, our household's very small, but even so
It doesn't run itself alone.
We have no maid, I have to knit and sew
And cook and clean, all day I'm on my feet;
My mother wants it all so very neat   965
And tidy, too.
She doesn't really need to scrimp and save at all,
We have far more than many others do.
My father left us well provided for –
A little house, a plot outside the city wall.   970
But still, it's very quiet here, it must be said;
My brother is a soldier in the war,
My little sister's dead.
She gave me so much trouble while she lived, and yet
I'd do it all again for her, the little pet,   975
I loved her so.

FAUST   An angel, if she was like you.

MARGARETA I brought her up, she loved me dearly too.
The little thing was born after my father died;
We feared the worst, my mother was so ill.
We nursed her, I was always at her side,   980
And slowly she recovered, by God's will.
But then she couldn't even think
Of feeding the poor creature at her breast,
And so I had to do my best
And gave it water mixed with milk to drink.   985
She grew up in my arms, smiled up at me,
And squirmed and wriggled when I held her on
                                               my knee.

FAUST Those must have been such happy times for you!

MARGARETA Yes, but we often had our troubles, too.
Her cradle always stood beside my bed;   990
She only had to stir once in the night,
I'd wake up, and she wanted to be fed.

I'd take her into bed with me and hold her tight,
And if she wouldn't settle, out of bed I'd creep,
Walk up and down and rock her back to sleep.   995
Then in the mornings I would have to sweep
And wash and cook, and go to market, too;
All day and every day I had enough to do.
It's hard work, and there's not much time for fun;
But then, we eat and sleep the better when it's done.   1000
                                        [*they walk on*

MARTHA   On all your travels, Sir, you mean to say
           You never lost your heart along the way?
MEPHISTO. Proverbially, of course, we're told,
           A good wife and a home are worth their weight
                                                in gold.
MARTHA   But have you met no one for whom you really care? 1005
MEPHISTO. I've always found a civil welcome everywhere.
MARTHA   I mean, have you been seriously committed?
MEPHISTO. To trifle with a woman's heart is not permitted.
MARTHA   Oh, you don't understand!
MEPHISTO.   You mustn't mind;
           I understand – that you are very good and kind.   1010
                                        [*they walk on*

FAUST   My angel, so you knew me at first sight
           The moment that I came in here tonight?
MARGARETA You must have noticed how I hardly dared to look.
FAUST   And you don't mind the liberty I took?
           You weren't disturbed by what I had to say   1015
           When you came out of church the other day?
MARGARETA I *was* put out, I thought it rather rash.
           I thought: there's something forward, something brash
           About me that this gentleman's detected,
           To talk to me like that. It was so unexpected   1020
           To be approached so boldly in the street
           Like any common girl, it seemed so indiscreet.
           I was confused, I must admit, but still
           I couldn't bring myself to wish you ill.
           And I was angry with myself, because I knew   1025
           That I could not feel angry towards you.
FAUST   My sweet love!

MARGARETA	Wait a moment.
	[*she picks a daisy and plucks off the petals one by one*]
FAUST	What is this?
MARGARETA	You'll laugh at me, it's just a game.
FAUST	But what?
	[*she plucks and murmurs*]
	What are you whispering?
MARGARETA	[*half aside*] He loves me – loves me not –
FAUST	You sweet and lovely vision of heaven's bliss! 1030
MARGARETA	[*continues*] Loves me – not – loves me – not –
	[*plucking the last petal, joyously*]
	He loves me!
FAUST	Yes, my dear child. Let the flowers spell
	The judgement of the gods, for it is this:
	He loves you! Loves you more than he can tell! 1035
	[*he takes her hands in his*]
MARGARETA	I'm shivering!
FAUST	Oh no, don't tremble! Let this look,
	Let one touch of my hands convey
	What words cannot express.
	Just trust your feelings, don't resist 1040
	This ecstasy that has to be for ever!
	Ever! To end it would be to despair,
	No, it must never, never end!
	MARGARETA *presses his hands, tears herself away and runs*
	off. He stands for a moment in thought, then follows her.
MARTHA	It's getting dark.
MEPHISTO.	Ah yes, and we must go.
MARTHA	I'd ask you to stay longer, both of you, 1045
	But it's a spiteful neighbourhood, you know.
	You'd think these folk had nothing else to do
	But watch their neighbours like a hawk –
	And how they talk!
	You can't turn round before the whole street knows. 1050
	And our young couple?
MEPHISTO.	Fluttered off up there
	Like wanton butterflies!
MARTHA	He seems quite fond of her.
MEPHISTO.	And she of him. And that's the way it goes.

A SUMMERHOUSE

MARGARETA *runs in breathless, hides behind the door, holds
a finger to her lips and peers through a crack in the door.*

MARGARETA He's coming!
FAUST You're teasing me, I'll catch you yet!
[*he kisses her*]
MARGARETA [*puts her arms around him and returns the kiss*]
Oh dearest man, I've loved you since we met. 1055
MEPHISTO [*knocks*]
FAUST [*stamps his foot*] Who's there?
MEPHISTO. A friend.
FAUST A beast!
MEPHISTO. It's time to go, you two.
MARTHA Yes, Sir, it's late.
FAUST May I not come with you?
MARGARETA What would my mother say! Goodbye!
FAUST I'll have to leave you, then.
Goodbye, my love.
MARTHA Good night!
MARGARETA Until we meet again.
[FAUST *and* MEPHISTOPHELES *leave*
MARGARETA Dear God, I'm sure I never heard 1060
A man so clever, so well bred,
And I can only nod my head
And scarcely say a single word.
It makes me blush – I just can't see
What he finds in a simple girl like me. 1065
[*exit*

GRETCHEN'S ROOM

GRETCHEN *spinning, alone*

My peace is gone,
My heart is sore,
It's gone for ever
And evermore.

Whenever he   1070
Is far away,
The world for me
Is cold and grey.

And my poor head
Is quite bemused,   1075
My scattered wits
Are all confused.

My peace is gone,
My heart is sore,
It's gone for ever   1080
And evermore.

It's him I look for
On the street;
It's only him
I go to meet.   1085

And in his walk,
Such dignity.
His gracious talk
Bewitches me.

And when he smiles   1090
At me, what bliss
To feel his hand –
And ah, his kiss!

My peace is gone,
My heart is sore,   1095
It's gone for ever
And evermore.

My very loins,
God, long for him!
And if I could   1100
Belong to him,

I'd hold him and kiss him
All the day,
Though in his kisses
I'd melt away!   1105

MARTHA'S GARDEN

MARGARETA, FAUST

GRETCHEN	Tell me something, Heinrich.
FAUST	Gladly, if I can.
GRETCHEN	What is your faith? I feel I ought to know.
	You're such a good and kindly man;
	You seem to have no true religion, though.
FAUST	Oh, do not ask! You know I love you well, indeed 1110
	For those I love I'd hazard life and limb,
	And never seek to hurt their feelings or their creed.
MARGARETA	But that's not right, you must believe in Him! [96]
FAUST	Must we?
GRETCHEN	I wish I could persuade you to
	Respect the Holy Sacraments as I do. 1115
FAUST	I do respect them.
GRETCHEN	Yes – but is your faith sincere?
	You don't go to confession or to Mass, I fear.
	Do you believe in God?
FAUST	Dear child, who can
	Say such a thing?
	Go ask the cleverest priest, the wisest man – 1120
	Their answers only mock our questioning,
	And mock us too.
GRETCHEN	You have no faith, I see.
FAUST	Sweet child, you misinterpret me.
	For who can name,
	Who can proclaim 1125
	Belief in Him?
	Who can reveal
	He does *not* feel
	Belief in Him?
	All-embracing 1130
	And all-preserving,
	Does He not hold
	And keep us all?
	Is not the vault of heaven above us,

The earth's foundation here below?   1135
Do not the eternal stars
Ascend the skies around us?
And when I look into your eyes, do you
Not feel how all things
Flood your heart and mind all through,   1140
And weave their everlasting spell
Unseen, yet visible beside you?
Just let it fill your heart, and when
You feel the highest bliss, why, then
You call it what you will: 1145
Joy! Heart! Love! God!
I have no name for it.
Feeling is all,
A name's mere sound, a haze that veils
The radiance of heaven from view.   1150

GRETCHEN I dare say that's all very true;
The catechism says the same thing too –
Only it sounds a little different there.

FAUST You'll hear it spoken everywhere,
As far as heaven's light can reach,   1155
All hearts, all languages will teach
That message; why should I not speak in mine?

GRETCHEN Yes, put like that it all sounds very fine,
But still it doesn't seem quite right; you see,
It's not what I think of as Christianity.   1160

FAUST Dear child!

GRETCHEN   It's always troubled me
To see you in that person's company.

FAUST But why?

GRETCHEN   That man you call your friend
Is deeply hateful to me, and I can't pretend
To like him, for in all my life   1165
I never saw a face so grim;
His look goes through me like a knife.

FAUST My sweet, you mustn't be afraid of him.

GRETCHEN His presence chills the very blood in me.
I always think the best of folk, but he –   1170
Although I long to be with you, I swear,

	It makes me shudder when I see him there.	
	I've thought he was a villain all along –	
	May God forgive me if I do him wrong.	
FAUST	He's odd – no more than many others, though.	1175
GRETCHEN	How you can live with him, I just don't know.	
	He only has to come in here	
	With such a mocking look, a sneer	
	About his lips, and you can tell	
	He cares for nothing, wishes no one well.	1180
	It's written on his face, it's plain to see	
	That he could never love his fellow men.	
	I feel so safe when you are holding me,	
	So free, so loving and so warm, but then	
	I freeze and shiver when I feel his presence.	1185
FAUST	You angel! Ah, what knowing innocence!	
GRETCHEN	It overwhelms me more than I can say.	
	I even think, whenever he is here,	
	My very love for you might ebb away,	
	And I could never pray when he is near.	1190
	That is what really tears my heart in two –	
	But Heinrich, you must feel his menace too.	
FAUST	You have a loathing for him, that is clear.	
GRETCHEN	And I must go now.	
FAUST	Ah, my dear,	
	If only we could have one hour tonight	1195
	To lie together, hold each other tight.	
GRETCHEN	If I were on my own, for sure,	
	I'd willingly unlock my door.	
	My mother sleeps so lightly, though;	
	I'd die upon the spot, I know,	1200
	If she should come and find us there.	
FAUST	My angel, we can easily prepare	
	For that; you only have to take	
	This bottle, put three drops into her drink tonight,	
	And she'll sleep undisturbed until daylight.	1205
GRETCHEN	What would I not do, Heinrich, for your sake!	
	You're sure it won't be dangerous for her?	
FAUST	My love, would I suggest it if it were?	
GRETCHEN	Oh dearest man, my love for you is such,	

| | I would do anything you asked me to. | 1210 |

I would do anything you asked me to.   1210
For your sake I've already done so much,
There's little more for me to give to you.   [*exit*

MEPHISTO. [*enters*] The little monkey!

FAUST   Eavesdropping again, I see.

MEPHISTO. I have been listening most attentively.
Was that the catechism I heard you reciting?   1215
I trust Herr Doktor found it to his liking.
These girls are keen on simple faith and piety,
They think: if he's had a religious education,
He's much more likely to resist temptation.

FAUST   You monster, you have never known   1220
How an angelic child like this,
Whose faith is pure and whole,
Whose faith alone
Sustains her hope of heaven's bliss,
Could fear the one she loves might lose his soul.   1225

MEPHISTO. What supersublimated sensuality!
A little girl has got you on a string.

FAUST   You misbegotten spawn of hell-fire and depravity!

MEPHISTO. She's good at reading faces too, the cheeky thing!
She feels a bit uneasy when I'm there;   1230
She looks at me, and seems to see
A touch of genius, a certain flair –
She might even suspect some devilry in me.
Well, and tonight?

FAUST   That's no concern of yours.

MEPHISTO. I like to have my fun – it's all in a good cause.   1235

AT THE WELL

GRETCHEN *and* LIESCHEN *carrying pitchers*

LIESCHEN	And what about Barbara? Haven't you heard?
GRETCHEN	No, not a word; I don't get out as much as you.
LIESCHEN	Sibyl told me today – it's true!
	At last she's got what she deserved,
	Miss Hoity-Toity!
GRETCHEN	What?
LIESCHEN	It stinks! 1240
	She's feeding two when she eats and drinks.
GRETCHEN	Oh, no!
LIESCHEN	Oh yes, she came a cropper in the end.
	That man she always went about with,
	The one she boasted she was 'walking out with',
	Going to fairs and dances with her 'friend' – 1245
	She always had to be the first in line.
	He treated her to cakes and wine,
	She thought she was so very fine.
	And all those presents he gave her, too –
	I'd be ashamed to take them, so would you. 1250
	And all those cuddles in the wood!
	Well, now her flower's gone for good.
GRETCHEN	Oh, the poor girl!
LIESCHEN	Now don't be soft!
	While you and I were spinning in the loft
	Because we weren't allowed out after dark – 1255
	She was with her lover in the park.
	Behind the house and in the alleyway,
	For hours they were together, every day.
	Next time she goes to church she'll have to do
	Her public penance in the sinners' pew! 1260
GRETCHEN	But he will marry her, for sure.
LIESCHEN	He's not so daft as that. And he's a likely lad
	Who'll want the chance to look around for more.
	And anyway, he's gone.
GRETCHEN	Oh, that's too bad!

LIESCHEN   And if she does catch him, she'll still be had.   1265
            The boys will snatch her wreath, and at the door
            Instead of flowers we'll throw bits of straw.   [*exit*

GRETCHEN   [*walking home*] If some poor girl got into trouble, you
            Would always scoff and gossip like that too.
            And you were always quick to lay the blame   1270
            And wag your tongue at someone else's shame!
            And though their sin was black as black could be,
            It never could be black enough for me.
            I crossed myself and felt so proud –
            And now my own sin cries aloud!   1275
            But what I did, dear God in heaven above,
            It was so good – and it was all for love.

A SHRINE

In a niche in the city wall a sacred image of the Mater Dolorosa with vases of flowers in front of it. GRETCHEN *bends to wash out the vases at a nearby well and fills them with the fresh flowers she has brought with her.*

Our Lady, thou
So rich in sorrows, bow
Thy face upon my anguish now!   1280

Thy heart transfixed,
Thy gaze is fixed
Towards thy son upon the Cross.
The Father beseeching,
Thy sighs are reaching   1285
To heaven to assuage thy loss!

Who can feel
And who reveal
Such pain, such bitter woe?
Why my heart with fear is shaking,   1290
Why it's yearning, why it's quaking,
Only you can truly know.

Wherever I may be,
I feel such misery
Within my bosom aching.   1295
When I am on my own
I weep, I weep alone,
My fearful heart is breaking.

The early sun was shining
When I rose from my bed.   1300
In grief and sorrow pining,
What bitter tears I shed!

The boxes in front of my window
Were watered with the dew
Of my tears as early this morning   1305
I picked these flowers for you.

Help! Keep me safe from death and blame!
Our Lady, thou
So rich in sorrows, bow
Thy gracious face upon my shame!   1310

CATHEDRAL. REQUIEM FOR GRETCHEN'S MOTHER.

GRETCHEN *and all her relatives. Mass, organ and choir.*

EVIL SPIRIT	[*behind Gretchen*] How different, Gretchen, you felt
	When you, still all innocent,
	Came here to the altar
	Thumbing the well-worn pages,
	Lisping your prayers, 1315
	Half childish play,
	Half pious worship.
	Gretchen!
	What's on your mind?
	And in your heart, 1320
	What misdeed?
	Are you praying for your mother's soul, which
	Through your doing is now in purgatory?
	And there below your heart,
	Can you not feel it quickening, 1325
	The shameful stigma of a sinful birth?
	That fearful presence, boding ill
	For both of you?
GRETCHEN	No! No!
	If only I could rid myself 1330
	Of these oppressive thoughts
	That swarm around me!
CHOIR	*Dies irae dies illa*[97]
	Solvet saeclum in favilla. [*organ music*
EVIL SPIRIT	Dread fear grips you! 1335
	The trumpet sounds!
	The graves gape!
	And your heart,
	From the ashes
	Where it slept 1340
	Awakes to hell-fire
	And quakes!
GRETCHEN	I must get out!
	The organ seems

	To stifle me,	1345
	The chanting voices	
	Melt my heart within me.	
CHOIR	*Iudex ergo cum sedebit*	
	Quidquid latet adparebit	
	Nil inultum remanebit.	1350
GRETCHEN	I'm suffocating!	
	The pillars	
	Press in on me,	
	The vaults above	
	Are crushing me! I need air!	1355
EVIL SPIRIT	You try to hide!	
	If only your sin and shame	
	Could be hidden!	
	Air? Light?	
	Woe on you!	1360
CHOIR	*Quid sum miser tunc dicturus*	
	Quem patronum rogaturus	
	Cum vix iustus sit securus.	
EVIL SPIRIT	The blessed	
	Turn their faces from you.	1365
	The pure	
	Shudder to reach out	
	Their hands to you.	
	Woe!	
CHOIR	*Quid sum miser tunc dicturus.*	1370
GRETCHEN	Neighbour! Your salts!	

[she falls in a swoon

NIGHT

In front of Gretchen's house.
VALENTIN, *a soldier, Gretchen's brother*

VALENTIN   When I was drinking with the rest,
They used to argue who was best
Of all the girls they ever knew,
The way that soldiers always do.   1375
And then they used to fill their glasses
And drink a toast to all the lasses.
I'd sit there with a quiet smile,
And let them brag on for a while;
I'd stroke my beard and hide my thoughts,   1380
And when they'd finished, I'd fill my jar
And tell them: Well, it takes all sorts.
But of all the lasses near and far,
Not one could hold a candle to
My sister Gretchen – ain't that true?   1385
He's right, they'd shout, let's drink a toast
To little Gretchen, she's the one,
She's the girl we all like most.
And all the boasters sat there dumb.
But now! It drives you to despair,   1390
It makes you want to tear your hair;
The neighbours talk, the gossips sneer,
And every lout thinks he can jeer.
All I can do is look away,
Dreading every word they say.   1395
And even if I knocked them flying,
I couldn't tell them they were lying.

FAUST. MEPHISTOPHELES

FAUST   Through that church window softly gleams
The warm reflection of the sanctuary light;
But here outside its ever fainter beams   1400
Are smothered in the darkness of the night.

That darkness, too, encompasses my heart.

MEPHISTO. And I feel like a tom-cat in the dark,
Up on the roof-tops by the fire-escapes,
Padding along the walls and roaming free,   1405
A bit of thieving, getting into scrapes,
Screwing around – that's just the life for me!
Come on, cheer up! Why all this gloom?
You're going to see your girl tonight,
And not to meet your doom!   1410

FAUST The promise of a night of heavenly bliss,
The thrill, the warming passion of her kiss
Cannot relieve my miserable plight.
I am accursed, a homeless refugee,
An aimless outcast driven relentlessly   1415
Like a cascading torrent over rock and precipice,
Raging and seething into the abyss.
And in a peaceful meadow by that stream
She lived her simple life, her daily round
And all the childish thoughts that she could dream   1420
In that small world were safely hedged around.
And I, whom God has cursed,
Was not content to thunder
In a foaming rage and burst
The tumbling rocks asunder.   1425
I had to undermine that girl's tranquillity –
That was the sacrifice that hell required of me.
What must be done, let it be quickly done;
Now, Devil, help me end this agony.
My fearful destiny and hers are one,   1430
And she is doomed to share my fate with me.

MEPHISTO. Oh, what a boiling stew we're in again!
Go in and comfort her, my friend.
A fool like that just needs to lose the plot, and then
He thinks the world is coming to an end.   1435

FAUST. MEPHISTOPHELES

FAUST   In misery and despair! Pitifully wandering the country
all this time! That sweet, hapless creature shut up in a
dungeon as a criminal, exposed to appalling suffering.
For so long! And you kept this from me, you treacherous,
despicable demon! Yes, stand there rolling your malevolent devil's eyes at me, stand and defy me with
your insufferable company. In prison! At the mercy of
evil spirits and the pitiless judgement of humanity, in
irredeemable misery. And meanwhile you lull me with
vulgar pleasures, you conceal her growing misery from
me and let her perish helplessly.

MEPHISTO.   She's not the first!

FAUST   You hound! You vile monster! Oh infinite Spirit,
change him, change this snake back into his dog's
shape, when he would delight in trotting ahead of me
in the night, rolling at the feet of harmless wayfarers
and leaping onto their shoulders as they fell. Turn him
back into his favourite shape, so that he crawls before
me on his belly in the sand, and I can crush the
depraved creature under my feet! Not the first! Oh,
misery! Misery such as no human soul can grasp, or
understand how more than one creature has been
plunged into such wretchedness, that the writhing
death-agony of the first was not enough to atone for
the guilt of all the others in the sight of eternal God!
The suffering of this one creature sears me to the
heart, and you grin calmly at the fate of thousands.

MEPHISTO.   How high and mighty! So we've reached our wits' end,
the point where you gentlemen lose your head. Why do
you seek our company, if you can't handle it? You want
to fly, but your head goes dizzy. Well – did we force
ourselves on you – or was it the other way round?

FAUST   Don't bare your ravening fangs at me, it revolts me.
Great, glorious Spirit, you deigned to appear to me,
you know my heart and soul, why did you have to
fetter me to this infamous companion, who feeds on

mischief and delights in destruction?

MEPHISTO. Have you finished?

FAUST Save her, or woe betide you! The most atrocious curse on you through all the ages. Save her!

MEPHISTO. I cannot undo the bonds or draw back the bolts of retribution. Save her? Who was it that dragged her to her ruin? I or you?

FAUST [looks wildly about him]

MEPHISTO. Are you reaching for thunderbolts? It's just as well they were not given to you miserable mortals. That is the only trick you can think of to clear your confused minds – to crush any innocent person who gets in your way.

FAUST Take me to her! She must be freed!

MEPHISTO. And what about the risks you run? Don't you realize that you're still wanted for murder in that town, that avenging spirits still haunt the grave of the man you killed, waiting for the murderer to return?

FAUST I have to hear that from you! You monster, may the deaths and murders of the whole world come on your head. Take me to her, I say, and rescue her.

MEPHISTO. I'll take you there, and let me tell you what I can do. I don't have power over everything in heaven and earth, you know. I will drug the gaoler, you take the keys and release her by human hand. I will keep a lookout and have the magic horses ready for you. That I can do.

FAUST Away then!

NIGHT. OPEN COUNTRY

FAUST, MEPHISTOPHELES *storming past on black horses*

FAUST	What's going on around the gibbet there?	1436
MEPHISTO.	I don't know what they're stewing and brewing.	
FAUST	They're swaying about and stooping and bowing.	
MEPHISTO.	A witches' coven!	
FAUST	They're sprinkling and blessing.	1440
MEPHISTO.	Ride on! Ride on!	

A DUNGEON

FAUST *with a bunch of keys and a lamp,*
in front of a small iron door

FAUST   A long forgotten shudder seizes me, the deepest dread a
man can feel. Here! Here! Come! Your hesitation brings
death nearer.
[*he takes hold of the lock, from within a voice is heard singing*]

> My mother, the whore, she's [98]
> Murdered me.
> My father, the villain, he's
> Eaten me.
> My little sister found
> The bones that lay around.
> In a cool place she laid them down.
> I turned into a little bird that day.
> Fly away! Fly away!

FAUST *trembles, staggers, controls himself and unlocks the door.*
He hears the rattling of chains and the rustling of straw.

MARGARETA [*cowering on her bed*]
No! No! They're coming! Bitter death!

FAUST   [*softly*] Hush! I've come to rescue you.
             [*he picks up the chains to unlock them*]

MARGARETA   [*resisting*] Go away! It's midnight! Executioner, isn't
             tomorrow morning early enough for you?

FAUST   Come!

MARGARETA   [*writhes in front of him*] Have pity on me and let me live!
             I am so young, so young. I was beautiful, I am a poor
             young girl. Just look at my flowers, look at my crown.
             Have pity! What have I done to you? I've never seen
             you in my life.

FAUST   She is distracted, I can't stand it.

MARGARETA   Look, the child! I must feed it. It was here just now.
             There! I've fed it! They took it away from me and said
             I'd killed it, and they sing songs about me. It's not
             true, it's just a fairy-tale that ends like that, their songs
             aren't about me.

FAUST   [*throws himself at her*] Gretchen!

MARGARETA   [*jumps to her feet*] Where is he? I heard him calling, he
             called 'Gretchen!' He called to me! Where is he? Ah,
             through all the wailing and gnashing of teeth I know
             his voice, he's calling 'Gretchen!' [*she throws herself at
             his feet*] Man! Man! Give him to me, bring him to me!
             Where is he?

FAUST   [*seizes her desperately by the shoulders*] My love! My love!

MARGARETA   [*sinks to the floor and hides her head in his lap*]

FAUST   Get up, my love! Your murderer is your rescuer. Get up!
             [*during her swoon he unlocks the chains from her hands*]
             Come, we shall escape this dreadful fate.

MARGARETA   [*leans against him*] Kiss me! Kiss me!

FAUST   A thousand times! Just hurry, Gretchen, hurry!

MARGARETA   Kiss me! Can't you kiss any more? What? Why? You're
             my Heinrich, and you've forgotten how to kiss? Once
             I felt all heaven overwhelm me in your arms. You used
             to kiss as if you would stifle me and kill me with
             passion. Heinrich, kiss me – or else I'll kiss you! [*she
             seizes him*] Oh, no! Your lips are cold! Dead! They
             don't respond!

FAUST   Follow me, and I will hold you to me with a thousand
             passionate kisses. Just follow me!

MARGARETA [*sits in silence for a while*] Heinrich, is it you?

FAUST   It's me, come with me.

MARGARETA I don't understand it. It's you? My chains are undone!
             You're rescuing me. Who are you rescuing? Do you
             know?

FAUST   Come! Come with me!

MARGARETA I've killed my mother! I've drowned my child! Your
             child, Heinrich! Dear God in heaven, was that not a
             dream, then? Your hand, Heinrich! It's wet − wipe it
             off, please! There's blood on it − put your sword away!
             My head is confused.

FAUST   This will be the death of me.

MARGARETA No, you must live, you must survive us all. Who would
             look after the graves! In a row, please, like this: my
             brother there, beside my mother. Put me over here,
             with my little one at my right breast. Give me your
             hand on it! You are my Heinrich.

FAUST   [*tries to drag her away*] Can you not feel my hand, hear
             my voice? Come, I'm here, I will rescue you.

MARGARETA Out there?

FAUST   Freedom!

MARGARETA Out there? Not for all the world. If the grave is out
             there, come! If death lurks out there, come! From here
             to eternal rest, but not a step further. Oh Heinrich, if
             only I could go with you out into the wide world.

FAUST   The cell is open, hurry!

MARGARETA They're waiting for me on the road by the wood.

FAUST   Come out! Come out!

MARGARETA Not for my life. Can you see it wriggling? Save the
             poor little thing, it's still wriggling! Go! Quickly! Just
             over the bridge, straight into the wood, left at the
             pond by the fence. Go! Save it, save it!

FAUST   Come, save yourself!

MARGARETA If only we were past the hill, my mother's sitting there
             on a stone, her head's lolling. She can't wave, she can't
             nod to us, her head is too heavy. She was meant to sleep
             so that we could stay awake and be happy together.

FAUST   [*takes hold of her and tries to drag her away*]

MARGARETA I'll shout out loud and wake everybody.

FAUST   Day is here. Oh, my love, my love!

MARGARETA   Day! It's day! The last day! My wedding day! Tell
             no one that you were with Gretchen last night.
             My wreath! We'll meet again! Listen, the people are
             shuffling along the streets! Listen! They're talking
             in whispers. The bell tolls! Crack, the staff breaks! [99]
             Every neck feels the sharpness of the blade that bites at
             mine! Listen, the bell.

MEPHISTO.   [*appears*] Come away, or you're done for, my horses
             are shuddering, it's dawn!

MARGARETA   Him! Him! Get away from him, send him away! He
             wants me! No! No! Into Thy hands, O Lord; may Thy
             judgement come upon me! Save me! Never, never
             again! Farewell for ever. Farewell, Heinrich.

FAUST   [*throws his arms round her*] I won't leave you!

MARGARETA   You holy angels, protect my soul – you horrify me,
             Heinrich.

MEPHISTO   She is condemned!

                     [*he disappears with* FAUST, *the door clangs shut*
             [*a voice is heard, dying away*]

             Heinrich! Heinrich!

NOTES TO THE TEXT

NOTES TO PART ONE

1 Line 21. Nearly all editions published during Goethe's lifetime have '*mein Leid*' (my sorrow); one of Goethe's literary executors 'corrected' it to '*mein Lied*' (my song). Many modern editions print the (erroneously?) corrected version. The dedicatory poem is in *ottava rima*: hendecasyllabic lines rhyming abababcc – a form generally used by Goethe for solemn or formal verses. The first sixteen lines of the Poet (59-74) are in the same stanza form – to ironic effect.

2 Sign of the Macrocosm: an astrological diagram representing the forces and influences linking the heavens, earth and mankind.

3 Lines 1042-8: terms relating to alchemical processes.

4 Solomon's Key: The *Clavicula Salomonis*, a sixteenth-century book of magic spells and formulae.

5 Evidently Faust here makes the sign of the Cross, or holds up a crucifix, and subsequently threatens to invoke the Trinity (lines 1318-21).

6 Pentagram: a five-pointed star associated with magic and witchcraft.

7 In the German text, *encheiresis naturae* (a trick or device of nature): an eighteenth-century term used to describe certain chemical processes.

8 *Eritis sicut Deus*: the Vulgate version of Genesis 3: 5. The Authorized Version has: 'and ye shall be as gods, knowing good and evil.'

9 At the time Goethe studied in Leipzig, the town and university set the tone for fashions in French manners, taste, and culture.

10 Formal laws governed the display of clothes and jewellery in public according to social status in sixteenth (and eighteenth) century Germany.

11 *Sancta simplicitas!* ('Holy simplicity!'): words attributed to Jan Hus when about to be burned at the stake, on seeing an old woman carefully replace a bundle of sticks that had rolled away from the pyre.

12 An approximate version of Ophelia's song in *Hamlet* (IV: 5).

13 These and the following lines from the Requiem Mass are translated in the Missal as follows:

> Day of wrath and terror looming,
> Heaven and earth to ash consuming . . .
> Then the judge will sit, revealing
> Every hidden thought and feeling,
> Unto each requital dealing . . .
> What shall wretched I be crying,
> To what friend for succour flying,
> When the just in fear are sighing?

(*The Missal in Latin and English*, ed. J. O'Connell and H. P. R. Finberg, 2nd edn, London, 1957, p. 230).

14 Spookybum (*Proktophantasmist*, or The Man with the Haunted Backside): a reference to the ageing pundit of the German Enlightenment Friedrich Nicolai, a critic, novelist and writer of travel books with whom Goethe had some literary scores to settle. In 1797 it was reported that a large house in Tegel (Berlin) was haunted; the rationalist Nicolai sought to combat such superstition by announcing in a public lecture that he himself had fallen into a fever some years earlier in which he had imagined he had seen ghosts – but that he had been cured of such fantasies by the application of leeches to his backside. This was a source of great hilarity to an irreverent younger generation.

15 Mieding: Johann Martin Mieding, cabinet-maker to the Weimar court, also worked as stage manager for the amateur theatrical entertainments staged by the court – most of them scripted and directed by Goethe. Indeed, the Walpurgis Night's Dream is in part a parody of such entertainments. The satirical verses are also derived from Goethe's and Schiller's polemical *Xenien* or satires (see lines 4303-6), directed at contemporary individuals

or types. Some of the individuals are identifiable; few are figures of any great distinction, and are included simply because
they fell foul of Goethe's and Schiller's polemics. August von
Hennings (lines 4307-18) was a minor belletrist who published
a literary periodical, *Spirit of the Age*, and a collection of poems
entitled Musaget (Leader of the Muses); the Inquisitive Traveller (line 4267) might be Friedrich Nicolai in another guise; the
Crane (line 4323) is probably Johann Caspar Lavater, a former
friend and mentor of Goethe's, with whom he fell out; lines
4343-62 represent a parade of philosophical ideologies, and lines
4367-86 appear to represent social and political groups from
the period of the French Revolution. Further specific identific-
ations are speculative and uncertain.

16 A puzzling passage – possibly a survival of early material that
was discarded.

17 From a well-known German fairytale *Von dem Machandelboom*
(The Juniper Tree).

18 A white staff was ritually broken above the victim's head immediately prior to execution.

COMMENTARY AND NOTES TO PART TWO

[*Because of the complexity of the symbolic action of Part Two, and in order
to keep explanatory notes to a minimum, I have included an act-by-act
commentary.*]

Act One: Commentary

After Faust's recovery from the horror of the Gretchen tragedy by
means of a therapeutic sleep of oblivion provided by beneficent
nature spirits, he wakes refreshed to a symbolic new day. His first
gesture is a characteristically Faustian attempt to look directly at the
sun – as it were, to experience truth in absolute terms. His vision
of the rainbow reflected in the flying spray of the waterfall teaches
him that the absolute can only be perceived indirectly, in mediated
form – as simile or symbolic reflection. His conclusion that 'our
life is in that colourful reflection' marks his settling for empirical

human experience as a metaphor of absolute truth, and stands as a motto over his experiences in Part Two. It is answered by the Chorus Mysticus at the end of the drama, which indicates a transcendental sphere where that which is relative and inscrutable becomes absolute and knowable: 'All that is mutable / Is but reflected' (literally: 'All that is transient / Is but a likeness'). Faust's lines are spoken in the metre of Dante's *Divine Comedy*: hendecasyllabic lines rhyming aba, bcb, cdc, etc. – a repetitive but fluid form that Goethe evidently considered appropriate for Faust's vision of the 'constant flux' of the rainbow reflected in the waterfall.

The following 'imperial' scenes appear to be set at the court of a late medieval or Renaissance Holy Roman Emperor; indeed, in his early draft scenarios, Goethe specified it as the court of Maximilian I or Charles V. But as always in Part Two, the historical colouring conceals a modern allegory: that of a régime threatened by corruption, bankruptcy and the breakdown of law and authority. Goethe's fear and loathing of war or civil unrest, and in particular of the French Revolution, is well documented; at the same time, he acknowledged its causes in the decadence of the *ancien régime*, while never being able to accept its effects. Mephistopheles manipulates himself and Faust into a position of influence at the court by usurping the role of court jester, and contrives to undermine the state by the introduction of unsecured paper money. The carnival masquerade is exploited by Mephistopheles to mask his fiscal schemes and to introduce Faust to the court in the guise of Plutus, god of wealth: an initially conventional court pageant is taken over by uncanny and magical forces with the entry of Plutus and the Boy Charioteer – an enigmatic allegory of poetry in the service of a wealthy patron. Plutus' masquerade is a dire warning of chaos to come; he foresees, albeit in a cryptic and heavily coded allegory, an impending breakdown of law and order (lines 5968-9). His warning falls on deaf ears: Mephistopheles' illusory paper wealth provides a brief and precarious solution to the empire's problems, and the immature young Emperor continues to demand amusement. The crisis of the *ancien régime* in eighteenth-century Europe is adumbrated in this sixteenth-century allegory.

The Emperor's demand to see Helen and Paris marks the beginning of Faust's long quest for Helen that occupies Acts Two and Three – during which the action leaves the political milieu for an extended cultural allegory. For the moment, Mephistopheles sends Faust on a forbidding journey to the Mothers in order to retrieve the forms of Helen and Paris. Critical opinion is sharply divided on the nature and function of these inscrutable deities; for the majority, they are awesome symbolic powers, archetypes of formation and transformation, a repository of cultural forms and memories, from whose remote and insubstantial realm Faust can retrieve mythical figures. For others (including myself), they are Mephistophelian inventions; the Devil hypnotically induces Faust to believe in these extravagant creations, so that he may all the more convincingly play his role in summoning up the spirits of Helen and Paris before the court (see J. R. Williams, 'The Problem of the Mothers', in *A Companion to Goethe's 'Faust'*, ed. Paul Bishop, pp. 122-143). Such conjurations by charlatan miracle-workers were common enough in the eighteenth century; here, as elsewhere in Act One, Goethe is casting Mephistopheles as a Cagliostro figure. Cagliostro (Giuseppe Balsamo, 1743-1795) was a notorious master of fraudulent schemes and spirit séances, whose pseudo-masonic activities were for Goethe a subject of fascination and revulsion; Goethe believed him to have been implicated in the diamond necklace scandal of 1785 which, he was convinced, fatally undermined the prestige of the French throne and contributed directly to the Revolution. Faust, caught up in the illusion he himself is helping to create, and besotted with the vision of Helen, attempts to intervene in the spirit séance; the result is an explosion that knocks him unconscious – a state he remains in until his feet touch Greek soil.

Act One: Notes

19 Aeolian harps: wind harps, supposed to produce chords of natural harmony.

20 The Lord Chancellor is evidently also Archbishop; his dual role is clearer in Act Four.

21 Guelphs and Ghibellines: proverbially warring papal and imperial factions in medieval Italy.

22 Here and elsewhere, the Astrologer's words are supplied by Mephistopheles. If they mean anything, they might refer to the alchemists' dream of manufacturing gold and silver (Sol and Luna) – often fraudulently produced by alloys of quicksilver (Mercury) and copper (Venus), or of iron (Mars), lead (Saturn), and tin (Jupiter).

23 It might seem puzzling that Mephistopheles, via the Astrologer, should offer such apparently prudent advice; but it is part of his strategy that the carnival should go ahead so that he can introduce and distribute his paper money.

24 Zoilo–Thersites: Mephistopheles in the double mask of Zoilos, an Athenian critic who pointed out errors in Homer, and Thersites, who mocked the Greek heroes at Troy, and was beaten by Odysseus with his staff (*Iliad* ii: 212-77).

25 Mephistopheles kneads a lump of gold into a phallus.

26 Great Pan: the Emperor and his courtiers in carnival costume. Goethe wrote many such (though more decorous) masquerades for the Weimar court.

27 Just as Mephistopheles prompts the Astrologer, so too Faust/ Plutus leads the Herald.

28 Thetis and Peleus: parents of Achilles.

29 Motifs and themes from the Arabian Nights are frequent in Part Two; Goethe knew the tales from an early age.

30 There were numerous financial scandals in the eighteenth century, from John Law's policies as Louis XV's Minister of Finance to the South Sea Bubble and the issue of paper *assignats* by the French revolutionary government. Goethe was no economist; but he had experienced the inflation of Prussian and Austrian currency, and was profoundly uneasy about credit and paper money.

31 Foot will heal foot: a reference to S. C. Hahnemann's homoeopathic doctrine 'like is cured by like'; Goethe was highly sceptical of any such 'miracle' cures. Here and elsewhere in Act One, Mephistopheles' activities recall those of Cagliostro as quack doctor and miracle-worker.

Act Two: Commentary

[I have not supplied notes to all the classical and mythological references in Acts Two and Three; they can be found in any good dictionary of mythology. David Luke (1994, pp. 289-307) provides an excellent index of classical mythology and a map of classical Greece.]

Returning with the unconscious Faust to Faust's old study, Mephistopheles briefly revisits academic life, where he encounters not only the deferential Famulus, Wagner's assistant – who represents an earlier, scholastic tradition of learning - but also the very student he had gleefully teased in Part One, now a bumptious graduate who patronises and disconcerts the Devil in a hilarious exchange. This scene can be read not only as the older Goethe's comment on rebellious youth (he had experienced frequent episodes of self-assertiveness among students at the local University of Jena), but also more specifically as a satire on German idealist philosophy – on Fichte, perhaps, or Schopenhauer. Goethe knew both well – indeed, he had adopted the young, recently graduated Schopenhauer as a willing disciple in his campaign to refute Newton's colour theory; but their collaboration was short-lived, at least in part because of Schopenhauer's overweening sense of self. In spite of severe provocation, Goethe for a time tolerated the philosopher's outrageous solipsism; and this may well be reflected in Mephistopheles' tolerant judgement on the rantings of the young idealist.

At this point Goethe introduces one of his most baffling creations: the 'homunculus', the product of Wagner's crazed experiment to create living matter *in vitro* – one of the dreams of medieval and Renaissance alchemists that is alarmingly close to realisation today. The immediate dramatic function of this enigmatic 'little man' is clear: to read, since he is so freakishly well-informed, Faust's unconscious dream of the conception of Helen in the encounter between Leda and the swan Zeus, and to prescribe the cure for Faust. This is to take him to Helen's homeland, to the Classical Walpurgis Night which, as it happens, is taking place that night. Not only Faust, but also Homunculus (and even, more haphazardly, Mephistopheles) will find fulfilment in Greece; for Homunculus, artificially created as he is, is pure spirit, lacking bodily substance – he longs for a physical existence.

Just what Goethe intended Homunculus to represent is less obvious. There is hearsay evidence that he is meant to be 'pure entelechy', a term used by Goethe, in his more mystical pronouncements, as virtually synonymous with soul or spirit: the indestructible part of any powerful human personality that might become reincarnated in another existence by a process of metempsychosis. In the context of Act Two, he is spirit in a state of pre-existence; in the course of the Classical Walpurgis Night he seeks – and appears to find – a way into organic life by the consummation of his 'marriage' with the ocean, the fecund source of all life. Driven by a powerful erotic urge, he smashes his glass phial on Galatea's scallop-shell chariot and pours himself into the waves – thus beginning a quasi-evolutionary progress through the scale of creation towards an uncertain destination.

Once Faust touches Greek soil – for the moment, not in Helen's homeland of the Peloponnese, but in Thessaly – he regains consciousness and begins his journey through a crowded theme-park of classical antiquity; he experiences his classical education, as it were, in the pre-history of primitive Hellenic myth that ultimately led up to the 'most unique' figure, Helen. He encounters the centaur Chiron, who taught the fabled heroes of antiquity, and is handed on to the sibyl Manto, who will conduct him to the underworld to petition Persephone to return Helen to the world above. Mephistopheles, wandering uncomfortably and aimlessly through this alien pagan and classical landscape, also finds a suitable goal in the ineffable ugliness of the Graiae, daughters of Phorkys. It is in this hideous female guise, as Phorkyas, that he will confront the classical beauty of Helen in Act Three – indeed, as Phorkyas he will manipulate and orchestrate the whole encounter between Faust and the emblem of Hellenic beauty.

The extraordinary episode within the Classical Walpurgis Night involving the eruption of a mountain through the efforts of Seismos is generally understood as an allegory of revolution, even specifically of the French Revolution – a subject never directly addressed by Goethe in literary form, though he did write a handful of minor plays and one major drama, *Die natürliche Tochter* (The Natural Daughter), that address the causes and effects of that political upheaval. He frequently referred to the Revolution as an earthquake or volcano; and in his literary imagery, political turbulence was often associated with, and expressed in terms of, the prevailing geological doctrine of vulcanism, which explained the origins and formation of the earth's crust through volcanic and igneous processes. Goethe was, by temperament and by scientific conviction, a neptunist; for him, volcanic activity was a late and superficial factor in the formation of the earth – neptunists held that rocks were principally formed by sedimentation in water, in the primaeval ocean.

The same gradualism also informed Goethe's political convictions. Here, Thales and Anaxagoras, figures based loosely on Greek historical models, are respectively the champions of neptunism and vulcanism. The vulcanist Anaxagoras is discredited as a lunatic, the horrid brood of creatures thrown up by the seismic upheaval – the 'sans-culottes' pygmies, who slaughter the aristocratic herons – is obliterated, and the way is clear for Homunculus to proceed to the marine festival on the shores of the Aegean, which culminates in his fiery 'marriage' with the ocean and his birth into a physical existence. This fluid, lyrical and musical celebration of the sea is a hymn to the 'neptunist' creed, a parade of elemental creatures and divinities; not the Olympian pantheon of classical Greece, but a more primitive, earlier and more enduring substratum of eastern Mediterranean myth that was in Goethe's day being discovered and studied by mythographers – at whose expense Goethe indulges in some recondite satire. The whole tumultuous pageant reaches its climax in the annual epiphany of Galatea – a scene generally associated with Raphael's painting of The Triumph of Galatea, but probably drawing on all manner of visual sources – and with an ecstatic paean of praise to the four elements. After this noisy and jubilant climax, Act Three begins with the lone voice of Helen announcing herself, as the action modulates into a reconstruction of Attic tragedy.

Act Two: Notes

32 Probably a reference to Lot's wife (Genesis 19: 26).

33 The rape of Leda: possibly based on Correggio's painting of Leda and the Swan, and/or on other pictorial sources.

34 Pharsalus, in Thessaly, was the site of the decisive battle that marked the end of the Roman Republic with the defeat of Pompey by Caesar (48 BC). The ghostly vision of the battle

evoked by Erichtho soon fades and gives way to 'the legions of Hellenic legend' (line 7028).

35 See Lucan, *Pharsalia* vi: 507 ff.

36 Antaeus: a giant slain by Hercules, who derived his strength from the earth. See also lines 9609-11.

37 This enigmatic characterisation of Mephistopheles appears to be a classicised version of the Lord's definition of his role in the Prologue in Heaven (lines 340-3).

38 This and other references to Mephistopheles' deformities reflect Goethe's notorious pronouncement that he considered the classical 'healthy' and the romantic 'sick'.

39 On the lower Peneus: topographically, the action of the Classical Walpurgis Night begins on the Pharsalian Plain on the upper Peneus or Peneios (strictly, on its tributary, the Enipeus), moves downstream through the Vale of Tempe (the lower Peneus) to the foot of Mount Olympus, returns to the upper Peneus after line 7494, and moves eastward to the shores of the Aegean for the final scene.

40 A reiteration, this time as Faust's waking dream, of the rape of Leda.

41 On Pherae: an incongruity. Achilles was posthumously united with Helen on the island of Leuce – as Goethe well knew (see also lines 8876-8). Pherae (in Thessaly) was the kingdom of Admetus, whose widow Alcestis offered to take his place in Hades. Goethe writes '*on* Pherae' ('auf Pherä') – thus deliberately conflating two myths.

42 'Here' (very approximately) is the site of the Battle of Pydna (168 BC) between Rome and the Macedonian King Perseus, which marked the rise of Roman republican power.

43 For a mother to give birth: Leto, mother of Apollo and Artemis.

44 The Cranes of Ibycus: agents of nemesis in Schiller's ballad 'Die Kraniche des Ibykus'.

45 References to features of the landscape around the Brocken in the Harz Mountains.

46 Diana, Luna, Hecate: the triple aspect of the lunar deity – respectively on earth, in the heavens, and in the underworld.

Thessalian witches were said to be able to draw the moon down to earth by magic incantations.

47 The Cabiri were obscure pitcher gods (see lines 8219-20), the subject of a treatise by Goethe's contemporary F. W. von Schelling. Their cult centre was Samothrace; Goethe appears here and below (lines 8168-205) to indulge in some persiflage of Schelling's mythological studies.

48 Since Venus went from us: the Classical Walpurgis Night, and the marine festival in particular, is devoted not to the classical pantheon of divinities, which did not survive the Greek and Roman civilisations, but to more primitive elemental cults (the Cabiri, the Telchines, the Psylli and Marsi, and all kinds of sea-creatures and demigods) that survive historical change (see also lines 8359-78).

49 Chelone: a nymph changed by Hermes into a turtle.

50 Telchines: legendary aboriginal inhabitants of Rhodes, famed for their skills in working metal. Worshippers of the sun god Apollo (the Colossus of Rhodes).

51 Psylli and Marsi: aboriginal inhabitants of North Africa and Italy, famed as snake charmers and for their skill in healing snake-bites. Goethe reinvents them as the guardians of the cult of Aphrodite on Cyprus.

Act Three: Commentary

At the beginning of the Classical Walpurgis Night, the Thessalian witch Erichtho had announced herself and the episode in a verse form quite new in *Faust*: in unrhymed lines of six stresses that are the modern equivalent of classical iambic trimeter (i.e. lines of three 'dipodic' feet), the metre of the Greek tragedians. This is the language of Helen, though this first scene in Sparta (from line 8909) also includes lines of trochaic tetrameter (lines of four dipodic feet – or, in its modern form, of eight stresses) – notably at moments of tension or agitation. Interpolated among these long lines of dialogue are the odes of the chorus which at times are arranged, in the manner of Attic tragedy, in a triadic form of strophe, antistrophe, and epode; strophe and antistrophe are metrically identical or near-identical, while the epode is in a different metre. This triadic pattern is, however, varied. In lines 8697-753, for example, the chorus recites a remarkable series of metrical responsions constructed as: strophe 1, antistrophe 1; strophe 2, antistrophe 2; epode; strophe 3, antistrophe 3; strophe 4, antistrophe 4. Classicising devices such as stichomythia, double and even triple stichomythia, are also exploited in this scene (lines 8810-25, 8850-81).

The time and place of the action concern Helen's return to Sparta after the Trojan War, uncertain of her fate at the hands of her husband Menelaus. The dramatic action concerns Mephisto-pheles-Phorkyas' efforts to drive Helen and her chorus of captive Trojan women into Faust's protection. This is achieved in two ways. Firstly, Phorkyas questions and undermines Helen's sense of identity by reciting the myths and legends that have grown up around her. For Helen is no longer a historical individual, not even the mythical heroine who was the *casus belli* of the Trojan War; she has become an icon, an emblem of classical beauty and Hellenic civilisation that will be assimilated by subsequent cultures and become the common property of a transmitted neoclassical herit-age. Secondly, Phorkyas uses the threat of Menelaus' jealousy and revenge: he will surely execute his faithless wife and hang her en-tourage from the rafters.

At this point Goethe exploits an extraordinary episode of medieval history: the establishment in the thirteenth century, after the Fourth Crusade, of Frankish rule in the Morea (as the Peloponnese came to be known) at Mistra, a hilltop fortress only a few miles from the abandoned site of ancient Sparta. This short-lived Frankish settlement in the heart of the Byzantine Empire is the symbolic meeting place of the classical Helen and the 'medieval' Faust, and of their respective cultures. This is the refuge that Phorkyas offers to Helen and her women; she explains how a race of warriors from the 'Cimmerian' north has established itself in that fortress. After all, she adds, with laconic understatement, they had almost twenty years to do it; in the symbolically condensed timescale of Act Three – which, as Goethe wrote, covers some 3,000 years from the fall of Troy to that of Missolonghi – 'twenty years' stands for more than two millennia.

Phorkyas' scheme succeeds, and the scene is magically trans-formed into Faust's medieval fortress – as Goethe remarked half-seriously, there is a 'higher' unity of time and place operating in this act. Faust greets his guest with the elaborate courtesy of chivalry, offering his protection – and his hand. Appearing as a medieval knight, he speaks (anachronistically) in blank verse, unrhymed iambic pentameter – the modern, Shakespearian form that also became the idiom of the German classical theatre in the late eighteenth century. Astonishingly, Helen at once replies in the same form (lines 9213-17); it is as if she is replying to Faust in his own language. And from this point begins the cultural rapprochement between the Hellenic and the western European world (or rather, perhaps, the appropriation of classical culture by the West), expressed in the delicate wooing of Helen by Faust in terms of prosodic symbolism. That is, Helen, intrigued by the unfamiliar (unclassical) use of end-rhyme by Faust's servant Lynceus, is taught how to rhyme by Faust: in lines 9377-84 she responds to his rhyming iambic pentameter, and their bond is reinforced by the further *internal* rhyming of lines 9411-18.

Phorkyas disrupts their intimacy by announcing an attack by Menelaus – at which point Faust appears to divide up the Morea by enfeoffing not his Frankish vassals, but the tribes of the Germanic migrations: Germans, Goths, Franks, Saxons and Normans. Once again, the symbolic anachronisms of the third act suggest that the whole history of encounters between north-western and south-eastern Europe is being resumed in, as Goethe put it, a 'phantasmagoric' sequence. Helen and Faust, defended by their encircling allies, withdraw to Arcadia – geographically, a barren region in the central Peloponnese; culturally, the emblem of an idyllic *locus amoenus* in a long tradition of classical and modern literature and painting.

In the third scene, the symbolic action moves from the medieval to the modern period. In this progression, the union of Faust and Helen in Arcadia stands for the cultural watershed of the Renaissance – for Goethe, unquestionably the highest point of western civilisation since fifth-century Athens. Helen and her Trojan women are assimilated into modern culture – Phorkyas tells them that their polytheistic culture is past (lines 9679-86), and from this point to the death of Euphorion, Helen, Faust and the chorus speak not only in rhymed verse, but in exchanges in the style of an operatic libretto – for which, indeed, music is specifically prescribed. We are in the context of eighteenth-century neoclassicism.

The figure of Euphorion, the child of Faust and Helen, is an allegory of poetry, more specifically of modern, Romantic poetry (though it has been argued that Phorkyas' characterisation in lines 9625-8 reads more like a tribute to Mozart's genius than to a poetic talent). Towards the end of the scene, however, Euphorion assumes wilder, more extravagant, and indeed bellicose characteristics; and this, together with the stage direction after line 9902, suggests an increasing association with Byron, the maverick poet Goethe described as 'the greatest talent of the century.'

Certainly, the moving threnody of the chorus at Euphorion's death (lines 9907-38) reads as an unmistakable, though not entirely uncritical, tribute to the philhellene poet who died during his campaign in the Greek Wars of Liberation. But the simple equation Euphorion = Byron is insufficient; Euphorion appears to represent the restless, wilful spirit of Romantic poetry, what Goethe regarded as its self-destructive tendencies – as indeed were exemplified in the life and fate of the English poet.

After the death of Euphorion, the classical and modern elements separate out; Helen returns to her 'native' verse form of iambic trimeter, Phorkyas to blank verse and rhymed iambic pentameter, and the chorus to ode forms. Helen joins her son in Hades, and Panthalis follows her. The chorus, unwilling to join their mistress in the underworld, are permitted to become spirits of 'ever-living' nature, and the act ends with a Dionysian celebration in the dynamic forms of trochaic tetrameter. Faust's classical experience is over; modern cultures have, it seems, failed to match or sustain the impetus of the classical tradition that peaked in the Renaissance. Goethe's and Schiller's high-minded classicism, for all its literary achievements, did not last; and in the following act the action returns to actual political and historical reality – to post-Revolution Europe, to the Napoleonic invasions, and to the restoration of the ancien régime that had, for some twenty-five years, been shaken by wars and revolution.

Act Three: Notes

52 Euros: the east wind.

53 A reference to the tradition, exploited in Euripides' *Helen*, that the Helen whom Paris abducted to Troy was a phantom;

the 'real' Helen was said to have been in Egypt during the Trojan War.

54 See note 41.

55 Taygetos: four syllables (Taÿgetos).

56 His fortress: Phorkyas compares the 'Cyclopian' masonry of Mycenaean buildings unfavourably with Faust's medieval Gothic castle.

57 Hermes: *psychopompos,* conductor of the dead to the underworld.

58 Lynceus may be referring to successive barbarian invasions of the Peloponnese (Dorians, Gauls, Goths, Slavs, etc.) – or, specifically, to the thirteenth-century crusaders, who came from the east (i.e. from Constantinople).

59 Again, the exact historical reference is unclear; cautiously, and in the context of the Frankish settlement of the Morea, we might suggest that Menelaus represents the forces of the neo-Greek (Byzantine) Empire. The Frankish Guillaume de Champlitte divided the Morea among his vassals in 1209 – but Mistra was reconquered by the Byzantine Emperor from his successor Guillaume de Villehardouin in 1259. It subsequently became a centre of Byzantine culture and learning, playing a seminal role in the emerging Renaissance.

60 The son of Maia: Hermes, who was, among other things, the patron god of thieves.

61 Euphorion: in the traditional Germanic Faust legend, Helen of Troy bears Faust a son named Justus Faustus. Euphorion was the name of the son born from the posthumous union of Achilles and Helen (see lines 7435-6 and 8876-8).

62 A puzzling episode – possibly a reference to Byron's *mores*.

63 Increasingly, the references appear to be to the liberation of Greece from Ottoman rule – which Byron did not live to see.

64 *exuviae*: spoils or clothing taken from the body of a fallen warrior.

65 The four sections of the chorus become respectively nymphs of trees, mountains, streams and vineyards. The frenzied celebration of lines 10030-8 may well be derived from paintings of Bacchanalia by Poussin, Titian and others.

Act Four: Commentary

Although this act is set firmly in modern Western Europe, Faust's grandiose opening monologue is spoken in unrhymed classicising trimeter; he is, as it were, still speaking Helen's language. The first section of his speech (lines 10039-54) is his valedictory tribute to his ephemeral classical experience and, perhaps, Goethe's own tribute to the brief but richly productive period of 'Weimar Class-icism', the years of his collaboration with Friedrich Schiller. The cloud that carries Faust from south-east to north-west - the reverse of the journey undertaken at the beginning of Act Two – separates into two types. One is the majestic 'castellated' form of cumulus, massively dominating the eastern horizon and emblematically rep-resenting the classical shapes of Juno, Leda, and Helen; the other rises as cirrus into the upper sky, symbolising Gretchen and the western Christian culture that she stands for. It also prefigures her intercession for Faust at the end of the drama. The symbolic struc-ture of this speech is informed by Goethe's study of cloud forms inspired by Luke Howard's classification (*On the Modifications of Clouds*, 1803).

With the entry of Mephistopheles, cued by a bizarre stage direc-tion after line 10066, the action switches from the classical culture of Helen to the political reality of early nineteenth-century Ger-many. In other words, it reverts to the milieu of Act One; and the verse forms of this act, until the final scene between the Emperor and his princes, revert generally to the rhymed iambic lines of four or five stressed syllables – the prevailing metre of most of *Faust*.

The burlesque exchanges between Faust and Mephistopheles on the origins of mountain ranges touch once again on the geo-logical theories of vulcanism and neptunism, of violent upheaval and gradualism that had informed the Anaxagoras-Thales debate in the Classical Walpurgis Night. As so often for Goethe, the to him repellent vulcanist doctrine is also a metaphor of violent political convulsion; and it is unsurprising that the Devil is here the proponent of (heavily parodied) vulcanist theory. Rejecting Mephistopheles' 'Sardanapalian' temptations, Faust reveals his final ambition: to conquer the sea, to tame the fruitless elemental ebb and flow of the tide, and to establish new territories. The opportunity to fulfil this ambition immediately presents itself: the young Emperor, who had failed to heed Faust's (admittedly heavily encrypted) warnings about the responsible governance of his realm, has seen the country descend into anarchy and civil strife, and a rival emperor has emerged who threatens to depose him and reform the political system.

If Act One had charted the decadence and frivolity of the *ancien régime* (whether in France or the 'Holy Roman Empire of the German Nation'), Act Four traces the historical consequences: discontent, insurrection, and the invasion of the Empire. The parallels with European events from 1789 to 1815 are there to be drawn: revolution, counter-revolution, the rise of Napoleon to terminate the process of revolution, and his invasion of Prussia, Austria and Russia as imperial ambition gained the upper hand. Prussia suffered its greatest humiliation at Jena in 1806 (within the Duchy of Sachsen-Weimar, Goethe's adoptive homeland), and the Holy Roman Empire, long since politically defunct, was formally abolished by Napoleon in the same year. Not until 1813 did the central European powers come together to inflict a decisive defeat on the invader at the Battle of Leipzig ('Battle of the Nations'); and the Congress of Vienna established the restoration of the old order. Many Germans, at least initially, perceived Napoleon not as a foreign invader, but as a liberator who might reform the ramshackle structures and institutions of the decayed Empire. Goethe himself held Napoleon in high esteem; he met him on three occasions, and wore with pride the order of the *Légion d'honneur* presented to him by the Emperor. Indeed, Goethe's notorious indifference to the 'liberation' of the German territories in 1813 was rooted in his admiration for Napoleon and his scepticism towards the political maturity of the German nations.

The broad lines of European political events are discernible behind the allegorical battle of Act Four, in which Faust and Mephistopheles contrive the restoration of the old order with the help of dubious allies and sinister forces. The final scene in particular concerns the restoration of secular and religious power; it is based on Charles IV's Golden Bull of 1356, which confirmed the offices, privileges, the succession by primogeniture and the traditional rights of the German Electors, but which also formalized the decentralization of the Empire, perpetuated the particularism of independent princes, and checked imperial power and authority. The restoration politics of the Congress of Vienna also confirmed particularism, creating the decentralised patchwork of states in the German Confederation under the watchful control of Metternich; and Goethe's sceptical view of the new Europe created after the defeat of Napoleon can be discerned in the heavy satire of the scene enacting the carve-up of the old empire. This scene, with all its comical ceremony and faintly ludicrous formal titles, its pomp and sycophancy, is written in a parodic formal language: the verse form is the alexandrine, the rhyming couplets of French classical tragedy, that was also the favoured form of the German Baroque, as well as of mid-eighteenth-century German classicism in its slavish imitations of *tragédie classique*. By the early nineteenth century this verse form, which in its heavily cadenced German form has little of the flexibility it has in French, had come to be regarded as stilted, rhetorical and pompous – an appropriate form for a scene that re-creates archaic privileges and powers.

Act Four: Notes

66 Seven-league boots: presumably to indicate the cultural and geographical shift of the action from south-east to north-west, as well as Mephistopheles' satisfaction at leaving the alien environment of pagan classicism.

67 Ephesians 6:12: here and elsewhere, Goethe marked the biblical references in his manuscript in pencil. It is not certain that he intended them to be printed; but his literary executors included them for publication.

68 Sardanapalus: a proverbially hedonistic Assyrian tyrant. Perhaps a further tribute to Byron, who dedicated his drama *Sardanapalus* to Goethe. Mephistopheles' description of an extravagant palace and lifestyle suggests the court of Versailles under Louis XVI, and/or its many imitations by eighteenth-century German princes.

69 Many precedents have been cited for Faust's reclamation schemes: Julius Caesar's plans for canals and land reclamation around Rome, Frederick the Great's drainage projects on the Oder, the creation of Porthmadog by William Madocks (1807-1814;

Goethe read an account of this in 1830), and the reclamation of land along the Dutch and North German coasts.

70 The German Romantic movement of the early nineteenth century inspired a revival of interest in medievalism (see also lines 10554 ff and 10768 ff), which took on a national colouring during the wars of liberation against Napoleon (against the perceived neoclassicism of French culture). The Gothic revival in Germany was also enlisted in the cause of national unity, culminating in the completion of Cologne Cathedral (see note 75 below). Goethe maintained a sceptical reserve towards these tendencies.

71 The Sabine necromant: the Sabines of Italy were reputed sorcerers. Goethe read of the burning of a suspected sorcerer in Florence in 1327; this obscure figure is here exploited as a convenient pretext for Faust's strategies.

72 Mirages (*fata morgana*) occurring around the Sicilian coast. St Elmo's Fire (see lines 10599 ff), an electrical discharge around the masts of ships, heralded the calm after a storm, and was attributed by sailors to the Dioscuri (Gemini: Castor and Pollux).

73 Mephistopheles calls the elemental forces of water and fire to his aid. In terms of the historical allegory, both played a significant part in the Battle of Leipzig: many of Napoleon's troops were drowned after the premature blowing of the Elster bridges, and murderous artillery fire (see lines 10750-55) was also a decisive factor.

74 In Charles IV's Golden Bull, the Elector of Saxony was appointed Lord Marshal of the Holy Roman Empire; the Elector of Brandenburg was Lord Chamberlain, the Count Palatine was Lord Seneschal, and the Elector of Bohemia Lord Cupbearer. The Archbishop of Mainz was also Lord Chancellor.

75 Within the modern historical allegory, this could well be an oblique reference to the project to complete Cologne Cathedral, which had been left unfinished since the fifteenth century. A national and religious movement to complete the building started around 1814; for all his scepticism towards Romantic medievalism, Goethe, urged by his friend Sulpiz Boisserée, one of its prime movers, took a distant interest in the project, which was not finished until 1880.

Act Five: Commentary

In this act, the action moves beyond the political settlements of the post-1815 European Restoration into the commercial, industrial and technological developments of the early nineteenth century. Faust has been granted quasi-feudal privileges over the tidal territories (although Goethe did not, in the final version, include the formal enfeoffment scene he had planned for Act Four, this is made clear enough in lines 11115-8). Having reclaimed his territories, once again by dubious and apparently supernatural means – Goethe was at once fascinated and alarmed by the accelerating pace of industrial and technical progress towards the end of his life – Faust has become a merchant prince, a ruthless trader and 'coloniser' whose grandiose utopian vision cannot mask his egotistic ambitions. The old couple Philemon and Baucis are, in Ovid's *Metamorphoses*, figures of proverbial kindness and hospitality who, in return for sheltering the gods Jupiter and Mercury, are granted one wish; their mutual devotion is such that they ask that neither should survive the other. Goethe's version is a brutally ironic reiteration of the legend: they perish simultaneously at the hands of Faust's henchmen. They stand here for any victims of ruthless ambition, expansion, or social and technological 'progress', and perhaps more specifically for the destruction of a centuries-old rural tradition by industrial advances.

Faust is now very old (Goethe suggested a symbolic age of one hundred). Confronted by Care, the accumulated burden of a lifetime of ruthless self-assertion, he is defiant; but since he appears for once not to resort to magic, he is exposed to the infirmities of old age. Blinded, he urges his workers to extend and improve his territories; but they are in fact digging, not his dykes and canals, but his grave. In a final exalted vision he anticipates the realisation of his schemes, a moment at which he *might* be able to bid the passing moment stay. Although the terms of his wager with Mephistopheles have been fulfilled only provisionally and conditionally, he dies as he experiences his 'highest moment'.

Nevertheless, the battle for Faust's soul is still to be fought. Mephistopheles, confident that his contract gives him the right to claim it, but unconfident that his rights will be respected, summons the legions of hell to snatch it as it leaves the body; but the battalions of heaven intervene, and in a scene of ribald hilarity the devils are routed and Mephistopheles succumbs to his own pederastic lust. Smitten by the epicene angels, his passion distracts him and allows the heavenly host to filch Faust's soul; the issue of Faust's salvation, it seems, is so finely balanced that only a form of theological sleight of hand, an angelic subterfuge, can save him from perdition.

The still fiercely controversial final scene shows Faust's soul (or his 'immortal part') in its progress towards heaven. Goethe – an avowed non-Christian – here uses the imagery and iconography of Christian mystical traditions and doctrines of love and grace, as he is reported to have said, as poetic vehicles or metaphors for a higher sanction in order not to lose himself in vague abstraction. He draws on visual sources, on the figures of patristic theology, on Dante and Swedenborg, on biblical and devotional accounts, to suggest Faust's transfiguration through eternal love, as the penitent 'once called Gretchen' intercedes for him; and he is drawn onwards and upwards by the enigmatic attraction of the 'eternally feminine'.

Goethe's apparent justification of Faust's morally dubious 'striving' remains utterly controversial. In particular, judgements of his final utopian vision have, especially in German scholarship, reflected a historical spectrum of political, cultural and literary perspectives. Celebrated by nationalist critics, whether Wilhelmine or National Socialist, in the cause of political ambition and territorial expansion, or by Marxist critics as a proto-socialist vision that would be realised in the German Democratic Republic, it has been reviled by others as illusory, vainglorious, and egotistic. Few non-Marxist German critics since 1945 have cared or dared to evaluate Faust positively; and indeed, as David Blackbourn has shown in a recent study of German reclamation schemes from Frederick the Great to the present day, the taming of nature has frequently served ruthless social and political resettlement programmes (*The Conquest of Nature: Water, Landscape and the Making of Modern Germany*, Jonathan Cape, London, 2006).

Goethe was evidently unwilling to conclude his drama on the burlesque tactical victory of the forces of light over the forces of darkness; but he was also unwilling to present Faust's salvation uniquely in terms of the solemnly transcendental religious mystery of the final scene. He was not prepared to give the Devil the last word, or to concur with Mephistopheles' sterile and cynical nihilism; but he evidently felt that the moral debit or credit of Faust's life was beyond human legal or ethical judgement. Faust's salvation is not, as Goethe is reported to have said, an idea that informs the whole work or each particular scene; it is only the final and most striking of the ironies and paradoxes of the figure and theme of Faust.

Act Five: Notes

76 Philemon and Baucis: see Ovid, *Metamorphoses*, viii: 624-724.

77 Lynceus: the reintroduction of the keen-eyed Argonaut at this stage seems incongruous, as does his megaphone. Luke (1994, p. lxiv) suggests that his function here and in lines 11288-337 is to report events that take place off-stage – the classical device of 'teichoscopy'.

78 Lemures: not nocturnal mammals (Lemurs), but Roman spirits of the dead (here embodied as half-decayed corpses). Their songs draw on the gravedigger's song in *Hamlet* (v: 1) – or on 'The Aged Lover Renounceth Love' from Percy's *Reliques of Ancient English Poetry* (1: i, 2).

79 Evidently a reference to the use of *castrati* in church choirs – a practice still common in Goethe's day.

80 Holy anchorites: based on late medieval paintings of the *Thebaid* genre (hermits in the Theban desert) – here associated with the *Patres* (Fathers) of the early Christian church.

81 Blessed Boys and Pater Seraphicus: Gaier glosses this bizarre section with references to Dante and Swedenborg (Gaier, vol. 2, pp. 1138-40).

82 In a manuscript version, Goethe wrote 'Angels . . . carrying Faust's entelechy' (see commentary to Act Two). Faust's transfiguration from corporeal substance to spirit (or entelechy) in the final scene is the reverse process of Homunculus' birth into physical existence at the end of Act Two.

83 Goethe enclosed these two lines in quotation marks, evidently for emphasis. The angels declare Faust's striving to be a necessary, but not sufficient, condition of salvation. According to Eckermann, Goethe declared that these lines contain 'the key

to Faust's salvation': 'in Faust himself an ever higher and purer activity to the end, and from above eternal love coming to his aid' (conversation of 6 June 1831). Critics now tend to treat Eckermann's reports as not wholly reliable; the idea may be his as much as Goethe's.

84 *Acta Sanctorum*: a seventeenth-century calendar of saints and martyrs that relates the story of the 'Egyptian' Mary, a prostitute who was prevented by an invisible hand from entering the Church of the Holy Sepulchre, did solitary penance in the desert for forty years, and before her death wrote a message in the sand asking the monk Socinius to bury her and pray for her soul.

NOTES TO THE UNPUBLISHED SCENARIOS

85 i.e. the Black (Dominican) and Grey (Franciscan) Friars.

86 'G.' could stand for Gesang (singing) or for Gretchen (as the phantom victim).

NOTES TO THE *URFAUST*

87 See note 2.

88 How nature beckons me: 'die winkende Natur' (*Urfaust*), 'die wirkende Natur' (*Faust*, Part One). The former is presumably a copying error.

89 See note 7.

90 See note 8.

91 A free rendering of the *Urfaust* text (literally: 'a grasshopper pie stuffed with oak leaves from the Blocksberg, delivered by a skinned hare with a cockerel's head, and no greeting from the nightingale').

92 Free rendering of the original. 'Hans Arsch [arse] from Rippach' was a figure of Leipzig student ribaldry.

93 Sometimes thought to be bowdlerised lines (either by Goethe

or by Fräulein von Göchhausen), and therefore counted in line-numbering, these dashes are more probably pause marks – perhaps to indicate protracted sobbing by Martha.

94 See note 10.

95 See note 11.

96 For no very clear reason, the text of the *Urfaust* and *Faust* Part One changes from Margareta to Gretchen and back again at various points.

97 See note 13.

98 See note 17.

99 See note 18.